Here's what readers and reviewers are saying about

THE LEGEND OF THE FIREFISH

Book One in the Trophy Chase Trilogy....

"Swashbuckling is the best way to describe Book One of the Trophy Chase Trilogy. Without wasting time, Polivka's first novel drops readers into a fantasy world filled with action, where chivalry is alive and well, and sword fights are frequent....With the nonstop action that cuts between multiple story lines, readers will be flipping pages eagerly."

—PUBLISHERS WEEKLY MAGAZINE

"A ripping yarn with the feel of the open sea and glimmers of eternal wisdom."

—KATHY TYERS,
AUTHOR OF *SHIVERING WORLD*
AND THE FIREBIRD TRILOGY

"*The Legend of the Firefish*, first in the Trophy Chase Trilogy by George Bryan Polivka, is a winner....filled with action, adventure, danger, intrigue, surprise, suspense...The characters Polivka created are fresh and interesting...A must-read for fantasy lovers, and a highly recommended rating for others who want a good story.

—REBECCA LUELLA MILLER,
A CHRISTIAN WORLDVIEW OF FICTION WEBSITE

"A seafaring tale of lands before the time of Internet technology and modern news media...like a foundation myth handed down through generations...Swashbuckling...and very much fun. Good for anyone in middle school through adult."

—ARMCHAIR INTERVIEWS

THE HAND THAT BEARS THE SWORD

George Bryan Polivka

HARVEST HOUSE PUBLISHERS

EUGENE, OREGON

All Scripture quotations are taken from the King James Version of the Bible.

Cover by Left Coast Design, Portland, Oregon

Cover photo © Steve Cole / Photodisc Green / Getty Images

THE HAND THAT BEARS THE SWORD
Copyright © 2007 by George Bryan Polivka
Published by Harvest House Publishers
Eugene, Oregon 97402
www.harvesthousepublishers.com

Library of Congress Cataloging-in-Publication Data
  Polivka, Bryan.
  The hand that bears the sword / George Bryan Polivka.
    p. cm. — (Trophy Chase trilogy ; bk. 2)
  ISBN-13: 978-0-7369-1957-9
  ISBN-10: 0-7369-1957-0
  I. Title.
  PS3616.O5677H36 2007
  813'.6—dc22

2007002494

Printed in the United States of America

07 08 09 10 11 12 13 14 15 / LB-SK / 12 11 10 9 8 7 6 5 4 3 2 1

For all those whose Kingdom is not of this world

ACKNOWLEDGMENTS

I offer heartfelt thanks to Nick Harrison, without whom the stories of Packer and Panna would still be known only within a very tight circle centered on a dusty space on a study shelf. His innate understanding of, and respect for, the various people of Nearing Vast has helped to guide their paths and shape their destinies such that, if they could know, they would be forever grateful.

Lifelong thanks to Jim and Nancy Polivka, out of whose nurture and from whose nature grew worlds of possibilities, the joy in the fight, glory in victory, perseverance in defeat, and solace in the rich mercies of hearth and home, regardless.

And eternal thanks to Jeri, my life's partner, my great, true love, my earnest and best critic, who has seen the worst and believed the best, soldiered on when obstacles eclipsed consolation, trimmed the wick when enthusiasms overflamed judgment...and whose heart has always, always sailed with true devotion, destined for faraway shores where good remains untarnished, where the spirit rejoices only in the truth, and where love and peace reign on as natural as sunrise—those shores that some bright morning we will raise at last, visible over a familiar, scarred, and sea-worn bowsprit ever pointed true by the firm and loving hand of our immortal Captain.

Contents

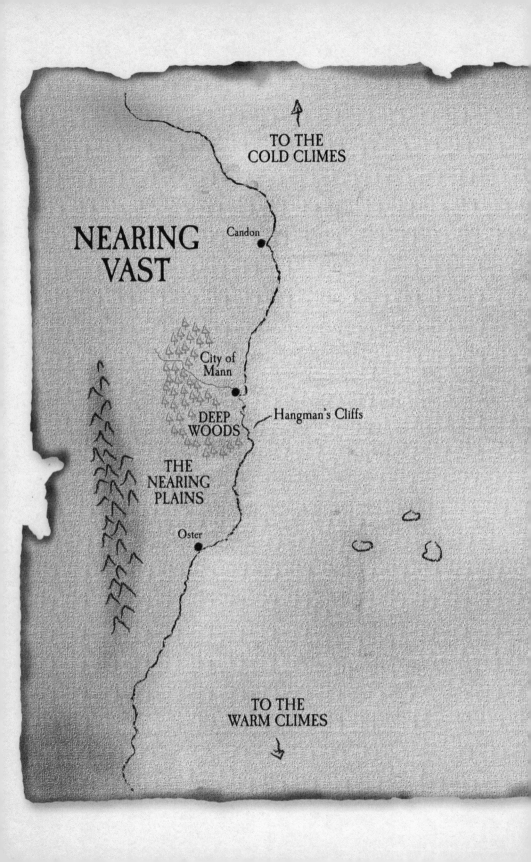

ACHAWUK
ISLANDS

UNCHARTED

THE
VAST
SEA

TO URLAH

Hezarow
Kyne

KINGDOM OF
DRAMMUN

TO SANDAVALE

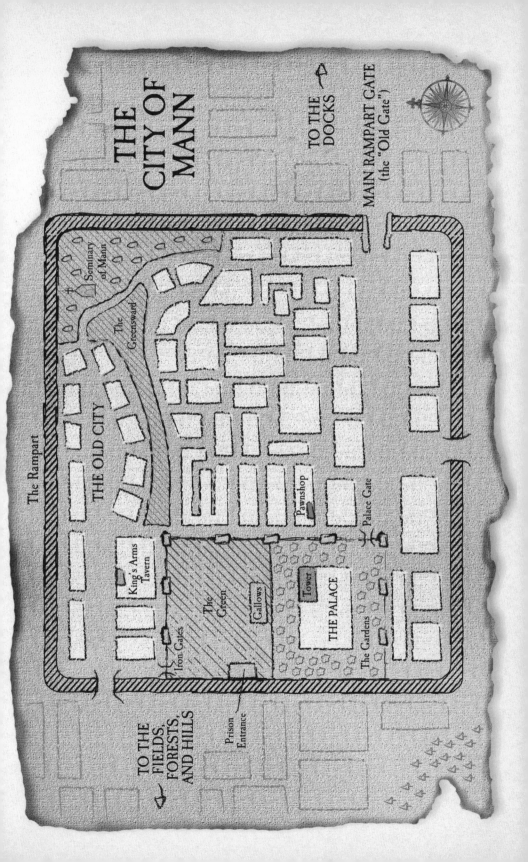

Doubt swells and surges, with swelling doubt behind!
My soul in storm is but a tattered sail,
Streaming its ribbons on the torrent gale;
In calm, 'tis but a limp and flapping thing:
Oh, swell it with thy breath; make it a wing,
To sweep through thee the ocean, with thee the wind
Nor rest until in thee its haven it shall find.

—GEORGE MACDONALD, *DIARY OF AN OLD SOUL*

CHAPTER 1

The Proclamation

"He never even fought."

"Never fought!" The friendly innkeeper just laughed, and kept on pouring. "You don't give up easily, do you? He bested a hundred warriors, maybe more. Rolled 'em off the decks!"

Dog Blestoe shook his head, watching his mug fill again with amber liquid. "I just got back from Mann. Met some men who were on that ship. And they say he hid up in the rigging until the fight was over. Never did draw his sword."

Cap Hillis set down his pitcher, wiped his bald head with a tattered dishrag. He glanced around the tavern to be sure no one had overheard. No one had. Laughter and loud conversation filled the small space. His inn was packed, every table full, more standing. It was a godsend.

"Hey, Cap!" a fisherman yelled from across the room. "These folks here want to know how Packer stabbed the Firefish!"

"You tell it!" Cap called back with a dismissive wave.

"No, I can't remember. Someone got eaten, right? Come on, Cap!"

More voices joined the chorus. "Aye, tell it!" "Tell the story, Cap!" Then someone added, waggling an empty mug, "And we'll all buy another round!"

Cap grinned and nodded. "Be right there!" His guests laughed and raised their mugs in toast. "Hen, more ale by the windows!" Hen Hillis hurried toward the appointed table, a clay pitcher sloshing in each hand.

It had been this way, more or less, since early spring, since news got around the kingdom about the *Trophy Chase*, the victory over the Achawuk, the slaying of the Firefish, the duel with the assassin, and most of all, the great school of beasts that Scat Wilkins would pay men in gold to go hunt.

As the legend grew with every telling, people came to Hangman's Cliffs, the hometown of the young hero who could swim under a ship's length in one breath and outduel an assassin who could outduel a swordmaster. And so Cap recited the stories again and again. Packer wouldn't speak of these things himself to his own townspeople, let alone to strangers, but all knew he had told Cap everything. The innkeeper's word was final; he was the loremaster, keeper of the flame.

Now Cap turned back to Dog, leaned in, spoke in a loud whisper. "Some men in Mann! Only you could find folks who might say such a thing. The boy's a hero everywhere. And he's sure a hero here!"

"Fine. No harm you making a little coin on tall tales. But Tooth and me, we know what's what." Dog nodded knowingly at his old drinking partner, Fourtooth.

"Yeah," the old man said thickly, "we know what's what." But he glanced glumly at the crowd of patrons, all having a better time than he was.

Packer had been recruiting for Scat Wilkins while wedding plans were being made and a little cottage in the woods fixed and painted. It didn't take much doing. Winter had been mild up and down the coast, and while the stream through Cap's little pub in Hangman's Cliffs had slowed, it had never frozen over. Not just fishermen came, but dockworkers, sailors, farmers, tradesmen, and drifters, all to enroll in the famous Firefish venture. Packer would ask a few questions, write down some names, and send them to the City of Mann, to John Hand.

As the weather grew warmer and the stories of the *Trophy Chase* spread wider, men who had no intention of enrolling arrived, then wives and children came with husbands, widows came alone, as did men of means and women of uncertain affiliation. Cap and Hen Hillis had started renting out rooms and drawing up plans to build

The Hand That Bears the Sword

more. It seemed that everyone wanted to be in Hangman's Cliffs, to hear firsthand about the voyage, to meet the hero, or if not the hero, then the heroine, the girl who had followed her true love into great dangers and escaped them all, cleared Packer Throme's name, and won his heart. And whoever they were, however or why ever they came, they all ended up in Cap's pub. Those who would and could, also ended up in Will Seline's church on Sunday mornings.

Not a single fisherman had sailed to find a single Firefish as yet, but the streets of Hangman's Cliffs were already being paved, if not with gold as Scat Wilkins had predicted, then at least with the footprints of men and women weighted down with the stuff and willing to spend it here, just to say they'd bought ale or cider or soap in a neighborhood of such historic dimensions.

Now the general clamor in Cap's pub grew intense, and faces were drawn to the front windows. A few words filtered through the din: "Carriage!" "Royal crest!" and "King!"

Cap threw his towel over his shoulder and pushed his way to the door. He stepped outside to find a gleaming black carriage trimmed with light blue, mud-spattered but brilliant, parked directly in front of his inn. It was emblazoned with the royal coat of arms: the intertwined initials *N* and *V* laid across a ship's wheel, pierced with a sword.

Horses whinnied and stamped. Cap felt a surge of panic. He wiped his hands fiercely on his apron as he assessed the sorry state of his little place of business: the warped and mud-trodden boards of his small stoop, the chipped and cracked plaster of his front wall, the faded and peeling sign of the Firefish above the door. He was planning to fix all this, plaster it, paint it up. But now that he had the money, he didn't have the time.

And now a royal coach…was it really King Reynard himself?

But before he could scourge himself as thoroughly as he would have wished, the driver opened the carriage door, and out grunted a very wide man wearing pale-gray silk clothing that looked a lot like pajamas. He had a royal-blue velvet vest trimmed in a sky blue, and he trailed a royal-blue cape. He was perhaps sixty years old, his face clean-shaven, puckered, and pallid, his eyes deeply bagged. His expression was one of either extreme discomfort or unfiltered disdain, Cap couldn't tell which.

The Hand That Bears the Sword

The man stood unsteadily for a moment, then put a hand to the small of his back, wincing as he stretched. "Awful way to travel," he said.

That being a royal sentiment if he had ever heard one, Cap took a knee and bowed his head dutifully. He wished he had a hat to remove.

"Yokels," the man said.

Cap looked up, startled.

"Stand up, man! I'm not the heavin' king."

Cap struggled to his feet.

The stranger eyed Cap carefully, then spoke in confidence. "He's much fatter than me."

Cap nodded. "Yes, sir."

"I'm his herald." The man said it as though the job had been punishment for some offense. "You have ale inside, I hope?"

"Yes, sir. Sure do. Good ale, too. Come in, come on in!"

The pub hushed as all eyes followed the royal visitor to the bar. He ignored them as best he could, even as they made way for his bulk. Cap hurried around behind the bar, filled a mug, and handed it to his guest. "Won't you sit down?"

"Mmm," the man shook his head as he drained the drink in three swallows. He set the mug down, and put both hands on his stomach. He paused, then belched deliberately. "Not bad."

"Thank you." Cap was pleased. "Another?"

"Hmm."

As Cap refilled the mug, the man turned around to look at his audience. He nodded, then sniffed. "Any of you Packer Throme?"

Each man shook his head silently. Except for Dog, who rolled his eyes.

"Well, anyone know where I can find him?"

They all nodded, but no one spoke. The man looked at the floorboards, apparently willing patience into himself, then looked at Cap. "I know you can speak."

"Sorry, sir, we're not used to having men of such...high esteem as yourself around here. We're just poor fishermen who rarely—"

The herald cleared his throat.

"Yes, Packer Throme. Well. He's a bit indisposed at the moment. Well, more than a moment really. And more than a bit. You see, he's just gotten married. Two weeks ago or so I guess it's been now, right,

Hen?" Hen nodded, the flesh of her face jiggling in vehement agreement. "Right," Cap continued, "but he's still in his honey month, and there's not man nor woman here who would interrupt him unless—"

"He's in his what?"

"His honey month. It's a tradition around here. After the wedding, the bride and groom, ah, well, they need a bit of time to themselves, you know? Most of us can't afford to go off on a grand trip, so we all pitch in and make sure they have food brought to their door. And other than that, we don't expect to see them. For a while."

For the first time, a trace of a smile crossed the herald's face. The smallest tip of the corner of his mouth crept slightly upward. "A month?"

"Give or take." Cap smiled sheepishly. "I guess we're not so busy out here as you are in the city."

"Sounds like the Thromes are plenty busy." Laughter filled the pub. The king's messenger raised his mug, squared himself, and suddenly looked quite regal. "Well, then…here's to Packer Throme and his new missus," he boomed, "and to this village! Greetings and honor to you all, direct from Mann and His Majesty the King!"

The room erupted into relieved and delighted cheering. They all raised their mugs and drank, inspired by the power in the herald's voice, and the sudden prestige that had engulfed them all. Even Dog drank, before he remembered himself.

The herald raised a hand, which silenced them. "I have a royal proclamation to read to you, which I shall do one hour from now on the front stoop of this fine establishment!" The pub erupted again, this time into an excited buzz as the herald turned back to the bar, motioning Cap close. "I'll need Mr. Throme here at that time."

"But…"

The herald stared, his eyes suddenly hard. "Orders, directly from Crown Prince Mather."

"Yes, sir," Cap said. "One hour."

Hen Hillis, appointed to be the messenger of the messenger, waddled up the winding path to the Throme cottage. She did not like this task, not one bit. In her hand was a basket covered with a bright red cloth, with fresh baked bread and hot turtle soup inside. She carried a bottle of wine in her apron pocket. But she felt these were tokens.

Bribes. Her mind raced, trying to find the right words, which simply would not come. She had a terrible feeling. It was never a good omen when a honey month was cut short. She did not like being the one doing the cutting. Not at all.

"I was not arguing," Panna said evenly.

Packer smiled. "Well, you weren't agreeing."

"I was simply expressing my views. Because mine don't agree with yours does not mean I was arguing. You cannot count that as our first argument."

He thought, tapped his chin, then nodded. "Okay. It wasn't an argument."

"Good. Thank you."

"But then this is our first argument."

Panna's mouth dropped open, and she hammered Packer's shoulder with her fist, laughing.

"Hey, watch the coffee!" he said with a smile, holding the mug away from her.

"Our first argument will not be an argument over an argument! We have to do better than that."

Packer laughed and put his cup on the small table that sat between them. The sun streamed in through the open bay window of their bedroom, catching his wife's hair from behind. Shadows from high leaves rippled across the sun, making her seem to be in motion. He moved a strand of hair from her cheek, tucked it behind her ear, let it fall on the thick white cotton of her robe. He looked into her eyes, those deep brown pools, the ever-present fire behind them all alight.

He was about to concede her point, when Hen knocked on their front door. It was an odd, intrusive sound. They stared at one another, listening. Food and drink had been left for them twice a day, morning and evening, for more than two weeks, but in all that time no one had knocked. A broom handle left leaning against the window was the only sign that a visitor had come and gone.

They heard the knock again. Then a voice drifted up from below. "Panna? Sorry to bother you two. Really sorry. It's me, Hen. Hen Hillis? I have a message."

Panna closed her eyes and shook her head. Packer laughed. "It's for you."

Their discussion, which may or may not have been an argument, was entirely theological. Like most disputes of that nature, though, it had highly practical ramifications. They were talking about the need for work. In the Garden of Eden, man and woman had lived in bliss. On this, Packer and Panna were in harmony. But Packer's position was that even before the Fall of Man, people had worked. Work, whether it was naming animals or tending fruit trees, was in the nature of human beings.

Panna's stance, however, was that Eden was bliss, but work was not, and therefore could not have been part of life before the Fall. However, since redemption through the blood of Christ meant reconnection with God, then through God's grace the descendents of Adam and Eve were given permission to return to such innocence, if only for brief times. A honey month, she felt, would qualify as such a time. They could let the cottage, and the dishes, and the dusting go.

It wasn't that Packer wasn't content with the way the last couple of weeks had gone. The contrary was true; it had been beyond any human happiness he had ever expected to be possible. The truth was, it had taken Packer a long time and much contemplation to accept the full measure of this good fortune. He knew what he deserved, and it was not this. He had presumed on the grace of God and joined up with pirates, putting in motion events that had led to catastrophe and near catastrophe. In full possession of the truth, knowing the path he should take, he had chosen disobedience, as thorough an act of anarchy as Adam had ever committed.

And yet, here he was. Alive. Blessed beyond measure. Living in the very Garden of Eden, revisited.

Packer looked at his marred right hand, now permanently curved into a clawlike grip. His entire palm and the inside of his fingers were a smooth, hardened mass of scar tissue. At the heel of his hand was the white circular scar where the Firefish had struck him with its lightning. He could use this hand for most things, but it throbbed constantly, and stabbed him with pain at the most awkward moments.

Often when it hurt him and he looked at it, as he did now, a scrap of Scripture would stray into his head: "Ye are not your own. Ye were bought with a price." He had begun to see his hand as the sign of that truth. These scars were a brand, a mark of ownership.

He was grateful for it, to the depths of his soul.

"What is it, Hen?" Panna asked through the cracked door. Her heart was light, and the worry creasing Hen's face couldn't reach her.

"I'm so sorry," Hen answered, chins quivering. "I'm just bringing the message." She held out her colorful basket. "Here."

Panna took it. "This is the message?"

"No, no!" Hen flushed, pulling the bottle of wine from her apron as she tried to find the right words. "Here, take this too."

Panna accepted it. "There isn't a message in the bottle, is there?"

"Land sakes, no! I'm just bringing you the soup and the wine along with."

Panna waited a moment. "Along with what, Hen?"

"Why, the message!"

Panna smiled, waited, but finally had to ask, "Which is…?"

"Well, there's a herald in town. From the king." Hen's eyes were wide, awaiting Panna's reaction.

Panna felt a twinge of alarm, but smiled through it. "Yes?"

Hen nodded vigorously. "He wants to see Packer."

"That's kind of him." Everyone who came to town wanted to see Packer.

"No, but he commanded. He has a proclamation he'll read in little more than half an hour. Packer has to be there. That's what he said, child."

"I see." Panna spoke gently into the beehive of worries that was Hen Hillis, but she couldn't keep the alarm within her from growing. "It's all right, Hen. Packer will be there. We'll both be there."

"But your honey month…"

"Just a short interruption. I'm sure we'll be right back here afterward. Please don't worry."

Hen nodded, much relieved. "I want so much for all to be well with you two, after all you've been through. Everyone does."

"Everyone has been so kind. Especially you. Thank you, Hen. We'll be fine, really."

Panna said her goodbyes and closed the door. But the inside of their little cottage seemed less cozy somehow. Darker. In need of attention. She carried the basket and the bottle upstairs in one hand, holding her robe closed at the throat with the other. She felt quite anxious, suddenly. She felt like there was work to be done.

"Now hear this! A message from King Reynard of Nearing Vast, to all citizens of the Kingdom!" The herald's voice rumbled like thunder. He stood atop a small polished black dais of three steps, created and brought with him for the purpose, placed in front of Cap's inn. The carriage had been rolled to one side, where impatient horses stamped and whinnied. He held a scroll of parchment in his hands. His mammoth girth now seemed built for this work, an enormous bellows that blew his words with effortless efficiency to the farthest reaches of the crowd, which at the moment numbered considerably more than the population of the town.

His face beamed purpose; its pallor was gone, replaced with a burnished red glow. The tucks and puckers of his jowls and cheeks now seemed as noble as a flag's folds waving in the breeze.

He was the Crown. He was the nation.

"Be it known to all present," he began in a low rumble, "that naval ships of the Kingdom of Drammun have, in most heinous fashion, attacked the marked and flagged ships of our Royal Navy, the Navy of Nearing Vast."

The townspeople gasped in unison. Packer and Panna, hand in hand, looked at one another in astonishment. They stood at the very back of the crowd, having lingered on the wooded path just in sight of the tavern until they saw the herald climb up on his small stage. They had, until this moment, been laughing quietly together about the uncomfortable nature of their clothing. But now the herald had their attention. Their hands clasped together more tightly.

The herald waited for whispers to die away. "In dark deeds well documented, the Emperor of Drammun, known in his nation as the Hezzan Shul Dramm, sent last summer an assassin deep into the very heart of our beloved capital, the City of Mann, who did seek out and kill our beloved Swordmaster, Senslar Zendoda."

"Oh, dear God," Panna breathed out. Packer closed his eyes. What was this? Talon was a lot of wicked things, but she was sent to shore by a pirate, not an emperor.

"In response, we, King Reynard of Nearing Vast, dispatched our peaceful envoy, under protection of several vessels of the Royal Navy, to the shores of our neighbors across the sea. This we did in order to make known with both civility and strength our grievances, and to seek peaceable redress."

The herald looked up at his audience, saw a decided lack of

comprehension. He cleared his throat and spoke less formally. "He sent a few ships over to ask some questions." Several within his audience nodded appreciatively. The herald went back to his parchment.

"On arrival," he boomed, "in open waters, our royal ships were surrounded by forces superior in number and, while under the white flag of parley, were fired upon, overrun, burned, and sunk."

Gasps and moans of shock rippled through the narrow streets.

"Our noble and God-fearing sailors and marines, the sons and brothers and husbands and fathers of our beloved land, were without exception killed or captured." More gasps. "Those captured were subjected to the most degraded and inhuman conditions."

The crowd boiled with murmurs.

"This news has now reached us with full confirmation, from brave souls who at great risk effected their own escape, and whose tales of mistreatment at the hands of the barbarous Drammune would, were they to be repeated here, chill the very blood of all Christian men and women!"

Gasps.

"Therefore..." and here the herald paused for effect.

"Uh-oh," Pastor Will Seline said aloud. Others looked at the big man in gray, but he clamped his mouth shut and stroked his beard. Panna's father had no great trust for government in general, and for this government in particular. He foresaw what was written next on the herald's scroll.

"Therefore, we have declared that a state of open war now exists between the Kingdom of Nearing Vast and the Kingdom of Drammun!"

Cheers erupted, full-throated, and with passion. This was an emotional release years in the making, years that this village had suffered from dropping prices and thinning catches, blaming all the while the Drammune, the foreigners who plied their harvesting techniques near Vast waters and then sold their goods through black markets in Mann. Will Seline bit his lip.

Packer and Panna stared at the herald in wide-eyed shock. They had the same thought, the same question, at the same time. Why, with this terrible news, did the king's herald want to see Packer Throme?

The herald continued. "We invite, entreat, and indeed command all able-bodied men within the Kingdom of Nearing Vast to do their duty to God and to country, to stand with us against this evil enemy, and to avenge the blood of our countrymen!" The herald lowered his parchment and boomed out the question: "Will you do so?"

"Aye!" "Yes!" "We will!" the men who gathered there all cried with a single voice, arms raised in fists of defiance. More than one wife hoped silently that the military would pay more than the market.

The herald returned to his script. "We hereby humbly beseech and verily command all good and able men, particularly all seamen of any description, and all who own and can handle with skill any weapons, whether swords, pistols, bows, or muskets, to gather in the City of Mann within one week of the reading of this proclamation. Here you shall present yourselves, your weapons, and your ammunition at places to be clearly marked and well known within the limits of the City of Mann. May God bless you, and may God bless this kingdom. Signed, King Reynard of Nearing Vast."

"May God bless the king!" someone called out.

"God bless the king!" the crowd answered in unison.

"May God bless Nearing Vast!" another voice shouted.

"God bless Nearing Vast!" came the roaring echo.

Then someone else yelled, "And may God curse the Drammune!"

An echo started, but was overcome with laughter and cheering. Excitement, anger, and determination now energized them all.

Panna and Packer turned toward one another, Panna searching and questioning, Packer distant and reflective. She could see the resolve growing within him. She could see him leaving her again. "Packer!"

Packer just shook his head and looked up at the sky, streaked red and orange in the fading moments of sunset. But before he could say a word, they both heard the herald ask in a loud voice, "Now where's this Packer Throme?"

"I'm here!" Packer called out, looking again at Panna. Then to her he said, "I have to go."

She grew determined. "Then let's go."

He smiled, nodded. Hand in hand they walked through the crowd, which quieted and parted as if the Thromes, too, were royalty. Dog stood aside, but eyed Packer warily as he passed. Then the citizens folded back quickly, in behind the two, following them, anxious to hear what further news the herald might have just for this couple.

The big man in the cape looked mortal again, even weary, as he stepped unsteadily from his perch. "Dangerous contraption," he muttered. He gathered himself on solid ground again, then looked up at the couple walking toward him. His eye lingered on Panna just slightly longer than Packer appreciated, but when he cut his gaze to Packer he was all business. "Packer Throme, I presume?"

"Yes, sir."

"Mrs. Throme." He bowed.

She curtsied. "Sir."

He looked Packer in the eye. "You're wanted for the war effort. I'm to take you with me to Mann."

The men in the crowd started to cheer, but were elbowed to silence by their wives, who were watching Panna.

"What?" Packer asked, reflexively.

The herald was impassive. "Did I mumble?"

Packer swallowed. "When?"

"A better question. The answer is *now*. I'll have one more ale while you pack. Bring your weapons and one change of clothes."

"But I have none," he said, then quickly explained himself. "I mean, I have no weapons." The townspeople, men and women, laughed aloud. Packer turned a deep shade of red.

The herald smiled for the second time this trip. "Well, bring whatever you do have. You're to come with me."

Packer felt the command like shackles around his heart. But he would obey; he had no choice.

It was over, then. Eden was gone. The flaming sword of war had suddenly been set at the gate, and he and Panna could not re-enter, not for a moment. And at their feet lay some new and awful path that wound through the dark, cursed lands beyond the Garden.

CHAPTER 2

Commandeered

"The king, may he live forever, is an idiot."

Packer's mouth dropped open. The speaker was a man he'd never seen, but recognized instantly. He was five years older than Packer, dressed in the finest silks, lace at his throat and his shirt cuffs, gold braids winding down his light blue coat. His hair was oiled, pasted almost flat to his scalp, his thin beard trimmed tight except at his jawline, where it was shaped carefully in a futile effort to enhance a receding chin. This was the Crown Prince of Nearing Vast, Mather Sennett.

"Listening to him is what put us in this predicament," Mather continued. Panna had described the prince as being unctuous, too slick to be trusted, but he was anything but that now. He was speaking with unvarnished anger, so far oblivious to Packer's presence. "We listen to him, and we'll all be on our hands and knees in front of that monster, the Hezzan Shul Dramm. And all our women will be his wives, or whatever they call that particular godless arrangement they prefer."

Mather's audience was made up of two men, both seated in his chambers as he paced the floor. One of them was Captain John Hand. The other was a person Packer had met briefly but significantly at the docks upon his last arrival in port: Bench Urmand, Sheriff of Mann.

Mather suddenly caught sight of his visitor. The valet at Packer's left, a bent old man who had been paying no attention whatever to the content of the prince's conversation, took the opportunity of a pause in the conversation to announce in a wheezing monotone: "Your Highness, Packer Throme." Bench and Hand stood, both glancing at the prince and looking concerned.

"Thank you so much, Stebbins," the prince said a shade glumly. "Once again, you have proven your inestimable worth to the Crown."

"Thank you, my lord," Stebbins grunted, missing the irony entirely. He bowed deeply, teetering as though he might fall over, then straightened up quickly and shuffled off.

"Packer Throme!" the prince oozed, recovering instantly and walking up to him with an arm out wide in welcome. He threw off a laugh. "Thanks to dear Stebbins, you caught us at an awkward moment. But never mind, I'll explain. I've been looking forward to this meeting for months now!"

Packer went to one knee, but when the prince reached him he took him by both shoulders and raised him up. "Ah no, the honor is all mine. The favorite son of Nearing Vast, hero of the fishing villages, the toast of all the kingdom." Elegant warmth, sharp intelligence, and genuine admiration poured forth from his voice, his face, his very being. "I'm ashamed we haven't had a banquet in your honor, renamed a street or two, declared a national holiday! Certainly you are due all these things."

"I...I didn't...Thank you, sir."

The prince smiled for a moment. "You're not a talker, I can see that. Few words and great deeds! Well, make yourself comfortable. You know John Hand, of course."

Packer looked up, relieved to be absorbed into the familiar, smiling face of the captain, who had followed his prince to come greet Packer. John Hand's eyes crackled, wrinkling at the corners; his beard and shock of hair both showed more salt than Packer remembered. He seemed to have aged somehow. Or perhaps he was just tired.

"You've sent us some good men, Packer. Your recruiting has helped to staff up the Firefish venture."

Packer nodded, shook his hand. "Thank you, Captain." He wasn't sure that was the right response, as he had been paid well for his efforts.

The Hand That Bears the Sword

"Admiral!" the prince announced proudly. "John Hand is now Admiral of the Fleet of the Royal Navy."

Packer was impressed and surprised. "Congratulations, sir."

Hand waved it off. "We've got some new business, and I need your help. The war has changed things, I'm afraid."

Packer could hardly disagree. John Hand in charge of the fleet? Packer understood a little better why he had been summoned, but he was at a loss as to how or why a captain serving under a pirate could gain such a lofty title. "I will do whatever I can, sir."

"Of course you will," the prince said, a little too easily for Packer's comfort. "And Bench Urmand, lately Sheriff of Mann, is soon to be announced Minister of Defense."

Packer struggled to find an appropriate response as he shook the sheriff's hand, also firm and equally painful. These seemed like field promotions. Emergency measures. "My congratulations, sir," he finally said.

"Thank you, Packer," Bench said. His eyes burned with zeal for his new position. His head bobbed once. His square chin and packing-crate shoulders, the oak tree of a neck that connected the two, and his powerful arms combined to make Packer feel quite small. Bench Urmand was purpose poured into a granite mold. "We were talking about you down at the office just yesterday," Bench continued. "We're quite sure you made the transition from wanted outlaw to national hero more quickly than any man in the history of the kingdom."

"And that would include Rake Mann and his brothers," the prince added pleasantly.

Packer shook his head, amazed to be mentioned in the same breath with Rake Mann, for whom the capital city was named, and about whom every schoolchild learned in history classes, if not on a parent's knee. "I'm not sure I deserve to be called either."

"And he's humble as well!" Mather proclaimed. "Excellent, then—shall we sit? Stebbins!" He clapped his hands loudly.

The old man had creaked back into the room by the time the foursome had found their seats. "Sir."

"Bring the usual assortment."

Stebbins knew his business. The four men barely had time to exchange pleasantries before several servants appeared behind rolling carts covered with steaming cakes, pitchers of coffee and cream, bottles of dark purple port, hunks of cheese in just about every shape and color, sliced ripe apples, and bunches of burgundy grapes. A small plate overwhelmed by several huge cakes was put into Packer's left hand, and a huge mug of coffee into his right. Cream poured from a white pitcher into Packer's cup almost before he could nod to the valet that he wanted it.

Once the foursome were settled, seated in the same area where Panna had been invited to sit almost a year ago, the prince looked hard at Packer, who was sitting opposite him. Then he turned to John Hand, on the sofa to his right. "Do you want to begin?"

Hand nodded, swallowed, wiped crumbs from his beard, and grew serious. He leaned forward toward Packer. The prince looked grim. Bench Urmand stirred his coffee slowly. "We're going to take you into our confidence, son. But what we say here cannot be repeated to anyone, cannot be discussed with anyone but the three men here with you now."

Packer nodded.

"Not even your wife," the prince added with a raised eyebrow.

Packer swallowed involuntarily as John Hand continued. "The Royal Navy is no more. It's been obliterated."

Packer's brow furrowed reflexively. He looked to the prince and Bench for confirmation. He found it in both faces. "When?"

"Actually, last autumn."

Packer was dumbfounded. Six months ago? "How?"

"Ah, but let me tell it," the prince cut in, clearly feeling the need for more of a story. "In response to the assassination of our sword-master, my father the king, may he live forever, sent our beloved but somewhat beleaguered Navy to the coast of Drammun. It took several months for the preparations, the fleet not being quite the nimble fighting force of our storied past. Years of peace and neglect had allowed it to settle into something of a state of, shall we say charitably, decline."

"Very charitably," Hand added with a grimace.

"But eventually," Mather continued, "sixty ships were sent to answer a single murder. A show of strength, my dear father called it. Some of us pleaded with him to send but an envoy. Two or three ships at most, on a diplomatic mission. But my father has ever harbored deep resentment for the Drammune. The fishing trade has been a thorn in our side for years. Oh, but you know about that, don't you?"

Packer nodded.

"There have been other provocations—irritants, mostly—but continuous, and in the face of several formal requests to desist, the most recent one rather terse. Some would even say, threatening. So, the king considered the killing of Senslar Zendoda an act of war, which of course it was, and therefore he determined to answer it as such."

"But it wasn't," Packer blurted.

"Excuse me?" The prince waited.

Packer now spoke more carefully. "I'm sorry. But Scatter Wilkins sent Talon to get revenge on those who had helped me stow away. When she found out Senslar Zendoda was my swordmaster, she went…a little crazy. But the Drammune didn't send her."

"Perhaps not. But it doesn't matter," the prince went on, waving a hand in the air. "The thing's done. Our king made his decision with all the knowledge he had available." Now the prince scooted to the edge of his seat and put the tips of his fingers together. "What does matter, Packer, is how we deal with the current situation. And the situation is dire. We are at war with a great naval power. And we have no Navy."

"But six months ago…" Packer didn't quite know how to ask the prince what his government had been doing since the sinking of the Fleet.

He didn't need to. "We had no news for months. Our ships did not return. Then we sent spies, who also did not return. And then winter came and we had no choice but to wait. Finally this spring, we were able to confirm our worst fears." The prince shrugged. "And so here we are. The Navy had left back here in Mann, what, four ships?" the prince looked at the admiral.

John Hand shrugged. "Six warships, including a couple in dry dock that might be ready in time, if the war lasts. We're building more, of course, but it takes a year per ship, at the fastest pace we could hope to manage it."

Packer's coffee and cakes would go uneaten. He set them both on the low table in front of him. His stomach had settled somewhere down near his knees. He had thought, for months now, that the storm he had unleashed had passed, that it had left in its wake fertile, watered soil. He had thought the Firefish industry would take off, and prosperity would return to the villages. It certainly seemed to be happening. But now he knew that the consequences of his choices had never stopped rolling. The boulder had been bouncing down the mountainside unseen, picking up force, just so that it could let loose this full landslide of destruction. Rather than ending, the path of devastation was widening.

"Bad news, I'm afraid." The prince's smile was a sad one.

Packer shook his head. "The entire Navy. But the proclamation said a 'peaceful envoy'—"

"Proclamations are for the people, Packer. The one you heard was meant to raise a new Navy, to refit the Army, to embolden the citizenry. We do not want to send them sprinting toward the Mountains in fear for their lives."

Packer shook his head.

The prince just smiled. "Hard for you to imagine, I suppose, that a king's proclamation should be anything but sterling truth, shining down from heaven to mere mortals. But imagine this," and the prince's voice grew dark. "Imagine your reaction, the reaction of your townspeople, had these truths been proclaimed for all to hear: 'The king has erred in his vain old age! The Navy is sunk! Mann is defenseless, and the Drammune are coming!' What sort of terror would that have engendered? The truth is simply not as helpful as we would like it to be at the moment, Packer. We have a duty to our people that supersedes telling the brutal truth."

This did not lessen Packer's sense of dread. "Are they?" he asked, somewhat more fiercely than he intended.

"Are who what?" the prince countered.

"Yes, they are," Bench answered flatly. "The Drammune are coming."

"Oh, almost certainly," the prince chirped. "We believe their Armada has left the capital of Hezarow Kyne already."

Packer stood and turned his back. He closed his eyes. There would be war on Vast soil; there was nothing to stop a full invasion. And this was a message to be delivered over cakes and coffee? Suddenly, his hand ached, pounded. He looked at it.

He turned back to face the three men who would run the war. "Whatever you want me to do, with God's help, I will do it."

The prince nodded. That was the sort of talk he hoped to hear from the young man proclaimed as a hero throughout Nearing Vast.

Captain Scatter Wilkins allowed the king's maidservant to light his cigar. He then took the small, ornate lamp from the young woman's hands and examined it, ignoring her as she walked away. It was an ingenious, self-contained thing small enough to carry in one's pocket. Under a close-fitting cover was a flint wheel that could be turned with the thumb. "Works like a Firefish lure," Scat said aloud. But it wasn't brass. It was made of gold. He set it down on the table beside his chair, eyed it a moment, then leaned back. Finally, he looked at the king of Nearing Vast critically. "What do you know about the prince's plans?"

The king's herald had spoken truth in at least one respect: King Reynard was indeed the fatter of the two men. Reynard filled his throne the way a hen fills a nest, and looked to be much harder to displace. He had been studying the pirate, and found it interesting that he paid more attention to the golden bauble than he did to the attractive young woman who gave it to him. Interesting, but not surprising. "What do you know?"

"I just came from Mather's quarters, not an hour ago. He had Bench Urmand and John Hand with him."

"Hmm. Our new admiral, and our new minister of defense, or some such. They're rebuilding the Navy."

"With my ships!" Scat's outburst ended in a cough, then a wheeze.

"You are not well, Scatter. You should let my physicians examine you."

Scat waved the thought away with his cigar. But he could not speak for a moment. He waited for the constriction in his chest to pass. He hated being ill. His heart had gone bad; he knew that. It had given way on the decks of the *Chase,* and it had not healed. No physician could fix it. They all said the same thing: slow down, quit smoking, quit drinking. Quit being Scatter Wilkins. He had no use for such advice. After a year, he had concluded it would never heal; he would simply learn to live on half a heart.

"He wants my ships," Scat repeated when finally he could.

"Of course he does. He will commandeer them. He has few of his own."

"You can stop him."

The king looked incredulous. "And why would I do that? So you can continue to rake in coins while the kingdom falls?"

"I rake in coins, you rake in coins. And you need 'em. But more than that, you need what those ships can deliver."

"Your price is ridiculous. John Hand will deliver the same goods as part of his duties. The Firefish trade is now owned by the Crown."

Scat just stared at him. The king had made a bad choice in the past. He had chosen the outrageous duties the *Chase*'s prizes could bring him as exports, rather than pay what Scat demanded in order to keep the Firefish trade within the boundaries of Nearing Vast. "I'll do the prince's bidding, same as John Hand. Just let me keep those ships."

"It's Mather's war now. He'll fight it as he sees fit. He doesn't trust you. He trusts Admiral Hand."

Admiral Hand. Scat grimaced. King Reynard's will had grown soft. His mind, which had never been his strength, seemed duller now than ever. "A man tries to make an honest living, and what happens? The government comes and takes it all away."

"Ever the lament of the businessman."

Scat blew a swath of smoke toward the unsympathetic king. "Piracy was simpler. All right, he can have all the ships I've bought and fitted. I won't fight him."

"How gracious of you. You'll be paid fairly."

"Ha. I doubt that. But I want to captain the *Trophy Chase*."

The king grunted. "You'd sail under Hand?"

Scat nodded. "No one can sail that ship like I can. He knows it."

"And did you ask the prince about this?"

"I did."

"And?"

"He said no. I swear to you, Reynard, I will die before I let another man have that ship." Scat left unsaid the obvious fact that he would kill as well.

"Don't do anything rash, Captain."

"Rash?" Scat's tone grew ominous. "Your Highness. You have the power. You can give me command of the *Chase* and save you and your...admiral," he said the word as though it tasted bitter, "a lot of trouble."

The king sighed. Once a pirate, always a pirate. "You can't blackmail me, Scatter. I told you, it's Mather's war."

Scat Wilkins' eyes threw fire. "Your son is taking your power."

King Reynard looked away. It was true. But he couldn't summon a desire to fight against his own son, not now, not with the grave errors he himself had made. "I love my son." He turned back to Scat. "And I'm proud of him."

The Hand That Bears the Sword

"Then give him your throne and be done with it. Either you're the king or you're not."

Reynard's eyes flashed. "I am still king enough to have your head. I have spared you from the hangman for years. Do not forget that."

"Then hang me!" Scat's voice cracked. "I'm not going to start fawning like those rattlesnakes you call nobles."

The king softened, and then he laughed. It was a genuine, affectionate laugh. "This is what I like about you, Scatter. I'd have done well to surround myself with more like you, blunt and honest men who would argue rather than bow and scrape. You have no son, do you?"

"No." He shrugged. "None that will claim it."

The king smiled again. "But you have John Hand, your closest confidant and friend."

Scat waited.

"And he is taking your power away, just as Mather is taking mine."

Scat grimaced. Then he sighed. *So this is how power flows from one generation to the next,* he thought. *This is why men retire.*

He hated it. Scat Wilkins, for one, would not go quietly.

"We're putting to sea tomorrow."

The words stopped Panna, who had rushed to the door when she heard Packer enter.

"We?"

"The *Trophy Chase,*" he added quickly. "Under John Hand."

She raised her chin. "Did you ask about me? Did you tell them I can work? Did you ask to put me on crew?"

"No," he told her painfully. "It's just too dangerous, Panna."

Her eyes grew defiant. "Then I'll talk to the prince myself."

"Panna. You don't understand."

She crossed her arms, her gaze flitting from eye to eye, searching. "Then explain it."

Packer's resolve began to crumble. He turned away and sat on the satin-covered love seat just inside the apartment door, feeling desolate.

They had been put up in a sumptuous apartment called the Blue

Rooms, off the main hallway of the newest part of the palace, and they had wanted for nothing, nothing except some quiet and some privacy. Panna had finally ordered all six servants out. They left baffled as to how the couple would eat or sleep or bathe or dress without their attentions.

Packer looked up at Panna. "I have a duty to make this right. This war started because of me."

"The prince said that?"

"No. I'm saying it."

She sat next to him, turned his face to hers. Her expression was velvet but her words were steel. "Do you believe God could have stopped this war? Does He have that power?"

He nodded.

"Then stop blaming yourself. God can protect you. He can protect me. He can protect both of us together."

"Or separately. Panna, the situation is very bad."

"The war."

"Yes. The war." He could not keep eye contact.

She took his scarred hand in hers. "Tell me everything."

He shook his head. "There are some very dark secrets they confided in me."

She grew alarmed. "What secrets?"

Packer felt riven within. He had promised. But the status of the Fleet and the mission on which he was being sent burned him, burned inward. Did he not have a greater bond with Panna? Had he not made a greater promise to her?

Panna studied his eyes, his face, saw the barrier, and was frightened by it. This was not right. She had imagined there would never be a wall, a fence, or even a veil between them ever again. "You aren't going to tell me."

"I can't." He shook his head. He did not want this to be their first argument. Or possibly their second.

Nor did she. "How do you mean dark? Dark in what way?"

He shook his head. She needed something. "This war is likely to be short."

"But that's a good thing, right?"

He shook his head. "A very bad thing."

She swallowed hard. "Something's gone wrong already."

Packer didn't move.

Panna felt a shiver run through her. "So what is it they want you to do?"

He shook his head. Then he sighed. "They want me to be a hero."

"Again? How?"

"They want a figurehead. To give hope to people."

"Well, that's a good thing. Right?"

He thought a moment about his mission, about the *Chase*'s quest. Then he grew urgent. "Panna, you should leave the city. Go to the Nearing Plains. No, go farther. The Mountains. Get your father, and just go."

She was incredulous. The Mountains were weeks of hard travel from Mann. "It can't be that bad already."

He swallowed, his moment of hope gone. His shoulders sagged. "I don't know where the safest place is." Was it only yesterday the two of them were in Eden, with a full, rich future together stretching out before them? And yet, even then this war had loomed over them. He remembered the shadows that played on her hair, cast from high above as they sat together.

"Panna. Why would God give us a time together, like we had, only to wrench it to bits like this?"

"Because He's gracious."

Packer studied her.

"He didn't have to give us any time at all. But He did. And no one can take that time away." Her will was iron.

His heart welled up into his eyes. And then he kissed her. Her gentle kiss led to an embrace.

In her dream, Panna saw Packer standing atop the Hangman's Cliffs, facing out to sea. Five hundred feet below him, spreading out as far as he could see, the waters were packed with ships, warships and traders, fishing boats and freighters, each deck a mass of people. The entire citizenry of Nearing Vast, it seemed, floated below. And all the people cheered.

On Packer's left stood the king, waving and smiling. Beside the king stood the prince, proud and pleased. On Packer's right stood Panna, absorbing the moment, reveling in the adoration they heaped on Packer Throme from below.

But when Panna looked at her husband, she saw only fear in his eyes, and a terrible discomfort. She reached for his hand to assure him that it was right, that he deserved all this, that he should enjoy what God had brought him. But as she grasped his damaged palm, he pulled it away, and she could see the scars were not scars, but raw flesh. She heard him wince in pain, and saw him look at her as if to ask why, why would she hurt him?

But before she could say anything, before she could assure him, the king's hand slapped Packer firmly on the back, just at the base of his neck, and then, the king still smiling, that hand pushed him roughly, unceremoniously, over the edge. He fell without a word. Panna saw a rope, heard it zipping past, a blur as it fled over the edge of the cliff. It was tied to Packer!

She grabbed at it, and her own hands burned, burned with fire as Packer's hand was burned, but she held on tight and the rope stopped. She had saved him! Her own hand was now a mass of raw flesh. But she heard the loud cheers grow louder, lustier. She looked down at the cliff's face. There she saw Packer...with horror she saw him far below, dangling, a hood over his head, a noose around his neck, his hands tied behind his back.

The crowd cheered on, but now they screamed out in that joyous guttural, horrible cheer heard only at public executions. And Panna let go of the rope, but it was too late. It stayed where it was, immovable. And Packer was gone, this time forever, and she had been unable to save him.

She wept bitterly, and woke up weeping. Packer was there beside her, real and whole and alive and warm. She held him close and he told her not to worry, not to be afraid, that it was just a dream. She held on to him, sobbing, held him as close as she'd ever held anything in her life, and she prayed as hard as she had ever prayed, that it was, in fact, just a dream.

But she remembered her dream of Talon, the dark-haired murderess, and how that dream had come true.

"I want to sail aboard the *Trophy Chase*. I want to go with my husband."

"So he told me," the prince said to Panna, successfully hiding his amusement. "But I'm afraid it cannot be."

"But why? I'm strong. I've been on boats before. I can learn almost any task. You let women on board your ships."

"But not warships."

Panna wrapped the housecoat she was wearing more tightly around her. She hadn't taken the time to dress; as soon as Packer had gone back to sleep she'd stolen away, putting this quilted silk robe over her nightgown, and gone in search of the prince. She felt appropriately dressed; she had found the housecoat in the closet of the Blue Rooms, and it was more beautiful than almost any garment she owned, and covered her flannel nightgown from neck to ankle. Besides, she knew the prince; she had gone to him before.

She would make her case. If the answer was yes, she would tell Packer what she had done. If no, he would never need to know.

Finding the prince had been more difficult than she had imagined. She didn't remember the way to his private chambers, and neither the servants nor the guards were pleased about her request. But through sound argument and sheer determination, with only the slightest hint of the damsel in distress, she finally convinced one of the younger guards to see if the prince was awake. Not to awaken him, but only to see if he was awake, to ask if he would speak with her.

And, thankfully, he was an early riser.

"Would you like some coffee? Tea?"

"No, thank you."

"This is beginning to be a bad habit with you, Panna Seline, coming to me for help and then refusing my hospitality."

"Throme."

"Excuse me?"

"It's Panna Throme. Your Highness."

"Of course, forgive me." He thought about asking her to sit, but remembered how poorly that had gone the last time.

"I cannot bear it," Panna began, "to let him sail away again, if there is any chance whatsoever that I could get a berth with him. I'm not asking to be put up as a passenger, but taken on as crew. I can cook, I can clean, I can sew, I can certainly scrub decks, bail water, run errands, whatever it is that needs doing."

"A ship's boy."

"Yes! A ship's boy. Or girl. You must have positions like that."

The prince smiled gently. "Did Packer tell you the nature of this voyage? The mission of the *Trophy Chase*?"

She looked at the marble floor. "No."

The prince wasn't sure he believed her. It was hard enough for him to deny this young woman, but what would it take to deny her if she was deeply in love, as she clearly was with Packer? He swallowed hard, surprised at his own reaction to this thought. "I can't let you," he said flatly. "It is a dangerous mission. Packer knows this. He wants you to be safe. As do I."

"But I don't care about my safety!" She was desperate now. "I would be there for Packer, to help him as he helps you win this war." She saw no softening in the prince's eyes. "The Drammune women fight! I can fight with my fists as well as a man. You know that's true. I can't fence, but I could learn to shoot."

She had indeed fought—if not well, certainly more fiercely than an old fisherman. "I don't doubt any of that," said the prince. "But even if you were a Mortach Demal like Talon, you would be a great distraction to him. He would be worried about you rather than his mission. He would want to protect you."

"But I don't need protecting!" Couldn't anyone understand this? "I would rather die with him than live on safely without him!"

Her eyes were deep, intense, full of the fire of love and the anger of being denied. Her flowing hair was unkempt from a poor night's sleep that could be read in her eyes, and in the lines beneath them. The prince rarely saw a woman who had not made every conceivable effort to beautify herself. Panna seemed to make a habit of appearing before him rumpled and unkempt, and he found her all the more attractive for it.

"No. I am your prince, and that is final. You will stay here." And by that he meant, though she did not understand it yet, that she would stay in the palace.

Panna saw there was no hope whatsoever of her going to sea with Packer. She fought the sting of tears, and dropped her eyes. "I'm sorry to have bothered you, then."

"It was no bother at all, Panna. I mean that. It will be hard, I know. But you have my ear whenever you wish it."

She did not look back up into his eyes. The futility of her mission now made her feel foolish. But he was gracious, and she appreciated that. "Thank you, Your Highness." She curtsied. "If I may take my leave."

"Of course."

She did not look back.

The order placing Scatter Wilkins' new fleet under the command of John Hand was delivered to the pirate in his small apartment above the cobblestone streets, in an extremely rough area of the docks known as Plank's Wharf. Entry to his private rooms could be achieved only through the establishment known as Croc-Eyed Sam's, a notorious pub even here.

Scat had ensconced himself on the second floor, having convinced Sam, with a combination of coercion and coin, to sleep at a nearby inn for the duration of the pirate captain's tenure. No fewer than three grizzled sailors, Scat's pirates, sat in constant watch at the tables by the front door, heavily armed, sipping not ale but tea, coffee, or the occasional ginger beer, which kept them both alert and in a very sullen mood. They watched, studying any and all who might enter, freely accosting anyone they didn't know.

The circular wooden stairway up to Scat's quarters could not be accessed without passing behind the bar, the entrance to which was guarded by two more of Scat's men. One of them was almost always Scat's scowling, thick-browed right hand, Jonas Deal.

Because of Scat's presence, Sam's place had never been busier. To get a glimpse of the famous pirate, the man who'd first learned to take the Firefish, who captained the *Trophy Chase,* who'd been saved by Packer Throme in the Achawuk territory, was apparently worth the risk of spending a day or a night drinking among the most dangerous citizens of Nearing Vast.

But Scat rarely appeared. The pirate entered and departed infrequently and quickly, nodding politely to any female who called out to him, but otherwise ignoring the clientele, going out the front door and into a waiting coach, and then returning through the front door and climbing the stairs, each time as quickly as he could manage it.

Today the sheriff's contingent charged with delivering the formal Notice of Confiscation to one Mr. Sandeman "Scatter" Wilkins was led by Bench Urmand himself, who arrived armed just as heavily as any patron in Croc-Eyed Sam's. He entered with a pistol in each hand, drawn and loaded, his jaw set, followed by three sheriff's deputies decked and armed in the same form and fashion.

The front table, which happened to have four pirates on duty at this moment, stood and drew on Bench the instant he was inside the door. Bench and his men held their ground. Since each lawman had a pistol in each hand, and each pistol was aimed at a pirate's head, each pirate therefore had two pistols aimed at him. The net of this simple equation was that even though the two sides were equally matched, the pirates felt outnumbered. This prevented them from firing on the sheriff's crew, but it did nothing to improve their disposition. The two foursomes bristled in silence on the very cusp of extreme violence.

Then Bench spoke in a crystal tone of command, through smiling eyes and gritted teeth. "Stand down, gentlemen, this is royal business, no need for gunplay. I have a paper to deliver to Scat Wilkins. I intend to deliver it and go my way."

"So you say," a greasy pirate countered. "You put yer weapons down, maybe we'll believe you." This string-haired veteran of Scat's ships, at whom Bench pointed one of his pistols, was Zeb Bones. He had missed the last voyage of the *Trophy Chase* because of a particularly dire case of dysentery, and he was looking to prove his mettle.

Both of Bench's arms were locked out straight, the muzzle of one flintlock inches from Zeb's nose, the muzzle of the other the same distance from another pirate's ear.

"I'm the Sheriff of Mann, friend. Show me you mean no harm."

The pirate hesitated, then slowly lowered his weapon. Bench instantly did the same. All parties followed suit. No one put his pistol away, however.

"I need to deliver a paper to the man himself," Bench said easily. "Either I go up, or you fetch him down."

The string-haired pirate ran his tongue along the inside of his cheek, considering. He looked away from Bench to Jonas Deal, seated at the bar.

Jonas grunted, then tucked his own enormous pistol, his hand cannon, back into his belt, and climbed the creaking stairs.

A quiet, tense moment later, Jonas climbed back down. "Captain Wilkins is not interested in your paper. Leave what you want, but he ain't comin' down." Then Jonas, his enormous brow furrowed with the preparation for a fight, actually growled. "And you ain't goin' up."

The three deputies with Bench all felt sweat on their pistol grips.

Each in turn stole a glance at their leader, but he betrayed not the slightest trace of concern. "Scatter Wilkins!" he yelled, a deep bass that shook the timbers. "This is Bench Urmand, Sheriff of Mann. Do you hear me?"

After a pause, the sheriff shouted louder. "Do you hear me?"

The pirate answered quickly and irritably, clearly audible in none too loud a voice. "I hear you."

"I'm under orders from the king. I must put this in your hand."

"Well, I'm under no orders to receive it," Scat called back.

There was a pause. Then the sheriff spoke slowly and clearly. "I've thought of you as many things, Scat Wilkins. But I never thought you a coward."

The silence was thick and ugly. Pistols cocked.

Bench continued. "You're not afraid to loot unarmed citizens and shoot men in the back. Loot and burn their ships, leave women and children to drown on the seas. But you can't face a simple piece of parchment?"

Jonas growled again, this time following it with a mumbled oath that verbally dismembered the visitors and their mothers. Someone from a back table whistled two low notes that said "uh-oh."

The sound of feet on a creaking floor above them led to the sight of battered boots on a creaking staircase, and then to a whole and wholly irritated pirate, unarmed, but looking every bit the dangerous leader of bloody-minded men, descending the stair. He wore a simple woolen vest over his white sleeved shirt; his trousers were clean but stained with sweat or blood or both. His speckled beard was carefully trimmed, his hair oiled and pulled back off his scarred face, which was pale and blotchy. But it was not his look but his stature, the sense of an unexploded shell with which he carried himself, the dark danger he could conjure with a glance, that marked him as a singular man, one accustomed to having his way, and to having his way at the cost of human life.

"Give me your heavin' paper, then," was all he said. Bench reached into the leather pouch at his waist and produced a leather scroll, tied with a royal-blue ribbon, and marked with the seal of the king. He handed it to the pirate.

"Is that all?" Scat demanded, staring death into the sheriff, who met his gaze with easy, unmasked animosity.

"That is all for now," Bench said. In fact, he was disappointed that it was all, disappointed to have seen Scat descend the stair unarmed. Had there been a shootout, Bench had no doubt he and his men, the best-trained of his office, could have routed this rabble in an instant, cleansed the city of so much refuse. The sheriff had harbored in his mind the faint hope that this errand would end with the pirate dead; a hope dashed the moment Scat appeared weaponless.

"One day," Bench could not resist saying, "one day you will hang for all you've done. And I will gladly pull the lever."

Scat's stern look melted into a broad grin. "It's nice to know the lawmen of the civilized world still recall me fondly." There was laughter in the pub, and a couple of whoops. "What's your name again?"

The sheriff's jaw tightened. "Bench Urmand, Sheriff of Mann. You'd best not forget it."

Scat's grin melted away. "I've seen you brave young men before, with your righteous need to rid the kingdom of such like me. I've seen you come and go for decades. But you're just an actor on a stage. You know that, don't you? You and your kind are necessary because the king needs the good people who pay his taxes to believe his laws are being justly enforced."

"And so they are."

"That so? Then why don't you arrest me, Bench Urmand, Sheriff of Mann? You say I've robbed unarmed men, killed women and children, shot men in the back. And I'll admit it. I have done that and more. So tell me, why don't you arrest me for all I've done? Tell me, Sheriff of Mann."

Bench stewed, but couldn't speak. He knew why as well as Scat did. The king had ordered otherwise.

Scat snorted, looked around the pub, and turned his back on the sheriff and all he stood for. "Nice show," he muttered. "Come on boys, give him a hand." Scat put his hands together. One man clapped, and then another, and then a robust round of applause ensued as the pirate returned to the stairway and climbed up out of sight.

"How about a drink, Sheriff?" the man behind the bar called out cheerily as the applause died down. It was Sam himself, a black patch not quite covering the gruesome scar, the flattened skull where his right eye and most of the socket had been forcibly removed by a crocodile. Or so the tale was told. "We got whiskey and ale. No hard feelin's. On the house for you and your men."

Bench's face was still red. "I'd sooner drink horse urine," he said darkly.

Sam picked up a bottle that was half-full of caramel-colored liquid, swirled it around. "I don't believe I have any a' that, but this stuff here comes pretty close!" The pub erupted in howls of laughter. Bench Urmand glared at Sam, then quickly left, his men following him out.

"Pimm, read that," Scat ordered, and the jumpy servant took the leather scroll from the table where Scat had thrown it. The pirate captain sat heavily on the wooden bench beside the table, exhausted from his trip downstairs and back. His hands trembled; his forehead glistened with sweat. He had needed to summon all his willpower to pull off that small excursion as though he were still in his strength. He would not let his own minions, or the sheriff's, believe he was too ill to defend himself.

Scat hadn't bothered to change much about Sam's quarters, but he had made sure it was thoroughly cleaned, and he had brought in a few items of his own, most of them with the ability to fire a projectile at deadly velocity. He looked at the half-empty rum tumbler on the table and pushed it away with his fingers.

"Can I get you something?" Pimm asked, watching Scat's hands shake.

"Just read the festerin' paper."

"Aye, sir." Deeter Pimm did not like this task at all. He was perhaps the only man yet alive who knew that Scat could not read. When he'd heard the angry sheriff downstairs say that Captain Wilkins was afraid of a piece of parchment, Deeter's insides had bunched up in a painful knot. Scat was, in fact, afraid of pieces of parchment. Because he couldn't read them or write them himself, he treated documents as if they were magical spells, capable of binding him in unpredictable and harmful ways. To have words stained into a paper, unspoken, waiting to be spoken at a later time and work their power far from the speaker of those words, just seemed wrong to him. Dangerous and wrong.

Pimm untied the ribbon, unrolled the leather, took the parchment from within it, and cleared his throat. His voice creaked. " 'Be it known to all men that King Reynard of Nearing Vast hereby confiscates all seaworthy vessels in the ownership of one seaman known as Scatter Wilkins, commandeering them in exchange for fair payment to become warships for His Majesty's Navy. The seventeen ships listed here below will be turned over to Admiral John Hand at the time and place of Admiral Hand's choosing, for use as he alone sees fit, by his sole discretion.' "

"Those are John Hand's words!" Scat snarled, pointing. "That's not the king's voice. 'His sole discretion,' that's Hand speaking right out of that parchment."

Deeter nodded in agreement, not knowing what else to do. "Aye, sir. Should I continue?"

"Yeah, continue."

" 'For fair payment, the king has deposited in the accounts of one Scatter Wilkins five hundred gold coins, which shall be increased to one thousand when the ships named hereunder are manned and manifested under the direction of Admiral Hand, and proven seaworthy.' "

"A thousand coins? The *Chase* alone is worth that!" Scat gnawed that thought for a moment. "A simple man robs his neighbor and hangs, but a king! A king can rob a whole country and reign on in peace."

"Shall I continue?"

"Yeah, continue." Scat stewed. He opened the cigar box beside him and angrily pulled a cigar from it, bit the end off, and spat it out. It could hardly get worse.

" 'All officers and crews shall be chosen at the sole discretion—' "

"Of Admiral John Hand, yeah, yeah, read on."

Pimm cleared his throat. " 'Of Admiral John Hand. To this order I place my royal seal, this twenty-sixth day of—' "

"Forget that. What about the list? Read the ships."

"Very well, sir. '*Rake's Parry, Black-eyed Susan, Poy Marroy, Homespun, Danger, Marchessa, Wellspring, Blunderbuss, Candor, Campeche, Gant Marie, Forcible, Bonny Anne, Swordfish, Windward, Gasparella,* and *Trophy Chase.*' "

Scat chewed on that list a while. Then he frowned. "Not the *Seventh Seal*?"

"It's not listed, sir."

"Count 'em. Is that seventeen ships?"

Deeter counted. "Aye, sir."

A gleam came to Scat's eye. "He's left me a play, then." Scat searched his vest pocket and found the small, ornate gold lighter, recently relieved from the king's employ, and lit his cigar. He coughed, a deep and scratchy thing. "Fetch me Jonas Deal," Scat said when he could. "We've got a ship to sail."

CHAPTER 3

Muster

The muster of Nearing Vast began. As intended, King Reynard's proclamation brought almost the entire able-bodied male citizenry of the kingdom into the City of Mann. The plan was simple. Recruiting stations were set up in stores, post offices, taverns, street corners, anywhere the recruiters felt they could post their signs and lay out their papers effectively. Lines formed, and the recruitment began. When a man presented himself, the recruiter would take a look at him, ask a few questions, and decide on the spot: in or out.

If in, the inspired new recruit would be given a small green ribbon for Army, or a blue one for Navy, and sent to one of two muster stations established for this purpose within the ramparts of the Old City. If out, the dejected man was sent back home to plow or fish or sell dry goods.

That was the plan. As it was implemented, however, several complicating factors intervened. First, the location of the recruiting stations remained a mystery to a good portion of the public interested in finding them. In some parts of town there were six or eight within spitting distance, while in others men searched in vain for anyone who knew where to apply. Within a few days it became known, or at least rumored, that the number of recruiting stations tended to increase in direct proportion to the number of taverns. Word of mouth then brought the majority of the male population of the kingdom into those sections of the city where the primary economic engine was the sale and consumption of ale, whiskey, rum, and nog.

Which led to the second complication.

The simple task of determining who was fit to serve and who was not became more guesswork than assessment. The recruiters, mostly retired military men, were forced to make judgments based on their best guess as to what a man standing before them might look like, or say, or be able to do, when sober. And as the recruiters were being paid by the head, they had little incentive to let a small thing like intoxication stand in the way of patriotic duty. So a large contingent of men of steady purpose but unsteady comportment were given their ribbons and their instructions and pointed in the general direction of service to their country.

Which led to the third complication.

The men had trouble finding the muster stations. This was in part because they were unable to follow the directions they were given, but it was in larger part because they had little desire to go looking for the muster stations. On one sunny afternoon within three weeks of the king's pronouncement, a significant portion of the newly arrived recruits, the new martial forces of the kingdom, the hope of Nearing Vast, could be found gathered or camped or sprawled in the streets, singing in taverns, and occasionally retching over horse railings. Celebration was in the air, and the streets were littered with hundreds of little green and blue ribbons.

The recruiters, quickly having lost all control of the situation, were left to salvage what they could by ensuring that the general tone and spirit of the revelry was as patriotic and martial as it could be. In other words, they felt it their duty, if they could not discourage the men from drinking, at least to encourage the right sort of drunkenness.

Which led to the final complicating factor.

The recruiters joined the recruits. Rolls were misplaced, papers went missing. Entire recruiting stations disappeared, unrecoverable. What had been planned as an orderly and simple process to raise a new and noble fighting force had degenerated with dizzying speed into an ale-sodden celebration of the past and future glories of Nearing Vast and the unworthiness of their despicable enemy, the Drammune.

It was in this precise environment and on these precise streets that the indefatigable Bench Urmand spent his first days on the job, having finally been announced as minister of defense. He coolly assessed the situation, and quickly took action. He started at one end of one street, and with five good men began to clean it up saloon by saloon, pub by pub, inn by inn.

After the first day's work, he had succeeded in filling one tiny jailhouse with eight belligerent offenders, and filling with anger and indignation a hundred times that many citizens, none of whom appreciated his authority over these matters—and all of whom were, after a bit of soggy recollection, quite sure they were already in the Army, or the Navy, and therefore also sure this man was diminishing the very military might of Nearing Vast.

Drunken outlaws Bench could handle easily enough, but he found he could make little headway against the stubbornness of drunken patriots. So he took to appealing to the pub owners and the saloon-keepers to shut off the spigots. And just as quickly, they took to treating him as a dangerous madman, someone who needed to be appeased until he could be convinced to go elsewhere.

After two days, Bench Urmand gave up in extreme frustration, took his men, and rode away cursing the weaknesses and stupidities of human nature, despairing of how such a rabble would ever become a fighting force, much less become so within weeks.

But the great forces that move history would soon conspire with the mean realities of personal economics to accomplish what the just and upright minister of defense could not. Eventually, the men ran out of money. And when they did, the spigots were shut off more finally and effectively than any decree of any king could ever accomplish. Men without ale being generally sober men, they began gathering their wits and their possessions. Most were able to locate their wits again, and most of their possessions. Their weapons and ammunition, however, were long gone.

Sadder if not wiser, they had nothing remaining to do but blame the Drammune. And then, with their new brothers-in-arms, they all joined the trickle, which became a flow, and then a flood, toward the long-neglected muster stations. They picked up ribbons they found in the streets along the way, or just went without, rightly assuming they would not be turned away from their glorious destinies just because they happened to misplace a small bit of colored cloth.

And thus the Kingdom of Nearing Vast would replenish its armed forces and prepare to return to its former glories in the face of the inevitable onslaught of the highly disciplined, thoroughly trained, battle-hardened, and merciless Drammune war machine.

As the citizens' supply of pistols, muskets, swords, and ammunition dwindled, Scatter Wilkins' stockpile of arms grew. His pirates drank but did not celebrate; instead they pilfered, and what wasn't sold or hocked made its way into the armory of the *Seventh Seal*. The captain was making preparations for his own war, and though his was on a smaller scale, it was also a far more efficient operation.

Scatter stood on the deck of his latest and perhaps—or so he feared—his last flagship, overseeing the provisions being lowered by ropes and pulleys into her hold. He was in a dark mood; he had been for days. He couldn't help but brood over the turn of events that had led him here to this fallen place, a sick man leaning on a rail for support, leading a band of cutthroats on a desperate mission of vengeance, sailing a dark and troubled ship, unwanted by a Crown desperate for ships. He put a hand to his chest, felt the beating of his damaged heart.

How had he gotten here, from that moment mere months ago when he stood in his strength, with the vision of a million gold coins dangling before his eyes, so close he could touch it, as he captained the greatest ship ever built toward the greatest glory a man had ever conceived?

All that was left him now was one last, savage stroke. If unsuccessful, it would be his undoing. This ship might well be his coffin. And if successful? He would return to his traditional line of work, seeking out the fat prizes that scurried across the seas during wartime. He would sail under the black flag once again, without plans, without politics, and without a pathway to legendary riches.

And who had done this to him? That was a question that smoldered in his bad heart like coals, ready to flare up with the slightest breeze, the smallest kindling. And as he watched and thought, he was able to supply not only kindling but fuel, and by the boatload.

King Reynard had done Scat wrong. That fool had sent the Navy off to be destroyed. Had he been even marginally intelligent about it, Scat's fate would be far different than it was. Scat had invested all his earnings, every penny of his hoarded gold, into buying and refitting this fleet so he could go harvest the Firefish at their feeding waters.

And King Reynard had paid him next to nothing; the ships had been stolen from him to conduct a war that could not be won.

Prince Mather had also done Scat wrong. That cunning upstart had taken not only his ships but most of his men. The taking of his ships Scat actually understood. But to cherry-pick his men, to order them to sail on the *Chase* without Scat, this was a humiliation he could not bear. But Scat would have his vengeance. His men were loyal. The prince would regret it.

John Hand too had done Scat wrong. "Admiral Sole Discretion" was disloyal to the point of mutiny. Scat couldn't stomach this for an instant. He'd killed men for far less. More to the point, he'd never let a man live who had wronged him so fully.

Talon! She had definitely done Scat wrong. That uncanny witch had undone him by murdering Senslar Zendoda. "Take your pleasure of vengeance," Scat had told her. But he had been talking about an innkeeper in Hangman's Cliffs. She had shown Scat up. She had started a war. That murder was a stab at Scat's heart, to make him pay for sending her ashore. And he had paid dearly.

And Packer Throme. There was the root of it all. Why had Scat sent Talon ashore? Because of Throme. "Trust him at your gravest peril," Talon had warned. He came aboard with the stated purpose of taking away Scat's monopoly, of putting him out of business. So why had Scat trusted him? Here was a bone to gnaw.

Talon had forced Scat to choose between her and Packer, and he had made a bad choice. But if he had chosen otherwise, if he had let Talon kill the boy, Scat would never have known the location of the feeding waters, would never have sailed in among the Achawuk, and therefore would never have seen that glorious sight, an entire school of Firefish feeding. No, Packer was the reason for both his greatest hope and for the dashing of that hope.

And this is what kept Scat's gloom growing deeper. He could find no path he should have taken, could have taken, that would have led anywhere else but here. He was trapped, channeled down this canal to a dead-end swamp, destined by his own lust for coin and Firefish to do precisely what he had done, with no one to blame but himself and God, or whoever or whatever planned out the order of the universe. He had played the hand he was dealt, and he had lost. Here was the end of it.

But it wasn't *quite* the end. Scat would write his own ending.

He would not die a sick old man spinning tales of former glories. Here was one pirate who would not retire to the Warm Climes to drink and play cards. He would not end up like Fishbait McGee and Skewer Uttley. He would rather hang, like Belisar the Whale. Let Bench Urmand pull the lever. Fine. Someone had to do it. Better the noose than dying of this terrible sickness in his chest.

But Scat could evade such a fate for a good long while, if he just had the *Chase* under him again. And if he couldn't succeed in taking her back, then Scat might remake his legend aboard the *Seventh Seal.* He looked at the triune motto he had had carved into a rough wooden plaque and nailed to the base of the mainmast.

Vigilance. Precision. Vengeance.

The day the *Trophy Chase* set sail was warm and sunny. The sky was a deep crystal blue, so clear it seemed a wonder stars were not visible. The *Chase* rocked and tugged at her mooring, creaking and groaning as though impatient to get to sea. Her hull was draped with heavy blue and white bunting all along her freshly repaired rails; her gangway was carpeted red. A dais had been constructed on her decks, so that those making speeches on this historic day could be seen, if not always heard, by the crowds gathered on the docks, as well as in and around and on top of the buildings lining the docks, and even on the hills beyond.

It was not yet noon, but the crowds were already in fine spirits. They could catch sight of Prince Mather, who was dressed in his finest, a white coat with golden epaulets and golden cords, powder-blue breeches and matching sash and gloves, a softly gleaming sword and scabbard at his side. There on his left stood Bench Urmand, in a dark-green suit crisp and pressed, the medallion of his new office around his neck. And on the prince's right stood Admiral John Hand, his white dress uniform brilliant, with vest and tails, and medals from naval services rendered almost twenty years ago gleaming on his chest. On his shoulders were five gold bars, the top one looped, the bottom one as wide as the top four combined: the insignia of the Admiral of the Fleet.

Behind them were the few officers who had retained their commands—a handful of men who had managed to keep the trust of their prince and pass muster with their new masters. Among them were three aged generals, but no admirals. In a seat of honor in front of them and to their right was the High Holy Reverend Father and Supreme Elder, Harlowen "Hap" Stanson, the sunny and genial leader of the Church of Nearing Vast. He was dressed in a white robe with a bright yellow hood and sash, with the small, inverted golden chalice that represented his office hanging from a braided gold chain around his neck.

A few steps from the church leader, and just out of sight of the crowd, hidden by the ship's wall below the quarterdeck, stood Packer and Panna Throme. Packer wore the simple dress whites of a Vast naval uniform, with the single gold collar bar of a newly minted ensign. He wore white gloves, the right one custom-made by the prince's own tailor to slip easily on and off his scarred and cupped hand. Panna was dressed in her only finery, the robin's-egg-blue dress that had been the disguise so artfully used by Talon, though it was now cleaned and pressed and repaired, and sparkled like new.

Lined up along the gunwales were marines, the soldiers of the sea, all bearing muskets and swords and wearing matching blue blazers with the familiar white sashes that signified their rank. Filling the decks and the rigging were the regular sailors of the Nearing Vast Royal Navy, dashing in their new white uniforms, the disciplined crew of a naval vessel.

Or so it appeared.

In fact, the marines and sailors were the longstanding crew of the *Trophy Chase,* with a few huntsmen from Scat's Firefish venture and some newly recruited adventurers thrown into the mix. They had all been formally drafted and then hastily outfitted. The ability of Andrew Haas, Mutter Cabe, Smith Delaney, and their ilk to stand at attention and present an impression of martial bearing tested the very furthest reaches of their military discipline. Those ashore who looked carefully could pick up on clues—the telltale tug at a collar, the half-concealed scratch of an uncontrollable itch, the shrugging shoulder or fidgeting leg that hinted at the deep, obscured misery of pirates in pressed pants and starched shirts.

"Countrymen!" Mather called out, and the scene below erupted into wild cheering. Will Seline, standing on the docks amid the shoulder-to-shoulder throng, thought, *This is going to take a while.*

And it did. Not that the speeches were long. Mather's was short and stirring, a song of dire times, heroic deeds, and certain future glories. It took time because the crowd responded with full hearts and full throats, almost sentence by sentence. The prince knew how to present a dark problem, draw out its drama, and then punch home the profoundly simple solution provided by good people doing simple but heroic deeds in accordance with their faith and their duties and their historic natures.

Panna and Packer listened, hand in hand, their hearts pulled along by this portrait of sacrifice and suffering and ultimate victory painted by their prince. Then suddenly, Panna squeezed Packer's hand so hard it made him wince.

She spoke aloud. "This is wrong."

Packer ignored the pain, but lowered his brow at her. *This is not the place for…* But the look in her eyes was far away, as though she were thinking of something else entirely, watching something only she could see. "What?" he asked.

Panna had become resigned to parting with Packer. There was no other course, regardless of how much she wanted him to stay, or her to go. But something had been tugging at her all morning, something grim and foreboding, pulling at her from within the dark secrets the prince had insisted Packer keep from her. Now, standing on the deck, with crowds gathered and the moment of parting near, she realized her dread was more specific. She had been listening to the prince talk about glories on the sea, and she had looked out into the bay. There she saw only waves catching the sunlight, seagulls careening, and a few small sailboats canted against the sky. That's when it hit her.

"Where are the other ships?" she asked.

Packer swallowed. "Not now, Panna."

She had had a picture in her mind of this parting, of the *Trophy Chase* joining the Fleet of the Royal Navy. She remembered stories told of the Comitani Wars by old men when she was young, descriptions of the Vast Navy filling the Bay of Mann with billowing white sails. She realized, just now, that in her mind's eye she'd expected this day to look like that. And the ships were missing. "How many ships are sailing today?"

"Three," he whispered. "The prince just said that." The *Marchessa* and the *Silver Arrow* and the *Chase* were lined up, ready to cast off. "Listen to the prince; he'll explain."

But the prince chose that moment to introduce the next speaker.

The Hand That Bears the Sword

53

"…a career as storied as any in our history, medals of honor, a chair at our Royal Academy, and lately the strategic mind behind the most celebrated business venture of our times, the hunting of the Firefish—"

Prince Mather had to wait for the cacophony to recede. When it finally did, he hurried through the rest of his introduction so as not to be interrupted again. "A man who has found success in the military, the academy, and in commerce, I give you a great and worthy captain of the *Trophy Chase*, as she takes her first voyage under the flag of our Navy: Here is our new Admiral of the Fleet, John Hand!"

The admiral was resplendent in his dress whites, doffing his cap, nodding dutifully, even humbly, waiting for the cheering to die away. When it did, and he began speaking, Packer looked at Panna. "Admiral of the Fleet," she said softly, eyes wide and distant. "I see the admiral. But where is the Fleet?" Her heart thumped in a hollow chest.

Packer's spirits fell. "Not now, Panna. Please."

She closed her eyes. A short war.

John Hand spoke somberly, and his voice, not a natural bass, nevertheless carried, and carried weight. He was confident, serene, grave, and earnest, as though born for this moment. "Today," he was saying, "we sail this great ship and her escorts out of our beloved bay, and worthy as she has proven to be, she is but a token of the iron will of the people of Nearing Vast." He had a steadying affect on the crowd.

"We will bring all our strength to bear against our foe. And such focus will be required. For ours is an enemy taught to believe that killing us gives them the right to our lands, and all our possessions. They do not want to rule us, but to replace us. Think about that, good people. They want to kill us in order to claim all we have." The only sounds heard were the tense creak of ropes pulling on pylons, the lazy flap of bunting blown in the breeze, and the plaintive squeak of wooden hulls chafing against leather padding on the docks.

"But they will find that we are not anxious to accept that little exchange." Breaths were taken, and laughter heard. "They will find that we have within us the rocks against which their dark dreams will be dashed, and sunk."

"Aye, Captain!" men called out, and "You said right!"

John Hand's voice grew in strength, like thunder rumbling closer and closer. "They will find that all they hope to claim will fight against them. Not only our naval vessels, but our merchant vessels, our fishing vessels, every boat and every cannon, every musket, sword, knife, bow and arrow, every stone and every clod of dirt in this great land will rise up against them! They will find every ounce of our will bent and trained on them, our singular enemy, until we, by God's grace, prevail!"

Wild, sustained cheering followed.

He's good, Packer thought. He glanced at Panna. *But not good enough.*

Now the prince stepped forward. He shook the admiral's hand, beaming his pleasure. He turned to the crowd and raised an arm, taking in the *Trophy Chase* and her sailors. "This is the ship, and this is the crew that slew the Firefish!"

Exuberant cheering.

"This is the ship, and this is the crew that defeated the Achawuk in their strength!"

Thunderous cheering.

"This is the ship, and this is the crew, that will slay the Drammune!"

Delirious cheering, whoops, roars, pounding.

"She will cast off today, by God's grace, with that mantle, that cloak of invincibility, that wreath of glory so recently hung around the neck of one of our own citizens, a humble fisherman and the son of a fisherman, who showed us all the true spirit of Nearing Vast. By strength of spirit and force of will he became a hero. I'm speaking of none other than our own native son, Packer Throme!"

And as the applause grew to a deafening roar, as the citizens pounded their feet and clapped their hands and raised their mugs with raw and ragged voices, Prince Mather looked over to Packer and held out his hand, beckoning.

But at that moment Panna clutched Packer's arm with both her hands. "Packer, don't go!" she pled. Packer looked at her in shock. Her face was pale, bloodless. She stared at him with eyes empty, dark windows into her fear.

"Panna, I have to."

She had heard it; had Packer not heard it? The prince had said it! He had called it a wreath of glory, but he had said it was hung around Packer's neck. And when he had said it, she saw the dream,

The Hand That Bears the Sword

saw it coming true. It was the side of a ship, and not a cliff; and it was a prince and not a king; but the cheering throng was here, and Packer and Panna were here, and Packer the hero was now pushed to the fore.

The prince's eyes narrowed. He stretched out his arm again, beckoning, providing Packer's cue a second time. Packer grasped Panna's right wrist firmly, intending to pull her hands away, to pull himself free. "Panna," he said.

"Oh, Packer," she answered, the words escaping her like a last breath. And she let go of his arm.

Had she clutched him more tightly, had she insisted, had she cried out, he would undoubtedly have torn himself away. But she breathed out heartbreak; it was the sound of love punctured, a heart deflated. She dropped her hands, as though dropping her claim.

And so he could not turn away. Instead he turned toward her and took her by the shoulders. He looked into her eyes, searching for the life, the spirit, the heart he knew was there. "Panna," he called gently. And she responded. Light came back into her, from her, into her eyes, and they searched his.

He would choose her over glory, over fame, over duty, over everything else in the world. She knew that now. And she would therefore let him go.

The prince was not impressed. He covered the five steps to the couple in three. Out of view of the crowd now, his face was wholly given over to anger. "Packer!" He put a hand on Panna's wrist, to disentangle her from her husband. Panna's eyes darted to him, cold and hard, and she yanked her hand from his grasp.

Mather was not accustomed to being disobeyed, nor was he accustomed to receiving such looks from his subjects. He blanched.

Packer didn't take his eyes off of Panna. "Are you all right now?"

"Yes," she nodded. "Yes, go."

The prince grabbed Packer's arm and spun him around. Plastering a smile onto his face, he marched Packer onto the platform, his hand on Packer's neck.

Now Panna heard the crowd again, cheering wildly. She stepped out from behind the ship's wall just far enough to see them in their frenzy, their zealous applause for a hero they knew not at all, could not know, not as she did.

Prince Mather stood aside, turning now toward Packer, clapping along with his subjects. But he was thinking how dangerous it was to put his trust in this young man. This humble-looking boy with the scruffy hair and pockmarked face had shown a missionary's zeal to serve, just yesterday. But now he was completely willing to make his prince look like a fool. Packer had insisted his wife join him here, and then he had ignored his duty, his commander, his prince, and quite literally, his country, in order to wrap himself in the embrace of that hardheaded creature he'd married. Which could only mean that Packer himself was softheaded, letting his marital desires overwhelm his martial instincts.

He was too unpredictable to be trusted.

Packer saw nothing as he looked out over the crowd. It was a blur to him, this cheering, exulting throng. He could not make a connection between their fervor and himself, or anything he'd ever done. They cheered something, but he was sure it was not him. They cheered for the defeat of the Achawuk, but that was a thing he had not accomplished. They had not seen the bloody melee on the decks of the *Chase,* this very deck where he now stood. They had not been struck by the horror of it, as he had been. They did not see how God had rushed in and changed the outcome. Perhaps they cheered God. Yes, perhaps they cheered God's deeds, without even knowing it.

"Wave to them!" the prince whispered through clenched teeth. Packer was just standing there like a stone.

Packer put his right hand into the air. The crowd renewed its efforts. There would be so much more death, Packer knew, now that the circle had widened into war. Unless God intervened again. Scat's greed had sparked Packer's dream of glory, which had lit the fuse on Talon's vengeance, which had now exploded into war. And for this, Packer stood as a hero, lauded by a roaring populace. Why? Because they wanted this war. But he knew they wanted a victory only God could bring them.

Out in the crowd, a few recruits who still retained their muskets and pistols fired them into the air, small fireworks with white smoke plumes exploding violently skyward. This was the beginning of the great campaign, they now knew, the mobilization of Nearing Vast onto the field of honor, the noble field of battle, where history would be written by their deeds. They would be warriors! They were warriors already. Prince Mather had said it, and Packer Throme confirmed it. What better proof of their own valor than this boy, this young man, a fisherman of humble birth just like each of them, who had gone to sea and made his name glorious? If God was with him, then why not with them? And if God were with them, then victory would be theirs!

A few spectators did not join in the revelry. There were a handful who did not see this event as a talisman of good fortune, but as a portent of doom. Among them were two men who watched from the darkened back window of the rooms just above Croc-Eyed Sam's, a window that looked out over the docks, over the heads of the roaring crowd, not sixty yards from the spot chosen for the *Trophy Chase*'s send-off. Scat Wilkins sat at eye level with those on the dais, his boots up on the windowsill, his wheel-lock pistol in his hand. Next to Scat stood Jonas Deal, a deep scowl seared into his face.

Neither man said a word. There were no words, none dark or foul enough, that could give adequate expression to this moment. Scat's ship, the thing he loved most in the world, the all-but-miraculous *Trophy Chase*, was draped in blue-and-white bunting and given like a wrapped package to John Hand. The glory she had won under Scat's leadership, at the cost of his blood and his sweat and his health, the dual glories of killing Firefish and defeating Achawuk, were now draped around the shoulders of a stowaway bilge rat, a boy who didn't fight and could barely sail, and who had collapsed in sobs under Talon's torture.

All the renown that was rightly Scat's, all Scat had done and built, would be wasted, was already wasted on this, all sold for this one moment, which was meant only to generate a passion in the peasantry that would not make one whit of difference when the Drammune warships appeared on the horizon. Nothing could keep this war from being short and brutal, from ending with Scat's commandeered fleet at the bottom of the sea or in the hands of the Drammune. Nothing could keep the foreign armies from ransacking the City of Mann.

But that was not Scat's concern. He was concerned only with saving the *Trophy Chase*. And he had a plan. Nearly a third of that crew, the ones now starched and shining like beacons of all that is upright in the world, were sworn to be loyal to him. His men understood who owned the *Trophy Chase*. They understood whose glory Throme was stealing. They would act, at the proper moment.

Scat rocked slightly in his chair, his face blank of all expression. Then he raised his pistol casually, closed his left eye, and aimed carefully at Packer Throme's heart. It was not an easy shot from this distance, but it was one he could make nine times out of ten.

Bang, he mouthed. And he lowered the pistol again. "Raise your hand, accept all the glory, little stowaway rat. This is far from over."

Then to his right-hand man he said, "You better get going, Mr. Deal. We don't want our precious hero facing the Drammune without a good first mate aboard."

When Deal smiled, his teeth were almost as dark as his intentions. "No, sir. We sure don't."

When the admiral finished speaking, Mather was in a hurry. All had gone exactly according to script, and now he wanted to push the *Chase* and her escorts to sea, while the crowd was in full throat and energized.

But there was one ceremony yet to perform, one that had been designed very carefully. As the applause for Packer died away, the prince turned to face him. When he spoke, it was in the carefully practiced, loud and precise voice meant to carry to the ears of the kingdom.

"Packer Throme," he said with great gravity, "you were awarded a special sword by our late beloved swordmaster, Senslar Zendoda. That sword won great victories against the Firefish, the Achawuk, and the swordmaster's assassin, the Drammune warrior known as Talon."

Packer opened his mouth as the crowd cheered, but he did not speak. Precisely none of those feats were accomplished with that sword. Packer had handed the sword given him by Senslar Zendoda to Scat Wilkins on his first day aboard the *Chase*, receiving it back in time to face only Talon, before whom he had dropped it, never to pick it up again. None of what the prince had just said was true.

If Mather read Packer's misgivings, he didn't seem to mind. He continued. "And after your sword slew your nation's enemy, its work was done. It was lost at sea in the burning conflagration that was Talon's tomb. And so, it is my pleasure," he said, unbuckling the sword at his own hip, "to present you with this." He held aloft the sword by its scabbard. It was a rapier, in an unadorned, soft golden sheath.

The people cheered again. Packer studied the sword. The hand guard was not a cup, but a crosspiece. The gleaming thing the prince held high, its hilt upward, looked like a crucifix.

And just then the prince beckoned to the High Holy Reverend and Supreme Elder, who stepped up to the dais between the two. Mather passed the sword, still held aloft, to Father Stanson. The churchman, taller than Mather by four inches, held it near its tip and raised it even higher. The crowd hushed. Hats came off; heads bowed. Now the symbolism could not be missed. The highest priest in the land held aloft a cross.

Hap Stanson raised his left hand and boomed, "Let us pray." He craned his neck upward and spoke with gusto, with passion. "Almighty God, You are our defender and our salvation. You alone determine the fate of men. Have mercy on us, and give us strength in the battles ahead. We ask You to multiply our strength, as You have done over the ages, as You have done with this ship, this crew, and this young man, Packer Throme. Help him to wear this sword well, in the honor of service to his country. Help us all in our time of trouble, give us hearts like lions, souls like lambs. Give us victory, and we will give You all the glory and the praise forever. Amen."

Packer accepted the sword. He held it by the scabbard with two hands and looked at the hilt. The handle was wrapped in a light, almost golden leather, dyed to give the impression it was all metal, one with the scabbard and the crosspiece. A cross that is a sword. A sword that is a cross. A thousand thoughts careened through his mind, but he couldn't come to grips with any of them. He didn't know what this meant. Finally, he rested on the simple fact that the prince had given him a new sword.

"Draw it," the prince said in a tone of command.

Packer put his gloved hand on the hilt. It fit his disfigured grip perfectly, as though made for it. And in fact, it was. He slid the rapier from its casing. It was shorter than his previous sword, and lighter. The blade was silver-gold in color, with the soft gleam of a pearl rather than the stark mirror finish of polished steel. It was straight and true, and unadorned but for the unmistakable mark of its creator, Pyre Dunn, at its base. It struck him as being pure. He swung the blade once, twice; it moved through the air as though his thoughts propelled it. He held it aloft, the point skyward.

The crowd saw a swordsman plying his craft in preparation for battle. He was their swordsman! He was their hope. Heartfelt, deeply emotional cheering erupted. Grown men had tears in their eyes. Those who had them drew their own weapons and raised them high. Those who didn't raised fists, hands, mugs, and bottles. They raised them to Packer, to the *Trophy Chase,* to Prince Mather, to John Hand, to Nearing Vast, and to God. Certainly nothing could defeat them now.

Will Seline, shoulder to shoulder with the throng, grimaced, then wiped away the ale that had been sloshed onto his robes by a drunken patriot.

Once the speeches and ceremonies ended, Prince Mather wished everyone well, shook hands all around, and then descended the gangway. The crowd cheered on, and a band, more exuberant than talented, pounded away at "Long Life to King and Kingdom." At the foot of the gangway Mather stopped and spoke briefly to his bodyguard, a huge young man wearing the light blue hauberk that signified the Royal Dragoons, the palace guard of Nearing Vast. The big man nodded and climbed up to the ship's deck. Jonas Deal followed him up the gangway.

"I can't believe you're leaving," Panna whispered. "And I'm not going with you."

Packer could say nothing. He held her close.

"Promise me you'll come back," she said. "*Promise* me."

"I'll make the promise," Packer said, "but only God can keep it."

She heard his heart break. "Then promise me you'll ask Him."

"I will. Every day."

"And I'll ask every hour, and every minute." They embraced a long while in silence, ignoring the big dragoon, now standing inches from them.

Finally the soldier spoke, in a surprisingly high and nasal voice for such a behemoth. "Excuse me, ma'am. Sir. Time for the missus to go."

"Panna," Packer said, looking her in the eye. "Don't stay in the city. Go home, but stay packed. Be ready to run to the Mountains. Promise me."

The Hand That Bears the Sword

"I promise."

He embraced her again.

"Excuse me," the bodyguard said, less patiently. He was watching the activities on deck, saw mooring lines loosened, sailors unfurling sails. He looked worried. "It's time."

Packer turned his eyes in the dragoon's direction, but didn't measure him, barely saw him. He turned back to Panna. "You're going to be all right?"

She nodded, smiled through tears.

The bodyguard spoke with an insistence they could no longer ignore. "Now."

Packer sighed. "You have to go."

"I know." She wiped her eyes. She had been determined not to cry, not to leave him once again with the image of the red-eyed, rumpled, tearstained girl. But the tears came anyway.

And so did his.

The instant she stepped back, just half a step, the big dragoon took her firmly by the arm just above the elbow and walked her away. "I'm sorry, ma'am."

And then catcalls, boos rose up from the docks. The crowd had been watching the couple's goodbye, and they now loosed their wrath on the dragoon, who was so surprised he stumbled and almost lost his balance. Panna recovered more quickly; she smiled and waved at the well-wishers. The boos turned to cheers.

Packer watched her leave, walking in her casual, innately elegant way down the gangplank. She looked back over her shoulder. Her smile was warm and sad and determined, a crushed heart resigned to an impossible duty.

Then she was on shore. The instant she stepped on solid ground, the gangway was pulled. The dragoon put Panna into a waiting carriage and closed the door. He then climbed up beside the driver.

As the coach wound its way slowly through the milling crowd, people pressed around it, touching it, peering in on tiptoe, waving, calling. Panna did not wave back. Her head was down, and Packer feared she was crying. When the carriage turned a corner, Packer thought he saw another person inside. He let the thought go. It was probably the prince. That was very kind of him. He'd make sure she got home safely.

Will Seline watched from amid the throng on the dock. He saw his daughter descend from the ship and he tried to move toward her, but the crowd prevented him. Something about the way she had been maneuvered into that carriage struck him as wrong. That she didn't stay to watch the ship sail was wrong as well. Will could clearly see the prince inside the carriage, saw him smile. Why did that seem so wrong? He was the Crown Prince of Nearing Vast. Panna was safer now than anyone else in the kingdom. Wasn't she?

CHAPTER 4

Broadside

"Now that's what I call a beauty!"

Packer looked away from the sword in his hand and up at the voice, saw a familiar grin beaming down on him from the footlines. "Delaney!"

Delaney scrambled the last ten feet and dropped like a cat onto the deck. Packer shook his friend's vicelike hand, carefully, and clapped him on his narrow shoulder. Then he held out the sword. "It is beautiful, isn't it?"

"I wasn't talking about that stick a' metal, ya ninny. There's not a man aboard could keep his eyes off the beauty you fetched as a wife."

Packer felt a stab of pain shoot through his hand. "I shouldn't have left her."

Delaney's eyes went wide. "Well, that's sayin' the ocean's blue. But you did it. A man like me wouldn'ta never been able to leave her ashore." He saw Packer's dark look, then spoke quietly, as though in confidence. "But a girl like that wouldn'ta never married a man like me, so there's the end of it."

Packer smiled. "I wish you'd dropped in earlier to say hello. Or goodbye. She would have been glad to see you again."

Both his eyebrows shot up. "Me? Naw. She only said three words to me at your wedding." He closed his eyes, concentrating as he ticked them off. " 'Hello,' 'Delaney,' and 'Pleased to meet you.' " He opened his eyes, then sighed. "I never once left a good impression on a intricate woman such as her."

"You're wrong. She thought you were delightful."

He furrowed his brow. "She didn't say that."

"But she did," Packer assured him.

He smiled oddly, his eyes losing focus. "Delightful," he repeated, turning the word around in his mind the way a child turns a piece of candy in his mouth.

Packer laughed aloud. "Delaney, I thank God you and I are in this one together."

Delaney puffed out his chest. "Well, me too. And Marcus is aboard here somewheres." He leaned in, brow furrowed once again. "What'd she say about Marcus?"

"Hmmm, let me think. I believe she said he seemed like a fine young man."

"And that he is! But she didn't call him delightful?"

"No."

Delaney nodded, sniffed. A highly satisfactory report. "Well, then. We're away." He looked at the dock receding behind them, its people but colorful specks already. "I don't imagine any voyage could be so much trouble as the last one we three sailed."

Packer just nodded, hoping it would prove true.

"Get to work, you two!" A familiar, angry voice cut into them. Standing on the bridge, glaring down at them, was Jonas Deal.

"Aye, aye," Delaney sang, and scampered back to the ratlines.

Packer just stared at Deal, disbelieving. He hadn't seen him come aboard. He wasn't wearing the dress whites every other sailor wore; he seemed like an apparition, materializing from the bad dream that had been their previous voyage.

Deal descended the stair, walked up to Packer, focused and menacing. He smelled of sweat and ale and old tobacco. "You may be a retchin' hero on shore, but you're still nothin' to me but a stowaway rat." Then he leaned in and whispered in a sneer. "If I get half a chance when no one's lookin,' I'll do what Cap'n Wilkins should a done a long time ago. Just one blind moment is all I need, and the next mornin' you'll wake up missing. Think on that, Mr. Throme."

Packer nodded, doing his best.

"Where is the Fleet?" Panna asked the prince. The cheering of the crowd had died away behind them, and the clip of the horse's hooves on the cobblestones could now be heard crisp and quick in front of the carriage.

"Excuse me?" he answered easily. His oiled black hair clung immaculately to his scalp. His gentle, pale-brown eyes smiled. He had had a good morning, and was in a good mood. She wouldn't spoil it quite this easily.

"The Fleet," Panna repeated firmly. "My husband is sailing out to sea with but three ships against the Drammune Armada. How will they be protected?"

The prince was not the least put off. "The *Chase* needs no protection. Haven't you heard? God is with her. But do tell me, what did Packer tell you about our Fleet?"

"He told me nothing, or I wouldn't be asking."

The prince nodded. "But he said something."

"Only that there were things he'd promised not to say."

"So, if he felt he couldn't tell you, what makes you believe I will?"

His smug confidence was irritating. "Something's happened, hasn't it?" Panna asked. "The war will go badly because something's happened to the Fleet."

He grimaced. She might get to him after all. "You are truly the most amazing woman, Mrs. Throme. You have a bright and agile mind, not to mention a wicked right hook. But think a moment. If something had happened to the Fleet, and you knew it to be true, what good would it do you? What could you possibly do with such information that would help the kingdom in this war?"

"The people need to know!" Panna retorted. "Didn't you see them? Half of them were half-drunk with ale, celebrating like this war was already won."

He smiled. "Half of them were half-drunk with ale," he repeated, amused. "But all were half-drunk with enthusiasm. Is that such a bad thing?"

"They are being asked to join up for a war they don't understand, and you are doing nothing to help them. How are you going to win this war with a drunken mob blind to reality?"

The Hand That Bears the Sword

"But that's my problem, isn't it? It wasn't an accident that the recruiting stations were found near the pubs, Panna. Better to gin up the fervor now, while they commit themselves to the fight. They'll have time enough for seriousness when musket balls start flying."

Panna's eyes went wide. It seemed so…manipulative. "So when will you tell them?"

He looked at her with an air of infinite patience. "Tell them what? The condition of the Fleet? That is confidential information even in peacetime, and we're at war."

"They'll find out."

"Perhaps. But not from you." His look was a dark promise. Suddenly, Panna realized her error.

"Of course, I won't tell anyone."

The Prince felt a pang of regret at seeing her falter. She was a beautiful woman, but even more so when she was full of confidence and spirit. "That is true. You won't. But don't worry, I'll make sure your confinement is quite comfortable, until your Packer returns."

That night, the *Seventh Seal* slipped her mooring in darkness, in silence, without a single lamp lit, without so much as a shout from the bosun. The crew moved on deck and in the rigging like so many trained thieves, stealing the wind for their own purposes, pilfering the tide, appropriating the current. The *Seal* was a small ship, her length overall barely two-thirds that of the *Chase,* and in spite of a greater beam, she was nimble and quick. And her master knew how to sail her the way an assassin knows how to wield a dagger.

"Right there!" Packer straightened up, lowered his sword. "That's when you do it. Did you see how I got to your belly?"

Delaney shook his head. "No."

"Anyone else see it?" Most of the men standing around them in a circle had their arms crossed, striking poses of indifference. They had stripped off their offending dress whites before they had cleared the Bay of Mann, relieved beyond measure to return to their accustomed variety of ragged apparel that shared only its tendency toward a sun-washed and faded gray-green color. The officers, including

Packer, still wore their "war whites," as John Hand called them. He wanted to salvage something of a military bearing for his ship.

"Someone saw it," Packer insisted. "How did I get to him?" The men may have affected a lack of interest, but they were truly baffled. Packer had beaten Delaney easily, and had even had the skill to slap the older swordsman in the chest with the flat side of his blade. *Mostly magic,* more than one answered him silently.

"He opens up. After he lunges." Everyone looked to Jonas Deal. His craggy face and darkened teeth loomed down from above, from the quarterdeck rail.

Packer waited for Deal to say something more, something brutal and insulting, but it was not forthcoming. "That's right. That's right, Mr. Deal." The first mate shrugged. Packer turned back to Delaney. "It's not just the lunge, but almost any thrust you try. You're too far forward. Too aggressive."

"Too aggressive," Deal said with a smirk, as though such a thing were not possible.

"Too eager, then," Packer countered easily. "Not every thrust will be deadly, whether you want it to be or not. Keep your feet under you. Okay, now lunge again, but this time move your lead foot another six inches forward, get lower. Lunge, but don't reach."

Delaney nodded and gave it a try. It felt awkward to him. But after three more attempts, he was grinning. "I feel the difference!"

Packer nodded and smiled. "And your belly will feel the difference in battle."

Delaney pulled his shirt up to show off his scars. Two white slashes in a rough X marred an otherwise unimpressive chest. "Maybe I won't be getting a third one of these!"

The men laughed, but couldn't help be impressed. Delaney was the best of them with a sword. If Packer could help him, he could help anybody.

"It's Drammune we'll be fighting," Jonas Deal cut in once again. "Better off learning how to reload a pistol. Or swing an axe." And he walked off.

"Big struttin' bully is what he is," said Delaney when Deal was out of earshot. "Can't fathom what the admiral wanted him around for."

"To fight, I'm guessing," Packer offered. "So," he said as cheerfully as he could, "who's next?"

The men looked at one another, and for a moment Packer was afraid Delaney would be both his first and last student. But their hesitance, it turned out, came from a desire not to appear too eager.

Packer was an ensign in the Royal Navy, but his official title aboard ship was mate-at-arms. He assumed John Hand had invented the title, but the admiral insisted it was real, if somewhat rusty with disuse. As it turned out, mate-at-arms meant pretty much that he was the ship's swordmaster. After his demonstration with Delaney, he had a steady stream of students.

The sailor in the crow's nest of the *Trophy Chase* squinted into the glare of the setting sun. He adjusted the kerchief that kept his stringy hair from blowing into his eyes, and then raised his telescope.

Zeb Bones watched the tall ship on the horizon coming up from behind, directly out of the sunset. She was moving fast. She unfurled no flag, displayed no signals, lit no lamps. This was a ship on the attack, and headed straight for the *Trophy Chase*. Zeb scanned the seas. The *Marchessa* and the *Silver Arrow* were far off on the horizon. He looked down below him. The admiral was not on deck. That was good. The quarterdeck was patrolled by Mr. Deal, who was now chatting quietly with the helmsman. That was even better. The rest of the sailors were busy about their work at the end of a long shift, unaware and unwarned. Excellent.

The lookout put his eye to the telescope again, watched the dark ship as it bore down on them. He could make out figures on the distant deck now but couldn't distinguish them. One of them would be Scat Wilkins, no doubt. Zeb pulled a polished steel mirror from his pocket, and signaled.

Scat stood at the prow of the *Seventh Seal*, his own telescope pressed to his eye, trying to hold the thing steady as he absorbed the all-clear from his man in the crow's nest. The *Chase* at sea was a welcome sight, but even though her lack of vigilance played into his hands, her old captain couldn't help but feel a pang of regret that she was so poorly sailed. The great cat was not prepared for his approach. He could see sails luffing. Scat was quite sure that John Hand was sitting with his feet up in the captain's cabin, Scat's cabin, drinking Scat's rum and planning, planning, planning while his ship wandered ineffectually under lesser men's guidance.

Scat took another look through his scope. Bunting! He could

hardly believe it, but there it was: the heavy blue-and-white ceremonial bunting still hung from the *Chase*'s rails. Two rows of it across her stern, one at the afterdeck rail, one under the captain's windows. What nonsense was this, carrying to sea such pomp and tomfoolery? The *Chase* was not vigilant, was without precision—and if this was John Hand's idea of glory, he had lost whatever sailing and fighting instincts he had once had.

Scat swore. He would rather see his beloved ship with Achawuk spears pricking her hide again than see her all gussied up like this. A lioness with a bow around her neck. A Mortach Demal corseted and painted and powdered for a royal ball.

John Hand did not deserve her. The prince, the king, none of them knew what they had in the *Chase*. Scat had summoned every ounce of strength left in him and focused it on this one mission, this single goal. There would be no glory, in Scat's mind, no gold, no riches, unless he had the *Trophy Chase* under him again. He would win her back, or die in the attempt.

Scat's guess was off the mark in one regard. Admiral Hand did not have his feet up on the table. But he did have a cup of rum in one hand and a pupil across the table from him. He also had a small, polished briar pipe in his other hand. The sweet, pungent aroma of tobacco smoke hung thick as he watched Packer's eyes. He felt the need to see into the young man, into his mind, into his heart.

Ensign Throme swished the cup of rum in his own hand, smelled it, touched the liquid to his lips, but did not drink. He was uncomfortable here in the captain's saloon, a place he had been more than once and never under pleasant circumstances.

"The people ashore believe you are touched by God," Hand said.

Packer watched the amber liquid swirl. He said nothing.

"A lot of the men aboard think the same."

No response.

John Hand drew on his pipe, creating a quiet crackle, and then he blew out a thick swath of smoke. He needed to know how much of all this Packer believed about himself. It would tell him how far the young man could be trusted. "Let's see the scar."

Packer instinctively closed his fist, his spirit writhing within him. This was the mark of his failures, and the mark of God's mercy. But with that thought the verse came to mind. He was not his own. The mark was not his to hide. Packer opened his right hand, holding his palm out, revealing the scarring and the almost perfect "O" of the electrical burn.

John Hand had seen the boy's instinctive recoil, thought it a bad sign. But Packer's willingness to obey without a second prompting was good. The admiral set down his cup, held Packer's hand to the light of the sunset streaming in from behind him. "So that's where the lightning of the Firefish entered you?" he asked.

"I really don't remember."

Hand again looked Packer in the eye. "Do you believe you are touched by God?"

Now Packer looked at his captain. "God saved us from the Achawuk, and from the Firefish."

"In order to save you?"

Packer shook his head. "God does what He wants to do."

"You believe in fate, then."

"No. I believe if we will get out of His way, He will do a lot more than if we stand against Him. And I believe that if we ask Him, He will do a lot more yet. But what He does is what He wants."

Hand sat back, crossed his arms. " 'His thoughts are not our thoughts,' is that it? 'Nor are His ways our ways.' "

"Yes." Packer caught the reference. From the Book of Isaiah. Did John Hand know Scripture?

"And you do that? You get out of His way, and you ask Him to do things for you?"

Packer nodded just slightly. "Not just for me." Now Packer watched the admiral. Why was the man suddenly concerned about God and spiritual matters? "What do you believe? If I may ask. Sir."

Hand scratched his beard. Then he picked up his cup, took a slow drink of rum. He set his cup back down. "I'll tell you the truth, son. I don't really know."

Packer waited.

Hand took another pull from his pipe and squinted through his own haze. "I grew up in a religious home. I came to see that a whole lot of what the Church teaches makes no sense. At least not to me. But it also seems certain there's more than sheer logic at work in the universe."

The Hand That Bears the Sword

"You mean faith."

Hand shrugged. "Call it that. I'm just saying that what may seem logical, even unassailable, in the comfort of a classroom or a parlor over port can fall to pieces in the cauldron of reality, when what a man believes is what he dies believing, or what helps him survive by believing."

"That's why you left teaching? To live in the cauldron?"

Hand laughed. "I suppose if I could have brought sailing into the classroom the way Senslar Zendoda brought swordplay, I might have stayed on. But theory only works in theory. And sailing only works on the sea."

In fact, the cauldron of reality was precisely where John Hand wanted to be. His mind tended to work forward and backward, harvesting ideas and thoughts and facts from the past, from ancient writings and teachings, from recent history, from his own experience, then linking these with the circumstances and knowledge of the present, and then using the result to construct potential futures. All that, though, was academic. What John Hand loved best was to play it all out, to add human will and time and desire, in order to blend people, places, things, and ideas into some new reality, to coax or drive or ride the resulting wave. He loved bringing into existence what had not ever existed before.

But as he rode the unseen, there were always powers at work, or perhaps currents under the surface, that took him in unexpected directions. Packer embodied one of those intrusions, and it was an enormous one. Since the blond-haired stowaway had arrived on board the *Chase,* everything had changed. He had to understand this current better.

Zeb Bones watched the *Seventh Seal* carefully, as Scat Wilkins watched the *Trophy Chase.* And below both ships, far beneath the surface of the seas, in the dark, cold gloom of endless, eternal salt water, the great beast, the trophy for which the *Chase* was built and named, and for which she would forever be remembered, watched them both.

Like a lone hawk looks down from above in a silent, circling vigil, taking the measure of every movement below, with its predator's brain clicking through a thousand calculations a minute, waiting patiently for a spark, for a moment when its senses and instincts isolate one movement among many—one spot of color, one shape, size, and motion that means opportunity—in the same way from far beneath the surface the Firefish looked up from the echoing depths. Every movement above was being watched. The ancient predator moved freely, keeping its constant vigil, seeing and assessing every creature between it and the light, whether fish, eel, ray, shark, or whale.

And now, from far below, its brain clicked through the calculations: size, shape, color, and speed. The Firefish would circle, and circle, and rise, and circle, and watch, waiting for its moment. And as the hawk would spiral tighter and tighter, riding on the wind, measuring, assessing, confirming, until it knew, absolutely, that this was the prey, and now was the moment, then plunge, gravity pulling it to earth at unstoppable speed, its perfect shape cutting through the wind and air like a knife until it reached the earth and turned, talons out, to slam into its prey, to break and to grasp and to squeeze and to kill, so would the Firefish circle, pinpoint its target, and fly upward at unimaginable, unstoppable speed, mouth agape, to slam into, to shock, to bite, and to devour.

This beast had never known anything but hunger. It had never feasted in the Achawuk waters, had only ever roamed the seas in a solitary search, with one thought, one focus, one need: to feed. To feed, it needed to kill. To kill, it needed to hunt. To hunt, it needed to stalk. And so its very hunger drove its patience.

The beast had been keenly aware of several large creatures on the surface of the ocean tonight. It had circled in the deep below them. They moved, turned, swam in a pack, as a school of fish or a flock of birds might. There were only three of them, but the beast had no ability to count. In the darkness of its primal brain it knew only that more than one was a school, and a school of such large creatures was something to study, to understand. To stalk.

These were creatures large enough that, should they turn together in attack, as a pack, the beast could not be sure of victory. They moved fast enough that, should they panic, they might escape entirely. So the beast followed, watching from below, circling, waiting. If it could find one alone, then it might be possible to kill it.

It stalked its prey for a long while, from deep below, alert for any motion that might signal weakness, any scent that might signal opportunity. But it sensed nothing.

And then, suddenly, two of them moved off, leaving one alone. The beast circled below, watching them all, then followed the one. Here was its chance. The lone one was sleeker, longer than the others. It had a very long, deep ventral fin. It had been the fastest of the three, but now, alone, it slowed. It moved listlessly, without purpose.

It was vulnerable.

"The outcome of events cannot be forced, Packer, at least not for long," John Hand said. "Sheer willpower, the power of fear, of violent action, can only shape the future for a time. Even then, it builds it into blunt and angry shapes that people cast away at the first opportunity. Scatter Wilkins does not understand this. To him, the future is something to be grabbed by the throat and beaten into submission."

Packer smiled at the image, but John Hand did not.

"The great leaders of people, Grot Wimboller of the Urlish, the Hezzan Tul of the Drammune, our own King Fram the Fifth, and before him the Brothers Mann, all of them learned to maneuver within the ebb and flow of time and history. They inspired admiration and love, as well as fear. They took with them entire nations who were grateful to be led through hardship and bloodshed to a better end." Packer's intense stare told Hand that he had, at least for the moment, a willing student. "The Hezzan Shul Dramm is such a leader."

"The Drammune emperor?"

John Hand nodded. "He is a fearsome enemy. The Drammune have no religion but Drammun."

"They're like Talon."

"A lot like Talon. But they have ancient ways they believe in, and follow. They have a book of law called the Rahk-Taa, written by the first emperor, the Hezzan Tul, many centuries ago."

"But the Dead Lands. They believe in an afterlife."

"An afterlife, but one a lot like this. No God determines it, but each of us travel an endless journey. The Rahk-Taa defines how to live in this world and prepare for the next. *Rahk* means 'law.' But it isn't a collection of laws like you or I know them. It's a lot more like commandments. The Rahk-Taa defines what it means to be Drammune."

Packer looked confused. "Commandments without God?"

"The word *Drammun* means 'worthy.' The Drammune are quite literally the 'Worthy Ones.' The rest of us are therefore, by definition, unworthy. All who are not Drammune are *Pawns*—a rough translation of their word for *worthless*. We are the worthless ones. To be used or cast aside."

Smoke hung in front of John Hand's eyes as he watched his student grapple with this. Then Packer said, "And so they have the right to all we own."

He smiled. "Ah, you were paying attention. Yes, to quote the Rahk-Taa, 'The Law commands the Worthy Ones to rule. Therefore the Worthy One who takes the life of the Unworthy earns all his titles and treasures.' That's what they call the Right of Transfer. *Kar Ixthano,* in Drammune. Friendly little concept, isn't it?"

Packer pondered it. "Sounds a lot like piracy."

Hand laughed once. "If you think Scatter Wilkins is a fierce foe, wait till you meet the Drammune."

Finally, the invitation to attack could not be resisted. This prey had its guard down. And so the Firefish circled, circled again, and then, its brain and body locked onto its prey, made its decision. It shot upward, mouth agape, scales glowing yellow, for the kill.

Now, at last, it would feast.

Hand pulled on his pipe, found it had gone out. But at that moment a loud splash could be heard astern, a cannonball striking the water outside the admiral's quarters. A fraction of a second later, the boom of a cannon. A dark shadow passed in front of the sun.

Hand's eyes grew wide, not in fear or surprise, but in excitement. "Finally!" He jumped up and ran to the double windows of his cabin at the stern, threw them open. The setting sun made the *Seventh Seal* look darker than she was, sails fibrous and translucent as she cast her shadow on the *Chase*. She was three hundred yards away and closing fast.

As the beast flew upward on its attack path, it detected another creature approaching. An attack! Its instincts told it that it had been lured, that the deep-finned one had lured it, and its companion was attacking from the flank. Pack behavior. But the beast, ablaze with the light of the attack, ignored the intruder. It would kill, then turn and kill again.

But then, an amazing thing—a surprising thing that had no precedent in the beast's mind or memory. Thunder, a flash of lightning, a storm closer to the surface of the waters than the beast had ever felt or heard or seen.

To be at the surface when the sky cracked, when the fire struck the waters: This was death even to Firefish. With a great effort, with the fear of the greatest powers of nature turning it from its feast, it broke off its upward surge. It whipped itself downward. As it did, the tip of its tail struck the deepest part of the deep fin. It was a slight blow, but enough to convince the beast that this was no fleshy creature. This was a shellfish.

The beast dove, and circled again, deep down, to watch. To wait. To learn. And then to stalk again.

The ship lurched and shuddered. "What was that?" Packer asked.

John Hand ignored the question. "The bunting, Packer!" Somehow John Hand had a knife in his fist and was cutting tie lines with it, the ropes that held the colored bunting across the stern of the *Chase*. "Cut away the bunting!"

A flash from the prow of the approaching vessel was followed immediately by a cannonball that whirred through the open window between Packer and the admiral. It traveled through the captain's quarters and exploded against the far wall of the saloon behind them. The impact of the blast knocked Packer against the window post, toward the water, almost tumbling him out. He ducked his head against a horizontal rain of debris that stung him like sleet.

John Hand looked at Packer, saw he was alive, and bellowed his command again. "Go cut the tie lines! Release the bunting!"

Packer looked out the window and saw blue-and-white bunting float down into the sea behind the *Trophy Chase*. The admiral had already cut the bunting away. Packer didn't understand.

Hand grabbed Packer by the collar as another flash erupted from the *Seventh Seal*, yanked him hard to the floorboards. A tremendous crash jarred them both as the cannonball exploded against the hull just under the open window. The admiral was on his feet now, pulling Packer back up.

"Go cut the bunting away on the afterdeck rail above us!" Hand now seethed, his face a knot of frustration, inches from Packer's. "Go!" And he threw Packer toward the saloon door.

Finally comprehending what his orders were, though having no clue as to the reason behind them, Packer left at a dead run, glancing briefly at the splintered pile that a moment ago had been a table supporting two cups of rum.

The *Seventh Seal* had fired her first cannon before any loyal sailor aboard the *Chase* had seen her approach. "To arms!" one of those in the rigging finally managed. "To arms! We're under attack!"

The benighted helmsman, understanding at last the danger, began spinning the wheel, turning the ship to starboard. He looked at Jonas Deal, but the first mate standing beside him was silent, and still as a post. "We're under attack," the helmsman repeated, pleading with the first mate. Deal turned a stony look toward him, but did not act. "All hands!" the helmsman yelled, turning away with a grimace. "Battle sta—" he started, but never finished the command. An explosion at his right ear threw him to the deck in a pool of blood. He was dead. Jonas Deal's pistol smoked.

Deal caught the spinning wheel and calmly eased the ship back onto its former course.

The helmsman's last instinct had been the correct one. The attacker came from upwind, starboard astern. Scat had meant to take out the *Chase*'s rudder as he approached, then rake her starboard hull with a full broadside as he passed. Turning into the attack would have made a rudder shot more difficult, would have given the *Chase*'s cannon a chance to fire on the approaching ship. Most importantly, it would have forced the attacker to choose between ramming the *Chase* and veering to port, giving the *Chase* the upwind position, the advantage known to seamen in battle as the "weather gauge."

Scat would indeed have yielded that advantage rather than ram his beloved ship. But now he had no need. The *Seal* would pass as she pleased.

"Siege! To arms!" came more cries from the rigging. These calls, with the report of Jonas's pistol and the cannon shots ringing from astern, finally roused the sleepy *Chase*. But the great cat's reactions were confused and slow. The first sailors to reach the armory found it locked, and no one seemed to have a key. The three-man crews that operated each cannon had trouble forming; each seemed to be missing at least one man.

The last thing Scat wanted was to sink the *Chase*. But he would do anything short of that to take her prize. He would not aim his cannon at the waterline, but at her hull, her cannon, her decks. Some men aboard the new flagship of the Fleet were aware of Scat's intentions; some were not. But every man was attuned to one brutal fact: The *Seventh Seal* would let loose a broadside in a matter of minutes, and the *Chase* was completely unprepared to return fire.

Packer came to a sudden halt as he exited the captain's quarters and found Jonas Deal reloading his pistol. The lifeless, bloody form of the helmsman lay at Deal's feet. Packer instinctively drew his sword. He stood that way for a moment, watching Jonas Deal ram the ball home. Reloaded now, Deal looked up and calmly pointed his pistol between Packer's eyes. Packer settled into the guard position, his body moving of its own volition. Deal readjusted his aim, and clicked back the hammer. At that moment an explosion from behind Packer crashed a musket ball into Deal's scowling brow. The man stood as though dazed for a moment, uncomprehending, then dropped his arm and his weapon and crumpled backward, landing splayed out and face up across the helmsman's body.

The admiral walked past Packer and pulled the sword from the first mate's belt. When he stood up, he faced Packer, shook his head, and then smacked Packer hard across the chest with the flat of it. Where was the boy's fire now, now that it mattered? "The bunting!" Hand pointed up, behind Packer. "The afterdeck!" The admiral walked away and calmly began cutting tie lines at the quarterdeck rail.

Packer looked at the sword in his hand. He felt like he was in a trance. But somehow he managed to scramble up the ladder to the afterdeck. He brought the edge of his blade down on the tie lines that held the top row of bunting across the ship's stern, above the captain's quarters. His blade was razor-sharp, and the bunting fell easily away.

The swivel cannon on the *Seal*'s prow flashed again, just as Packer cut the final tie. The ball struck the *Chase* and exploded not three feet below where Packer stood, jarring him so he needed to grab the handrail to keep from falling overboard. He looked down at the hull to assess the damage.

And then he saw it. He finally understood what John Hand was doing, why the bunting needed to be cut away. His heart leaped. He looked up at the *Seventh Seal.* Her bowsprit was now almost even with the stern of the *Chase.* Below the prow of the attacking ship Packer saw clearly her figurehead, the bust of an angel, a dark, grim angel carved with an outstretched right arm. Yellow and red painted flames rose up from her open right hand, an offering of fire.

Now musket fire rang out from the *Seal,* from the sailors on her prow. Musket balls pattered into the *Chase*'s hull and whistled through the air. Sailors aboard the *Chase* returned fire, multiple cracks traced by plumes of blue smoke that lashed out at the attackers. Packer felt a calm energy now, certainty and clarity. He knew his role, and he knew the reason for it. And he knew the *Chase* would prevail. He looked up to heaven, deeply thankful, and then, with a guttural yell that came without being summoned, he hurtled over the afterdeck rail, sword in hand, and landed on the quarterdeck. He ran past John Hand, who was cutting away the bunting there, and sprang down onto the main deck. Packer's hand burned as he moved down the rail, attacking the tie lines as though each were a bitter enemy to be dispatched.

The gathered folds of the bunting fell away. Sailors moved back to give him room, eyes wide at his determination, at the speed and precision of his work, but to a man baffled as to his purpose.

Packer was already amidships when the *Seventh Seal* began firing her cannon. She was close, not twenty yards away, and she let loose a long, sustained volley, explosion after explosion, an enormous and ponderous string of fireworks that would rip the *Chase* from stern to bow. The blasts were hideously loud, cracking and booming like a thunderstorm inside a cave. The *Chase* staggered and shuddered as blast after blast exploded from the *Seal* and tore into her.

Near the prow of the *Chase,* Packer went down, unable to stand, his legs kicked out from under him as though he had been standing on ice. The *Seal* was firing directly below him now, at the ship's hull just under him. But he had finished his task; the bunting along the starboard rail was gone.

The booms turned to a high-pitched whine as Packer's ears stopped themselves up, refusing to process the sounds. The ship beneath him jarred and rocked. He tried to hold onto the floorboards, but was batted against them again and again as they slapped him into the air. And then finally, the *Seventh Seal* had passed by, and the air went still.

The Hand That Bears the Sword

Packer sat up, stunned by the sheer, violent chaos of the broadside, the shriek in his ears otherworldly. He tried to take in the scene. Acrid-sweet blue-white clouds of gunpowder smoke draped a haze over everything, burning his eyes and his throat. Men ran, reloaded, knelt over fallen comrades. Then he saw John Hand, saw the admiral stride swiftly to the main-deck gunwale. He looked up at Packer, a gleam in his eye. Smiling! He mouthed some words Packer couldn't hear, couldn't understand, but he grinned back anyway. It had worked. Of course it had worked.

"Look, men!" Hand called, pointing down, and now Packer could hear him. "Take heart, lads, there is no damage to the hull! Come about, prepare the cannon! We'll cut her to shreds in the next pass!"

The admiral's words were more shocking to the crew than the broadside had been. They rushed to the rail to see if somehow it might be true.

And it was true—utterly so. Not a single cannonball had penetrated the *Chase*'s hull. Where bunting had been cut away, wide and overlapping strips of gray metallic material now lay unfurled. Not even a pock or a bunch showed where the cannonballs had struck it. It was pristine. Word passed through the ship, a single thought that seemed to strike every sailor's brain at once. They knew now what hung along their hull...it was Firefish scales, the hide of their great enemy and their great benefactor, their prehistoric predator, their highly profitable prey.

The thin, impenetrable material had been rolled up under the bunting, hidden there, waiting to be unfurled by Packer Throme and John Hand just in time to protect the ship. The men aboard reacted with unrestrained delight. John Hand had outwitted Scat Wilkins. Packer Throme, with his furious sword, had clothed the *Chase* with armor just ahead of the cannon fire.

But before the men could unleash their joy, even as swords went into air and mouths opened, a loud call came down from above them. "For Captain Wilkins!" shouted the lookout. Zeb Bones had unfurled the white skull and bones hovering over a black field.

Silence fell as all the men looked up at the pirate flag under which they now sailed. The blue and red flag of Nearing Vast, with the kingdom's great seal, the interlaced initials *NV* emblazoned over a ship's wheel, fluttered casually away to port, down, into the waves. The silence aboard, and the confusion that drove it, ended with a gunshot from the afterdeck. The body of Zeb Bones tumbled from the crow's nest. Lifeless, he struck the forestay of the mainmast and pinwheeled into the sea. The men watched, frozen in astonishment.

John Hand lowered the enormous pistol, Mr. Deal's reloaded hand cannon, its barrel smoking once again. "Pirates," he said under his breath. Then, "Somebody strike that flag!" Four men scrambled up through the lines, racing for the privilege.

"For John Hand!" shouted Andrew Haas. "All loyal men fight for the admiral, and for Nearing Vast!"

Swords came out, but remained held high, or pointed toward the decks. Sailors aimed their pistols downward as well, just below one another's feet, not wanting to give offense to an honest brother. All waited for some evidence that would betray a mutineer.

Packer looked out to the ocean, to the spot where Zeb Bones's body had splashed into the sea. Then he looked farther, and saw the *Seventh Seal* turning sharply in preparation for another pass. "Where is the *Marchessa*?" Packer asked aloud, to no one in particular. "Where is the *Silver Arrow*?" He scanned the horizon, and finally found two small white dots, the *Chase*'s escorts, tacking into the wind in an attempt to join the fray. They would be no help.

The tense, awkward moment was finally broken by another shout from above.

"White flag! White flag!" called the sailor who had scrambled into the vacant crow's nest. He pointed at the *Seventh Seal*.

John Hand shook his head. "Now there's something I thought I'd never see. Captain Scat Wilkins wants a parley."

The storm on the surface raged, and the Firefish watched from deep below. And then, another surprise. A small bit of something drifted down from the deep-finned one. The great predator waited. The morsel would come down to it.

CHAPTER 5

Parley

Panna quickly learned to despise the palace and its atmosphere, its cold marble and shining, polished wood, where everyone dressed and behaved as though they were going to some fabulous event every minute of every day, where everyone judged everyone else by their ability to look and act as if their own fabulous events were more fabulous than anyone else's fabulous events. Panna rebelled against all this, refusing to wear anything but her peasant dress. This distressed the prince, which in turn pleased Panna. She avoided him as much as possible anyway. She tried to get to know the servants, but the older ones were standoffish, as though born to a privilege she could never achieve, and the younger ones were skittish, speaking politely with her, but with eyes always scanning, looking for an exit. The prince had them all well-trained.

The dragoons were the worst. Big, hulking, angry-looking, they were henchmen in fancy uniforms, starched blue with shiny brass buttons, carrying huge pikes and spears, or what looked like enormous meat cleavers on the end of long poles. They were everywhere, and they watched her always. Only when she was in her rooms, the Blue Rooms, with doors shut and windows shuttered, was she free of their glare. Even on her porch, they watched her from the ramparts. If she were to try to escape in the dark, to climb over the stone railing, they would wait for her, politely and impassively but forcibly returning her to the palace. This she learned the hard way. Eventually, she grew accustomed to their dark, cold stares. She learned to ignore them. But she was never at ease.

She truly loved the library, with its histories and travelogues, philosophers and political thinkers. Here she could lose herself, and forget for a while that she was a captive. This one room opened up worlds to her she had never known existed. But she didn't spend as much time there as she would have liked, because Mather was always coming and going there, looking up a battle or something about Vast or Drammune history. And whatever topic it was, he always wanted to chat about it, as though he felt it his duty to tutor her in the ways of war and good government.

Her saving grace was that the palace sat on some twenty acres of well-tended paths, ponds, and flower-covered hills, so Panna could, and did, spend most of her days outside in the gardens. She found these distressingly sterile as well, with their perfect, perfectly unnatural grooming and shaping, but at least plants grew at their own pace, and flowers ignored royal commands, blooming only when they were good and ready. And then they wore precisely the blooms they wanted, as God intended. They were arrayed, as the Lord promised, more fabulously than any of the fabulous finery within the palace walls.

Panna had found a relatively secluded pond—not far from the palace but far enough away, and off the walks and bridges—where she could sit and read and think. It was not too far from a wide, open expanse, a grass-covered amphitheater called the Green, but here a shady, gently sloping lawn allowed her to take off her shoes, feel cool grass under her feet, dip her toes in the water, and listen to birds singing. If she closed her eyes she could imagine she was on a hillside somewhere in the real world. But when she opened them, she always remembered that she was not. A quick look around would reveal some grim dragoon watching from between two trees or from behind a hedge.

Just before noon on one of a series of otherwise identical days, the Princess Jacqalyn, Mather's sister, the eldest child of King Reynard, wandered into the garden to chat. Panna had met her before, and knew she was the wife of a mostly absent baron. The introduction had been formal, of course, and the princess had made Panna feel very uneasy. Her fabulous events seemed fit for no one but Jacqalyn, and she eyed Panna like the girl were some rare species, a captive bird from a distant locale, not very exotic or interesting, but unusual nonetheless.

Now Jacqalyn in all her glory strolled nonchalantly down to the lip of the pond where Panna was sitting with her peasant dress hiked to midcalf and her feet blissfully bathed in the coolness of the pond. She had a book in her hand and two more lying beside her.

"Something from the library?" Jacqalyn asked, by way of hello.

Panna started to stand up.

"No, please! Please sit. In fact," Jacqalyn looked around her as though someone might be watching, "I may just sit here with you!" She said it with an air of conspiracy. Then she carefully arranged her dress and skirts and lowered herself to the grass nearby. "Well, how about that?"

Panna had no idea what to say in response.

"What are you reading?"

"Mark," Panna answered with a smile.

The princess nodded serenely. Her long, thin face was attractive in a severe sort of way. "Mark who, dear?"

"The Gospel of Mark."

"Ah, quite." There was a long pause, as it became evident that Jacqalyn in turn had no idea what to say. But she maintained her cheerfulness. "You know, it's rather lovely out here. I haven't had a seat on the grass in ages."

"I find it very comfortable."

Again the princess was silent. She had been raised here in the palace, and had left the grounds only for holidays and outings and two extended trips abroad in all her thirty years. The palace was her domain, and she fit it like a goldfish fits a fishbowl. In Jacqalyn's world one might sit on the grass for a number of reasons, but comfort could not possibly be among them. Panna's words made no more sense to her than if the girl had said, "I find the lawn quite dangerous." Certainly, the grass could not actually be comfortable, no more than it could actually be dangerous, unless someone or some circumstance made it so. And Panna had not made it so; she had simply plopped down upon it.

Regrouping her thoughts, the princess looked for a way to broach her chosen subject.

"The prince thinks well of you," Jacqalyn said at last.

"That's nice of him," Panna replied, unable to respond in kind. In fact, she did not think well of him at all.

"Is it?" the princess asked.

Once again, Panna had no idea how to answer.

"You don't know my brother very well, do you?"

"No. No, I don't."

"And you don't seem too keen to get to know him better."

"Is it so obvious? But I suppose not. I'm only keen on going home."

"Home. Yes—to Hangman's Hollow, I believe?"

"Cliffs. But yes. Do you know of it?" she asked hopefully.

"It's all the talk, of course. Packer Throme and the Firefish and the *Trophy Chase* and all."

Panna nodded. Of course. It meant nothing to Jacqalyn.

Now the princess looked at Panna very carefully. She felt a need to be blunt. She wet her lips, pursed them slightly. "Dear Panna. The prince thinks…well…of you. Very well. Do you understand my meaning?"

Now Panna's heart sank. "Perhaps you should explain."

Jacqalyn nodded. "Of course." Even blunt wasn't quite blunt enough for this girl. "My brother is complicated. He is very ambitious, focused on his career, determined to someday be the best king this grand empire has ever known. Our younger brother and I are not quite so ambitious, and he looks down on us for our own little weaknesses. But he is under a great deal of pressure now. And he is showing some signs of weakness himself."

"The war."

"Yes, of course, the war," Jacqalyn said, too quickly. "It puts us all under a strain. But there is more. He has taken to walking the halls at night. Perhaps you've heard him outside your door?"

"My door? No, not at all."

"Ah, that's good then. I'd hate for him to wake you up. He's been irritable. Late for meetings of state, which is highly unlike him. Something is distracting him."

Panna looked at her coldly. "And what is that?"

"Well, it's you, of course."

Panna rolled her eyes. "But I've done nothing. Literally. Why doesn't he just let me go home, then?"

Jacqalyn looked at her with amusement. Had the girl not heard her? The prince was not about to let Panna go. "Well, I'm sure you don't mean to lead him on."

"Lead him on?" The words were shocking.

"I said I'm sure you don't mean to. I'm sure young women in Hangman's Falls wander about in their bathrobes all the time."

Panna's face went white. "You mean that housecoat I found in the closet? He thought that meant something? Gracious, that's more formal than anything anyone back home even owns!"

The sing-song sweetness of the princess's voice was unaltered. "I'm sure that's true. And I'm sure young, attractive women show their ankles quite often in the fishing villages." Panna pulled her feet out of the pond, tucked them under her dress. Now Jacqalyn giggled. "Yes, I'm sure it's true. You really don't mean a thing by it, do you?"

"Of course I don't! Of course not!" Panna looked at her urgently. "Does he really think I—"

"Lord knows what he thinks, Mrs. Throme. I'm sure he understands just as I do, as everyone does, that you are a freer spirit from a simpler world. But he is drawn. I believe he is smitten."

"Smitten?" Panna felt the word like a knife. "I'm a married woman."

"Aren't we all."

"But that's just wrong. That's wrong of him! Someone should tell him so." Panna closed her mouth before she said more. This princess would not take kindly to being lectured by a peasant girl.

But Jacqalyn heard the unspoken words clearly enough. "Me?" She laughed. "As though he doesn't already know. Of course he knows it's wrong. That's why he is in turmoil, of course. He's a man of conscience. That's the only reason he feels guilty about it. He knows you are the bride of the hero, pure and spotless and true. He knows what your Good Book there has to say about neighbors and neighbor's wives. But just like King David on the rooftop, he watches anyway."

"What do you mean, he watches?"

"But glance up at the third-floor balcony, over to the left."

Panna did. The palace was some thirty yards away.

Jacqalyn spoke without taking her eyes off Panna. "You see a dark figure near the hydrangea?"

Panna saw smoke rising from a shadow.

"Those are his private quarters, Mrs. Throme. You are out here every day."

Panna flushed. "Oh my word. I...I had no idea. What should I do?"

Jacqalyn smiled. Yes, she was quite sure now, Panna had had no inkling of the affect her simple charms were having on her complicated prince. It was an amazing amount of innocence to carry so far into womanhood. "What you do about it is your business, of course. Do as you please. Lord knows, that's what I do. I'm just here to let you know." And she stood, a bit clumsily, but then rearranged her skirts until they were perfectly in order. "Good day, Mrs. Throme." She nodded, turned, and glided away, once again enwrapped in her usual splendor.

Panna stood quickly, glared angrily at the hydrangea, picked up her books, then grabbed her shoes and dashed out of sight of the palace before stopping to put them on. She would no longer spend her days in the garden, that was sure. At least, not where she could be seen by someone on that porch. But more importantly, she thought as she pulled angrily on the laces of her soft leather shoes, she would have to find some way to convince the prince and everyone else that she was precisely what she was: entirely unavailable, and entirely uninterested in anything and everything except leaving this place and going home.

Firefish scales. The ultimate protection. The one substance no sword, no musket, no cannon, no weapon could penetrate. Word spread on the *Seventh Seal* every bit as quickly as it had on the *Chase*. How would they ever prevail?

Scat Wilkins' demeanor, however, was more critical to his men's morale than any setback in battle, even one of apparently insurmountable proportions. His orders to run up the white flag of truce were accompanied by a fiery determination they were glad to see. They could see his relish in the fight, see how it strengthened him, and they concluded quickly that he was not surprised by this turn of events. Parley did not mean surrender.

And Scat was not, by any means, surprised. Nor was he finished. He stood on the quarterdeck, legs under him, shoulders square to the *Chase*, square to the fight. His chest hurt him, and he breathed delicately to avoid coughing, but these were minor irritants, shoved to the back of his mind.

At the forefront was the draping of an entire ship with Firefish armor. That was Scat's idea, discussed with John Hand late at night over port on the way back to Mann from the feeding waters. John Hand had been dismissive at the time; the cost would be ridiculously high, he thought, and the results questionable at best. Firefish hide was surprisingly thin, and difficult to tan and treat without losing the scales, which of course provided the protection. It was not just the scales themselves, but the mechanics of how they interlaced, how they reacted to sudden pressures, and that was all related to how the scales were attached to the thin skin beneath them. Small swatches of the stuff was all they'd ever been able to manage. But obviously, his admiralship had now worked it out. It was exactly the sort of detailed problem he loved to solve. And cost was clearly no object now, now that he had Reynard and Mather and the entire royal exchequer at his disposal. And blast if it didn't work.

No matter, Scat's battle plan would succeed. No amount of protection on the outside could withstand an attack from within. And that was Scat's goal, the point of the parley. He had infiltrated the admiral, gotten past the *Chase*'s scales and into her muscle and sinew and bone. He only needed to get close enough to give orders.

Within a few minutes the two ships were hove to alongside one another, with large, three-pronged grappling hooks tossed from one ship to the other, lines held taut to keep the ships close, and with sounding poles held by crewmen of both ships, pushing against the opposite hull to keep the ships at a distance. Close enough to parley but not close enough to board. Not yet, anyway.

So the gunwales of both the *Chase* and the *Seal* were lined with sailors. Those not holding ropes or poles aimed their weapons across the short span of water. The *Chase*'s cannons were now loaded and ready, angled down at the decks of the smaller ship. The *Seal*'s cannons had all been reloaded as well, and were aimed high at the rails of the *Chase*, above the shimmering gray armor that now slapped lazily against the ship's hull.

Scat Wilkins climbed up to the forecastle of his ship; John Hand stood on the main deck of his, so that they were roughly at eye level with one another. "What do you want, Scat?" John Hand called. His voice was gruff and commanding. "The *Chase* is no longer yours. You want her, you're going to die trying to gain her."

Scat was silent a moment. He looked around. To execute his plan, he needed only to get the two ships closer together, or at least to get lines passed from one to the other so his men could board. "You're right. You win. I got a good ship under me. Give me any men who choose to sail with me, and I'll go."

John Hand watched the reaction of the sailors carefully, his own and Scat's. There were no murmurs, no grumbling, no sense of surprise. All were poised for battle. "I know you better than that," Hand called out. "Let's fight now, and be done with it. I can't be worried about you sneaking up on me. There's a war on. You may have heard."

"Did hear something 'bout that. You won't last long against the Drammune, if you let a ragtag bunch like us overtake you. But it's your war, not mine." Scat fumbled in his vest pocket, pulled out a cigar, bit the tip off. "I tried. I failed. I'm done with you." He spit out the small tobacco plug. "Give me my men."

Hand shook his head, disbelieving. "I have the upper hand, here and now. Give me one reason I won't regret letting you fight another day."

Scat took a deep breath. He put a hand to his chest, raised his chin. "Because I can't beat the *Trophy Chase*. Not today. Not any day."

John Hand had his doubts. But he had never heard Scat Wilkins talk this way. "I want your word, in front of all these men, that should our roles ever be reversed, you will do me the same courtesy. Swear that you and I are at truce, now and in the future."

One corner of Scat's mouth rose. "Aye, my old friend. You and I."

John Hand saw a moment he could use. He gestured for Packer Throme to join him at the quarterdeck rail and Packer obliged, standing silently as the admiral turned to face his own crew. "Any man wants to leave, join up again with Scat Wilkins," Hand ordered, "do it now. It's no mutiny; I'll let you go. But if you stay, and I hope you do stay, you forswear piracy and your former captain."

Here the admiral paused, raised his right hand. "You heard him say it—the *Trophy Chase* cannot be beaten. Joining with us here means you become part of the legend of this ship. Stay, and you join yourself to the light. You fight with the very power of God on your side.

You all know the miracles." He put his hand on Packer's shoulder, as if that gesture proved the truth of his words. Packer looked at John Hand in astonishment.

"Stay with us," Hand continued, "and sail with God. Join with Scat, and sail to the devil. The *Seventh Seal* will be your tomb. The name of that ship, gentlemen, comes from the Book of Revelation, the greatest prophecy of the Bible. That angel at the prow is pouring out the fire of God's wrath. The *Seventh Seal* means the end of the world. It'll be the end of your world. So choose today: God's favor—" he patted Packer—"or God's judgment." He pointed to the prow of the *Seal*.

Packer looked at the men on the decks of both ships. Their eyes wandered from Packer to the angel and back. They were all focused, poised, at perfect attention. Packer had the strange impression they were listening very carefully to a voice from far away, a voice with an important message they couldn't quite make out.

"Now pass the lines," John Hand commanded.

Scat Wilkins laughed low. "Nice sermon, Reverend. Aye, pass the lines." Quickly, from the top of the yards of the *Seventh Seal,* three, then five, then seven ropes were thrown to the deck of the *Chase,* ostensibly for Scat's loyal men to swing from Hand's ship to Scat's.

Not one sailor took hold of them.

Scat sniffed, unruffled. He would have been surprised had any of his men taken this offer. They were awaiting his orders. He gnawed his unlit cigar. Then he smiled. "Seems you win again. But you of all people should know, Admiral," he said with a sneer, "that nothing's ever all it seems."

The moment hung on the silent portent of Scat's words as the two captains assessed one another and their situation. The two ships were lashed together so close that the *Chase*'s cannons, though aimed menacingly down at the *Seal*'s decks, could not be aimed at her hull. Regardless of the carnage they unleashed, the *Chase* could not sink the *Seal* from here. The *Seal*'s cannons were aimed upward, but they could not hit the decks of the *Chase*. The best they could do was take out rails and sails and masts, but the hull of the greater ship was armored, and safe. Both commanders knew that a fight from this distance favored the *Chase*, whose crew had the high ground, and therefore cover. But Scat still counted on greater numbers, with his sailors aboard the *Chase* just itching to fight against John Hand.

The old pirate took the cigar from between his teeth, and scanned the faces lined up against him. He nodded, satisfied. Now was the time. Now he would set the dismal errors of the king and the prince to rights. Vigilance was his. As was precision. And now he would have vengeance. Now he would have the *Trophy Chase*. He smiled.

"Loyal men, stand firm!" Scat called. And then with a roar and a snarl, sounding almost like the pirate captain he once was, he commanded, "Take back the *Chase*!" The men of the *Seal* cheered and fired with muskets and pistols, taking out first the men who held the poles that kept the two ships apart.

Hand's face contorted into a blaze of anger as his men returned fire, not waiting for orders. "Open fire!" he commanded, his voice lost in the din of exploding black powder.

Now the great cat roared, showing no trace of her former sleepiness. Cannon blasted down onto the decks of the *Seventh Seal*, cracking and thundering as great tongues of flame and smoke lashed out.

The smaller ship staggered under furious blows. The cannon rained down fire and smoke, while blood and splintered wood turned her decks to a deadly maelstrom almost instantly. Scat's sailors peppered back with small arms as best they could, and the cannon blasted upward, grapeshot and canister ripping what it could reach. But the crewmen of the *Chase* took cover simply by lowering themselves to a knee and ducking their heads. When the cannon blasts ceased, the sailors on the taller ship fired down on the unprotected cannoneers of the *Seal*.

Scat was unconcerned with this initial volley. He figured he would weather it. He knew that while fifteen cannonballs might do a great deal of damage, they could take out no more than twenty or thirty of his men at the very most. He would lose a few more to small arms. But he had as many men loyal to him on the decks of the *Chase,* who would already be thinning his enemy's ranks there. As soon as this initial volley ended, he would order all his men across, to overrun her, like Achawuk, fighting hand-to-hand.

Scat's protégé, business partner, and one-time friend, however, had prepared for the same battle. He had ordered the *Chase*'s cannon loaded not with cannonballs, nor even with grapeshot, but with scrapshot. Each blast left not a single hole or crater, but rather a wide and bloody swath of destruction from ten pounds and more

The Hand That Bears the Sword

of scrap metal and shrapnel: nails, screws, buckshot, even the occasional knife or fork, loaded into cotton bags that disintegrated when fired, spreading their contents over the widest range possible, almost ninety degrees from the cannon's muzzle. This pirate's gambit, unexpected from a newly minted admiral or an old academic, more than doubled Scat's worst-case casualty count. Hardly a man aboard the *Seal* was left unbloodied. And when the volley finally ended and the smoke began to clear, Scat ordered far fewer men aboard the *Chase* than he had hoped.

And far worse news for Scat's battle plan, there was now no way for them to cross. The grappling lines had been cut away during the fusillade, and the lines from the *Seal*'s yards had been tossed off the *Chase*'s decks. Without orders, without a word, the men of the *Chase* had cut the cords away, lines falling into the drink, severed hooks falling silently to decks amid the great booming of cannon fire.

Worst of all, not a single sailor aboard the *Chase* had lifted a sword or a pistol or a musket against his fellow. Every one of them had chosen instead to line the gunwales, to face the *Seventh Seal,* and to deliver deadly fire down onto her. To a man, they had chosen John Hand over Scat Wilkins. To a man, they had chosen Packer Throme over the Angel of Death.

Few of them, truth be known, had chosen God over the devil, at least not in any lasting way. A few, but very few, would later claim to have seen the light of God as dusk fell on that dark summer day. But pirates were a superstitious lot of men, and so John Hand's sermon had had a profound impact regardless. A prophecy of doom was an ominous cloud that could not be wished away. The admiral's appeal to unreasoning fears had hit its target.

Scat, not John Hand, had erred. The admiral had left Scat this one play, and this one ship, for a reason. He had wanted to confront Scat, to be rid of him once and for all, but he could not do it on land, where the king's decree made such a confrontation dicey at best. So he had left Scat one ship, an ugly and sinister ship, knowing it would create the starkest choice imaginable for the men who sailed her. Scat's first error was to take the bait.

But Scat's greatest mistake was to underestimate what it meant to pirates to be honored. They were celebrated as heroes by all the kingdom. They had been cheered, lauded to the heavens, as they sailed away aboard the greatest ship ever built. It was in part John

Hand's sermon that had turned them, true, and in part Packer Throme, but it was in largest part the *Trophy Chase* herself. They had been raised up to the heights on these decks, and did not want to be lowered down again to the depths on those of a lesser ship.

So now instead of obeying his orders, instead of taking the *Chase*, Scat Wilkins' own handpicked men raised their pistols and their muskets. They took aim. And on John Hand's command, they acted in accordance with their natures and their habits, and their chosen profession. They fired.

In fact, most of the would-be mutineers missed their targets. They hit whatever they aimed at, but they were more interested in appearing loyal to their new captain than they were in actually killing off the crew of their old one. Still, twenty men who had weathered the scrapshot fusillade now dropped to the decks in the smoking sights of muskets held by John Hand's loyal crewmen. The crew of the *Seventh Seal* was decimated. More than two-thirds were dead or seriously wounded within the first minute of the battle.

"Hold your fire!" Admiral Hand ordered, knowing this fight was already over and won.

Scat stood on the foredeck of the *Seal,* dumbfounded. His unlit cigar hung loosely from his mouth as he surveyed the carnage on his own decks. Then he looked at the battered rails of the *Chase*, drifting slowly away.

"Fight for me, you rat badgers!" he cried. He looked across at familiar faces, questioning, boring into eyes he recognized, eyes of men he had commanded, men he expected to command still. A few lowered their gaze as Scat's withering look caught them, but none raised a hand. "You gut-slitting slackdogs, take back my ship!" Scat's voice cracked on the last syllable. It was a pitiful yelp.

"Hold!" John Hand countered, in case any were tempted.

The sailors on board the *Chase* shifted from one foot to the other, mostly embarrassed for their old captain. Those still alive aboard the *Seventh Seal* were as unmoving as statues, watching their leader, wondering what had happened to him. Where was the unmistakable, unstoppable power of Scat Wilkins, the infamous pirate of legend? Who was this old, sick man, hands trembling, voice cracking? As they stood still, they felt their confidence drain away, replaced by an unmistakable, quite unaccustomed, and utterly unwelcome draft of fear. It grew, filling their chests, throttling their willpower.

"Jonas Deal!" Scat fairly screamed. "You mutinous blaggard, where are you?"

"Give Scat his Mr. Deal," John Hand instructed quietly.

Packer joined three other sailors in picking up the body. He fought back a wave of nausea as he tried to get a grip on the clammy, flaccid flesh below the knee of this once fearsome man, now nothing more than a heavy, gelatinous bag of bones. They wrestled what was left of him overboard.

A *ka-thunk,* then a splash, and then silence. Every man looked to Scat Wilkins. They saw the dark look, the set jaw, the mouth turned down. They saw his soul writhe in the twitching of his face, as murderous ire grew there like a flame following a trail of gunpowder. He looked back at the *Chase,* at the row of sailors still aiming, ready to let loose another angry cloud of blue-white smoke and yellow fire. The *Seventh Seal* had drifted far enough away now to allow the *Chase*'s cannon direct aim at her hull. One by one, each cannon had been reloaded with round shot, cannonballs, then re-aimed and readied. Torches hovered over touchholes. The next volley would sink the *Seal.*

"I will kill every one of you," Scat seethed. His voice was a steel rasp on a pine box. "Every last mother's son. And I'll bury your mothers with you. Double-cross *me,* you blaggards!"

"Small arms," Hand ordered in a monotone. The admiral had been tempted to feel pity. But he knew Scat's treachery, his wrath, his need for vengeance, and it ran too deep for any act of mercy. Scat would not crumble. He would not bow. He would not quit. Only death would stop him. "Fire at will."

There was a pause, just a second or two, as Hand's men, all of those aboard the *Chase,* cocked their weapons and aimed. A doubt clung to the air; no one wanted to be the first to fire. And then a musket cracked. And then a pistol. And then came the flood.

Their aim this time was dead on target. Scat's threats were not idle, and they all knew it. They fought for their country, their captain, their mothers, their lives. The *Seal*'s crewmen dove for cover, but found little. A few returned fire with pistols and muskets, and one even coaxed a cannon to bark. But they could not keep up. The *Trophy Chase* poured deadly, drowning, all-consuming fire into the *Seventh Seal.*

The beast circled low, keeping far from the surface, watching,

The Hand That Bears the Sword

waiting for the morsel to drift slowly, maddeningly, down. In the thick darkness of the beast's mind, the idea began to form that these two creatures were not prey and predator, but equals, fighting. And then a murky thought worked through: Somehow the creatures had called forth the storm of lightning and thunder now passing between them.

Once planted in the beast's brain, the thought would not leave. Both of these creatures were predators, dangerous predators. The Firefish wanted to turn away, to swim off, to abandon any pursuit of these stormy creatures. But it could not. Not without testing the morsel that sank toward it, closer and closer. Not without tasting it.

And then came the smell of blood.

The beast rose instantly, its hunger a hot spike in its belly, a brilliant streak of fiery yellow in its mind. Its enormous mouth opened as it rose, frantically, to consume. It took the morsel. The beast's shock waves, its own lightning, created hardly a ripple against the storm above, and it attracted no notice.

But that morsel! Sweet and ripe and raw!

Now the beast rose farther, methodically, in complete control, circling, searching the storm creatures intently for any weak spot, any place to enjoin an attack, any way it could feast.

But each time the storm paused, it returned, louder and brighter.

Scat watched his last battle with a sense of disbelief so keen it crossed some internal line. He disengaged. This couldn't be happening. The scene around him was a stray thought to be rejected as soon as it entered his head, a preposterous, absurd idea: defeat. And not just defeat, but defeat at the hands of his own men who would not obey his command. He had the feeling he was standing in the wrong place. He simply needed to switch ships. If he could just get to the quarterdeck of the *Chase* then all would be well.

But he could not. His sailors fell backward, were blown backward; they pirouetted, contorted, sprawled, crawled through smoke and debris until their bodies covered the decks, piled up on one another, soaking everything red.

Scat stood alone on the forecastle, watching, distant, smoldering, trying to work out how this had happened, and how he might yet turn this battle and kill his enemies. He chewed his cigar. He felt his pockets for a small gold lighter that was not there.

John Hand turned his eyes toward Packer. The boy's look was intense, alert, the fire of battle burning in him once again, as it had in Prince Mather's quarters, as it had when he'd cut the tie lines of the bunting. His sword was in his hand once again. But Packer did not move. He stood silently, absorbing the carnage.

Packer was pondering this scene. He had seen bloody battle before. The death and dismemberment here was just as brutal, the blood flowed just as freely as when the *Chase* had fought the Achawuk. But this time it was different. It was gruesome, yes. It was hideous. But somehow this time it seemed…necessary.

Why?

"Resist not evil," Jesus commanded. John Hand and the *Trophy Chase* were resisting evil with all the firepower they had. "But whoever shall smite thee on thy right cheek, turn the other also." The *Seventh Seal* smote the *Chase,* even choosing her starboard side. So why did Packer feel so strongly that here, now, it would be utterly wrong to turn the *Chase's* port side to these pirates as well?

Was it his own hardness of heart that made this seem so different? Perhaps. But Packer felt no hardness within him. He felt the pain of Scat's loss. He felt the knife's blade of regret. Was there anger in Packer? Was that the difference? But Packer felt no wrath that needed to be appeased. He didn't hate. He felt no blood lust. He took no pleasure in any of this: not in any part of his heart to which he could find access.

I'll bury your mothers with you. That was it, then. It was that Scat simply had to be stopped because he could not stop himself. It was a government's role to bring justice, to protect its citizens, and Admiral John Hand was now the government. The *Trophy Chase* was no longer a pirate ship, or even a merchant ship; it was a ship of state. It had been attacked, and now it was executing judgment on behalf of the government, the one God had ordained for Nearing Vast. It was sad; it was ugly. But there was simply no other way.

"'But if thou do that which is evil, be afraid,'" John Hand quoted aloud, still looking at Packer, "'for he beareth not the sword in vain.' That's our duty."

Packer looked over at him with a start, realizing how rapt in thought he had been.

The admiral smiled. "Do you have a pistol?"

"A pistol?"

Hand nodded. Packer shook his head.

Hand pulled Jonas Deal's enormous hand cannon from his belt, looked at Packer, and grimaced. The boy wouldn't be able to handle the thing. "Go get my spare." He reached into his pocket for the key to his cabin, then saw the door ajar behind Packer. The damage from Scat's first cannonade was visible from where he stood. "You'll find it already loaded, in my desk drawer under the logbook."

Packer nodded. "Aye, sir. What should I do with it?"

"Why, use it, son." He watched Packer go. The intensity of the boy's face, the depth of purpose, these were things Hand had seen before in other men. Packer had iron in him, the fire to do what was right. He would likely die for what he believed.

But would he kill? The admiral needed to know the answer.

CHAPTER 6

Predators

Cannonballs now, Scat thought. His heart pounded away in his chest, every beat now striking him with pain, a hammer on white-hot iron. Yes, round shot at the waterline, to sink him. The *Chase's* crewmen were already aiming the big guns, preparing to fire. Scat knew he should order all his remaining men to the cannons. But he didn't do it. He wasn't sure he could muster the voice, with this horrible spike again and again through his chest, through his heart. But it wouldn't matter if he did. The day was lost.

He pondered the ship before him, the *Trophy Chase,* his prize and now his undoing. The sun was almost set, and the *Chase* had turned golden-red in the fading light. The haze of smoke around her was purple in the slanting rays. The Firefish hide glistened on her hull, its scales glinting. A beautiful ship. A gorgeous ship. A fast and fighting ship like no other, draped in the hide of its great quarry. This was the *Trophy Chase* in all her glory. Scat felt pride, love, and jealousy, emotions that could have been no more intense had the *Chase* been a treacherous woman he loved with unreasonable passion, and who had brought him to his knees, and then to his death. Yet he loved her anyway. It wasn't her fault. No, he had already fired his cannon at her, to no avail. He would not do it again.

It wasn't the *Chase* to blame, it was the men who sailed her, who stole her. They should be dying; they should be dead. This

Packer, this pretender, he had no right at all, no claim whatsoever to her heart, and yet he bound himself up with her...Fury rose in him, and he looked up and down her length in a jealous rage, trying to find him, that he might kill him. But Packer Throme was not there.

John Hand was, however. He had designed her, and so he did have some claim, but Scat found he hated him all the more for that. Scat would be dead, and she would be his, and everyone would think that was as it should be. Now Admiral Sole Discretion was on the quarterdeck, staring back at him. With little more than a tightening of the jaw and a twitch of one eye, ignoring the pain, Scat reached for his belt and pulled his pistol. Killing John Hand would make him feel better.

He tried to aim, but his pistol sight fluttered like a hummingbird. He cursed.

A hundred armed men aboard the *Chase* had seen Scatter Wilkins standing on the forecastle deck during the battle. Any one of them could have killed him. Any man could have aimed a pistol or a musket or even a cannon at the pirate captain. But none did. Not one even considered it. They each had an innate sense that it was not their place to take him down.

In the tight circle of vision that was his target, Scat now saw John Hand looking straight at him, taking his measure. Then he saw the admiral shake his head. Hand had the appearance of the professor he was, a schoolteacher rebuking a student, as though Scat were a favorite pupil in whom he was greatly disappointed. Scat sneered. Then he saw the musket. Hand raised it into view, and now carefully aimed it at Scat. The pirate could see it clearly. He could see the gray rim around the black hole of its barrel. He knew it was aimed true.

Scat pulled the trigger of his pistol just as he saw a yellow flash engulf the muzzle of John Hand's musket.

The deck jarred underneath him, and Scat went down. He fell as the barrage of cannon fire rocked the *Seventh Seal*. Almost the entire crew of the *Chase* watched him fall, and those who didn't would swear forever that they did. All, however, saw him lying on his back, his left hand across his chest, his right arm outstretched on the deck, his pearl-handled pistol still in his grip.

The onslaught paused, as though the battle itself needed to take a breath while this powerful presence, this guiding force, the dark angel that had overseen the harvest of so many souls, lay motionless. Every man waited to see if he would rise again.

Packer Throme found John Hand's pistol, but he did not rush back to the deck with it. The captain's log caught his eye. He read the day's entry. Under the heading "Battle Plan," John Hand had written several notations in his precise script.

Jonas Deal and Zeb Bones ringleaders; take them out early. Armor and Packer will convince others. Expect close quarter assault. Scrapshot in close, then round shot at the waterline.

Packer swallowed hard at the last notation:

Take no prisoners.

When the decks of the *Chase* erupted with cannon fire, Packer held tight to the writing desk, prepared for the return fire from the *Seal.* But only an eerie silence followed. He walked to a small porthole on the starboard side of the captain's saloon and opened it, his hands tingling. He would not have been surprised to see only smoke clinging to the water where the *Seventh Seal* had been.

But she was there. True to the admiral's plan, the cannoneers of the *Chase* had emptied their guns amidships and opened an enormous hole just at the *Seal*'s waterline. The ship was drinking in water, listing noticeably already, heeling over toward the *Chase.* Packer, and all others aboard the now victorious craft, could see Scatter Wilkins lying alone on the forecastle as that deck angled up toward them.

Scatter Wilkins' last glimpse of the sky was of a dark red-orange streak, a long gash with no beginning and no end. He would die now; he knew that. John Hand's musket ball had struck him just below the breastbone. He felt the wound, felt the blood under his fingertips. He could not move his legs. His back was broken.

He closed his eyes, and the bloody orange streak in the sky became a glowing white scar in his mind. The treachery of his own men rose up within it, filling him with the desire to retch. And then came the black bile of hatred, rising up against all those who had double-crossed him, put him on his back, helpless, for the world to see. At the top of the list now was John Hand. Scat had been killed by the treachery of a preening professor who used a king to steal ships.

Scat wrapped himself in this hatred, regretting nothing…nothing about his entire life but that it would not last long enough for him to avenge himself. He wished even now there were some way he could kill John Hand and the boy Packer Throme. He opened his eyes, tried to aim his pistol, but he had no control of it. He put his head back to the deck, closed his eyes again. Talon had been right. Trust him at your gravest peril. He could envision Talon ramming her sword through the lad's conniving heart. This was good. This was right.

And then, with that portal opened, that hatch into the hold of his own darkest soul, Scat's hatred expanded. It grew in his chest, up into his throat, and broke open and soaked his mind, his reason. From there it moved into his memory, into time itself, blackening all the circumstances of his life, all the lost opportunities, all the times he had been thwarted by lesser men and women, vain princes and idiot kings, scheming men and dangerous women. He hated everyone and everything that kept him from being what he was, what he was born to be: the richest, most powerful, most glorified man on earth.

And then in the heart of that darkness a darker revelation slid through him like cold, black water. The root, the wellspring of his hatred was that his glory was not inevitable. Some fate bound him to the finality of his losses, decreed he should fail. It was the way the world was built, the way it was managed that had frustrated him. He hated whoever it was who created and sustained this world.

Yes, yes! That was it. With that thought, the cold black water in his veins transmuted itself into powder, dry black powder. And that powder ignited. Hatred ripped through him like an explosion, as though that gunpowder had been packed away into every fiber of his being for a lifetime—and now it all flashed in an instant, enraging him, ripping him to bits like the scrapshot that had decimated his decks. Here, at the very gates of eternity, from his deepest, most hidden heart, from the very bowels of his being, he unleashed a full-bodied, fully formed blasphemy, delivered as richly and as furiously and as finally as he could deliver it, directly into the face of God.

The doomed ship creaked and groaned. Timbers cracked. A rush of wind, air escaping her hold, was followed by three or four enormous glugs from the holes now penetrating her hull, as though the *Seventh Seal* choked on seawater, as though the ship herself were drowning. The angle of her decks continued to grow more and more acute.

The decks of the *Trophy Chase* were still and silent. All sailors watched the forecastle of the *Seventh Seal*. Scat Wilkins was still rising toward them, as though being put on display. When the ship reached a severe enough angle, somewhere around forty degrees, Scat's right hand, still gripping his pearl-handled wheel-lock pistol, rose up from the deck. Gasps were heard along the length of the *Chase*. A few men stepped back in instinctive fear. Scat's elbow crooked, and the pistol hovered for a moment, pointed at the darkening sky. Anger flashed across his face. And then he went limp.

As his closed fist settled down on his chest, the barrel of his pistol nestled under his bearded chin for just a moment. Then the weapon fell away and skittered down the wooden deck, splashing into the sea. Scat lay with both arms folded across his chest for a few more seconds, looking almost peaceful, until the ship rolled over toward the *Chase*, bowing to her superiority.

With the accompaniment of a final breathy gasp from the *Seventh Seal* and a great series of loud groans and cracks, Scat Wilkins' limp body crumpled down to the gunwale; his left leg and left arm protruded grotesquely between the rail posts. And then, without ceremony or honor, the *Seventh Seal* rolled over onto him, burying him under her timbers.

Sailors aboard the *Chase* stepped back from the rails, fearing that the masts and sails of the *Seal* would come down upon them. But the tip of her mainmast slapped the cold water six feet from the *Chase*'s hull. There, the white flag of a broken truce sank into the black waters of the sea.

As if commanded, the *Seal*'s surviving sailors gave in, gave up, and leaped toward safety, splashing into the water wherever they could, swimming toward their executioners, calling out for mercy. As the sails sank into the sea, drowning pirates were caught beneath them, fighting yards of canvas for air. More fortunate sailors scrambled across the top of the sails and the rigging, clawing their way toward the *Chase*.

Packer watched it all through the porthole. It was over. These men were desperate now. They had abandoned their weapons and they swam toward the *Chase*, now become their beacon of hope. Their faces were stricken with fear, their voices ragged with panic. They begged for their lives. And yet Packer had seen the words: *Take no prisoners*. He felt he should fall to his knees and ask God to protect them, to save them from what was about to happen. But he didn't. He couldn't pull his eyes away. His mind spun; he felt dizzy, and he had the strange sense that the world had turned, that the *Seventh Seal* was still upright, and he, aboard the *Chase,* looked down onto her decks, hovering above, watching as the pirates climbed up the rigging toward him. He closed his eyes to regain equilibrium, and the pepper of small-arms fire began. His heart pounded, louder with each pistol report and musket crack. He opened his eyes to watch pirates swim, call out, raise their hands, stop swimming, and sink beneath the waves.

A thousand thoughts streamed through his head until they merged into a single river, a feeling deeper than thought, a sense of dread and helplessness that careened toward hopelessness. God's judgment was over. Scat was dead. Would John Hand have no mercy even now? None at all? How could he quote Scripture, call on God to rally his troops, and then slaughter men who were surrendering, denying them the most basic mercy of battle? Packer knew now he could not trust John Hand any more than he could trust Scat Wilkins. And John Hand was much smarter, clearly more cunning than any pirate had ever been.

In agony of spirit, Packer finally sank to his knees and cried out to God.

Pop, pop...crack!

It was still going on. But it had to stop. Packer couldn't keep praying, couldn't wait for an answer. He sprang to his feet and sprinted to the quarterdeck.

He ran toward John Hand, speaking before he thought. "Stop firing! Cease fire!" he demanded, not addressing the crew but the admiral. Packer's face was inches from John Hand's, his voice carrying a tone no one could misunderstand.

Hand was startled to the point of shock. Packer had simply appeared before him. The admiral had been watching his men take aim and fire, reload and fire again, but the swimmers kept swimming. Some of them went down, yes, but not many. His men reloaded with ponderous deliberation, and their aim was uncharacteristically bad. John Hand knew why, of course. They were not pleased with his order. The first of Scat's refugees had already reached the *Chase.* The man was crying out piteously.

Hand could hardly rescind his order. He had given it just moments

The Hand That Bears the Sword

ago, and precisely so his men would know their captain, would know that John Hand would execute judgment; he was every bit the fearful commander Scat Wilkins was. He had thought they needed to know this. The men would fear and respect this. That was the theory. But in the cauldron of reality, the closer the enemy got, the less enemy they seemed.

And then Packer appeared, an apparition, eyes piercing with that bright intensity, voice the essence of command. It took the admiral only a moment to understand the gift he was being given. "Cease fire!" he called out, not taking his eyes off Packer.

It was an order that needed to be given only once. In fact, it hardly needed to be given at all, as every man had ceased shooting when Packer had started shouting. Now, with John Hand's confirmation, the butt of every musket hit the deck.

"You would give quarter to our enemies?" Hand asked Packer. His voice was steel, but a sparkle glinted in his eyes.

Packer was taken aback. "Well. Yes. These ones, anyway. They're Vast, sir, not Drammune. They can fight. We'll need them. Won't we, sir?"

Hand nodded. "Mr. Throme believes we should show these blaggards some mercy!" he called out, still not taking his eyes off Packer. "All right, men, throw them a line!"

A cheer went up, then died quickly away as the crewmen went to work throwing coils of rope and rope ladders, lowering the ship's boats. Lines whirred and windlasses clicked metallically as the men buzzed with renewed enthusiasm for their work.

Packer felt dazed. That was all it took? He looked at Admiral Hand with such an earnestly quizzical expression that Hand laughed out loud. Packer found that stranger yet.

John Hand grasped Packer's shoulder, shook him gently, even affectionately. "You do have courage in you, son. Let's make sure you pour it out on the Drammune."

Packer nodded, then noticed blood flowing from the whiskers at Admiral Hand's neck. He pointed. "You're hit, sir."

John Hand felt the warmth on his neck, cold wetness on his shoulder. When he fingered his jaw, he realized that Scat's final shot had very nearly done its job. The ball had traced a crease just below his jawline, as near to the jugular as a shot could come without opening it. He granted his old friend and partner a nod of appreciation. The man could shoot.

"Help them aboard," John Hand ordered, nodding toward the men in the water below. He noticed that the boy still carried no pistol. He grimaced. Twice now, Packer had appeared from nowhere, calling for mercy: once with the Achawuk, and once with these pirates. Both times, it was the right thing to do. But John Hand still didn't know. And he needed to know. The men all loved and respected Packer Throme. They thought God was with him. John Hand had fed that belief. This was good, certainly, but only to a point. He had just sent Packer to fight, and again the lad had not fought.

The admiral looked at the blood on his fingertips, then pressed them back against the wound at his jaw. Strange as it seemed, as he navigated this small current of history, in the crucible of this present reality, John Hand found he strongly believed that the success of this voyage, and perhaps therefore the outcome of the entire war, hinged on the answer to one stark question.

Would Packer kill?

The beast had collected each morsel as it drifted downward. There was no need to shock these; they were but bits of flesh. No need to snap down on them. It just opened wide its jaws, left its mouth agape like a great net, and swam about scooping them all in. Blood scent was everywhere now, wonderfully rich, and the morsels were sweet. But the Firefish stayed low, away from the thunder on the surface.

And then it realized that one of the shellfish creatures had begun to dive!

At the surface the rotund creature had turned over. It made sounds—booms, cracks, and bellows. Its enormous fins, like great wings, settled into the water. It was submerging. It was leaving the surface. The Firefish circled, worried it might have been spotted. Was this storm creature diving to hunt, to attack?

No, this was not a dive. The creature was not swimming. It was sinking. Motionless but for the fluttering of its winglike fins in the current, it sank, just as the morsels had sunk. And then the beast knew. This storm creature was dead! The beast sped up to it, circled once. It was bloody. And its shell was cracked open!

And then the beast saw a single flailing morsel clinging to its shell, at one end of the creature. Here was the weak spot, then. Here was a place where the meat oozed from the shell. Here was where the Firefish could attack, break through the shell, and feast!

The beast swam down, turned upward, and saw the morsel flail. Yes. This was the place to attack.

Scatter Wilkins opened his eyes as the last glimmers of light filtered through the seawater. The crush and cold of the sea pierced him. The creaks and echoing cracks of his sinking ship reached into and rang within his ears. He was sliding downward. He was sinking with his ship. He was drowning. He tried to move, but succeeded only in waving his arms. He felt no desire to save himself. He felt quite peaceful. It was an unaccustomed sensation.

And then, from below him, he felt a rumble. It seemed vaguely familiar, this sound, this reverberation. Some distant memory tried to reach him, but it would not form in his mind. He looked down into the darkness toward which he drifted. As he did, he remembered the blasphemy he had uttered. It was comforting to him. He had cursed God. Now he would die. He marveled that he felt no fear. All his life he had feared what he would face on the other side of death. But now that he was dying, he felt nothing like that at all. He would go somewhere far from God, far down into the cold and black. He was content.

Scat felt the darkness below him grow darker yet, and thicker, colder. It seemed to him like a hole was opening, a pit into which he was falling, falling rapidly, not drifting down any more, but plummeting. It was almost as if the black hole were coming up at him.

And as that darkness grew, as he fell into it, he noticed, calmly, with a peaceful curiosity, that the hole was surrounded by white teeth. Odd. A hole with huge white teeth around its rim, growing so quickly, so rapidly, that it seemed as if the world were being swallowed by some great beast.

And then, like a lightning bolt searing through him, panic overwhelmed his entire being. His mind snapped awake as he realized at last, as he knew with utter clarity, what was happening to him.

Then his terror swallowed him whole.

John Hand walked to the quarterdeck rail. "What are our casualties, Mr. Haas?"

"Light, Admiral," Haas called up to him. "We lost Zeb Bones on lookout, Jonas Deal, and Mutton Caller. Those three for sure. We got four other men injured, Jack Mack and the bosun the worst."

"Stil Meander? How bad?"

"Got a nasty splinter in his thigh."

"A splinter?"

"Aye, about eight inches long and almost as wide. Jack took a ball below the elbow." Andrew shook his head. "We lost a good sounding pole overboard from that one. Stitch thinks the arm'll need to go as well."

"That's it?"

"That's all I know about for sure, but there's a bunch of men bleeding here and there."

John Hand's eyes widened. Maybe God really was with them.

At that moment a shudder came from under the water astern, from the place where the *Seventh Seal* had gone down. A huge bubble of water broke the surface, broken boards and kegs and bits of mast and sail coming up with it. Sailors who had been looking in that direction reported they'd seen an explosion beneath the surface.

"Must have had a whole lot of powder in that hold," Delaney said to Packer. Packer looked at him carefully, saw the doubt. What makes a keg of powder explode underwater? But they both chose to leave any other possibility unspoken.

"Line the prisoners up on the main deck!" Hand ordered, apparently unconcerned with the death throes of the *Seal*.

"What will you do with them, Admiral?" Packer asked.

He shrugged. "I guess we need to decide whether to hang 'em or jail 'em or just sign 'em up." But he smiled. "Do you have a suggestion?"

"I say sign them up, sir. If they'll join."

"Had the same thought myself."

Packer nodded appreciatively, then helped Delaney, who was struggling with a line, trying to haul a particularly large pirate up the side of the ship. Despite Packer's help, the wounded man lost his grip and crashed back into the sea. "Get yourself on the ship's boat, ye great side a' beef!" Delaney called down to him. "We can't haul ye!" Delaney turned his familiar grin toward Packer. "Man needs to be put on rations."

Packer laughed. He looked past Delaney, to where the *Silver Arrow* and the *Marchessa* approached from the west. "Now where do you suppose they've been?"

Delaney nodded. "Exactly. Puzzles me why Admiral ordered them off a great distance, just this afternoon."

They had been to sea for nearly a week now. Scat had attacked only just tonight, and only after the other two ships had been sent away. But the logbook explained it. Hand had lured Scat in.

Packer didn't let it worry him. The mood on the decks was light, and he soaked it in like a sponge. Victory had been won, an implacable foe defeated, and mercy had been shown. John Hand had ultimately done the right thing. Packer looked to the heavens, thankful. Then he threw himself back into the work of saving pirates.

Even at the farthest distance, with the sun all but set and the light fading, the *Chase*'s lookout could tell that the ships on the horizon were not Vast ships. Their sails were not the usual white, square-rigged sheets every Vast ship boasted. They were small crimson triangles, layered one over the other like scales. He focused his telescope, and shook his head.

"Drammune!" he called. "Drammune warships, due east!"

The light mood on deck vanished like a mist in a sudden gust of wind. Sailors rushed to the gunwales and into the rigging. One or two wet pirates, halfway up the side of the *Chase*, went back into the drink.

The crew had hardly begun to mutter the questions that rose in their hearts when the lookout cried again. "Drammune warships! Nor'east!"

The sailors scanned the horizon northward, feeling the cold chill of fear.

And then they heard, "Drammune warships, sou'east!"

Within minutes, the entire eastern horizon, as far as anyone could see, was speckled with blood-red sails.

"Well, condemn me for a hanged man," Delaney said softly to Packer, breaking a stunned silence on deck, "if it ain't their whole heavin' navy."

CHAPTER 7

Warrior

It was not the whole heavin' Drammune navy that sailed for Nearing Vast. But almost. How they came to be strewn across the sea in attack formation, headed toward the City of Mann with a full load of fighting men and women, ammunition, and every weapon of war available on Drammune shores, was a tale that several now watching wide-eyed aboard the *Trophy Chase* would have been amazed to hear told.

John Hand in particular would have listened eagerly, seeking to understand the genesis of these events, how the great and long-festering animosities between kings and kingdoms had converged with peculiar and particular fates, hopes, and ambitions of individuals, in order to bring these ships here, to him. If he could have, the professor would have stared deeply into this steaming cauldron, stirring it, testing it, trying to unlock its secrets.

It was a story that reached back to the bleak, cold months at the wane of the previous year, and would reach forward for many years to come.

"Tai eyneth." *Come with me*. The guard said the words gruffly, a command not to be questioned. He was dressed head to foot in dark chain mail. He wore a deep crimson helmet and carried a halberd, a pike as tall as he was with the blade of a battle-axe protruding from its shaft. His dress, his weapon, and the floor on which he stood all identified him as a member of the Hezzan Guard, the most feared of the Drammune fighting forces, the most loyal to the emperor.

The warrior to whom the guard spoke stood silently, nodded slightly, then followed through huge, crimson double doors. Each door was twelve inches thick, each a perfect crimson square divided diagonally by a black slash of bolted iron. The pair walked past four other guards and into the dark, rich chambers of the emperor of Drammun, the Hezzan Shul Dramm.

The Hezzan was reclining on leather pillows under enormous, towering windows, now shut and shuttered. A basket overflowing with fresh fruit lay at his right hand, strips of red meat steamed in a steel skillet at his left. A young woman, dressed in a fabric that looked like gauze but which suggested more than it revealed, knelt to pour wine into her emperor's silver goblet. Her dark hair was braided from her left ear to her shoulder; her eyes and face were painted. She looked up, startled.

The triple golden earring that pierced the flat of the young woman's left ear flashed in the lamplight, and by this the visitor knew she was one of the Hezzan's wives. The gauze-clad woman stood quickly, surprised and troubled by the disdain she saw in the warrior's cold look.

"Go," the Hezzan commanded. His most recent bride bowed dutifully and left, glancing back once, with fear.

The emperor was fifty-one, fit and muscular. He wore leather arm guards wrist to elbow, and a leather vest and kilt. His sandals were those of a warrior, thick-soled, hobnailed, with leather laces up to the knee. His beard was trimmed and dark, and his appearance, despite the gray that touched his temples, was altogether youthful. His eyes, black, sharp, and fierce, flashed in his scarred face.

"You have done well," he said to the warrior.

"I have always sought to do my duty to you, and to the Law of my kingdom."

The emperor took careful stock of the warrior before him, marking the leather robe and hood, the battle scars, the posture of pride, even defiance. "Bow to me."

The warrior obeyed, putting one knee and both hands on the polished floor, as was customary before the Hezzan. "I am at your command."

"You are worthy to command. And so you will become my wife."

A tremor ran through her, but the warrior did not look up.

"This does not please you?" he asked.

Now Talon raised her head. Her eyes were every bit as fierce as his. She pulled back her leather hood, revealing short, ragged hair that had grown in around the scarred flesh of her scalp, burned in her ordeal aboard the *Camadan*. "I did not dare to imagine myself... attractive to you."

He didn't flinch. "You shall be my sixteenth wife."

Talon knew better than to betray her emotions. "Words...fail me, Your Worthiness."

"The arrangements are made. You will join with me tonight."

She knew she could not keep the bitterness from her voice, could not hide it in her eyes, and so she said nothing, but stared down at the polished floor.

The Hezzan dismissed her. Talon was escorted by the guard back to her apartments in the palace, where a troupe of women, aides and servants, waited with baths, perfumes, face paint, and the gauzy garments she disdained.

Talon fought a burning rage. She had not foreseen this. She had earned a place of honor. She had been advising the Hezzan these many weeks, and had advised him well. She had done the kingdom great services, killing the Traitor, counseling the Hezzan in the sinking of the Vast fleet. She expected to do more. If she was to be rejected as a leader or an advisor, then certainly she should be a warrior. Not a wife!

To be numbered among those miserable concubines, fawning over the emperor in public, backbiting and clawing in private, a herd of cats caged for a single man's vanity? She was to be his conquest, then, and not his confidant. It was a bitter, bitter blow, a deep and raw humiliation.

Still in her leathers, she dismissed the dumbfounded gaggle of aides, who fled before her snarling orders like a pack of deer from a howling wolf. She walked to the balcony outside her small residence, built for guests of honor.

The view, overlooking the great capital of Hezarow Kyne, was breathtaking. The city's crimson, clay-tiled roofs covered the hills like armor plating, sloping down away from her to the shoreline in the distance. From here, Talon could see the masts of ships lining the harbor, the triangular crimson sails of Drammune warships out at sea.

But it would not be her city, not now. She would be worse than a captive here; she would be as one dead, this palace her tomb. To all but the Hezzan, she would be nobody. And even to him she would be but one of many. How could he not see that her skills, her capabilities, were far different from theirs? Men were always blinded by their desires, but this made no sense.

She would escape. She would run. She would return to the sea, to piracy.

As she looked past the city, past the bare masts of the harbor and out to the sailing ships, she thought about the *Trophy Chase*. She imagined that it yet plowed the waves, Captain Wilkins on the prowl for more Firefish. But much had changed since the days she'd sailed on that ship. She had left that behind, and felt no pull toward her old life. That she had survived at all seemed reason to believe that she had some destiny yet to fulfill.

She still wondered at how it had all happened. And how it might play into her fate.

When Talon had regained consciousness, she found herself lying on her back. Fire burned above her, burning cinders and ash swirled around her. She realized her hair was burning. She sat up, pain screaming through her as she stripped off her jacket and smothered the flames on her scalp.

The cracks and snaps of the fire were all but drowned by the roar of wind that fed the conflagration, sweeping up through the ceiling above her like a chimney. The heat was intense, but she was alive. She had fallen through the floor above and into the quarters of one of the ship's officers. She had hit something, or landed on something, that caused her great pain. Now she looked down to find her own knife, her dirk, piercing the flesh of her left hip. How had this happened? She felt dazed, unsure of herself. How had her knife gotten out of its sheath?

And then she remembered that as she fell, she had reached for her blade. With her right hand she had dropped her sword and reached out for Packer Throme, the very image of the crucified Christ, his face full of peace, compassion, and yet strong and determined. And at the same time her other hand, her left hand, had instinctively sought out her knife, drawing it as though she might still kill him. Where was her sword now? She didn't see it.

Smoke started to choke her. She coughed. She had to move; she had to get out. She pulled the knife from her side. Wincing in pain, bleeding heavily, she rolled to her knees. She kept her head low, below the smoke that flew past her, up through the fire above and into the night air. She crawled to the door, knife in her hand, and slammed it open. The room behind her exploded into flame, and she rolled out onto the deck.

Outside the cabin the air was slightly less smoky, but the deck was ablaze. She crawled across it, her leathers instantly as hot as the fire; she used her jacket to swat at flames and then she draped it over her head as she crawled on, through a single path that seemed to have been left open just for her. Halfway across the deck she found a sword. Packer Throme's sword. She grabbed it by the hilt, again using the leather of her jacket, this time as a glove. And then with a great effort, she stood and ran for the port railing.

The many sailors aboard the *Trophy Chase* who had gathered to watch the duel were now watching Packer, who, with Delaney, Mutter Cabe, and Marcus Pile, were swimming away from the burning *Camadan*. They did not see the dark shadow that passed along the deck amidst the flames. They did not see that shadow as it slashed the ropes that held the ship's boat. They could not have seen it tumble into the water on the opposite side of the ship, or climb from the water into the boat. It would have been impossible for them to see the pool of human darkness lying in the floor of that boat, drained and burned and bleeding. Defeated, but alive.

Talon drifted all night and the better part of the next day without food or water. She lay unmoving in the bottom of the boat, rising to consciousness only to find pain, failure, and emptiness, and then sinking again into darkness, where her dreams were of flames and swords, a great struggle for her life against innumerable foes, against Firefish, swordsmen, and pirates. Lurking in the background, watching every battle, never coming near but never out of sight, was Packer Throme. He would not fight her. He would wait to see whether she lived or died, whether she fought or surrendered.

She knew he would not approach her until she quit fighting. He wanted her to give up, to spread her own arms wide, as he had done, and accept her own death. But this she could not do. And so she fought on, wounded, bleeding, burning, barely able to move her feet or her arms, damaged and injured again and again and again.

Just as it seemed to her she would die of her wounds, as she sank to her knees unable to struggle further, she would awaken to a low, slate-gray sky, lightning flashing through the looming billows, and the patter of rain on the wooden gunwales, on her leathers, on her face, on her charred skull. And then she would sink again, only to begin the fight again.

Finally, she faced a foe she could not overcome. He was an enormous demon, with hollow eyes and muscles of stone. He stood before her with his scimitar already bathed in her blood, for he had hacked and hacked and refused to back down. His impassive face simmered with a calm satisfaction. She had worn herself out fighting him, but he could not be beaten.

Finally, she could fight no more. She could not raise her sword arm one more time. She looked at Packer, and saw the face she had seen on the deck of the *Camadan*. But it was no longer Packer; this was the very Son of God, robed in white, eyes like torches searing her, searching her, seeing her inmost parts. She was at the end of all her strength. She was exposed, and defeated. Yet in his look was a promise of comfort, of rest from all her struggles, if only she would take the hand he offered.

Then he spread his arms wide. She dropped her eyes to the ground, and then her sword. The demon's blade sliced through her. She closed her eyes; she felt nothing. She looked up, and the Christ was gone. She looked to the stone demon. His hardened form cracked, then shattered, then fell at her feet in slivers and shards of silver glass, as though he had been no more than an image in a mirror. Above her shone a bright white light, a light that grew until it engulfed her. She drank it in. It was warm. It was healing. It was youth and power and peace. She rose up into it.

"Talon! Wake up, now!" a voice commanded. At first, she thought it was the voice of the demon. It came from deep within the cavernous darkness now underneath her, and it called her back to the darkness, away from the light. It was a voice from far away, from long ago.

"Do not surrender, Talon. Do not give up. Fight!" The voice was a voice of command, speaking in the Drammune tongue. It was martial, and it struck chords, created cords, it bound her deep within. It was her duty to return. And so with a great struggle, she did.

The bright, cold sun shone down on her. She was lying on the deck of a ship, and a Drammune captain hovered over her. She recognized him. She looked around her. She recognized the shape of the vessel, the dress of the crewmen, the sound of the drums below deck, the splash of a multitude of oars working in unison. This was a Drammune slave ship.

She closed her eyes, knowing she was safe now, that she would not die. She did not feel within herself a trace of thankfulness for that fact. She simply accepted it. She would return to Drammun. What would come, would come.

Now, standing in the Hezzan's apartments on Drammune soil, Talon wondered if she would ever feel again the peace of rising into that light. Then a new thought came to her. The humiliation the Hezzan brought upon her…could it be a test? Was there an opportunity here for her to test the knowledge she had gained among the Vast? The Hezzan Shul Dramm was putting her in a place of weakness. And her confrontations with Senslar Zendoda, with Packer Throme, even with Panna had all taught her one thing: Great strength could come from great weakness.

She took a deep breath. She would need to consider this very carefully. The power of the God of Nearing Vast was great. This power had defeated her without a sword, without a weapon, and it had defeated her through the most unlikely of vessels. Could it be possible that she might learn the workings of that power?

"The meek shall inherit the earth." Is that not what their Son of God had said? Yes. She had been reading these stories again, stories that portrayed this man who died without fighting, who gave Himself up to death, and yet did not live in weakness. Rather, He had unimaginable power. Still, he chose to be humiliated. And yet greater power resulted.

The Hand That Bears the Sword

Yes, she determined. She would test his words. She would play the role of the meek. It would be a small test, not unto death. But then, Talon was not nearly so ambitious as the Son of God suggested she should be. She did not desire to inherit the earth.

She would be content with only the Kingdom of Drammun.

Surrounded by a handful of witnesses, with the Hezzan Guard stationed by the door, Talon was placed on her knees before the Hezzan. There, repeating words first written more than a thousand years earlier, she swore allegiance to him. In return, he spoke words that confirmed to the world that she was his wife, sealed and protected forever as, essentially, his legal property.

Sool Kron, the Hezzan's right hand and Chief Minister of State, enjoyed the ceremony thoroughly. Not because the wizened and long-bearded advisor liked weddings, nor because this one was particularly unique. No weddings in Drammun were unique. Sool Kron enjoyed it because it accomplished a very important purpose. He congratulated the Hezzan warmly, and then his eyes met Talon's. The minister's look was one of absolute, dominant victory.

Talon could only close her painted eyes and accept one more deep humiliation. In her mind, though, she saw her dagger in her hand, saw its blade slicing across Sool Kron's throat, saw his eyes go wide in surprise and then dull in death as her knife then reached up into his heart. But she let that image go. If there was a God who preferred weakness, who would step in to protect the weak, then she would benefit from that protection soon enough. Certainly, no one was weaker or more humiliated on this earth than the sixteenth wife of a Hezzan of Drammun.

The legal niceties over, the Hezzan retired with his bride to his chambers.

"You may change now," he said, waving her away.

As Talon turned away from him, head high, and walked toward the dressing room, she feared her humiliation was just beginning. But in the small vanity room she found her hooded leather robe laid out and her familiar leathers waiting for her, along with her sword and her dirk. Puzzled but deeply relieved, she put these clothes on and returned to stand before the Hezzan.

"Sit," he ordered. She sat down where he beckoned, on a small stool beside the enormous bed. He sat on the edge of the bed, still dressed formally in his loose leather tunic. "Now I will tell you why I wanted you to be my wife."

This, she wanted to hear.

"You have brought glory to our kingdom. You have slain the Traitor. By doing so, you have lured the Vast Navy to its destruction. You have counseled me wisely and well in its defeat. You are worthy of the greatest honor, and I am not a man who will bring dishonor where honor is deserved."

"Thank you, my lord," was all she could say.

"But you have also made many enemies among my advisors, the Court of Twelve. They conspire against you."

"Who conspires, my lord?"

"All of them." He watched her face, saw no reaction. She knew this already. "They hate you. They fear you. You have wounded their pride. They have banded together, determined to destroy you. They want to force me to choose between you, and all of them."

"I am sorry to bring this trouble on you."

"Enemies always follow in the wake of heroic deeds. Should we therefore regret the heroic deeds?"

"I regret only the trouble."

"I do not. I have solved the problem. I have married you. As a warrior, a Mortach Demal, you may fight, you may counsel others in the arts of war, and you may rise to any level in the military but one. Mine. As a warrior, you would be dishonored if I protected you from mere civilians. But as a married woman, you are under the protection of your husband. Such are our ways, and ever have been. Now, you have both the privileges of the Mortach Demal, and the protection of the Hezzan Shul Dramm. They dare not conspire against you."

Talon was dumbfounded. "You are changing the Law."

"I am not. I have studied the Rahk-Taa carefully. There is no prohibition here. I am simply reading it with new understanding."

She was speechless. "I...thank you."

"You are welcome." He said it without smiling.

Talon looked at her emperor in a new light. He was taking a great, great risk. Certainly, others would expect, as she had, as Sool Kron had, that her warrior status would be removed, negated by her newer status as wife. For Drammune women it was a choice of the starkest kind. This would be a new thing in Drammun, the first new thing in the Law since the Hezzan Kaltyne had enhanced the role of Mortach

Demal more than two hundred years ago, granting them full equivalency with men. It would be known and spoken about all over the kingdom. She would immediately be held in higher esteem than any other warrior, or than any other wife. She would be known forever, for generations to come.

Talon's heart pounded. She had accepted her humiliation. She had seen no way out of the obscurity it promised. And now she would be given power and honor she had not sought, more than she could have imagined. The universe had turned under her feet. Who had the power to do such a thing? Only the Hezzan, and only if the Hezzan was willing to bear a great burden, to create many enemies. No one could convince a Hezzan to do this. This was the answer to her test. It would seem that God did show His power in human weakness.

And as she looked at the Hezzan Shul Dramm, she saw in him something she had not seen before. For the first time in her life, she felt she was in the presence of a man who might truly be worthy. She felt a strange desire to give back, a desire to repay such an act. But she had no idea how.

The Drammune language had no word for romantic love, not as it was expressed and practiced in Nearing Vast. And the word as used by the Vast held no meaning for Talon. In the beginning, she simply respected the Hezzan, to whom she had been wed. She felt him to be worthy of honor. He was worthy of her time and attention. That was all.

He was different, yes, but only in degree. She had met many men in her life, and she respected some of them in some ways. Scat Wilkins was fearless, for the most part, and he knew how to lead, how to act, how to make men accomplish great feats. But he was also in many ways a boy, a child who had to have his own way. When Scat threw tantrums people tended to die, but otherwise the comparison was apt.

John Hand certainly was no child. Talon respected his mind, his craftiness, his creativity at sea. But he had no feel for the fight. He did not know how or when to be savage. He did everything in his head first, and sometimes failed to execute it later. Hand's associate, Lund Lander, the Toymaker, had brilliance, and honor, but lived in fawning obedience to his masters. The slave-ship captains she knew were strong and fearless, focused by necessity, but tended toward needless cruelty, cruelty that became their hallmark. All the other captains and leaders she had met had something worthy of respect, but much that was not.

The Hezzan Shul Dramm, however, struck her as a complete man, more so than any she had ever known. He was fearless and wise. He was patient. There was in him something that the Vast might call kindness, but there was no weakness bound up in it, no sweetness. No blindness. He could be brutal; he certainly relished the fight. But he was not rash. He wanted war with the Vast, and believed that war could be won. He knew men; he knew what motivated them, and he led them. Men wanted to follow him.

Without allowing a moment's doubt about who held the power, he gave those in his circle room. She saw how he gave them the freedom to do his will their way. If they did not do his will, of course they were disciplined. They might be put outside the circle, jailed, or hung, depending on the extent of their disloyalty. But he allowed each one to make the Hezzan's desires his own, to execute them with pride, to become one with the movement of the great ship that was the governing force of Drammun.

The Supreme Commander of the Glorious Drammune Military, Fen Abbaka Mux, might have been a superior emperor himself. The High Commander of the Glorious Drammune Navy, Huk Tuth, was almost twice the Hezzan's age, but served him dutifully, gladly. Others in positions of direct power were the same: the leader of the Infiltrators, who did the nation's spying, and of the Coinage Forces, who created and managed the Drammune currency and ran the central bank.

Only the Twelve were excepted. These men Talon did not respect; their conniving was beyond any man's ability to ennoble. This was a traditional body of advisors, a worthy group in the past, but they had no direct power and so had become mere politicians who schemed for their master's attentions and sought power through influence and, Talon firmly believed, treachery. They seemed to her hollow men, unable to see the quality of the emperor who led them. Fear kept them in line, when admiration should have been their prime motivator.

Talon's admiration for the Hezzan only grew. He had not required marital rights as she had assumed he would. Nor had he ignored any attraction as she had then assumed he would. Rather, he had come to know her and to understand her as she worked alongside him, as she learned how he thought, and how he ruled.

They spent, at first, just the same few minutes a day together that they had before the marriage. Nothing had changed, except that she now had his protection. She was one of many advisors he would seek out for discussions on various subjects. He spoke to her of Nearing Vast, of that kingdom's likely response to the crushing of their Fleet, and of the readying and fitting of his own Armada. The minutes they spent together grew as the weeks passed, as he learned the subtlety and the fearlessness of her mind. One day he took her to the docks to show her his preparations there, and to have an audience with the supreme commander.

Her first substantial meeting with Fen Abbaka Mux was the turning point in her fortunes, in both love and war.

It was deep into the year, and the weather had turned bitter. The Vast Fleet had lain at the bottom of the harbor of Hezarow Kyne for more than three months while plans for an unprecedented frontal attack on Nearing Vast, scheduled for the spring, were being made. Now the enormous and detailed preparations for this undertaking were underway. Almost the entire military might of a nation was to be transported en masse over the seas, in order to obliterate the defenses of their great rival.

In all these plans the Court of Twelve had played little part; it was a military operation, and being as huge as it was, it was also extraordinarily risky. As Talon pointed out to the Hezzan, politicians by their very nature would always and only shrink from such a bold and decisive move. They would oppose it, and news of the effort would leak; the Urlish would learn of it, and then the plans would need to be scrapped. No enemy could know what small percentage of the Drammune forces were to be left behind as protection. All and everything hung on secrecy. That a military undertaking was planned could not be hidden, but the size of it, the nature of it, could. So only a few, even among the armed forces, could know.

As the Supreme Commander of the Glorious Drammune Military, Fen Abbaka Mux was fully immersed in every detail.

"Abbaka Mux is of the old order," the Hezzan said as they walked the docks toward the flagship of the Armada. By this he meant that Mux was a Zealot, numbered among those who held in highest regard only the oldest teachings, those of the original Rahk-Taa, and who considered all additions since then to be illegitimate.

The Hezzan was covered in a wolfskin coat that reached to the ground, and wore a matching hat. Talon disdained such accoutrements for the lack of mobility, and therefore lack of defense, they guaranteed. She wore only her leather robe with her hood pulled tight against the bitter air.

"But he is a good judge of men," the Hezzan added. Talon remained silent, wondering at the wisdom of this meeting. In her experience, few men were good judges of other men, and even those who were had trouble seeing backbone if it was clothed in female flesh. Zealots, much like the pious of many religions, tended to be the worst judges of female character, fleeing from their own lusts into prejudice and calling that prejudice purity.

Talon knew she was hated by many of them. The nation as a whole was predictably shocked by the Hezzan's marriage. Women were either wives or weapons, but never both. But to the Zealots, the emperor's actions regarding her were beyond scandalous. They were an affront to the kingdom, to all that was right. Here was proof that the ancient values had been undermined by the elevation of the Mortach Demal to equality with men two centuries ago. The old teachings were simple and clear, defining the limits of what a woman might or might not do. Now, just as the Zealots' forebears had predicted back then, the doors had been thrown open and things were going from bad to worse. It was bad enough that the Hezzan had married her. But now it was far worse—he was treating her as an advisor, not just equal to, but superior to the advisory council demanded by the Rahk-Taa, the venerable Court of Twelve. This was offensive in the highest degree.

To the ultradevout leaders of the Zealots, the four men known as the Quarto, it was against all morality, all convention, and all decency. It could hardly have been more revolting if their leader had married a Vast.

Talon had little concern for the opinions of others, particularly the masses whose opinions ebbed this way and then flowed that way. But as she approached the supreme commander's ship, these thoughts weighed on her. She hesitated at the gangway. The Hezzan stopped, turned to face her. "What is it?"

"My lord. Tell me why you want me to meet with Supreme Commander Mux."

He looked at her with piercing eyes. "You do not fear him, do you?"

Her eyes were colder than the air. "I fear no man."

He smiled, doubting it not one bit. "You know ships."

"Yes."

He looked at the Armada's flagship, the *Rahk Thanu*. It meant "the fist of the Law." He gestured toward it. "Tell me about this one."

She glanced at the cut of its prow, assessed its beam, the length between perpendiculars, the masts, the hull at the waterline. "Is it fully loaded?"

"No. I'd guess its hold is half-empty."

"A standard keel?"

"Yes."

She nodded. "It's a strong ship. Faster than most. The cargo will need to ride very low to keep it steady at full speed."

"That's why I want you to meet the supreme commander."

She stared at him. "I'm sure he knows his ship better than I do."

"I don't want you to tell him about his ship. I want you to tell me about *him*. In precisely that manner, and with the same boldness."

She waited for more explanation.

"He has grown more and more devoted to the Rahk-Taa. He has become a Zealot. I need to know what he will do in battle. I want to see him react to you, and to me. And I want you to see the same. He may be an excellent judge of men, but I find your judgment better."

Talon felt a surge of confidence. She had assumed the Hezzan was testing her. But it was the other way around; he was testing Mux. "Of course I will tell you whatever I see, whatever I learn, as always, my lord."

"Good." He smiled. She felt a strange warmth within her.

The Hezzan entered Mux's quarters unannounced, a tradition among Drammune military commanders that kept all men on their toes, regardless of rank. It discouraged unworthy activities. He found the supreme commander with his back to the door, a leather glove on his hand, and a large brown falcon perched on that glove. Mux was feeding the bird raw meat.

"Can that bird make the trip from here to Nearing Vast?"

Mux turned, surprised to see his Hezzan, more surprised to see the Hezzan's infamous wife standing behind him, her eyes as searching and cold as any falcon's.

"No, my lord. She doesn't know the way." He answered the Hezzan, but he was looking at Talon.

Talon studied Mux. That he was a Zealot could be seen immediately. He wore the red sash around his waist under his clothing, with the telltale end visible at his right hip, cut and sewn at an angle, a red triangle. His beard was untrimmed, his hair as well, falling down around his shoulders as the Rahk-Taa commanded. Mux was a broad, strong man with deep-set eyes. He exuded a sense of peace and assurance and intelligence. He was a leader. He was worthy. He was Drammune through and through.

"It is my great honor to have you aboard the *Rahk Thanu*." He put a knee to the floor, bowing deeply to the Hezzan. But he did not look again at Talon.

The Hezzan took him by the shoulders, raised him up, locked eyes with him. "The honor is mine. This is my wife, the warrior Talon."

Mux nodded quickly in her direction but did not make eye contact. His discomfort was evident. "What would my lord have of me?"

The Hezzan walked to the falcon, admiring the bird as he spoke. "Talon has penetrated deep within our enemy's citadel and in single combat killed the Traitor, Senslar Zendoda." Talon watched Mux as Mux watched the Hezzan. The Supreme Commander did not even glance her way now. He knew all these facts; who didn't? His face was blank.

"She has brought us much honor."

Mux knew he must speak. "And for any honor brought to you, I am grateful."

The Hezzan nodded. "So what is the purpose of having a bird of prey aboard ship, if she can't fly to Nearing Vast?"

"She can fly from our enemy, from Nearing Vast, and return here with information. She can deliver messages to you, my lord. She is but a bird. That is all she should be asked to do."

The Hezzan shot a quick glance at Talon. Her face was calm, impassive, but her eyes danced. She caught Mux's double meaning. The Hezzan looked back at Mux and smiled. "Sit, please. We have wars to plan."

Mux obeyed, relieved to be past the niceties. "Yes, my lord."

"The *Trophy Chase* must be taken whole and her captain and crew alive. We cannot lose the knowledge they have gained." Talon spoke to the Hezzan as they walked back along the docks toward the horses they would ride to the palace.

"Do you think it will not happen so? Those are the very orders I gave Abbaka Mux, as you are witness."

Talon paused. "Fen Abbaka Mux does not like the idea of taking prisoners."

"It is a point of pride with him."

"It is also a point of faith."

"Faith? What do you mean?"

"I mean that his zeal for the Law is his religion."

The Hezzan shot a glance at her. She did not return it. "You have not become religious in your time with the Vast, have you, Talon?"

Unsummoned, the image of Packer Throme hung before her eyes, his arms outstretched. "The Vast believe that their God handed down their religious laws. And yet they keep them with much less devotion than a Zealot does his."

The Hezzan walked as he waited, but Talon did not elaborate. "A Zealot takes the Right of Transfer quite literally," he said in agreement. "It is a stark teaching as originally written, brutal and merciless. The qualifications added by Hezzans over the centuries to soften it are ignored by the Zealots. However, it is a powerful tool for an emperor at war."

"Powerful, but capricious," she warned. "The Worthy takes the life of the Unworthy and owns his titles and property. Simple enough when the Drammune is taking the life of the Vast in the name of the Hezzan. You then own all. But the Quarto also claims that they determine how Drammune a man is, or is not. They decide the degree of his Worthiness, as compared to the Rahk-Taa. Therefore, they alone can grant the Transfer of titles and properties. They are setting themselves up to claim that you, my lord, are not worthy to be Hezzan."

"Yes. Their followers already speak against me daily on the street corners because I am not Drammune enough for them. And that is why I need to understand the man who commands my forces, and follows these teachings."

"Yes," was all she said.

He glanced at her again. She was still reluctant to reveal her thoughts about the supreme commander, which made him all the more anxious to know them. He looked up at the ship they now walked past, captained by their naval leader, Huk Tuth. It was a ship called the *Kaza Fahn,* named for a particularly bloody commander of the Drammune past. "If our supreme commander were a ship, what would you say about him?"

Talon thought a moment. "A ship will sail the way it is built to sail. Handled properly, it will do more than expected. But a man-of-war will never be a cutter."

The Hezzan said nothing. She had offered him nothing yet.

Talon chose her words carefully. "Abbaka Mux is a man-of-war. He has little ability to be quick or nimble. This is not his way."

He stopped, looked at her. "Go on."

She turned to him, spoke face-to-face. His eyes were both piercing and calm. "So long as the seas are not too high, my lord, he will do his duty both to you and to his beliefs."

"And what would high seas look like?"

Talon looked away, so as not to be distracted. "Difficult choices. He will want to win the current battle in honorable combat, in accordance with his reading of the Rahk-Taa. He will want to crush his enemies." She looked back at him, and thought she saw something faraway, as though he himself were distracted. But it was gone in a moment. "If circumstances require him to choose the *Trophy Chase* over one of his own ships, my lord, then he will be a loaded freighter in a storm."

The Hezzan nodded. That was what he needed from her. But he wanted an equally straight answer to one more question. He stepped in front of her so he could look her in the eye. "Do you believe he will obey my commands?"

She looked at him for just a moment longer than was necessary. "I want to tell you what you want to hear. But I cannot. The longer the fetch, lord, the higher the waves."

The Hezzan looked out over his docks and pondered her answer. The fetch was the distance that wind and weather travel over open sea. She meant that the farther Fen Abbaka Mux ventured from the shores of Drammun, from his Hezzan, the less he could be counted on to make the correct choices. The obedient choices. He looked back at her. "Thank you for your honesty. You know ships, and you know men."

Ultimately, the Hezzan would trust Fen Abbaka Mux with his Armada, but only after several more war councils and many more explicit, written instructions. He was more than satisfied with his new wife's cautious candor, and so he began to ask her advice on a wider range of matters, taking her into his confidence on judgments regarding civil disputes, construction projects, and finally the intrigues of his own court. As Talon's confidence in her role grew, she began to point out to him the weaknesses of the Court of Twelve, individually and collectively. She believed they were irrelevant, and a dangerous hindrance to him. She did not counsel him to discard them, but to relegate them to a mere formality.

The more time Talon spent with the Hezzan, however, the more often her attention wandered. She found she was not always able to keep herself from thinking about him while she discussed the subject at hand. She found she liked to watch him as he made decisions, as he weighed matters carefully.

And finally, he caught her doing it.

"Talon?" he asked, with the smallest trace of a smile behind his eyes. And she realized she had not followed his train of thought; she had allowed her attention to drift to the man reclining regally before her. She was angry with herself. "Many apologies. Please repeat your question." And he repeated it patiently, as though nothing had happened.

But something had happened. Talon didn't recognize it as quickly as he did, but she finally understood what she wanted. And when she did, she realized he wanted the same. And from that moment on, the two were one, inseparable whether together or alone, whether in quiet conversation or in ruling a nation.

For his part, the Hezzan Shul Dramm discovered he had never understood—had not been prepared by his culture or his position or his experience to understand—what it meant to care so deeply for a woman. And he did care for Talon. She was unique. She was unlike any other woman he had ever met, certainly unlike his other wives, mere servants, now relegated to catering and catfights. She did not seem interested in making him feel like a god; she was truly interested in *him*. She was interested in his success, and she was interested in the success of his kingdom. She would not let him err in vanity. She was more insightful than any three men on his court. She was better with a sword than he was, better than any man he knew, and judging by her success with the Vast swordmaster, perhaps better than any man in the world. Her mind was worthy. Her willpower was worthy. She was valiant. She was cunning.

And given all this, it gave him great satisfaction to know that she required his protection, and that she had accepted it.

CHAPTER 8

Prey

"You have called us here in the Hezzan's absence to speak treason?" Daon Dendada, the Chief Minister of the People, launched the question from his seat at the huge, triangular table. Winter was over; spring had come. And though the preparations had taken months longer than had been hoped, the Drammune Armada had finally sailed. The politician's face was a wrinkled mass; he looked like an old bulldog. He held up both hands. "This was the Hezzan's decision. And the thing is done." He let his hands fall heavily back to the polished wood.

"I speak no treason. This thing is done, yes, but I propose to you it was not done by the Hezzan." Sool Kron's bony finger poked the air, his creaking voice uncharacteristically resonant with conviction. The group shifted uncomfortably in their seats. They knew what was coming.

"The entire Drammune Armada is one-hundred-forty warships," the Chief Minister of State continued. "The Hezzan has sent more than a hundred of them to war across the sea, leaving less than forty in reserve. And he has sent more than half our army along, packed into the belly of our troop ships. This, gentlemen, is madness! We are all but unprotected here on our own shores, in our own capital. Does that sound like the Hezzan's wisdom?"

Kron spoke to the entire Court of Twelve, whom he had summoned at this late hour to the Great Meeting Hall of the Hezzan. Marble floors glistened, and triangular vaults peaked fifty feet over their heads, flickering with lamplight from the floor below. "A defeat at sea puts an end to us. We must act."

"I don't see the crisis," said the Chief Minister of Justice, Zan Gar, a gruff cannonball of a man, in physical characteristics a younger version of the old bulldog Dendada. "Wisdom often demands secrecy. We are not unprotected. And even if we were, the Urlish and the Martooch could not possibly know it. The Hezzan's own Court did not know—how could they? We have destroyed the Vast Fleet. Why not attack them? The sooner the better, I say."

"Destroyed their Fleet? The Vast are not stupid," Kron said, turning on Gar. "Lazy and selfish, yes. But not stupid. If they could afford to send sixty warships for a parley, what did they hold back? Twice that number? Three times?"

"But our intelligence indicates—"

"Intelligence? Because a dozen spies cannot tell us the location of the remaining Vast warships, we call this intelligence? Where is common sense? The woman Talon has beguiled it from us all. And how do we know our dear friends to the east have not planned an attack on us, wholly ignorant of our designs with the Vast? The Urlish line our borders day and night, waiting for a sign of weakness. No, I do not speak treason, Ministers. I speak duty. I speak patriotism."

No one responded. Their triangular table was cut across one tip so the Hezzan could sit comfortably at the head. Four men sat at each side of the table, the Prefects of Justice to the Hezzan's left, the Prefects of State to his right, the Prefects of the People across from him. But tonight, their leader's seat was empty.

"Duty and patriotism," Dendada finally muttered. "But I must ask if you are not motivated by zeal for the Rahk-Taa."

"Zeal?" Kron was genuinely surprised.

"Yes. Speak plainly. You echo the charges of the Zealots, who day and night denounce the Warrior Wife as an abomination."

Kron looked at Dendada with a disarming smile. "Do not let your own fears obscure your vision. We are not speaking of taking away your seat at this table, Minister. That is the Zealots' desire, not mine."

Dendada looked like he'd been slapped. His greatest fear was, in fact, that the Zealots would win favor with the Hezzan, and then he would replace the four Prefects of the People with their own four leaders, the Quarto. The Zealots actively and publicly campaigned for this.

But Kron had no intention of letting this debate slide down the slope of domestic controversies. "Dear Ministers," he said soothingly, "we stand to lose much more at the hands of this one woman than at the hands of all the Zealots combined. They, at least, are men who seek to join with us in power. She is a woman who seeks to take away our power. They do not have his ear. She has…much more of him than that."

Wry smiles. "You have proof of her intentions?"

Kron closed his eyes, impatience furrowing his brow. "The Hezzan has sent more than half the Glorious Drammune Military across an ocean to attack the full strength of the Vast on their own soil. But has he consulted us together at this table? Did he consult any one of us separately or privately?" Kron paused and waited. Silence reigned. "He has ignored the Twelve! Certainly he speaks to us of taxes and bridges, of commerce, even of Vast spies caught and imprisoned. But of the greatest war effort of our lifetime? No! Silence! When has this been done? It is not his way; it has never been his way, nor the way of his father before him, or his before that. The Hezzan rules with the guidance of the Twelve! It has ever been so. Until now."

"The Rahk-Taa commands it be so," Zan Gar put in.

"So what do you recommend?" asked Daon Dendada.

Kron nodded. "The Hezzan, and the nation, must be freed of the Mortach Demal. Our great leader is utterly in her sway, and will not willingly part from her. So she must part from him."

"And how can she be made to do that?"

Kron shrugged. "We are at war, dear Ministers. The spies of Nearing Vast are among us. We know that she has killed their Minister of the Sword deep within their capital. I am quite sure the Vast have sent their assassins to return the favor. Quite sure."

"Do not speak in riddles. What do you propose?" demanded Gar.

"A well-aimed musket ball. Or an arrow. A knife between the shoulder blades."

"You suggest we kill the Hezzan's wife," Dendada said evenly.

"She is a warrior!" he countered fiercely. "Warriors die."

Silence. The wick of one of the great lamps popped twice, then a third time. "I concur," Zan Gar said, and every head turned. "The death of the warrior will rid this nation of the curse of that woman. The Law must be followed, if we are true Drammune."

Daon Dendada rolled his eyes. "Yes, well, let the Law kill her then."

Gar's eyes were ablaze. "You are a fool."

Dendada looked like he wanted to spit his disgust. "And you are a Pawn."

"How dare you—"

"Ah!" Kron clapped his hands, interrupting the suddenly murderous exchange. "Now this is how it should be," he cooed, opening his palms. "The Council, the Twelve, at one another's throats, determining the fate of our nation. And yet, gentlemen, while Talon lives, our quarrels do not matter. While she lives, we have no power. She has castrated us all. Dear Ministers, let us plot with one accord today, so that we may tear one another to pieces at our leisure tomorrow."

The nods, the grim laughter that punctuated Kron's final appeal told all. They would talk, they would debate, they would scheme, but the conclusion was foregone. The thing was done.

The Hezzan Shul Dramm rushed through the halls of the palace to his wife's aid. He did not need to know the nature of her concern to understand the depth of it. If she had sent a messenger asking him to join her in her chambers at this time of the month, something was badly amiss.

When he entered her rooms, he was attuned to danger. She was not. She was standing in front of the darkened window, moonlight streaming in on her shoulders, on her robe. She was not wearing her usual leathers, but soft crimson silk, tied at the waist. When she turned to look at him, her expression was impossible to read. It was not fear, but it was fearful. It was not joy, but it was joyful. She looked as though she were on the very precipice of some great step that would take her out into the infinite. She looked, he realized, altogether beautiful. Her great strength was there, but in repose, without its hard edge, without the knife's edge. She had hope in her, and promise streamed from her.

She put a hand to her belly.

And he knew. He smiled.

Then he heard a small click, like a twig breaking underfoot far away. The noise came from beyond the open window.

All his instincts shouted danger. "Step aside," he said quietly.

She did as he commanded. He waited a moment, then went to the window and spread his arms wide, taking hold of the wooden shutters to close them. As he did, Talon heard the faint hiss, and then three soft knocks, like knuckles rapping a melon. The Hezzan stood up straight, as though surprised. Then he closed the shutters, and held them shut. He looked down at his chest. Then he sank to his knees.

Talon knew before she saw the arrows, before she heard his last breath ease from him like a sigh, before she caught his slumping body, that he was dead. The arrows had hit him square, had buried deep into his chest. She knew from the sound of the impact, from the motion of his body, that they had struck him where no knowledge of the healing arts could save him.

His heart was pierced.

Talon held him close, his head to her breast. She felt the warmth of his body, which she knew would last but minutes more, and then would be gone forever. She trembled at the glassy stare when she turned his eyes a final time to hers.

"Not now. Not now," she said. "Oh, not yet."

But a desolate chill had engulfed the world. It caused her to tremble. The tremor turned to a quake, her chest heaving of its own accord, her breaths uncontrollably sharp, her mind darkened as if by a thundercloud. She did not understand; it seemed to her she was dying, as though her body were tied somehow to the soul of her king, her emperor, her lover, her husband. Only when she felt the cold wetness of tears on her cheeks did she realize she was sobbing.

She knew she should rise. She should fight. She was Talon, and enemies had killed her husband. But she could not. The training, the discipline that had saved her again and again was no help to her. The anger, the rage that should move her to vengeance did not come. All she could think was that these arrows were meant for her, and that she wished, she longed, she desired only in all the world that they had been shot true.

She could see the instruments of his death clearly now, ugly and short and black, fired from a type of Vast military crossbow that was now obsolete. She knew the weapon well, and so her mind could not help but calculate that with six inches still visible, six inches were buried, which meant they had been launched from more than thirty

yards away. The assassins were not on the balcony, but on the roof-
tops. She knew that from thirty yards at night, the Hezzan would
have been no more than a silhouette. He would never have been
expected to be in her rooms, not now, not during her time.

He had known the danger, had sensed it, had heard it approach
when she had not. She had been swept up in the moment. He had
guessed her secret and had moved her to safety, had moved their
child to safety. He had taken her place at the window. He had spread
his arms wide, and had accepted a death that was rightly hers.

And suddenly she understood the strength of such an act. Dying
of one's own volition, sacrificing oneself. He could not have known
with certainty that he would die in this act. But he was willing to risk
it, for her. And it was not an act of weakness, not at all. It was an act
of great strength. It was an act of great power. It was an act of great
love.

She touched the cheek of her husband and wished she could
bring him back. Perhaps the God who sacrificed Himself, who rose
from the dead, would bring her husband back to her as well. So she
asked Him. She begged Him, then and there, to put breath back into
her husband. She put her lips on his lips, and breathed. But the air
came back cooled into her nostrils, into her mouth, and no amount
of effort, no prayers, would ever warm it again. His life was gone.

She held him close, racked once more with sobs. Deep anger
was bound up in her tears now. This had been what she had fought
against all her life. Her rage had been all, and always, against this.
She had built a dam against this, brick by brick, to protect her from
the ravages of this moment, of this madness, of this horrible vulner-
ability, the excruciating power of this powerlessness. This was what
she had feared, and now it had come upon her.

It had sought her out. It had hunted her through Packer, and then
through Panna. It had stalked her through Senslar Zendoda. She had
hated him with an intense hatred; she had tracked him down and
killed him, and yet he had spoken only words of gentle affection...*My
little child! How I have missed you!*

And finally, it had conquered her. Love had arrived whole and
complete, created in full form and power, in the Hezzan. Her husband.

And now it had crushed her. It would leave in its wake, she knew,
precisely the desolation it had left one generation earlier. She could

not rise, and she could not dry her eyes, because it had happened all over again. In spite of all her efforts, a child would once again not know its father. A father would not know his child. A mother would never again hold the man she loved, the father of her only child. And a mother would be left to bring her child into a hostile, ugly world, an outcast, alone.

Talon stayed on the floor below the window, holding the body of the Emperor of the Kingdom of Drammun, rocking it gently, until her tears stopped flowing and her body ceased shaking.

When the madness finally ebbed away, when her mind began to function again, she considered the danger she was in. She was now a widow with no protector, a soldier with no commander, hated by the powerful, powerless in herself. And she was alone in her own rooms with the body of the slain Hezzan.

They would twist this around. Sool Kron and the Twelve had missed their target, but now they would find a way to blame her. *Talon has killed the Hezzan.* That would be their cry, and it would be the end of the Hezzan's child, the end of Talon, the end of everything.

She laid her husband's head gently on the floor. She kissed his forehead. She rose and went to her dresser, unlocked it and, blood staining her hands, her breast, she removed the tattered pages of Vast Scripture she had hidden there. The Hezzan's library held few books of any sort that were not about the arts of building, healing, or war. Those on the subject of philosophy and morality were few, most of them either copies of the Rahk-Taa or books written by later Hezzans who had interpreted the Rahk-Taa to their own ends.

Talon knew the Rahk-Taa well, as did all Drammune. It read like orders from an invisible authority, shot through with the plainest statements of right and wrong, good and bad, but with no origin other than the hand of a single man millennia ago. Its moral authority was of the most basic, iron-fisted, and despotic kind, almost as barren as the dry descriptions of the Dead Lands to which all were destined.

But the library had copies of several books from the Vast Scriptures. Talon had learned about some of them as part of her schooling, and had read more on her journeys. Compared to the Rahk-Taa they were rollicking histories, stories of great dangers, great defeats, great victories, deeply flawed heroes, and complex villains. Now she had in her hands two books: one written by a disciple of the Christ, a man named Matthew, and one written by another named John.

She had found Matthew's book astounding as she had read it these past months. If she assumed it to be a fable, as she had been taught to believe, she had to grant Matthew the Disciple a place among the world's greatest spinners of tales. Who but a genius could dream up a character like this Jesus? He was a hero who did no heroic deeds. He slew no enemies, fought no wars. Who but the most imaginative writer would have conjured a story in which one man had all the unstoppable power of an omnipotent God, and then did not use it except to bake bread for crowds and calm seas for fishermen? What writer would put the very Son of God into human history, insert Him into the most turbulent times of His people, and then refuse Him the right to shake off the yoke of His oppressors, to slaughter either His nation's enemies or His own? What writer would create a hero with such absolute power, and then not allow Him to wield it?

Yet in the entire yarn, first page to last, this Jesus never once slew even one enemy, not even when they killed His prophet. Instead, He died without overcoming His foes. And then, He came back from death with greater power yet and, amazingly, did not even then wreak His vengeance. Oh, He promised to. But it was as though the story ended in the middle, the beginning told, the climax almost reached… but then nothing. What writer would have the nerve to withhold from His hero, even then, the chance to destroy His enemies? And yet, this hero all but ignored them. Not even a taunt. It went against all reason.

And yet the tale resonated. It seemed to touch people in places no heroic tales of strong men defeating strong men with strength ever could. To create such a compelling tale would be a feat of fiction without parallel in history. If it were known to be written by the greatest poet, it would be a work so brilliant as to cause suspicion that God had indeed inspired it anyway.

But it was not written by a poet. It was written by a tax collector. A man who never wrote anything else. And more astounding yet, Matthew's book was but one of four, all by different authors, none of whom were writers, and all of whom told the same exact tale.

Talon could only conclude that it was not, therefore, fiction. It was an account of a life actually lived. What did that mean? She did not know. She had successfully tested the power that might be hers through an act of submission, in the manner of this passive hero. This much was sure: It worked. So she had to ask herself, was there a similar path before her now? She needed to know. So when she opened the sheets of parchment and read again, at this moment, with the body of her husband near her, how the Son of God taught men to live, she was in a very specific way looking for His help.

And that God, that Christ, said clearly in these pages that she should love her enemies. She should turn the other cheek, allow herself to be hurt by them. He was telling her she should sacrifice herself. She should die in the way He did. She should sacrifice her child the way God did His.

With the blood of her husband hardening on her robes, soaked through the silk fibers and drying on the skin that protected the life of her child, she considered this path very carefully. Turning the other cheek would mean allowing her enemies to do as they would to her. Like Packer, she would be dropping her sword and accepting her own death. Like God, she would be accepting her child's death.

To follow Jesus' teaching was to accept one's own demise on someone else's terms. Of that, there could be no doubt. He said so, just that plainly. This passive activity, this active, knowing, willful passivity in the face of one's enemies was precisely the option the Vast God, the Son of God, wanted her to choose.

She considered it very carefully, deep into that dark night. And she rejected it.

She had no love for the Court of Twelve. She loved the Hezzan, and she loved her own child. But she had no love for her enemies. She hated those who had killed the Hezzan. She hated Sool Kron. She could not pretend otherwise. This request, this mission the Vast God required was simply a higher calling than she could attain to. It was more than she was willing to attempt.

She could protect her child. She could fulfill the Hezzan's mission. She knew how to win his war, and to see the Drammune take their place as the leaders of the world, just as her husband had envisioned it.

She would choose the Hezzan over the Christ.

Talon closed the pages and put the books back into the drawer. She looked at them one last time before she shut them away. Perhaps one day she could live up to those standards. She would try to do justly, she told herself, as much as she could. She would try to reject bloodshed for the sake of vengeance, reject vengeance motivated by hatred. She would try to remember the God who spoke to her through the weakness of Panna, and of Packer, and through the death of her father and the death of her husband.

If that wasn't good enough for the Vast God, then He could kill her, and that would be the end. She would not blame Him. But no, she would not accept her own death, not at the hands of someone as devious and despicable as Sool Kron.

So she changed her clothes, put on her dark leather robe, and when she was ready, an hour before dawn, she called for the General Commander of the Hezzan Guard.

Talon's bargain with Vasla Vor was a simple one. He was a loyal man, loyal to his Hezzan at all costs, which was why he was chosen to protect the emperor. He detested politics and politicians, respected warriors, and loved the Hezzan more than any man on earth. Talon brought Vasla Vor to see the Hezzan, dead, lying on the floor where he'd been shot, the three grotesque arrows still protruding from his chest. Vor's grief and anger were barely contained, as she knew they would be.

She did not hide from him her belief that the arrows had been meant for her. She spoke of Drammune assassins who had known her movements, who had chosen a time and place she would be alone, when they believed the Hezzan would be nowhere near. They had not meant to kill the Hezzan; they had not wanted him near when they killed his wife. They had not wanted his anger aroused, blowing hot dry winds across the red coals of his grief.

She spoke, as they knelt by the Hezzan's body, of the deceitfulness of the Court, their lack of honor, their willingness to risk their country and their emperor's life, even the outcome of the war, over their petty jealousies. They would kill a woman, and for what? They would kill the wife of the Hezzan, who was under his protection, and for what? They would kill a Drammune warrior, and for what? They would kill the Hezzan, and for what? All in a vain effort to protect themselves, to regain favor they perceived they had lost.

As she spoke, the broad shoulders of this battle-hardened soldier rose. He did not take his eyes off his commander, his emperor. His jaw tensed, the lines of his forehead deepened, and his eyes narrowed. She spoke of the ineptitude of the Court. She spoke of the danger to the nation that they posed, their recklessness, their immorality. She spoke of them not as individuals, but as a single entity, a single enemy, a single mass of cancer.

Finally she went silent, and he turned his face to her. His expression was deadly. "Can you prove their treachery?"

"Here is the proof." She held her hand out, gesturing toward the body of her husband.

"Can you prove they conspired together?"

"I can. They do not yet know that they have slain their emperor. I will call them together, through the emperor's messenger. When they see me instead of the Hezzan, you will be there to witness their reaction. Then you will know."

"And if I am unconvinced?"

"Arrest me. Do with me as you please. But if you are convinced…"

He nodded at her.

"Ah, I see you've finally decided to freshen up your appearance," the prince said to Panna. He had sought her out in the cool of the summer twilight to confirm his plans for the evening. He found her not in her usual spot by the pond, which she seemed to have abandoned several days ago, but sitting on the back steps near the servants' entrance, chatting with several chambermaids. They all scattered the instant they saw their prince appear. He did nothing to stop them.

Panna had been something of a mystery to the servants. She had not given up talking with them, and eventually she had gotten several of the younger ones to let down their guard. When certain advisors of the Crown found Panna's visits to the maids beneath the dignity of a palace guest, the prince's mind was sought on the matter, and a simple order came back: "Let Mrs. Throme do as she likes."

Panna did have free run and though she was followed by the Royal Dragoons incessantly, the prince was clearly willing to make dramatic exceptions for her. This fact was daily displayed by her drab peasant clothes. The staff knew that the prince sent Panna a new outfit almost daily, hoping something would catch her eye and soften her resolve. The one elegant dress she owned she wore only to the formal dinners to which she was occasionally invited.

But last night, she had sent her peasant dress out in the evening to be cleaned, and it didn't return. Lost amid the royal wash, she was told. She questioned the chambermaids, but everyone was quite close-mouthed on the subject. Only the young servant girls with whom she had just been conversing would occasionally speak ill of the prince. In fact, they seemed to have no great love for anyone in the royal family. Panna had yet to get to the root of their disrespect, but she got the definite impression that it grew from the king himself. But Jacqalyn, she was told, was a known gossip, willing to spread the worst kind of falsehoods, while Mather's younger brother, Ward, was an all-around scoundrel.

"I have few things," Panna said to the prince, standing to confront him. "You have many. But what I do have, you feel the right to take away?"

For a moment, the prince was baffled by her intensity. "Of what do you accuse me, Mrs. Throme?"

"My dress. It's gone. I want it back."

Mather was relieved. For some reason he had feared she was talking about her husband. He waved a hand dismissively. "Perhaps one of the servants thought it a pile of rags," he said, a charmless sentiment, but uttered with his usual smile and wink and casual smoothness. He allowed his eyes to flutter briefly and admiringly toward the dress she now wore: robin's-egg-blue, her one stylish gown. "At any rate, the improvement in your appearance is immense, and I for one am grateful for it. Brightens up the place."

Panna seethed. "I am not a marble pillar or a stick of furniture," she said, her hands on her hips. "And I am certainly not interested in brightening up the place to please you. If you had any decency, you would let me go home, where I am respected and accepted regardless of what I'm wearing." She hoped she was being harsh enough to convince him she had no interest in him, should Jacqalyn's warnings turn out to be accurate.

"My, you're in a bad mood." The prince, attempting to be casual, hiked his trouser legs and sat on the steps. He sighed. "Look, I know what you want, Panna. But you know you can't leave. I'm trying to make this as comfortable for you as possible—I would hope you understand that. Why bring it up again?"

"But I will bring it up. Over and over until you set me free from this highly polished prison."

"The bird in the gilded cage is supposed to sing more sweetly. Somehow, this principle seems lost on you."

She crossed her arms. "I am not a bird. And even if I was, I would certainly not be your bird."

The prince looked like he had no idea why she spoke in this way. "No. Of course that's true. But this is my cage. And you are, do not forget, my subject, while I am your prince. That accident of social positioning does create some responsibility on both our parts. I seek to fulfill mine, and hope one day soon you will seek to fulfill yours. You are too hardheaded by half to be trusted not to tell what you know, or think you know."

"I live in Hangman's Cliffs. Hangman's Cliffs! It sits on the very edge of nowhere. All the men who can serve have gone off to fight your war. Who would I tell?"

"You are the hero's wife. People will find you. But enough of this. I came to tell you that tonight, dinner is at eight. Please try to be on time."

She stood, bowed briefly, and left him. Mather marveled at her ability to infuse such a simple gesture with such a subtle shade of hostility. He wasn't sure how she accomplished it, but he was quite sure she had perfected the sarcastic curtsy.

The *Trophy Chase* would not be caught by the Drammune. She had simply vanished.

The *Marchessa* was a good ship, well-crewed with sailors who had been aboard her for years, and well-captained by Moore Davies. But she was not nearly as fast as the *Trophy Chase*, and she could not keep up. Davies was not surprised when the *Chase* disappeared into the darkness. He knew the ship, knew her captain, and was glad to have such a weapon out there on his side. He didn't worry. What he couldn't outrun he was sure he could outsail, and the darkness of the night gave him every advantage.

But he worried about the *Silver Arrow*. She lagged badly.

The Vast warship was captained by Bebo Melloon, a Navy man with a fifty-year career strewn with commendations and decorations

The Hand That Bears the Sword

for honor and valor. But his most recent medal carried almost three decades of tarnish, rust, and dust. He was nearsighted to the point of blindness, forgetful to the point of dementia. He had not sailed with the Fleet to Drammun when King Reynard ordered his ill-conceived show of overwhelming force. Considering some of the decrepit captains who had sailed to their demise, this was notable.

But Bebo's self-assurance had waxed as his other faculties waned, and with the prince insisting that at least one Vast warship, one remnant of the Royal Navy, join this mission, Admiral Hand had finally agreed to appoint him to captain the third vessel. To hedge his bets, though, he had given Bebo a first mate of true distinction, a man named Orly Fine, who could sail rings around most captains. And, not insignificantly, who could remember what orders he had given his own men yesterday.

The admiral's command to Captain Melloon had been, "Orly will sail. You fight." And it worked out almost that way. Orly sailed, and Melloon fought Orly.

The crew was at first confused by the bickering, and then dispirited, and then apathetic, all of which resulted in something well short of a showcase of naval prowess. When the *Arrow* ran, she staggered. When she sprinted, she limped. She could make good time in short bursts, but then she'd falter, sails luffing like a winded runner.

Captain Davies' decision was a hard one, but the only one. He could not protect the *Silver Arrow* from a hundred warships. Admiral Hand had signaled them both with orders to run, not to stand and fight. So Davies ran, even as his crew looked astern with wide eyes, straining into the growing darkness as the pale sails of the *Silver Arrow* sank farther and farther back toward the blood-red teeth of the enemy's canvas.

Eventually, there was cannon fire. At this distance in the gloaming, it could be seen only as pinprick flashes of yellow light. It could not be heard at all. But through the telescope, from the crow's nest, every blast lit the low sky and illuminated the ship at which it was aimed. The lookout called out the action, and it was relayed through the rigging down to the deck.

"*Arrow*'s takin' it from two sides!" he announced. The news was repeated, received glumly. They had caught her, then, and surrounded her.

"She's givin' as good as she gets!" A grim hope grew.

"An equal exchange!" Crew members buzzed as spirits rose. Martial praise rose up from the decks. The old buzzard can still fight!

"The lee ship is listing! The *Arrow*'s got her!" The crew of the *Marchessa* whooped.

But then there was a long silence. And finally, "No, no—the lee ship was turning. The *Arrow*'s listing now."

And then, "She's takin' it hard."

The flash of cannon now clearly favored the Drammune, two blasts from the enemy for every one from the *Arrow*. Then four for one. Then ten. And then the cannon fire from the *Arrow* ceased altogether.

"She's done. No return fire."

The *Silver Arrow*'s mainmast came down, her sails settling over her like a sheet pulled over a corpse. The ship heeled terribly. Then she began to burn.

"*Arrow*'s aflame. It's over."

The crew of the *Marchessa* was silent and grim. Men took off their caps.

"That's it, men!" Moore Davies cried out, cutting through the moment with an unexpected energy. "Let's run, boys, or we're next!"

The sailors of the *Marchessa* jumped to life, putting their minds and backs into their own tasks. To falter meant death, and death was at their heels.

CHAPTER 9

Flight

All night the *Chase* ran in the dark. Once the signals had been sent to the *Marchessa* and the *Silver Arrow*, Admiral Hand ordered hull speed. All lamps were doused, and no pipes or cigars were to be lit. The men on deck draped themselves with muskets, pistols, swords, and knives. And excepting only the muskets, the men in the rigging carried the same accoutrements, maneuvering through the darkness with the clank and jingle of weaponry hung from belts or strapped across chests and shoulders. The cannon were charged and loaded, and cannoneers stood by, their torches soaked in oil and waiting on the unlit matches that were held in hands or chewed between teeth.

John Hand had not ordered silence, but the men were silent anyway, as though they might be able to hear over the slap of the waves and the creak of the spars some sign of their enemy. Or as though they might be overheard.

Once the sun had set, low clouds hovered, obscuring the moon, making the darkness seem unreasonably thick, giving the night a texture of gloom. Only rarely could moonlight be seen glowing above the heavy blanket that been thrown over the world. When light did occasionally creep through, not a man looked up to its source; every eye scanned the horizon for a trace of a crimson sail.

But the mood aboard ship could not stay as dark as the night, or as grim as the circumstances. More than half the men now aboard this ship had never ridden the *Chase* at top speed. She ran, they now knew, like an absolute lioness in full stride, smooth and easy and graceful, cutting through and over the waves with utter disdain for them, as though measuring each and absorbing it or hurdling it, bounding effortlessly. With her sails full, she heeled to starboard at an angle that for a lesser ship would have put sweat into the palms of her crew—but the *Chase* felt steady and sure under their feet. She gave off a palpable sense of power, of being at ease with power. Those who had sailed her before remembered why they loved her, and those who hadn't knew now they would never want to sail another.

The beast had gotten little more than a bellyful of splintered nothing for all its trouble with the *Seventh Seal*. One tiny morsel, no larger than the others. All the rest shell. In brooding darkness, it circled. It had not feasted. It had not dared to rise up into the storm to gather in the small morsels on the surface, though the blood scent was strong.

But it had learned. The only reason a shell would be empty was if something had emptied it. It now understood. The victor, once it had killed its prey, had eaten out the meat. Only the empty husk sank below the surface. To feast on the full flesh of these creatures, the Firefish concluded, it must attack the victorious creature. It was the long, deep-finned one that held the meat.

But before it could attack, it sensed the presence of many, many more of these storm creatures. These were of the same ilk, swam in the same straight lines. It was an enormous pack. In frustrated darkness the beast dove, and then waited. The pack approached the deep-finned one. Were they attacking? What would the deep fin do?

It did not take long. Very quickly, the deep fin turned and fled. And with amazing speed! The Firefish was not sure it could catch the deep fin, or even keep up. It watched, but did not pursue. The others, the smaller ones that had left the deep fin alone, these also fled from the huge pack. But these were much slower.

The Firefish watched as the pack surrounded, and then attacked a small, limping storm creature. A straggler.

Again, the thunder and lightning on the surface. Again, the Firefish watched, and learned. It learned that even the small straggler was fierce, throwing thunderbolts without stop, without rest. And then, a shower of morsels! The Firefish swam about, scooping them in. And again the loser, this time the little straggler, sank slowly beneath the waves.

But this time, the Firefish did not attack. It could not. As it considered its prey, the smell of burnt splinters reached it, a sharp and horrible stench, so wretched as to drive hunger itself away. No, the Firefish could not attack, not with this poison in the water. What if these creatures were full of this poison?

Another dive. More patience. More study.

That Prince Mather Sennett had a broken nose, nobody within the palace questioned. There could be little debate. The nasal quality of his voice and the purplish bruising below his eyes were evidence. A better sign, however, was the large white bandage tinged with red that covered the entire center of his face. But precisely how he had broken his nose was a matter of no small discussion among the servants. He claimed it had happened in a riding accident, though no one at the stables had seen him come or go, much less take a spill. If the prince wanted it to be a riding accident, then fine, it was a riding accident. But that didn't stop the talk.

All the juiciest speculation centered on what might or might not have transpired between the prince and the hero's young bride. It was too much coincidence that the day the bandage appeared, Panna Throme's free run of the palace ended. She was now confined to the Upper Quarters, in the northeast wing: "the Tower," as it was called.

The servants were quite sure that the prince's face had been aligned normally at the beginning of last evening's royal dinner. Others were sure the bandage was in place at breakfast. So whatever had happened, it must have happened some time between the two.

Smart money was on dinner.

Royal dinners were generally formal and ceremonial affairs, matters of state, with six to eight guests and at least twice that many political agendas. Panna's role, on the few occasions she was invited, was to be Packer Throme's wife, no more and no less. She had three approved topics: Packer's past exploits, her own faith and hope in his current success, and her confidence in the future victory of Nearing Vast over the Drammune. Otherwise, she was to smile sweetly and chew with her mouth shut.

She had no problem with the first two topics. But the prince had learned to approach her very delicately on the third. It dismayed him that when she was asked her opinion on the outcome of the war, she would quickly invoke the sovereign will of God or some such platitude, and then take a large, smiling bite of something that required significant time to work her way around. Mather had learned to speak for her, and she had learned not to contradict him when finally she could speak again.

This was the first such dinner since Princess Jacqalyn's revelation, and Panna was on edge, unsure she could manage even that much preplanned spontaneity. As she entered the Royal Dining Room, she was wondering why she had even come, why she hadn't pled illness, anything to avoid Mather. But she was quite dismayed to find only two place settings. They were both laid out at the far end of the royal table, with only the width of the table between them. The prince entered the room right behind her and closed the door.

"What is this?" she demanded, eyes blazing.

"Whoa." He held up a hand. "I have detected an unusual amount of hostility from you lately, and I thought it was important we get that behind us. It's a matter of importance to the kingdom. You and your husband are important assets to the winning of the war."

"There are only two place settings."

"And as luck would have it, there are two of us. But do not be mistaken, Mrs. Throme, this is a formal state dinner and your duty is to attend."

Panna's skin bristled with goose bumps; she could feel every nerve ending. No one else was in the room with them, not a dragoon, not even a servant. She recalled the warnings from Princess Jacqalyn with ice-cold clarity.

Mather looked puzzled. "Goodness, woman, I'm not going to hurt you."

Panna's heart thumped in her chest. "I am a married woman. This is not proper."

Mather looked confused. "I'm not proposing to you, Mrs. Throme. It's dinner. Have I not always treated you with the utmost respect? Of what do you accuse me?"

"Where are the servants?"

He smiled. "My. You are skittish." He snapped his fingers once, and a waiter appeared. Mather did not look at him. "Wine, please," he said, and the waiter disappeared. "Satisfied?"

Panna relaxed some. But she didn't like the situation any better.

A look of sudden enlightenment crossed Mather's face. "Wait. Did my dear sister put thoughts in your head?"

Panna didn't respond.

"She did!" Mather confirmed to his own amusement, and then laughed easily. "You must understand that dear Jacq has nothing at all to do. Nothing whatever. She spends her time weaving wild stories, trying to create intrigue where there is none. I personally think she's more than half crazy, but what's to be done about it? Please. Do not judge me by what my sister says or does."

Panna relaxed a bit more. The servants had said as much. And he was, after all, the prince. She had not been raised to confront authority. If in fact Jacqalyn's story was nothing but a story, then Panna had been quite rude. She looked at him. He seemed sincere. "You have always been a gentleman."

"There. I understand my place, and I understand yours. Not only are you married, but you are in love. Even were I completely smitten with you, I would understand it could never be." His eyes were sad. He seemed almost childlike.

She felt no danger from him. "Very well," she said. "Forgive me."

He looked surprised. "Dear Mrs. Throme, there's nothing to forgive. Please, let's sit."

The dinner conversation was pleasant, much more so than was the case in previous dinners. Though she had seen Mather pay close attention to the most tedious dronings and posturings around the most trivial subjects, awaiting his chance to steer the conversation his way, his attentions tonight seemed entirely honorable. They spoke of the Drammune, of the buildup to the war, and Panna learned just how long the hostilities between the two powers had simmered. She had questions from the books she had been reading, questions that surprised the prince. She wanted to understand the impact of the loss of fishing revenue to the kingdom, and what had been done about it. A book she had been reading said that fully half the economy of Nearing Vast centered on fishing. How, she asked, could the fishing trade grow weaker and weaker as the Drammune took over, and yet the results seemed to affect only the little fishing villages? Why was not the whole kingdom plunged into poverty, as had happened once before, almost a hundred years ago?

Mather was impressed by the question. "In a word, the answer to your question is, Firefish."

"Firefish?"

"Yes. My father, may he reign forever, was a silent partner with Scatter Wilkins."

Panna's amazement crossed into the realm of disbelief.

"The tax revenue to the kingdom from Scat's venture has been enormous," Mather explained, and then told her in confidence of the deal that kept Scatter Wilkins from hanging, and the kingdom from financial ruin. "War with the Drammune was not part of the plan." He suddenly looked weary. "He has lost his way."

"Who?"

"The king. I will take his place soon."

"How soon?"

"He wants it immediately. I'm the one holding him off."

Panna didn't know what to say. No wonder Mather felt so much pressure. "I had no idea. Princess Jacqalyn said you were troubled…"

"On that point, she is quite correct. But she sees the world through a dark lens." And then he talked about his family, about how he was raised, how Jacqalyn had become so cynical. She was the eldest, wise in many ways but always excluded from matters of state because of her sex. Eventually that fact had broken her down, but he hoped one day to draw her back into affairs of state.

Then he spoke about how his younger brother, Ward, had turned to drinking and carousing, always uncomfortable in the shadow cast by Mather. Ward had ultimately decided that his own duties mattered little, and had begun to abuse his privileges. Mather further confided how Ward had begun to use the secret passages to go in and out of the palace at all hours of the day or night, ancient passages designed hundreds of years ago for emergency escapes. The king knew of Ward's antics but said nothing, and so Ward grew more and more outlandish in his habits.

Mather avoided talking in any depth about his parents, however. He waved that subject away as if the situation were obvious and the conclusions unavoidable.

Then he spoke about himself. He had been raised and educated as though the very future of the world depended on him. He clearly

The Hand That Bears the Sword

had accepted that assumption. He was fluent in Drammune and Urlish, passable in Martooch and Sandavallian, almost as knowledgeable about their histories and cultures and religions as he was about his own. He was, of course, steeped in political strategy and economic policy. He had studied the sword under Senslar Zendoda, and seamanship under John Hand's mentor, Admiral Andrew "Anchor" Tammerland, the legendary captain of the *Far Horizon,* now lost with the Fleet. He had learned the strategies of war from retired General Mack Millian, who had devised the brilliant defense of Oster in the Comitani Wars, and who now advised Bench Urmand. He talked about being both honor-bound and destined to restore his kingdom's defenses, its economic vigor, and its status in the larger world.

Panna realized for the first time, really understood, that the man before her had no other purpose in life than to take his father's place. He had been tutored, trained, disciplined, and directed for that one role. Mather Sennett was born to be king. She felt a new respect for him, and wondered how any boy could bear up under such an upbringing.

But then suddenly, he changed the subject. He asked about Packer. He seemed particularly interested in the details of his childhood, which surprised and pleased Panna. She spoke easily and joyfully about days she remembered: climbing with him at the cliff's edge, building treehouses, organizing the village children in hikes and pirate battles. She was glad for a subject she needn't be careful about, or tread lightly around. She could not remember ever being without Packer, she told Mather, not until the day he left for seminary. She missed him tremendously then, as she did now. Talking about him made her hurt more and feel better at the same time.

After he had heard several stories, the prince said abruptly, "He saved my life, you know."

Panna sat up straight. "Who did?"

"Your husband. He wasn't that at the time, of course."

"Packer Throme saved your life?"

"He is lately a hero to many, but he has been a hero to me for many years."

"What are you talking about? He never told me anything like that."

"He shouldn't need to. You were there."

She was deeply puzzled, but he seemed to be serious.

"I remember you. You had long dark hair and dark, mysterious eyes, even then. You stood by the fire, where the water was being heated. You were, what, ten years old? I was fifteen."

Panna's mind raced. She couldn't imagine...

The prince smiled. "You helped his mother pour hot water into wineskins. But that wasn't what did the trick. It was him. I was dying of exposure. Packer's father had foolishly carted me all the way up to Hangman's Cliffs wrapped only in a blanket. His mother was the one to grasp the severity of my condition. She ordered Packer to strip to his skivvies and warm me with his own body."

Panna's eyes were wide as her dessert plate. "Oh, my Lord. That was you." She remembered him coming around, color returning, remembered him looking at her. She blushed.

The prince nodded. "Ah, so you do remember. Yes, I was that near-naked, shivering boy. But you couldn't have known it was me." The prince's attitude was breezy. His voice was smooth as the choco-laty dessert left behind by the waiter just before the prince dismissed him. "It was a secret." Mather paused, watched her.

Panna felt the floor shifting under her chair. "But that means... Packer's benefactor all these years, who sent him to seminary, and then to study the sword..."

"Yes. Packer's benefactor was the King of Nearing Vast."

"Packer doesn't know this?"

Mather shook his head. "No, he doesn't. Only you." Something inside him ached as he said those words. So he said them again. "Only you."

She suddenly felt trapped, unable to keep from going down a dangerous road with this prince. She did not like this shift in his demeanor, and she didn't want to share any secrets with him. Certainly not secrets Packer didn't know. She put her napkin on the table. "Thank you for dinner."

"What? But we haven't had coffee." He looked pained.

"I'm tired."

His look grew urgent. "Panna." He reached a hand out, to put it on hers.

She jerked her hand away. "No," she said instinctively, and stood.

"No what? What have I done?"

She gathered herself. "I'm just tired. Thank you for dinner."

The Hand That Bears the Sword

He stood, looking panicked. "There's something else I need to say."

She faced him, her instincts telling her to run, her sense of etiquette and duty telling her that would be rude. So she said nothing, and did not move.

"Panna!" he said softly, urgently, more hiss than whisper. "Help me here."

She felt a ragged lump of fear in her throat. "With what?"

He looked at her with unseeing eyes. "I... I can't get you out of my mind."

"No!" she said, shaking her head and backing away from the table. So Jacqalyn had been right! Panna should have listened. How stupid of her to believe Mather rather than his sister, who was at least a woman, even if she was cynical and jaded. "Don't say it, Mather. Don't say anything more."

"You feel it, don't you? You feel something for me, even though it can never be."

"No!" she repeated, and she turned for the door.

But he followed her, taking a parallel path along the other side of the long table. "Yes, Panna. You do, admit you do! You came to me in your nightclothes, you bathed outside my window..."

She ran.

He chased her.

At the end of the table he caught her, his grip hard on her elbow. He spun her around, intending to take her in his arms and kiss her, believing she would let him.

But she didn't let him.

She broke his nose.

It was a single blow, a solid punch, well-aimed, well-timed, fueled by the same mixture of fear and anger that had almost killed poor Riley Odoms. She put her legs into it, her back, her shoulder. She felt the too-familiar crack beneath her fist. But this time when her opponent went down, she didn't go on top of him. She watched him fall, watched his head bounce with an ugly thud on the polished wooden floor. She stood over his crumpled form, fist still balled, still angry, not knowing whether to kick him or hit him again.

He didn't open his eyes.

Her breathing and her pulse slowed as she began to consider what

The Hand That Bears the Sword

had just happened. And what it might mean. Something had just changed. No, not something, everything. Everything had changed. She put her hands into her hair and pulled. Why had he done this? What would happen to her now, now that she had struck the prince? This was not some old fisherman who wouldn't even recognize her. This was the Crown Prince of the Kingdom, at a state dinner. This was the very prince who had made sure all the charges against her were dropped the last time. And when he awakened, he would know exactly what had happened to him.

Assuming he would awaken.

For the first time she wondered how badly she had hurt him. With a chill she bent down and looked at him more closely. He was breathing. He wasn't bleeding too much, just a trickle from his right nostril, above his mustache and down his cheek. The swelling of his nose had already begun.

"You stupid man," she said to him. "You royal idiot. There are ten thousand women in the kingdom who would…" She grimaced at him.

She stood up and looked down at herself, at her dress. She seemed to be whole, in one piece, nothing torn, nothing much amiss. She looked at her right fist. Only a slight smudge of blood between her knuckles. She wiped it away with her other hand. She sighed once, took a last look at her captor and tormentor. His eyes were still closed, but he was moving now, writhing where he lay, a look of pain on his face as he came around.

She hurried out of the room, back to the Blue Rooms, to await the repercussions.

Prince Mather struggled up through a boggy marsh, looking for air. When he broke through, he came fully awake into a realm of black, dark agony. His head throbbed with the worst headache of his life; front, back, middle—his entire head seemed to be one sharp and focused, dull and pounding pain. He sat up slowly, and the pain increased, threatening to suck him right back under the surface.

By sitting perfectly still and concentrating only on waiting, on holding on, he was able to keep from falling over. The throbbing eased enough for him to take stock. It took him a few seconds to recognize that his nose had been broken. He touched it once, but then had to hold himself still again to wait for the pain to subside. It took him a few seconds longer to realize that the back of his head was aching, badly swollen. What had happened? He avoided the memory for as long as he could, but now it came.

Panna had hit him. Had hit him hard.

The image of her fist came back to him. He was backing away from it, but far too slowly. Her knuckles filled his vision, and then he saw a white flash, and then the carved wooden ceiling above him. Then nothing. She had most certainly hit him. And why? He knew he didn't want that answer to come back to him either.

But it came. He had tried to embrace her! She had seen it as an attack, and fought back. But it wasn't an attack. He had thought she would respond...differently. A deep shame filled him, raising his body temperature, making his head throb all the more, and opening sweat glands from head to foot. How utterly foolish. How completely asinine. How much wine had he had? Enough to lower his inhibitions a bit, but not near enough to plead drunkenness. He wanted to disappear, simply to crawl back into darkness and stay there.

He looked around him. The candles on the table had burned down but a little. He hadn't been out long. He was thankful he was alone, thankful he had made it clear to the servants they were not to return once he had dismissed them. He didn't need them to witness this.

But wait, he had given himself this opportunity. He had dismissed the servants on purpose, as though he had planned the whole thing. But he hadn't. Or had he? His heart sank further. Some part of him, at least, had fully intended to take that beautiful, infuriating woman in his arms. What was wrong with him? Was he two people, or one? What was going on within him?

Mather struggled to his feet, then sat gingerly on the nearest chair. Thank God she had hit him, he thought. Thank God he had not overpowered her.

What was he saying? What was there to be thankful about? And then he realized the extent of his own jeopardy. What if she told someone? What if this became widely known? She was a captive here precisely because he couldn't trust her not to talk. She would make this out to be something awful, something more than a moment's poor judgment. His instincts for survival now overcame his remorse, as he realized he had to make a move, now, to keep her quiet.

He would have time to consider later, time to figure out what had happened to his willpower, why he had misjudged the situation so badly. There would be time to work things out with Panna, get her to understand. But for now, she had to be silenced. For her own good. For the good of the kingdom.

He stood, calling for the dragoons who were certain to be stationed outside the dining room, somewhere within earshot. Panna needed to be out of harm's way. She needed to be controlled.

She needed to be locked up.

Yes—yes, he thought. She needed to be locked up where she could speak to no one, see no one. No one but him.

CHAPTER 10

Dead Reckoning

The *Chase* had been running southwest since the horizon had filled with the red sails of the Drammune. She ran at hull speed until somewhere near midnight, when John Hand gave the signal to turn due east. They sailed east for three more hours. And then, at around three in the morning, the admiral had given the command to turn again.

Now their heading was northwest.

"So we're sailing in a circle," Packer said to Delaney. The older sailor dropped down from the rigging, spry, like a young cat.

"A triangle, more like," Delaney nodded. He spoke in a whisper, looking up at the quarterdeck at their captain, whose hand held the ship's wheel as he studied the sea, the sky, the sails, the wind. "Been sailing all night by dead reckoning."

Packer looked up at the clouded sky. "You mean he's guessing."

Delaney nodded grimly. "That's the thing about dead reckoning. You don't know how much of it's guess till you're done and there."

"Or not there."

"Exactly. If John Hand is the seaman I think he is, he'll come out pretty close to there."

"And where is 'there,' do you suppose?"

Delaney looked at the sails, scanning them for cut and fill. He looked at the sky. The moon provided a sudden faint glow of grim light through the heavy blanket of cloud, and then was gone again. Delaney looked back at Packer. "If I didn't know how crazy it was, sonny, I'd say he wants to sneak up on the Drammune from behind."

Moore Davies was impressed by the quality of ships in the Drammune Armada. He had been confident he could outrun them, but now he knew he could not. He had held his lead over the ships directly behind him, but this was an illusion. The Drammune ships on the wings, both north and south of him now, had increased their speed and were flanking him. This could only mean that the ones directly behind were holding back. The Drammune were surrounding the *Marchessa.*

It was still well before dawn, and though Captain Davies knew his predicament, his crew did not, at least not yet. They were running hard and watching behind. In the next few minutes Davies would need to pick a spot, pick an enemy, stand, and fight. Otherwise, they would close in on him and he would be taken prize. Or, he would have to fight them all.

Abbaka Mux watched the *Marchessa* through his telescope. He was not impressed. The Vast ship was little faster than a Drammune freighter, built on a design Drammune engineers had surpassed five years ago. She was captained well, certainly better than the clumsy *Silver Arrow* had been. But this ship would go down just as easily.

The Vast were arrogant and lazy, living in the past, while the Drammune exceeded them in every way. Pawns, that's what they truly were. They were soft even for Pawns, though. "Sahr hund," the Drammune liked to call the Vast, to distinguish them from the Unworthies of other lands. *Salamanders,* hardly worthy even of being called an enemy. Mux was pleased with the opportunity he had been given to kill them, and claim their earthly dominions. Killing the Vast was his high calling. It was his duty and his privilege to take all they had. This was the great Kar Ixthano, the Right of Transfer, so central to war in the Rahk-Taa. Mux knew the passages by heart, as did all Zealots. He quoted the key passage silently now. *"The Law commands the Worthy Ones to rule. Therefore the Worthy who takes the life of the Unworthy earns all his titles and treasures."*

In the past, many Drammune had used those words to justify piracy and plunder, but those days were gone. The Zealots had higher

The Hand That Bears the Sword

ideals, and the future was theirs. For the sake of Rahk, the Glorious Drammune Military would slaughter many Pawns on this voyage. These salamanders would die while the upright Drammune assumed their place on the earth. This was right, and good. And besides that, it was wholly logical. Such a law ensured that Worthy men would always rule the earth.

Fen Abbaka Mux did not want or expect the spoils of war for himself. The dominion of Nearing Vast, by order of the Zealots, would be passed up the chain of command to the Hezzan, who had decreed their honorable slaughter. With this, Mux was more than satisfied. He would sweep souls into the Dead Lands tonight. And tomorrow. And for weeks and months to come. As the Drammune stormed the gates of Nearing Vast, the Unworthy would storm the gates of the Dead Lands, by the hundreds, by the thousands.

They deserved no more, he knew. They defied all that was right by teaching one another that humiliation and death were the highest honor, claiming this as a message from some Almighty God. This was absurd. Humiliation was dishonor by its very definition. It was like saying dishonor is honor, and honor dishonor. The babbling of lunatic minds. And death by crucifixion, that was dishonorable in the extreme.

Surely, even the Vast secretly knew their religion was false, for they refused to follow their own beliefs. They fought for their lives like animals; they plundered one another as if there were no law; they drank and murdered and sold themselves for money, taking whatever they could on this earth as their own, behaving as though hoarding treasure was their highest calling.

They were a miserable people. They deserved only death, and death they would have. Mux would assure it. He was Worthy.

As Fen Abbaka Mux focused his heart on slaughtering the Vast, Packer Throme focused his telescope on Mux's ship, the *Rahk Thanu*, watching its progress through the darkness. He tried to steady the long telescope against the new brass rail that circled the recently rebuilt platform high above the waves—the crow's nest, where Lund Lander, the Toymaker, had breathed his last. Packer's heart raced, and he suppressed fear that pulsed through him.

"That's her, dead ahead," Packer said as evenly as he could, certain he had located the flagship of the Drammune Armada.

"You see it?" Delaney asked. He had climbed up to the crow's nest to join Packer, to be of whatever help he could. Packer appreciated it more than Delaney knew.

"I think so. The one in the middle, behind. The signals are coming from her." Packer handed his friend the scope.

"It ain't a *she*," Delaney said as he focused on the trailing ship of the Armada.

"What?"

"Drammune don't call their ships like women. It's just a *it*."

Delaney saw the quick, bright flashes of communication Packer had seen. "They don't waste for letters, do they?"

"A code of some sort."

"You see the *Marchessa*?" Delaney asked.

"No. Do you?"

Delaney went silent for a moment. "They got her 'bout surrounded."

"What? Let me see." Packer couldn't believe he'd missed something like that. "Where?"

Delaney looked at him like the question was daft. "In the middle. You know, surrounded."

Packer scanned the dark waves. "I don't..."

"Look for sails. She'll have no lights burning."

Of course that was true. Now Packer saw her, very faint gray puffs against the dark sky. The Drammune had made a wide arch behind the *Marchessa*, with their flagship in the middle, at the keystone. The warships on the wings had spread themselves out and moved forward, and now were moving in, pincers closing on the fleeing ship. "They're gaining on her."

"They've already caught her. Just a matter of time now."

"We have to tell the admiral."

Delaney took the telescope, his face grave. "I'll watch. You tell him."

Packer climbed down the mainmast to just below the yardarm of the highest sail, the main topgallant. It's where he had left the boatswain's chair, kindly offered him by the bosun, Stil Meander, who was nursing his injuries and preferred to stay on deck.

Packer climbed into the sling, untied the lines, and thanks to the ingenious pulley system lowered himself at a much higher rate of speed than he could have climbed down. He had no trouble until the last twenty feet, when he lost control and swung well out over the waves, spinning once before slamming his hip against the rail. He paid no attention to the pain, though. He climbed over the gunwale and out of the chair, scrambling onto the deck as sailors nearby laughed at his clumsiness.

Packer cut his eyes at them, and they were silenced. But he wasn't angry; he barely noted them. He was thinking about what he had just seen, not on top of the waves, but under them, as he descended. He limped quickly up the stairs from the main deck to the quarterdeck, and found Admiral Hand scanning the sea ahead with his own telescope. He looked over at Packer.

"You okay?" he asked with a grin.

Packer's mouth was dry; his heart was pounding. "Sir. Their flagship is the one farthest back, in the middle. If we stay on course we'll run up on her."

"Good work." Admiral Hand looked at Packer more closely. He was white as a ghost. The boy was staring out over the port rail as though looking for something. "Anything else?"

Packer looked back at John Hand. "The *Marchessa,* sir, is ahead of them. They've got her surrounded."

John Hand nodded grimly. He suspected as much. "And the *Silver Arrow?*"

"No sign."

Hand nodded again. But Packer kept scanning the ocean. "Something else to report, Ensign?" Hand asked.

Packer sucked some moisture into his mouth. He pointed at the sea off the port side. "Aye, sir. We've got company."

Hand looked quickly at the seas, scanned them with his telescope. "Drammune?"

"No." The image Packer had seen as he spun over the ocean played in his mind. Dark waves with whitecaps, and then just under the surface, a long, gray-colored beast, its back laced with triangular fins. "It's a Firefish."

"Ah, that. Big one, isn't it?" the admiral said with a smile.

"You...you've seen it?"

"It's been running with us for at least an hour."

Packer was dumbfounded. Running with us? "What are you going to do?"

"What do you recommend?" The way John Hand asked it, it was clear he thought there was little or nothing that could be done.

A Firefish was swimming alongside the ship. It was going to do what it was going to do. They had lures and bait, but attempting to kill a Firefish right now did not seem the prudent choice, not when the *Marchessa* was in danger. And no matter how big the beast was, a hundred Drammune warships were a greater threat, certainly to Nearing Vast. Packer walked to the port rail and peered over the edge. He could see nothing.

Hand joined him. "Why doesn't it attack?" he asked Packer.

Packer looked at the captain with surprise. "I don't know, sir. I was going to ask you."

"If I knew, I'd be rich." He shrugged. "Richer, anyway. Could be it sees the Armada ahead, and doesn't want to attract attention. Or could be it's had a bit of dinner already."

Packer paused. "The *Silver Arrow.*"

Hand nodded. "And maybe the *Seventh Seal,* too."

"The explosion."

Hand nodded.

"Why is it waiting?"

"Scat probably gave it a bellyache." Hand laughed at his own joke. "Wouldn't that old pirate love to know that his rancid soul saved the *Chase* from being eaten?"

Packer ignored John Hand's cold-blooded comment. He took a deep breath, still looking for the monster, still seeing nothing. But the thought of the pirate captain inside that beast right now was, somehow, terrifying.

"I don't think he's going to hurt us, though," John Hand said.

"Who, the captain?"

The admiral laughed again. "The beast. Apparently it's content to wait and see what happens. They seem to like the aftermath of battle, if I recall."

Packer did recall—how could he forget the underwater river of fiery gold in the Achawuk territory, the yellow streaks of a whole school of these things following the trail of bodies thrown overboard? They had not waited then, but had attacked the *Trophy Chase.* The memory of that battle shifted his thoughts to possible battles ahead, where more bodies would be falling into the sea.

"Sir, are we going to attack the Drammune?"

"Aye, Packer. We do have our orders."

Packer thought a moment, then looked into the water again. "That's one smart fish."

Admiral Hand had few advantages, and he meant to use them all. The clouds had cleared and the sun was rising bright and crisp as the *Trophy Chase* approached the *Rahk Thanu* from the east. Coming out of the sunrise, it would be difficult for any aboard the Drammune flagship to make out details of her attacker, or to get a clean read on her distance. Hand knew he had the fastest ship on the seas, and could fairly pounce on his enemy. His ship also had impenetrable armor. And he had a battle-tested crew that bordered on the bloodthirsty. They had beaten the Achawuk. They had beaten Scat Wilkins. They believed they could beat anybody.

And, if all that failed, John Hand had God on his side. Or at least he had Packer Throme, who had God on his side. Or at least, the men believed it was so.

For John Hand, to attack and take down the lead ship of a vastly superior force in the midst of the Armada was but another test of what could be accomplished with foresight, knowledge, leadership, and an understanding of how to maneuver in the tides of time and human activity. Admiral Hand had no illusions about the difficulty of this battle. But he also had no intention of losing. This was not a suicide mission. It was an opportunity to harness and ride the powers that drive history.

He called the men to the main deck.

"Gentlemen!"

Several of the gathered crew looked at one another with sheepish grins.

"Warriors, sailors, men of action!" Now they nodded. That was better. "Not even we can defeat an entire Drammune Armada."

"But we'll give 'er a try!" shouted a sailor. Others laughed and called out their agreement.

"What we can do," Hand continued, "is destroy its leadership. Before the day is done, as God is with us, we will take down the Drammune flagship, and capture or kill the very leadership of that Armada."

Cheers rose.

"That done, we will leave the rest in disarray, and we will fly like the wind, like only the *Trophy Chase* can fly!"

More cheers.

"They're after the *Marchessa* now. They're close in behind her. I don't know if we can save her, but if we can, we will. Our target is dead ahead, the dark ship, the one called the *Rahk Thanu*. We will catch it in less than half an hour." He saw concern on their faces as they scanned the Armada, its flanks far out ahead. "We are not attacking them all, nor will they all turn and fight us. They are closing in on their prey. Calling off their attack to deal with a single ship would be Unworthy. If their commander is arrogant enough, he may even think he can take us alone. But regardless, with our speed, and his Armada so far out ahead of him and spread across the sea, we have a good chance at single combat."

The older hands squinted and nodded, winking at one another. Their new commander was not just a good seaman, but a wily warrior.

"So we'll attack him the way Scat Wilkins attacked us," the admiral continued. "And with no armor, and no ability to penetrate our armor, that little boat will go down, just as the *Seventh Seal* went down. Raise your swords, men!"

Swords went high in the air.

"Dead ahead are the very ships that sank a peaceful envoy of Nearing Vast off the shores of Drammun." Hand raised his voice to a shout. "Will we have vengeance this day?"

"Aye!" "Vengeance!" Swords crossed one another with a scrape and a clatter.

"One more thing. Packer Throme here," and he put his hand on Packer's shoulder once again, "has spotted an old adversary who is traveling with us as a companion. You may see the beast as we fight. It's a Firefish."

Mouths dropped open and eyes scanned the seas.

"It has been with us for hours, and it has not attacked. I take this as a good omen. If we can put blood into the water, then the Drammune will taste not only the wrath of Nearing Vast, but the wrath of God, through His most fearsome creature."

The looks on the faces before him blended astonishment with the passion of possibility. To fight *with* the Firefish, and not against it? It was a heady thought.

"All cannons are to be charged and primed, all fighting men are ordered to the starboard rail. We have defeated the Firefish. We have defeated the Achawuk. And now we make our mark for all time, for all history. Now, gentlemen, this day, we defeat the Drammune!" A guttural roar arose.

John Hand was satisfied.

Just after dawn in the great city of Hezarow Kyne, the Court of Twelve gathered in the Great Meeting Hall of the Hezzan once again, under the high, sharp vault of the ceiling. Again, the Hezzan's seat was empty.

The atmosphere in the room this morning was grim. Each of the robed and regal men knew why he had been summoned. They would together deny it, of course, under Sool Kron's leadership. They were prepared to turn their emperor's gaze on the many enemies the woman Talon had made among the Vast. That she had been shot with Vast arrows was proof sufficient that she was a casualty of war, tit for tat, and certainly the Hezzan would see this. And more certainly yet, no matter what he might suspect, he would also know that with his nation at war, upheaval in the governing council was the last thing a leader needed. They were confident.

They were surprised, however, when General Commander Vasla Vor entered the room, bowed deeply, and then silently took his place in the visitor's dock to the left and behind the Hezzan's empty chair. Looks were exchanged. Why was he here? Was the Hezzan planning to arrest them all? Or was he just protecting himself? It was the first sign that things would not go as they had planned.

The second sign was less subtle. Talon entered the room.

She wore her black leather robe, hood up, and her face was inscrutable. She walked to the Hezzan's chair and stood directly behind it.

She surveyed the faces of the Twelve silently as their mouths dropped open, their eyes darted back and forth, breaths were taken in, faces blanched and blushed, pulses quickened. But within seconds, the Twelve had composed themselves.

"What is the meaning of this?" asked the man immediately to her right, Sool Kron. He managed to lace this first question with suspicion. But his second question betrayed a deeper fear: "Where is the Hezzan?"

"He is dead," she announced, looking from face to face. "He was assassinated last night while he was in my chambers. The result of a conspiracy among his own advisors."

At this the composure of the Twelve disintegrated. Only Kron kept his head. Others put their heads in their hands, or leaned back in disbelief, or exchanged accusing glances.

"It is a lie," Kron proclaimed. "You lie. What have you done with him?"

Talon turned to Vasla Vor. The General Commander stood, then walked to the heavy curtain behind him, which closed off the larger visitor's gallery. Without a word he pulled the curtain back, revealing the third sign that the day would not go as planned for the Twelve. The body of the Hezzan lay on a table, face and hands pale, three arrows jutting from his chest.

"Here is the dark fruit of your conspiracy!" Talon hissed.

Oaths and curses erupted. Wails of anguish, cries of pain. Angry glances were exchanged, and low, urgent conversations filled the space. One man put his head on the table, his shoulders slumping as he sobbed.

"Silence!" Talon demanded. Her features were as intense, hawk-like, and predatory as any man alive or dead had ever seen them. "You are all implicated. You will all pay." She looked Kron in the eye. Her features softened. "Except for you, of course, Minister Kron. I thank you for your services. You are free to go."

Gasps. Then from Sool Kron, in a voice as thin as wisps of smoke from dying embers: "What are you saying?"

"I thank you for revealing the conspiracy to me. You will be rewarded with the power you seek. You are free to leave."

"No!" Kron shouted, eyes blank as he looked around him at the hard faces, the deadly outrage around the table. "She lies! Say nothing."

But it was too late. "It was his idea!" said Daon Dendoda, standing, pointing. "Sool Kron brought us to agreement in this! How dare you let him go!"

"Silence, you fool!" Kron seethed. But he knew it was already over, and the Warrior Wife had won.

"No, I will not be silenced!" The Minister of the People turned on Kron. "I will not allow myself to be accused of killing our emperor!"

He looked at Vor. "It was this concubine, this wretched female we targeted. And it was Kron who led us!"

"But you all agreed to the plot." Talon looked around the table. Now no one said a word. She looked at the general commander. He clapped his hands twice.

The Court's silence was now one of dread. In that silence, making it seem greater and not less, they could hear the footsteps of hobnailed sandals coming down the corridors toward them, the drumbeat of their demise. They looked aghast at Vasla Vor, then at the walls that reverberated with this unseen army, and finally their eyes turned toward the doorway.

"Vasla, you wouldn't dare," Sool Kron croaked. "You have not the power."

But he did have the power, and in seconds that power, the final evidence that the day would fall short of the hopes of the Twelve, flooded the room, swords and halberds and crossbows at the ready.

Kron pled on. "Vasla Vor, you side with this woman? You trade your nation for this witch? Hear our case first!"

Vor shook his head. "I have seen your deeds. You have all confessed them here together."

And so the entire Court was marched through the palace, then across the palace yard, and into the prison where they would remain prisoners, Talon's prisoners, until she had opportunity to question them.

This was a task she would undertake herself.

The men scurried about the ship, Andrew Haas ordering sailors back into the rigging while Stil Meander passed along orders to reef these sails, unfurl those. The *Chase* was heeled hard to starboard, and the admiral hoped to maintain full speed as she passed the *Thanu*.

"Packer," John Hand said, turning to the young swordsman. "I want you at the prow. Whatever prayers you have, pray them. But I want your sword in your hand. Do you understand? You are to fight on the decks this time. The wind is steady. There will be no breath of God today."

Packer started to protest; where else would he be? "I...I..."

John Hand looked at him sternly, then winked. "The men need to see you and your sword, leading this charge."

"Aye, aye," Packer concluded with a grim smile.

As he walked up to the prow of the ship, Packer felt a calm assurance he could not explain, then nor afterward. Somehow the insanity of what they were doing, what they were about to do, did not occur to him. He had no idea how such a battle might end, but when he began to pray he felt it was indeed possible that these events could become the stuff of history. Is that what God intended? Packer didn't know. He could only play his part, as ordered, and let God decide. And he had no doubt that God would decide the outcome.

Packer had orders. This gave him a firm and final sense of his duty. "The prince," Packer remembered from Scripture, as John Hand had quoted it, "bears not the sword in vain." In fact, the orders given to John Hand by Prince Mather were, verbatim, "At whatever price, whatever cost, delay the Drammune Armada from its arrival on Vast shores. Buy us precious days to prepare our defenses, and to fit our ships."

Packer wrapped his hand around his sword hilt. Pain shot through it. But the fit was perfect. He was thankful he was not his own. He was bought with a price, in blood. His soul, his body, his very life were not his to command, but God's. There was peace in that, even in wartime. Perhaps especially in wartime.

Packer stood at the prow as the *Trophy Chase* approached the *Rahk Thanu*. His sword was unsheathed. He could see the men aboard the enemy ship quite clearly now, warriors in helmets, moving along the rail, along its afterdeck. They, too, Packer knew, prepared their hearts in their own ways, readying for battle.

To John Hand's disappointment, the *Thanu* began a quick turn to port, to gain the weather gauge. Both ships heeled the same direction in the same wind, so whichever was upwind would present the least amount of hull to be fired upon, and could fire upon more of the enemy's exposed hull. A hole blasted in a hull might not sink the ship that owned the weather gauge, even if it penetrated at the waterline. When the ship righted, that hole would rise. But if a ship without the weather gauge received a hole in the hull at the waterline, she was sunk even as she sailed on. As soon as the wind abated or the ship turned, that hole would plunge below the surface.

John Hand reluctantly accepted the *Thanu*'s invitation. He steered the *Chase* easily to starboard as he ordered his armed men to the port rail. He had armor down to waterline on either side of his hull. But as a precaution, he ordered the sails reefed two points. He would level the ship some, lose a little speed, but expose less hull.

Now Packer saw hatches open along the stern of the enemy ship, and gun muzzles emerge. His heart raced. He felt the sweat under his arms, on his palms. More hatches opened along the stern, and now cannon protruded, three of them, all small caliber. Packer's pulse pounded in his neck. One fired, and a ball splashed into the water twenty yards ahead. In minutes, perhaps seconds, they would have the *Chase*'s measure.

The floorboards beneath Packer began to level. He felt the scudding of the waves as the *Chase* cut through them, as seawater sprayed in rhythmic cascades on either side of the prow. Now he heard low voices, words exchanged, and looked behind him. The rails to his left were lined with men, his shipmates, muskets in hand, aiming forward and past him. They pointed to one another and picked out targets, determining who should aim where so as not to waste ammunition. They knew their business.

Then Packer saw, halfway down the foredeck rail, Delaney and Marcus Pile with their heads bowed. Marcus's lips were moving in quiet prayer. A Marcus Pile prayer as they entered battle! Packer wished he were there to hear it, standing shoulder to shoulder, praying along with them. But he knew he was included in it, embraced by it. He closed his eyes and almost immediately felt a hard thunk, thunk, thunk through his feet. At the same time he felt a charge, a wave of excitement that was almost electric. His heart now beat like an entire drum line. Here he was, in the line of fire. On point. As exposed as any man, in as much danger as he'd ever been in his life. His mind spun, unable to settle on any one thought. He might live, and he might die, but God would play out this battle however He wished, just as He had against the Achawuk.

If I die, it is God's will, he thought. It did not calm him. He looked up. "Your will," he said aloud. A sharp lump grew in his throat.

And then he thought of Panna. She could easily become a widow this day. He hoped it would not be the case, hoped she would not feel that bottomless, endless ache. For her sake, he asked to live. "Your will," he said again. But he knew that only time would give him the answer, and not much time at that.

And then it occurred to him that this battle, this moment, might determine more than Panna's fate, or his own, or his shipmates', or his enemies'. The Vast Fleet was sunk, and the Drammune Armada carried troops ready and able to destroy and occupy all of Nearing Vast. If the *Chase* went down now, if nothing could be done to slow the Drammune, then a brutal victory over his homeland seemed inevitable. But if the *Chase* could destroy their flagship, if somehow Admiral Hand could take out their commander, then Nearing Vast had one more chance. A slim chance, perhaps. But a chance.

These thoughts, flying through his mind, emboldened him even further. Such great changes in history were surely, surely in the hands of God. It might be hard to believe that God was intimately involved in a routine breaking of a wagon wheel on the road to the docks, or the daily price of fish. But it was not difficult to believe that if God wanted an entire nation to survive, He would move to ensure it. This moment, this hour, might well be one of those points in history that men hang dates on, and schoolchildren recite.

But whom would God favor? The Drammune were not believers, did not acknowledge any God. But Nearing Vast was a dissolute nation in many ways. The God of the Bible had allowed His people to be carted off into slavery again and again, in order to teach them obedience, to sever them from their own sins. Would He do such a thing to Nearing Vast? Why would He not? He would, if that were His will and His purpose. Did the sins of Nearing Vast require it? Packer did not know.

His hand burned him again. He was not his own.

"For Nearing Vast!" someone yelled.

He heard cheers behind him, "For Nearing Vast!"

Flashes of fire erupted on the *Rahk Thanu* ahead, smoke plumes following. Packer heard musket balls whistle through the air, and heard them strike wood around him. Only then did he hear the muffled report of the enemy muskets. And suddenly in answer, the black-powder muskets behind him boomed again and again, a staccato drumbeat of absolute certainty. Packer fought an urge to duck for cover.

The *Trophy Chase* closed in on her enemy. The *Thanu*'s cannon barked, their shot striking water, or bouncing off the *Chase*'s armor. Packer saw Drammune reloading. He kept his sword in the air, felt the wind in his hair. And he felt peace.

Later, he would describe it as feeling the power of God within him.

It was as though everything up to that moment was the approach, the drawing near, and finally at that moment it arrived. Elation, all out of place, seemingly out of nowhere, overcame him. He did not know why, but he raised both hands, his sword still in his right as he looked up to the heavens. Your will! His heart sang out.

It was at that moment the most extraordinary event occurred. In years ahead, as the tale of the *Trophy Chase*'s attack on the *Rahk Thanu* was told and retold, as the details of this day were counted and recounted until they became distorted and embellished beyond all recognition, this one, singular event would stand out, difficult to exaggerate. It was the root and the foundation of the tale, the sign of victory that assured victory.

The Firefish surfaced.

The beast had circled beneath the great herd all night, watching. Stalking. Hungry. Frustrated. Once the stench of the dead storm creature had cleared, the Firefish realized it had lost track of the victor, the one that had fatted itself on the meat of the little straggler. These creatures all looked alike. And even if it had known with certainty, it would have waited. It would take something extraordinary to drive a Firefish to attack such a pack in its strength. Prey here was plentiful. There would be another straggler. The beast would feed.

Finally it heard and felt the approach of another lone creature. This one moved quickly, speedily, hungrily. The beast quickly recognized it as the deep fin. Here was the victor from the first stormy battle! This creature was still flying, still running at breathtaking speed. More than that, it exuded now a sense of power and determination that clicked in the beast's brain and said *predator, not prey. Hunter, protector, not straggler. Not victim.*

Curiosity, then discomfort formed within the beast's dark heart. The deep fin approached the pack with great speed, greater than any creature but a Firefish, and then only when on the attack. Why? Was the one hunting the many? Was the straggler attacking the pack? Such a thing could not be. Even a Firefish would not do such a thing.

But it was.

Its movement was fast and sleek as any Firefish, and it did not waver, did not change course. It ran, full speed, attacking. As the beast swam below, the great light above the waters dawned. And then the beast saw something more interesting still.

A flap of skin.

The deep fin's scales fluttered below the water. Swimming closer, the beast smelled something very unusual. And very familiar. The sunlight as it struck this skin showed something, something that twinged the predator's guts, made it feel uncertain. The beast watched, swimming alongside at high speed, closer and closer to the creature, wanting to understand—drawn, repulsed, and then drawn again.

It stayed near for quite some time, venturing to the very surface twice. There, it heard the creature growl: not quite a roar, but an exclamation, a voice that sounded like many voices. And the spirit of it! The sense of power in that growl, the energy of this animal was utterly unlike anything the Firefish had known. It was fearsome. And it was most certainly on the attack.

But what was it about that skin?

Finally, with a burst of speed and courage, it edged close to the creature, and nudged it. Immediately, an electrical shiver ran through it. Yes. Now it knew. This creature was...somehow...Firefish. Its scales were its own scales.

Confused, startled, hopeful, and drawn more powerfully yet, it swam with increasing excitement, an excitement that was no longer hunger, but something new to the beast, something primal and energizing, emboldening. The beast felt kinship. It felt jealousy. It wanted to be close to this creature.

The deep fin was a great creature. It brought thunder and lightning to the surface of the sea. It destroyed; it ate the meat and discarded the shells. It feared nothing, not even the Firefish. It was powerful. It was Firefish, and yet it was not Firefish. It was stronger, bolder. And with that thought, a dark, ages-hidden door opened within the beast.

It wanted to know this creature. It wanted to be known by this creature.

The Firefish glowed now with the yellow of attack. And yet it would not attack. Its skin turned to flame, and it nudged the deep fin. It nudged it again, and again, and again. Thunk, thunk, thunk... And then the thunder on the water began. Lightning and thunder, just above the surface. The Firefish wanted to turn, to dive, but the deep fin was not afraid, did not dive, did not run, but kept attacking. And so the Firefish stayed.

The Hand That Bears the Sword

And having decided not to run, the beast craved, longed to take part. It felt a deep, deep drive, an ache in its belly, in its mind, in its heart that was not hunger, was not for the hunt, nor for food, nor for procreation, but more powerful than any of these. The beast yearned for something it knew not. As it rose toward the surface, it felt it was being drawn upward. And as it broke the surface between the deep fin and the other, slower one, it felt the air, it raised its head into the light.

And it saw the very face of the deep fin.

The teeth of the deep fin were bared, the eyes wide and ablaze. The beast could not know this was but carved and painted wood. It saw and it felt only the passion of the lioness.

And then it saw the deep fin's wings, like clouds billowing up forever into the sky.

Then it felt before it saw, and then it saw, an intelligence, a mind so great it was as though an entire pack of creatures lived within this single creature, looking out from its eyes. Rows and rows of eyes. They stared back as the beast stared, lining the sides of the deep fin between scales and wings. And then, more astounding yet, a beaming source of light and wonder at the fore of the creature, just above its face, as though the deep fin's very heart stood shining there. Its eyes spoke of wonder, of possibility. This presence held high a single tooth, a pale and gleaming blade.

The Firefish felt its joy.

CHAPTER 11

Revelations

Packer Throme stood at the prow of the *Trophy Chase* with his arms upraised as the beast broke the surface to his left. It rose up slowly, almost methodically, seeming motionless as it matched the pace of the great cat. Its scaly, misshapen head dripped water; its jaws were closed, its teeth poked up randomly, menacing. Its eyes took in the figurehead below him, his comrades lining the deck behind him and then, piercing and aglow, they fastened on him.

Packer's heart raced as he stood eye to eye with the Firefish. As he looked at it he felt a sense of connection, something much like kinship, something that chased away his fears. He sensed a searching there, a longing in those enormous, terrifying, watery eyes. It was as though the beast wanted to speak. Even when its jaw dropped open, Packer felt no fear. He felt only its desire to communicate. To commune. He stood that way, emboldened, searching, until the ancient predator turned its great face away, eyed the oncoming *Rahk Thanu*, bared its teeth, and sank noiselessly back into the rushing sea. And then Packer felt a pang of regret, a desire for that moment to continue. His one thought, now that the beast was gone, was of his father. *If only you could have lived to see this. If only...*

All gunfire had ceased the moment the Firefish appeared. The Drammune stood slack-jawed. They saw the beast in all its radiant yellow, glowing like the sun behind it. They saw its face as it turned to them, its mouth agape, its teeth…Packer could see the Drammune gaping now themselves, fear flooding through them, terror emptying their souls through their eyes. They knew the legend of the Devilfish, as they called it. They knew it could take down a whole ship. But they had never seen one. The secret Vast trade in Firefish was known only to their leaders, and on this voyage, only Fen Abbaka Mux. So now they stared into the swirling seas as the prow of the *Trophy Chase* overtook them.

"Fire! Fire! Fire!" shouted John Hand, again and again and again until his crew awoke from their own trances and began to obey. When they did, smoke and flame erupted from the *Chase,* so thick and heavy it appeared to the Drammune that the Vast ship's gunwales simply flashed, barrels of gunpowder igniting and exploding all at once along her rails.

The *Chase* pummeled the *Thanu* with cannonballs and musket balls from every gun available and with every load possible, steel and lead and shot and scrap, raking and clawing and biting deep, a mad barrage, a blistering fire, a titanic drum corps that hammered the entire length of the hull and rails of the pride of the Drammune Armada.

The *Rahk Thanu* did not return fire.

Drammune sailors, clearly visible now in their crimson vests and helmets, took musket balls to head and chest and torso and limb, and were knocked away from the rails, away from their cannon, blown backward by cannon fire. Through the smoke now filling the seas behind him, Packer watched the *Rahk Thanu* take the full brunt of the *Chase*'s rage, saw wood splinters flying, saw the hull of the enemy ship open like hide being peeled away, leaving visible the skeletal framework of the hold, the decks, the timbers below the decks.

And then the *Chase* was by, just that quickly, unscathed, unharmed, barely even fired upon. The roar from the crew of the *Chase* was as deep and full as that of a whole pride of lions.

Packer looked behind him, saw Delaney and Marcus. Marcus's eyes danced, glassy in the awe of victory; Delaney looked at Packer, shook his head in wonder. Packer shrugged, eyes wide, half a smile turning to a full one. He had no clue what had just happened, or why.

Fen Abbaka Mux did not see the Firefish.

He had been standing on the afterdeck astern, where he had just given orders to begin firing on this crazy, suicidal Vast ship. There was nothing of a surprise in this attack; the Drammune commander had been notified of the ship when it broke the horizon in darkness, more than an hour ago. When he was sure the Vast vessel was by itself and that it was seeking out his flagship, he had ordered the *Kaza Fahn,* his rear guard and second in command, up to the line so the *Rahk Thanu* could have the honor of dispensing with this irritant.

He had been thinking, as he watched the ship approach through the first rays of the morning sun, that the Vast were truly, unequivocally the most naïve people on earth. This was an attempt to save the *Marchessa,* of course. The attacking ship's captain, whoever he was, undoubtedly had courage, at least in the foolish way the Vast defined it. But he had no wisdom. Why would a captain risk himself and his ship to save one other ship, especially when the ship in danger was far less capable than his own?

It never occurred to Mux that this could be the same ship that had slipped from his vision at sunset. That would be an impossible feat for the best Drammune ship, let alone a Vast tub.

The Drammune captain had walked away just as the musket balls began to fly, exercising good judgment. The Armada would not sail itself; the army would not land itself; they needed a commander like Abbaka Mux. His men would dispense with the Vast ship. Mux was already appointed to take command of the captured capital, to rule the City of Mann for the Hezzan. This early victory would make him seem anointed as well.

Mux had no idea why his men froze, why they feared, why the icy blast of approaching death seemed to sweep over his ship just as the prow of the attacker came alongside them. He screamed at his men; he shouted orders. They obeyed, but slowly and with trembling, as if in shock. This strange loss of nerve created just enough gap, gave the Pawns just enough advantage that when they began firing, his own men were on the defensive.

And the cannon blasts from the taller Vast vessel were devastatingly on target, ripping not just his hull, but his cannon placements, taking out two-thirds of his starboard cannon in one swift and brutal pass. Only when the attackers had passed by, and the stern of this flying ship came into view, did the commander bother to look at its name. His Vast-language skills were not good, and he could sound out only the first few letters. Still, those letters gave him a chill.

"Sailor," he ordered his first mate, who knew the Vast language. "What is the name of that ship?"

" '*Trophy Chase,*' sir."

Abbaka Mux closed his eyes. It was the ship his Hezzan wanted him to spare, to take alive! It took him less than five seconds to determine that this ship must be defeated at all costs. Capture her, sink her, burn her, it didn't matter to Mux. In the first engagement with the Drammune Armada, the Vast salamanders had made his men look like, well, like Pawns.

The Hezzan understood honor. If he were here, he would feel the same need to crush this foe for the sake of the war. For the sake of the Armada. For the sake of the kingdom.

"You bust udderstad, Padda, I ab dot all I seeb to be." The prince was unable to breathe through his nose, and the huge white bandage across his face made him look as ridiculous as he sounded. Panna felt an urge to laugh, but managed to stifle it. It would not have been a compassionate laugh.

"I know," the prince continued, as Panna grew more accustomed to translating the sounds of his nasal blockage, "that I appear to be calm and in control, but in fact I am often unsure of myself. There are things that…scare me. The king is not well; his mind is going. I have enormous pressures. I carry the weight of Nearing Vast and its future, especially now that we are at war. It is a harder thing than anyone knows."

Panna sighed, completely unsympathetic. She had thought a lot about what had happened, about where she was, and why. She thought about what Mather had said, and about what the servant girls had told her, and all the ugly things Jacqalyn had hinted at. And the conclusion she had come to was that she was, for the first time in her life, ashamed of her nation. The Vast were good people, she believed, had always believed. Now she had to doubt. If this was their leadership, if this was how their country was run, how could they be good? Mather thought his father was a fool, but what was Mather? How was he any less one? He lied to his people about the

Fleet; he purposefully got his new recruits drunk to try to gin up their fervor; he had made Panna a captive in his own home, and then in this remote corner of it. And of course, there was his loathsome behavior at dinner. And now he enters her rooms with dragoons in tow, spewing self-pity?

Panna was standing, arms crossed, in the center of the entranceway. She would not let him pass, would not let him believe he had any right to enter into her chambers, even if they were his. "So that's why you accused me of wanting your filthy advances? That's why you've locked me up in these four rooms as though I were a threat to you, instead of the other way around? That's why you brought these two…goons with you?" She did not look at the hulking dragoons standing behind Mather at the doorway. "Because you're unsure, and things scare you?" She grimaced. "Why am I locked up here? Tell me that."

The prince could see this was going to be difficult. He had thought about what he had done as well, had considered it all through the night and most of the day, and his conclusions were somewhat different. He had decided that his passion for her was, at root, quite pure. He had simply fallen in love. This was not his doing; how could it be? It simply was. He had made a bad mistake in displaying it at all, and a worse mistake in the manner he had chosen to display it. But the war and the pressure he was under, surely these were to blame for that. His manners had always been spotless before. Panna would understand this, certainly, as a momentary lapse in judgment. No one was perfect. She had had lapses in judgment of her own, including her decision to deck him, the Crown Prince of the land. He would apologize; she would apologize. He would then behave himself, as a true prince. She would promise to keep it all quiet, and all would go back to the way it was. This is how it would need to work out. Otherwise, things would stay…difficult. He was here to work it out just that way. He had planned his approach. Somehow, though, he had not envisioned standing in her doorway as he attempted to execute his plan. He had not expected her to position herself as quite the obstacle she seemed to be.

"May I come in to discuss this?"

"No, you may not."

He took a deep breath. "Fine." He smiled, but his voice betrayed

The Hand That Bears the Sword

irritation. "We'll chat here. Panna, I am not a bad person," he said. "But at the same time, I am not always the person I should be."

Panna glared. "I believe that last part."

"Yes, well. But who is, really? Of course you have little evidence of my better nature. I was uncouth at dinner, and I apologize for that. I am sorry. I understand your anger. But you know nothing of me except for a few stories over dinner. That is why I am here. I want you to know me better." He softened some, and then said the words he'd prepared so carefully, the strategy he was sure would win her favor: "I know you can help me to improve."

She rolled her eyes. "Look, Prince—"

Not the response he had anticipated. "Please. Call me Mather."

"You need a priest. You need a counselor. I'm your victim, not your pastor."

"Victim? That's a very harsh word." He was beginning to sense that this conversation would not end at all where he needed it to end. "Panna, you seem quite well, while I on the other hand have this horrible broken nose." He pointed to his "broked doze," as if she couldn't see it. "I didn't have you arrested, as I could have. Twice now I've saved you from the law. Surely that says something about my good intentions."

"Oh for the love of—listen to you! Do you have any idea how self-centered you are? No, of course not. How could you? No one will tell you for fear you'll have them locked away somewhere."

"What are you talking about? How am I self-centered?" He was happy to have finally engaged her in this line of conversation, even if she was being rather ill-tempered about it.

"Are you joking?"

He swallowed. "No. I am not joking. Nor am I arguing with you. I'm sure you're right. But I really don't know how to be anything other than what I am. Perhaps you can help me."

She stared at him. It was the last thing she wanted to do, but perhaps it would get him out of her rooms. " 'I want to talk about me.' 'I have this burden.' 'I want you to know me better.' 'I carry the weight of the kingdom.' 'I saved you twice.' *I, me, me, me, I, me,* and sometimes *you,* but then only because of *me.* For heaven's sake, Prince, maybe flattening your nose will help you see past it. I represent something you can't have, and so you want it more. I can't believe I have to say this to you."

He smiled, as though he weren't listening to her words, as though he was just admiring her spirit.

This irritated her. "You're hopeless. And to top it off, you are a total, unrelenting bore."

Now the prince grew sullen. Then a flash of anger glinted in his eyes.

She was glad to have gotten to him. "Let me guess, no one ever talks to you like that. And that means no one in your life has ever told you the truth about yourself. If they had, maybe you wouldn't be assaulting married women over dessert."

His eyes went wide, his voice went low. "I did not assault you."

She was defiant. "You did. And I will punch you again if you try it again."

Mather glanced at the two dragoons he had brought with him. They stepped forward in unison. Mather waved them back. But he also took a small step backward, just to be sure he was well out of her range. "Let's leave that behind us, shall we?"

"No, let's not. How long am I going to be locked up here?"

"Panna." He tightened his jaw. He would need to get stern with her. "I can't have you wandering about the palace telling people I assaulted you. You do understand that, certainly. I will be happy to give you free rein again when you can promise me that this little episode will always and only be between us."

She put her hands on her hips. "Our little secret."

"Yes."

"No. The answer is no. I will tell whom I please what I please."

He was incredulous. "But you know that means you must stay here."

"And how will you explain to your father, your brother, your sister, and the servants why I'm locked up here? How will that look to them?"

"You don't understand at all, do you? These things are not difficult. You're ill. That's why you're here."

She pursed her lips in anger. "And what about your dragoons? They know better."

"But they are loyal to me. They will not talk."

Now she looked at each of them. Their eyes were implacable. One of them was the same young man who had taken her from the *Trophy Chase* to the carriage, though she didn't recognize him. She

The Hand That Bears the Sword

shook her head, angrier yet. "You come up here pretending to be remorseful, offering apologies, saying you need my help. But all you want is to shut me up. That, sir, is revolting behavior for any man, but for a prince? True repentance doesn't arrive with armed guards. No, I will not let you get away with this. For your own sake, and for the sake of this kingdom. I will speak of the Fleet, and I will speak of how you assaulted me, to anyone and everyone I choose. You choose how to deal with my crimes."

He stood still, stunned.

"You should have let me go home, Mather, when it was just about the Fleet, when I truly knew nothing and could only guess. But you didn't, because you wanted to manipulate me like you do everyone else. Now I won't go away, not until everyone knows who you really are."

Mather just stared at her, wide-eyed. What was she trying to do to him? She was trying to destroy him. But why? "Panna, I haven't hurt you. Why do you insist on hurting me?"

"You can't see it. You're too blind. But you asked for my help, and this is the only way I know how to give it."

"Panna, there must be some way you can help me be a better man, other than ruining me."

"Perhaps if you truly repent, you will not be so ruined as you fear."

"I...have no idea what you're talking about."

This was the first thing he'd said that she believed. She looked at him a moment, then asked, "Do you have a copy of the Scriptures?"

"Of course."

"Read the Gospel of Matthew."

"Which part?"

"All of it."

"Okay. But tell me why."

Panna paused. "Because it's not about you. Read it. You'll figure it out."

The big young dragoon stole a glance at his partner, who smiled. Just slightly.

"Please, I know she's in there. I just want to get a message to her."

The dragoon was impassive, as all the others had been. But this one was young. Will Seline did not recognize him as the one who had shepherded Panna from the *Trophy Chase* to the royal carriage. He just hoped that because of his youth, he might still have a soft spot within him somewhere.

"Please," Will Seline begged. "She's my daughter."

The huge young man shook his head. "Give me the message, and I'll pass it along," he said in his high-pitched voice. "That's all I can do."

Will Seline waited for a carriage to clatter by. Then he spoke softly, leaning over the rail of the guard shack. "I've been giving messages to you guards for weeks now. I must have given notes to twenty different men." The rotation of these guards had frustrated Will to no end; he had yet to see the same man here twice. "They are not getting to her. Or if they are, no message is getting back to me. She's my daughter. I need to know if she's all right." The big man's was stony. "Do you have a daughter?" Will asked.

The dragoon shook his head again. He started to say something and then bit his lip.

"What?" Will Seline could read people. "For the love of all that is holy, man—say it."

The dragoon looked down the street. He looked at the pastor. "The King's Arms, ten o'clock tonight," he said under his breath.

"The King's Arms? What do you..." Then Will understood. "You want me to meet you there. Right. Okay. I'll be there. Thank you." He nodded twice, then hurried off to the inn where he was staying, anxious to find out where, and what, the King's Arms might be.

The *Trophy Chase* flew by the *Rahk Thanu*, traveled just far enough to be out of cannon range, then wheeled to port. Abbaka Mux saw it, believed it a serious tactical error, and ordered ramming speed. His opponent would be in irons in a moment; the ship wouldn't get halfway about before he was upon her, and he could sink his steel-plated prow deep into that arrogant ship's hull.

But Mux was wrong. He had never seen a tall ship that could maneuver so deftly. Within minutes, the *Chase*'s crew had dropped every sail on the mizzen so that all billowed full, and had trimmed almost every sail on both the foremast and the mainmast. Coupled with the hard port turn, the wind acted like a great hand, pushing her stern around. The one-hundred-eighty-degree turn was executed in less than five minutes, with the *Chase* in irons for less than half of that. During that time, Abbaka Mux and the *Thanu* had gained on her hardly at all.

Now all the *Chase*'s sails were dropped, and billowed full. She stood still for just a moment, seeming quite proud and aloof, before her sails popped, and she leaped forward toward the Drammune flagship.

The two ships sailed directly at one another now, prow to prow.

Mux's men were still not as sharp as they should be. They had weathered an unexpected level of fury from this Vast ship. They moved quickly, but without their usual dexterity, as they kept one eye on the water around them, trying to understand where the monster had come from, and to see where it had gone.

The Drammune crewmen were disciplined, though, and they did not speak. There was little whispering and no rumormongering, just each man swallowing his fear and doing his duty.

Mux called for his first mate, a man tall and thin by Drammune standards. "Helko, what happened to your men?"

The mate looked surprised. "Did you not see it, sir?"

"See what?"

"The great beast. The Devilfish."

Mux looked at his man as though he had lost his mind. "Speak," he commanded.

"It swam alongside the bow of the *Trophy Chase*."

It rankled Mux to hear his man call the enemy ship by name, though he did not know why. "You saw this?"

"I did. So did all the men."

Mux pondered a moment. He was tempted to ask what it looked like, but did not want to give the man's fear so much credence. "You think this thing came with that ship?"

"I...it seemed so, sir."

"Helko. We have a mission. We are at war, and we have a battle to fight. Let's fight it."

"Aye, sir!"

Mux left him, walked to the center of his quarterdeck, and bellowed out to his entire crew. "Men!" He had their attention instantly.

"I don't care what you saw! I don't care what the Vast throw at us! I don't care what the sea throws at us! The ship dead ahead is mortal. It carries the enemies of Drammun! I want all grappling guns on deck now! I want grapeshot loaded! I want swords and pistols and muskets! I want death and destruction and blood bathing the decks of that ship! And I want to send those Vast salamanders into the Dead Lands, now!"

The Drammune sailors did not cheer, but they were cheered. Their hands moved now with alacrity, their eyes and their minds focused sharply on their work.

They were Drammune. Fen Abbaka Mux was their commander. They would not fail.

His orders were to run, but they were now very hard to obey. Moore Davies, aboard the *Marchessa*, had watched the attack of the *Trophy Chase* through his telescope. He was elated. His crew was hoarse from cheering, and many of them were wiping tears from their eyes. The *Chase* had not only escaped, but had somehow flanked the enemy in the night, an awesome feat in itself, and then had managed, apparently, to sneak up on the flagship of the Armada! How or why the Drammune commander had left his rear unguarded was a mystery, but however it happened, the *Chase* had blistered him for it.

Davies and his men had not seen the Firefish. Their view had been blocked by the wider *Rahk Thanu*, and even had it not been, they were now looking directly into the rising sun. But they saw the *Trophy Chase*, that magnificent ship, their ship, the hope of the Vast; they watched as she bettered the flagship of the Drammune, then turned and, instead of running, stood like the lioness she was, facing down the entire Armada.

Davies obeyed his orders and kept the *Marchessa*'s sails trimmed and his ship at full gallop, but all eyes were strained to see what would happen next. It seemed to him that the whole navy was stunned. They had apparently forgotten about the *Marchessa*, and now she was putting distance between herself and her pursuers. This was their chance to escape, to take word back to Mann, back to the prince and the king.

But as the face-off diminished in the distance, and a hundred ships seemed to close in on the *Trophy Chase*, Davies' sense of excitement abated. What ship, no matter how great, could survive those odds?

Will Seline understood why the King's Arms was favored by the Royal Dragoons. Every square inch of wall space was covered by some implement of war, ancient or otherwise. There were muskets and rifles, a blunderbuss, derringers. There were swords and knives of every shape and size: broadswords, pikes, halberds, maces, sabers, scimitars, rapiers of every origin, Vast, Drammune, Urlish, Kambui, Martooch, Sandavallian. In a glass case near the entrance was a proud new addition, an Achawuk spear. A plaque beneath it commemorated the crew of the *Trophy Chase*.

The priest took a table for two in a shadowy corner, and ordered a pint of dark ale. He was not a drinker, nor did he much feel like drinking now, but in a place like this on a mission like his, he did not want to attract any undue attention by ordering ginger beer or gaseous water. In an effort to be invisible, he had even left his robes back at the inn, and wore plain trousers and the one work shirt he had brought with him, the type favored by fishermen. He noticed, however, that this was not much of a fashion statement on the streets of Mann. He might have been less conspicuous in his robes.

Will was anxious. A loud discussion was underway at the bar, where a red-faced old man in a full dress uniform with a colonel's insignia was telling a story of bravado and daring to a small crowd that hung on every word. Will couldn't follow the tale, however, so he sipped his mug of stout, wiped the foam from his moustache, and stroked his beard, thinking. At least that little gathering kept eyes out of dark corners.

The priest had come to Mann as had all other able-bodied, law-abiding male citizens, noting that the king's proclamation did not make exceptions based on either one's earthly or heavenly calling. He had not been untouched by the riotous, delirious nature of the recruiting process, rather he participated in his own way: He heard many confessions. All were heartfelt. Some were sober.

The priest had taken all this with his usual patient good humor. For the most part, these were men of good intentions who were frightened very deeply. They wanted to be worthy of Nearing Vast's martial history, and they wanted to protect their homes from foreign invaders. They simply had no idea how to go about doing either.

Their intake of ale provided a shortcut to community, allowing camaraderie to blossom in mere days where otherwise it might have taken months, even years. It broke down barriers.

Unfortunately, it also broke down doors, bar stools, horse railings, general health, and the short-term financial position of almost every man not wearing an apron or carrying a bar towel. Cap Hillis was one of those exceptions, at least for a while. The innkeeper would eventually be denied induction and make his way back home to Hen and hearth—and a far less prosperous pub than the one he'd left—but for many nights running Cap and Will teamed up in the big city much as they did back in the tiny village. Cap would send the depressed and the fearful and the heartsick to Will, who would do what he could to help them sober up and then find both forgiveness and, when possible, misplaced belongings.

But often the only help Will could offer was highly temporal: dragging a half-conscious man from the mud into the grass, locating a surgeon who could stitch a forehead, or shooing a barmaid away from the purse of a man passed out in a corner.

Will had, of course, joined the throng in sending off the *Trophy Chase*. If he'd had any advance notice of the event he might have gotten closer earlier, and might have had a chance to see and speak with Panna, or even to wish Packer well. At the time, the pressing crowd seemed like a minor irritant. Certainly, he would be able to get all the news from his daughter afterward. But Panna had been whisked off by the prince in a fancy carriage, and Will had not seen her since. The vague foreboding he felt then had turned out to be a grim foreshadowing of something…but as yet he did not know what.

He was stuck in Mann. The military would not accept him to fight, but the powers on high had yet to form a policy on the induction of military chaplains, so he was asked to stay in the city until policies could be set. Apparently, these were not high-priority decisions. Will took the cheapest room he could find, above the loud but well-managed inn where Cap and he had worked, and there he dedicated himself to prayer and to finding news about Panna.

This meeting was the first chink in the royal armor. He watched the door for half an hour, during which time he sipped down perhaps an inch of his ale. The old officer at the bar had finished two stories and had begun a third, when the big young man with the angry face entered. Will recognized him instantly in spite of the casual brown cotton shirt and trousers. He was clean-shaven as usual, but out of uniform he looked even younger, a mere teenager. A man-child.

The dragoon looked around the tavern. Will raised a hand. His target located, the young man skirted the group at the bar just as they burst into laughter. He looked at them with some alarm, then realized they were paying him no attention.

"Got delayed," he said by way of apology as he squeezed into the chair across from Will. "Baby's sick."

"Sorry to hear that. How is the little boy?"

The young man wrinkled his brow. "How'd you know he's a boy?"

"You told me you didn't have a daughter."

He squinted. Then he remembered. "Oh. Right. He's fine. Or will be. Croup."

"Your first child?"

"No, third. Oldest is five." The man eyed Will's pint thirstily. Will waved down a barmaid, and the dragoon happily ordered a stout.

"I appreciate you meeting with me," the big priest said. "I can't get any news of Panna. I don't know if you can imagine what that's like."

He nodded. "But I don't have any news," he said abruptly.

Will fought disappointment, and waited. There must be some reason the young man had come.

The dragoon glanced over his shoulder at the bar. "That's Prince Ward right there," he said. "Did you know that?"

Will blanched. "Which one?"

"The tall one, listening to Colonel Bird recite his stories."

Will watched a lanky, dashing young man pour the last drops of his ale down his throat, then take a mug from the barmaid's tray as she passed. It was the mug meant for the young dragoon. She smiled coyly at the prince; he winked at her. She wheeled around to get a replacement. "He comes here frequently?"

"Mm-hmm."

Will thought he detected a trace of disapproval. "If I was guessing, I'd say you don't think too highly of him."

The young man stared daggers at Will. "I can't talk about the royal family," he said with finality. "All I can say is, your daughter's fine."

The priest's face brightened. "So you've seen her?"

He shrugged. That was no secret. "Sure. Everyone's seen her."

"Well. That's news, then." The big priest put out a hand. "Thank you. My name is Will Seline."

They shook. "Stave Deroy. Friends just call me Chunk."

Will smiled. It was certainly apt. "Panna's well, then?"

The dragoon nodded once.

Will sensed there was more. But nothing else was forthcoming. "Anything more you can tell me?"

"No, that's it."

The priest nodded, but took a sip as he waited.

The barmaid came by with Chunk's drink. He scowled at it; it was still mostly foam. Impatient, he took a deep drink anyway, then used his shirtsleeve to wipe away the generous leavings. "She's being kept in the upper rooms right now. What we call the Tower."

Will's shoulders slumped. His voice grew low. "And why is that?"

Chunk sniffed, looked around the room. He took another drink, and then another swipe.

"Is she in danger?"

"No. Not that one. She can take care of herself."

Will grew alarmed. "I have to ask you, Chunk. Why would a young woman under the protection of the king need to take care of herself?"

Chunk stared hard. He took a deep breath. "'Cause it's the prince she's under protection of."

Will nodded. His worst fears, which he had hardly dared to think, he now put into words. "And he's taken an interest in her."

For the first time, the dragoon's eyes opened up to Will. He leaned in. "She broke his nose. But you didn't hear it from me."

The priest sat back as though he'd been punched himself. "She did *what?*"

"Don't know the how, can only guess the why. But she did it. So he put her in the Tower."

Will just nodded. "He was making advances."

"Oh, he was advancing. She was retreating." He thought a moment. "'Cept a course for when she was punching."

"He visits her there, in the Tower?"

The dragoon looked into his mug. His face now twisted into obvious disgust. "He's not a good man. I was there when he went to

The Hand That Bears the Sword

see her, after she hit him. I was supposed to protect him from her." He looked at Will. "Protect *him* from *her*. Can you believe that?"

Will's eyes closed. This was a nightmare. He couldn't imagine the ugliness of this for Panna.

"He said he'd let her go if she'd be quiet about everything, but she said no, she wouldn't. She'd tell who she pleased."

Will nodded, somewhat encouraged. That was his Panna.

"She said it was for the kingdom. That people needed to know how bad he was for his own good, and for the good of the war."

Suddenly the priest saw a flickering light, the hand of God behind these events. "And you believe that?"

Chunk got an odd look in his eye. "Well, yeah. How are we going to win a war with such as him running it?"

Will's heart ached. Chunk was a simple man, and a good man. And what he just said was foolishness in the eyes of many, who would separate out a man's character from his ability to lead, or fight, or succeed. But to Will, it was a shining spiritual insight. It was faith. "Not by might, nor by power, but by my Spirit, saith the Lord."

Chunk shrugged, took a swallow. "I'll die fighting. That's my job. But I'd rather know I'm fighting for the good. That's all."

"Death comes to every man, sooner or later, and we're all fighting in our own way, for good or ill." Chunk was studying his stout. Will was studying Chunk. "War is coming," the priest said. "Are you prepared to die? Are you ready to meet your Maker?"

Chunk looked earnestly up at Will. "I don't know."

"It would be an honor to help you, sir. If you would allow me."

There was a pause as the young man's eyes grew more earnest yet. "Okay."

Will smiled. "Do you have something you want to confess?"

Chunk nodded. He faced it now as his solemn duty. He looked thoughtful for a just moment longer. And then he told Will Seline every sinful thought, act, and deed that he could remember from his earliest childhood. When he had finished, Will Seline prayed with him to the God who forgives all sins, who paid for them all, and who ushers humble sinners into His Kingdom. With gladness.

The Hand That Bears the Sword

CHAPTER 12

Fight

The Drammune grappling gun was a small cannon, an inch in diameter, into which a three-pronged grappling hook was inserted. Tied to the hook was a strong, braided, lightweight line, which would reel out when the cannon was fired. Launched either above a ship's masts or in and among its sails and lines, the hook would be pulled back by hand until the prongs caught on something, and then that something could be hauled closer, for more intimate combat.

Grappling guns were not peculiar to the Drammune. But Fen Abbaka Mux had elevated their use to the warfare equivalent of high art. This fact was one that the Admiral of the Fleet of Nearing Vast would soon discover. As the *Trophy Chase* began her second pass, the crew of the *Rahk Thanu* loaded not three or four, or even a dozen grappling guns, but fully four dozen. The Drammune warship lined its decks with them. In front of each cannon was a fat coil of line. A warrior stood behind each, holding a small single-wick lantern with an open flame, and awaited the order to fire.

Like a number of sailors in the rigging, John Hand saw the activity on the deck of the approaching *Rahk Thanu* but did not comprehend its meaning. He was focused on attacking once again the *Thanu's* starboard side, where the damage was already significant, and where at least some of the cannon had been put out of action. He was not surprised when the other captain seemed willing to oblige. The two ships were on a collision course, prow to prow, until the *Thanu* veered southward, preferring to offer its wounded side once again rather than give up the weather gauge.

John Hand also guessed that his enemy had movable cannon placements and could therefore replace lost cannon with good ones quickly. He had heard of this innovation, and was anxious to see whether the Drammune had perfected it.

They had.

Twelve damaged pieces were dumped into the sea; ten were replaced with spares. The other two were not recoverable; the floorboards on which they had been mounted were obliterated. The sailors aboard the *Thanu* prepared themselves and their armaments well this time. They had steel in their hands and in their hearts, cannon loaded and ready at their feet.

Admiral Hand surveyed the set of the battle, the placement of the Drammune warships against his own. The quickness of his ship had left him in good stead. The next closest ship to the *Chase* was the *Kaza Fahn*. It had veered sharply north as the *Chase* passed by the first time, not pleased to be both in range and downwind of the attacker. Now the *Fahn* was well out of cannon range, in irons, stern facing the *Chase*. In a few more minutes it would complete its turn and be facing east, capable of pursuing. But in a few more minutes John Hand expected to have completed his second pass, west to east, and to be running like the wind with the *Thanu* crippled or sunk behind him. The *Fahn* would not catch him.

The other Drammune warships had slowed, some were turning, but none was capable of taking part in this battle unless it became a prolonged one.

So it was the *Chase* versus the *Thanu* again. The admiral was content.

Mux had his grappling guns out on his decks and in the forefront of his battle plan. The Drammune flagship's commander had honor to redeem, and he would redeem it at close quarters. He had decided against attempting to sink the *Chase*. Not only would that be counter to the Hezzan's orders, it would not be nearly vengeance enough. He wanted his men on the decks of that ship with swords in hand, where they would crush the soft Vast sailors, sledgehammers on salamanders. Then he could preserve that maddening but sterling vessel for his emperor, with or without her officers left alive. He wouldn't

The Hand That Bears the Sword

disobey orders, not directly. But the contingencies of war often confounded the best-laid plans, and the Hezzan would simply need to be content with whatever outcome Mux delivered.

John Hand gave Packer his spare pistol and its accoutrements, a bag of charges and musket balls, and ordered him to the starboard rail. No one on board now doubted Packer's courage. He had stood firm in the crossfire, stood tall when the Firefish faced him. Some, however, were beginning to doubt his mortality. How could a mere human summon the beast from the depths like that, look it in the eye...and the beast not attack?

The admiral was not among the doubters. He was quite sure Packer was perfectly capable of getting himself killed. What he still doubted was whether the boy was capable of killing. Packer had not yet drawn blood, and drawing blood was precisely the service required now. Packer Throme with pistol and sword, firing, fighting, a comrade in arms, that was what his men needed to see. It was what John Hand needed to see. A war-hardened Packer would be a great asset, far more practical than a haloed figurehead. And if Packer were to die—well, John Hand could use that as well. A martyr was always a great asset to any cause.

The *Chase* came under fire early as she approached the *Thanu*. The Drammune would not wait this time. Cannon belched, and grapeshot spattered the *Chase*'s hull and rails. A few men fell, a few men swore. John Hand called for small-arms fire in return, holding his cannon back, wanting to blister the *Thanu* once again at close quarters. But why grapeshot? Hand wondered. Did their commander know about the armor? So few cannon had been fired against the *Chase*, how could he...?

Then, suddenly, Hand understood. "Hard to port!" he yelled. He now realized what the activity on the decks of the *Thanu* was all about. His men looked at him quizzically, even as the ship's prow began to turn away from her prey.

"Fire at will!" Hand ordered, as soon as the angle of his hull allowed for direct shots. Cannon erupted, and the already damaged starboard hull of the *Thanu* took more damage yet. But this was nothing like the consuming fire of the first pass. The *Chase* was still almost fifty yards from her enemy; the cannon fire was sporadic as crews took careful aim, and not all the projectiles found a target.

Packer raised his pistol. He aimed at a Drammune warrior across more than forty yards of ocean and pulled the trigger. But the best that could be said about Packer's skill with a pistol was that he was good with a sword. The kick surprised him; this was a harder jolt than he had experienced firing his one round from the rigging in the Achawuk battle. His intended target was unimpressed and unaware; the ball struck the hull of the *Thanu* eight feet below him.

Packer dropped a charge packet into the smoking barrel, but as he put the ramrod down into it, the *Thanu*'s grappling guns fired their missiles.

It was an odd sound, a multitude of small, muffled pops. Because of the distance and the angle of the barrels, the reports were softer even than those of muskets. Packer saw the rising shower of hooks, slow, peaceful, almost gentle, each trailing a thin line like a spider's web rising upward. They arced high in the air and then began raining down from above, many clearing the uppermost sails, the sky and the main topgallant, many catching in lines and guys, on canvas and mast.

One sailor on deck cursed loudly and ripped an offending hook from his shoulder. He stared at it in wide-eyed dismay, as if it were some strange creature that had just bit him. Then, as if to prove him right, it leaped from his hand and began a quick, jerky journey across the deck, back toward the gunwale. Dozens of them did the same, spiders scurrying toward hidden nests.

"Cut the lines! Cut the lines!" Hand ordered, his anxiety unmasked. Others joined in the call, and swords and knives came out as any sailor near a grappling hook severed, or tried to sever, its lifeline.

The little things moved fast. The crewmen set a dozen free, but three times that many were caught in standing rigging, yards, guys, sails. The total number of grappling hooks astonished the crew as did the speed at which they went taut. Almost immediately, the seasoned sea legs of the crew could feel the *Chase* tremble as she was pulled toward the *Thanu*.

Crewmen who scrambled up into the rigging to release the spiders' grip were stopped by grapeshot from cannon and musket balls fired by marksmen on the *Thanu*, their long rifles perched on tripods for just this purpose. And these marksmen were tested less every second as the *Chase* was drawn closer and closer.

On the decks of the *Rahk Thanu*, Drammune sailors lined up in rows like men in a tug-o'-war contest, pulling on the thin lines like madmen, hand over hand, knowing that time was their enemy. The faster they pulled, they knew, the less time their enemy would have to cut the lines, and the better their chances would be to overrun their foes.

"Cannon, fire!" John Hand repeated, but now got little response. Crews had stopped reloading to marvel at the grappling hooks, and had then left these duties to follow the new orders, to cut the hooks away. Now they returned to their artillery, and a few cannon boomed, but the effect on the *Thanu* was slight.

Hand grimaced. There would be no quick pass. *The Fist of the Law* had caught them and was pulling them into a death struggle.

Then the *Kaza Fahn* surprised him as well. Long range guns blasted the *Chase* from across a span of water John Hand would not have believed possible. And their cannoneers aimed true. Concussions knocked his men to the floorboards, drew them away from the starboard rails.

"Charnak!" yelled the commander of the Drammune Armada, in a voice easily heard by John Hand and the Vast sailors. *Fire!*

Cannon roared again from the *Rahk Thanu*. Packer hit the deck along with many others who stood at the starboard gunwale. A few of them went down bleeding, but most went down of their own free will, out of the line of fire. Now splinters and wood chunks from the railings and masts and cabinets and cabins, anything above the protective armor, went flying all around them.

Now it was the *Thanu*'s turn to blister its enemy. The *Chase*'s decks quickly became a deafening, pounding battleground. Grapeshot shattered and skeletonized the Chase's structures like locusts passing over a cornfield. Endless cannon fire drummed out rational thought. Packer's cheek was pressed hard against the decking. He looked at his right hand and saw the back of it turn red with spattered blood. He wondered whether it was his own. In this maelstrom there seemed no way to know.

And then suddenly the cannon fire was twice as loud, twice as close. For a moment, Packer couldn't understand what had happened. Had the *Thanu*'s cannon moved directly onto the *Chase*'s decks? He covered his ears to protect them, but the firing seemed to come from within his skull.

Then, finally, he realized this was the sound of his own shipmates

The Hand That Bears the Sword

returning fire. Packer felt a sense of pride bordering on awe. How could anyone function in this smoke-choked hell? And yet they did.

Cannonballs from the *Chase* once again blasted the *Thanu*, cratering its hull, then its decks. But the cannonade was not thick and not prolonged. This time, Vast cannoneers were taking heavy fire, with casualties mounting quickly. By the time the cannon had been emptied, no more than two-thirds of the cannon crews were capable of reloading.

When the blasts finally slowed, Packer raised his head from the deck. He was shocked to see that the rails of the *Rahk Thanu* were no more than five yards from their own. Somehow, the Drammune had continued pulling those lines and had closed the gap in the midst of that thunderous volley. He looked up into the rigging, saw Drammune warriors swinging toward him, coming down from above.

The *Chase* was being boarded.

Packer leaped to his feet and drew his sword.

John Hand's voice cut through the fray. "Fight, men, or say your prayers!"

As the gap between the ships closed to mere feet, small arms erupted and men fell.

"Nochtai Vastcha!" Fen Abbaka Mux cried in his deep, resonate rasp. *Death to the Vast!*

Drammune warriors roared the refrain. "Nochtai Vastcha!" And then they came pouring across, up from the decks of the *Thanu*, a swarm of hornets.

Packer's first foe leaped across the gap, then struggled to climb up over the rail. He was grim and determined, helmeted, short, and built like a boulder. He was no more than an arm's-length from Packer. Without thinking, Packer rammed his blade into the man just below the breastbone.

But the sword did not penetrate; it flexed with the force of the thrust and then almost sprang out of his hand as it recoiled. Packer's wrist and hand exploded with pain. The man looked up at him with stunned anger in his eyes, a look that spoke of instant vengeance. Packer took an involuntary step back as the lumbering man cleared the rail. Then the man's short, curved sword came up, a sweep from Packer's left. Packer blocked it neatly, but his head spun, trying to understand how a man could...

And then it hit him. Where Packer's sword had struck, the color was scraped away in a gash, leaving a gray, mottled, metallic sheen. It was some kind of chain mail, steel mesh. The man's vest—a short tunic, really—was armor. It was a hauberk. That realization, slow as it was to make its way to his brain, ushered with it a great sense of relief. There was no magic here; the man was not made of iron. Packer immediately put his sword through the man's throat, buried it until its hilt struck the man's jaw. Then he shoved him away. The thick warrior collapsed backward and landed sitting on the deck, his back against the rail, eyes locked on Packer and frozen wide in surprise.

Packer's own expression mirrored the dead man's. But he couldn't think about what he'd just done. He needed to think about that armor. The man's helmet was made of the same crimson material.

"Armor!" Packer cried out. He remembered how Lund Lander had instructed his shipmates from the battle deck. "They're wearing armor! Go for the throat!"

But when he looked around, all he saw were his shipmates being cut down. Almost all of them had once been pirates, and were still as fierce in a fight as any Drammune warrior. Most were better with a sword. But the jabs that struck Drammune bellies, the cuts across heads and torsos, the thrusts into chests—none of them mattered. None of them penetrated. The Drammune fought on, pressing forward in their aggressive strength, backing bewildered Vast sailors into one another, into railings, into corners, where they died.

Mux stood on the quarterdeck rail and watched with growing satisfaction. Salamanders under sledgehammers, hammers wielded by the *Fist of the Law*. Mux was pleased. The Drammune were worthy.

Packer raised his eyes to God. The *Chase*'s crew was being slaughtered. No response came back. His heart thundered in his chest. Lives were draining away all around him; his countrymen, his friends. He looked at the sails. They were full, but bound with what seemed like a hundred cords. There would be no breath of God this time, just as John Hand predicted. *I want your sword in your hand*, he had said. It came into Packer's mind that he should fight harder, more fiercely. But it also came into his mind that no amount of effort would matter. They were destined to lose.

Packer dropped to his knees, put his head back, and closed his eyes. Fighting raged around him. He was completely vulnerable, but kneeling, he was all but invisible. "They're killing us!" he said aloud, looking up into the sails. "Is that what You want?"

Now he closed his eyes, and for a moment the sounds of fighting faded, and Packer was sitting on the edge of Hangman's Cliffs, looking out over the sea. Clouds were sprinkled across a blue sky, the sun peeking in and out of them. It was a memory, but a powerful one, and now it came to him like a waking dream, like a vision. Packer could feel the warm ocean wind in his hair, hear the waves crashing far below him, the cry of gulls. He was here, really here again, where all was peace and serenity, and the earth in its infinite detail spread out on an unimaginable scale.

And now Packer, as he had done so many years ago, asked his Creator, "What is it You want?"

And the answer came back once again, not in words, but in tenderness, in the peace of the moment, the breath of the breeze, that He wanted Packer's heart. And as he had done then, Packer gave it, instantly, wholly, willingly, without reserve, without condition. Life or death, ease or hardship, pleasure or pain.

And then Packer asked again, as he had done all those years before, "What do You want me to do?" And God told him, once again, as He had before, that Packer could ask whatever he wished.

And Packer remembered the joy he felt that the God of the universe would say such a thing. And Packer said now what he had said then: "I want to do good on the earth."

Then Packer realized that God had let him choose, had always let him choose his own path, so long as his heart was in God's hands. And with his head bowed now on the blood-streaked decks, he asked God, pled with the God of the Universe, the God of life and joy and peace, the God of time and eternity, for the grace to do a mighty work now, for a space of time, to help his shipmates, his country, and his king:

"I want to fight!"

He heard no voice, saw no visions. The sound of the deck returned to him in all its brutal ugliness.

"Fight!"

Packer looked up to the source of the word, the single syllable of command. John Hand stood at the quarterdeck rail, a pistol in each hand. The admiral pointed a pistol at Packer, and fired. A Drammune soldier fell at Packer's right hand.

Packer looked at the admiral and smiled.

Now John Hand could see fire in the boy. And not just in his face, not just in his expression—his whole being seemed alight. As Packer stood, Hand took a deep breath and turned his attention to another target. "Religion," he muttered, and fired again.

Packer stood slowly, his heart eager, and looked around him. Marcus Pile was struggling against the port rail, trying to hold off a much larger, much stronger Drammune sailor. Anger rose in Packer, but anger like a smooth flow of molten steel, a power that drove him forward without thought.

Blows were raining down on Marcus; his defenses were crumbling. Packer came upon the Drammune warrior from behind, his mind focused to a pinpoint, like blazing sunlight through a convex lens. He put his sword tip through the back of the big warrior's neck, just at the base of the skull. He didn't think about protocol or form. The honor of the duel did not cross his mind, nor would it for the remainder of the battle. All that mattered was that the battle end, that he stop the Drammune from killing his shipmates.

That he must kill to stop the killing was a simple fact. He would fight until there was no fight left within him. He pulled his sword free from Marcus Pile's attacker, now a body crumpled at the boy's feet.

The young man looked Packer in the eye, and Packer saw and felt his fear and his relief. "Thanks." A half a smile.

"They have armor," Packer told him. "Go for the throat." And then he turned, ready now to even the odds wherever he could.

As quickly as his reflexes and his training and his natural gifts would allow, Packer moved from one armor-clad Drammune warrior to the next. He had no concern about whom, or even whether, his enemy was fighting. It did not matter which way the man faced, or what his weapons were. Without conscious thought, driven to help his shipmates, to slay his enemies, he fought. He fought as though every Vast sailor was but a feint, a decoy put there to distract the enemy so Packer Throme could kill him. He moved like lightning, struck like thunder. All his training at the hand of Senslar Zendoda was preparation for this very battle.

But when he looked around again, he knew it would not be enough. Panting, he surveyed the decks of the *Trophy Chase*. He killed many. But he was only one man, and in the time it took him to stop five warriors, eight Vast crewmen had died. He questioned God once again. Why grant him this strength, this answer to prayer, and then let the Drammune win the battle anyway?

Fight! Had that not been John Hand's command?

Fight, Packer thought. *Not kill.*

Yes, yes, Packer realized, his stomach falling. His request had been to fight; the orders had been to fight. And now he realized he needn't kill. It would work the other way just as well. Perhaps better!

And even as the thought was forming, he was in motion. He moved even more quickly now, now that he wasn't dealing deadly blows, now that he was slashing at a neck, or skewering a knee from behind, loosing blows at legs, arms, shoulders, striking anywhere there was no armor, any opening, one strike every second, then two every second, inflicting blindside, blinding pain, pain that in every case was followed quickly by another Vast victory. Packer did the distracting now, pulled the enemy's attention away—and in the pause, the wince, the cry, Packer's shipmates finished it.

Packer had the speed, the training, and the motivation to attack a hundred men in this manner every minute. He could feel an enemy coming up behind him and know, without looking, exactly how much time he had before he needed to turn to face him. Packer could use each second to score another hit, two hits. One more strike, and then he must turn…Strike! Turn and strike! Move, strike, strike, yet another, feel the presence from behind, hear the footsteps, don't turn yet…Strike! Not yet…Strike! No need yet, the man has paused, he is unsure, strike another! And another! Now he's decided, turn and strike!

The Supreme Commander of the Armada stood at his command post and watched his Drammune warriors fall. He was appalled. The battle had turned suddenly, instantly. His sailors had been invincible, it was only a matter of time. But now they fell as though an angel of death passed among them.

And then he saw that angel, a white-clad, yellow-haired warrior who flicked among them like a hornet, fighting not like a man of valor, but like a coward. And yet he was winning the day for the Vast.

Mux pulled his pistol to take him down, but the boy moved too quickly. He was never still, never stopped moving, and his movements were all jerks and starts, smooth but without flow, rhythmic but without steady rhythm. It was impossible to draw a bead on him.

As the Supreme Commander of the Armada tried to find a clear shot, the Admiral of the Fleet took careful aim. Nothing stood

The Hand That Bears the Sword

between John Hand and Fen Abbaka Mux, and neither man was moving but for the gentle rocking of ships at sea. And these two ships were lashed together.

The salt-and-pepper-haired admiral with the long rifle in his hands came into Mux's line of vision. Mux saw the insignia, knew from his briefings that this must be John Hand. Certainly, it was not the pirate captain.

John Hand saw Fen Abbaka Mux, but he felt Scatter Wilkins. The dark-bearded commander now aimed back at him. The odd sensation of familiarity vanished, however, when Fen Abbaka Mux lowered his pistol and bared his teeth. He was taunting. "Nochtai Vastcha!" he cried.

John Hand understood the words well. He fired just as Mux lowered his head, a bull ready to charge. Hand did not miss. The musket ball struck Abbaka Mux square on the top of his skull and slammed him backward against the mainmast of the *Rahk Thanu*.

Hand lowered his rifle. But instead of watching the body of his enemy collapse onto the deck, he saw Mux raise his chin and snarl, enraged. His helmet had stopped the ball.

Now Mux raised his pistol.

Hand's eyes widened in surprise, and his head disappeared behind the wheel casing, just as Mux's musket ball took a spindle off the *Chase*'s wheel. The Drammune commander grimaced, lowered his smoking pistol.

That small distraction over, Mux assessed the scene again. He was still losing. The number of Drammune warriors continued to dwindle, and the fight was now spilling down onto his decks. In minutes, the *Thanu* would be overrun.

Mux looked for help from the *Fahn*, but that ship was out of range again, having kept moving while the *Thanu* tied itself, and its fate, to the enemy ship.

Cheers began to rise from the *Trophy Chase*. Mux growled aloud. Even the Pawns knew victory could be had. Somehow the salamanders were escaping his hammer.

He called the retreat. "Enahai! Enahai!" He was not naïve. His courage was tempered by realism. "Karba zhal!" *Cut us loose!*

The remaining Drammune sailors obeyed instantly, pouring back down over the rail, fleeing to their own ship, cutting as they came the lines that bound them to their otherwise-certain demise. The Vast warriors whooped their full-throated approval. They did not, however, follow their enemies onto the *Thanu.*

John Hand felt enormous relief knowing they would now escape with their lives, and the *Chase* would indeed outrun the Armada to safety. Then suddenly, he felt victory slipping from his grasp. Their commander would escape. The *Rahk Thanu* would survive. He had in front of him an opportunity, a moment in which he could not just delay the certain attack on Nearing Vast, but possibly affect the outcome of the war. This chance had suddenly bubbled to the surface of the cauldron, and he could not ignore it.

"Attack!" he shouted. "Board that vessel! I want their commander!"

The Vast sailors hesitated only a moment, and then followed Packer Throme, who now leaped down to the decks of the *Thanu.* The Drammune warriors gave Packer a wide berth, none wanting to venture close to that stinging sword.

"Enka charnak!" Mux called out. *Load and fire!*

But it was too late. The remainder of the *Chase*'s crew flooded the decks of the *Thanu*, fifty men chasing down fifteen. Within minutes, the Drammune had their hands in the air, and half a dozen *Chase* crewmen, including Packer Throme, surrounded their commander. Seven swords hovered at Fen Abbaka Mux's throat. Packer and Mux stood eye to eye.

Mux snarled his disdain.

"We got 'im, Admiral!" Andrew Haas called out. "What now?"

John Hand did not have time for anything elaborate. The *Kaza Fahn* was back in range. "Bring their commander, put the rest overboard alive. Find me their battle plans if you can do it quickly. But cut the rest of those grappling lines loose!"

Mux unbuckled his sword belt and held it in his hands, sheathed. He hated the Vast, hated the *Chase,* hated most of all this yellow-haired boy and what he had done to his warriors. Honor demanded he give his sword to the enemy commander who had defeated him. He would not give it to anyone of lesser rank.

The cannon from the approaching *Kaza Fahn* barked, and the *Chase* shuddered. "Hurry now, men! Let's fly!"

Vast crewmen took great pleasure in shoving, prodding, and otherwise inviting the beaten Drammune sailors over their own ship's gunwales and into the sea, calling out to them in gleeful taunts as they did.

As the Drammune floundered, Delaney came up from below decks with a leather-covered strong box. He was followed by Mutter Cabe, with Mux's falcon perched on his fist, riding on Mux's heavy leather glove. "Looky here!" Cabe announced to anyone who cared to pay attention. "Got me a hawk!" But just then the bird's great wings flapped and it rose from Mutter's fist, talons out, and attacked, going for his eyes. He ducked and shook the glove off his hand. The bird rose, glove now dangling from its leather thong, circled once, and then headed east toward Drammun.

"A gold coin to the man who kills it!" John Hand bellowed, fearing it bore some message. Several muskets and pistols barked. The bird's wings flapped in an ungainly effort to stay airborne. More shots rang out, and it plummeted into the sea. Arguments began immediately as to who was responsible, and who should claim the coin.

Mux snarled, hating to see his falcon's demise, hating all that was happening around him. He then made his way as slowly as he thought reasonably prudent to the bloody decks of the *Trophy Chase*. The decks of the *Thanu*, already emptied of Drammune warriors, were quickly cleared of Vast sailors as well. The two ships began to drift apart.

Mux handed his sword to a grim but respectful John Hand. His honor-bound duty accomplished, the Supreme Commander of the Armada and the leader of the Glorious Drammune Military then spat on the deck at John Hand's feet. "Nochtai Vastcha!" he seethed, and raised both fists in defiance.

John Hand quickly brought the hilt of Mux's sword up hard into Mux's jaw, stunning but not toppling him. "Noch*ta* Vastcha!" the admiral seethed as the cut he'd opened on Mux's chin dripped red into his dark beard.

The crew of the *Chase* looked at their admiral, amazed at his apparently perfect use of the Drammune tongue. But what was it he said?

John Hand turned to his crew and held high the Drammune sword. Then he looked at the Armada, still fanned out across the sea, but closing in. "NochTA Vastcha, you sons of the devil! Death FROM the Vast!"

The crew whooped. "NochTA Vastcha!" John Hand called out again, and then repeated it in a slow, staccato cadence that encouraged a chant. The crew picked it up almost instantly, adding their own flourish to the second word. "Knock-TAH Vast-CHAH! Knock-TAH Vast-CHAH!"

Freed from her tethering lines, the *Trophy Chase* bounded forward, almost instantly putting distance between herself and the *Thanu*. The surviving members of the crew, every man with breath enough aboard the *Trophy Chase*, whether loading cannon or unfurling sail, continued to call out the chant, the catcall, the taunt, *Noch TAH Vast CHAH!*

Death from the Vast!

Abbaka Mux trembled with rage as his blood ran down his neck. He wiped it away angrily and watched his own ship, the pride of Drammun, the very *Fist of the Law* fall back away, battered and desolate. Beaten.

And still these Pawns chanted.

From far below, the Firefish watched Deep Fin.

The creature had fled the surface after seeing that face, the eyes and eyes, the bright spirit with the single blade tooth. Then the flashes of lightning and roaring thunder intensified. The beast waited there beneath the waves, energized and alive with longing, anxious and patient. It saw and felt the thunderous first pass of the *Chase*, watched the great creature turn, stand, and begin a second attack. It saw Deep Fin close in on its prey, pulling it close even as the storm grew, and the thunder crashed. It knew that the great predator was killing its prey, destroying it, devouring it from its shell.

And then the beast smelled blood, blood that flowed from the feasting above. It wanted to attack the slow one, to join in the feast. But it did not. This was Deep Fin's prey. So it waited, trembling with anticipation. But now the great creature moved away! And morsels, lovely morsels floated down from the slow one. Splashing, flapping morsels floated on the surface around it. And so the Firefish could wait no longer. It had no reason to wait. Deep Fin had left meat behind! Deep Fin knew the Firefish, knew what it needed, what it wanted.

So the beast dove deep, deep, deep into the cold, black darkness. It turned for the surface and flew, flew fast and famished, mouth agape, up and up, directly toward the slow one. The speed of this beast, inspired as it was, far exceeded any speed it had ever attained before. When it hit the underbelly of its victim, its huge teeth formed a pocket that covered more than a third of its width.

The impact did not slow the monster. It did not raise the *Thanu* an inch from the waterline. The Firefish broke through cleanly, a cannonball through a thatched roof, leaving a Firefish-shaped hole. It hurtled upward through the decking.

It had aimed as best it could for the storm creature's heart, which in the beast's predacious brain meant a target roughly one-quarter of its length from its head. The beast lost some speed as it went through one, then two floors below decks, as it encountered and engulfed stores of rations, meat, and barrels of Drammune grog. Satisfying victuals. And then it hit the foredeck. It emerged between the foremast and the mainmast.

The chanting aboard the *Trophy Chase* died instantly as the loud crack of the *Thanu*'s deck produced a rising Firefish, aglow with the kill. The cannon from the *Kaza Fahn* went silent. All ships, all sailors, Drammune and Vast, watched as shattered boards and planking and splinters flew, as the great beast rose up through crimson sails, ripping them like bits of gauze, and went through the rigging, severing it like gossamer threads. It clamped its jaws on the frail bones of the slow one, swallowing as it did its bellyful of provisions.

Lightning leaped from the beast's mouth, jumping to the highest rigging, St. Elmo's fire in bright yellow, an image branded forever in the mind's eye of the sailors who saw it.

And up it went yet, slowing noticeably now, until its head was even with the crow's nest. The taper of its tail still had not cleared the deck when it paused, almost thoughtfully, hanging in the air. All the glistening, shimmering, golden-glowing body of the beast was visible, lit, ablaze even in the now-bright sunlight.

Then, at the apex of its climb, the beast turned its head and looked across the water to Deep Fin, watching the great creature as it sped away. And it opened its jaws again—as if, Packer thought, to speak. But it was silent.

Sailors aboard the *Chase* would swear they saw the beast grin, like a jack-o'-lantern afire. Packer would disagree. To him, it was the look of a howling wolf, sad and unfulfilled, unable to be fulfilled. And it began its descent.

It fell, inclined toward the *Chase,* never taking its eyes off Deep Fin. As it crashed downward, it split the *Rahk Thanu* from centerline to starboard rail, crashing through its decking as if the ship had been made of matchsticks and toothpicks. Then the *Thanu* broke in two.

A solid wall of water rose on either side of the beast as it crashed into the sea, obscuring everything. A hole in the sea opened, pulling the two halves of the Drammune ship down into it. And then just as suddenly, the hole filled, with a loud boom, a deep and melodious drumbeat, creating a fountain of water, then a mountain of water that rose twenty-five feet into the air.

The mountain filled the open wounds of the *Thanu,* and within seconds both the prow and the stern ends were under the waves. Masts splintered, yardarms cracked, canvas ripped.

And then the *Rahk Thanu* was gone.

The sea rose and fell, and then went calm.

The sailors aboard the *Trophy Chase* stood stock still, trying to comprehend what they had just witnessed. Where the *Rahk Thanu* had stood just moments ago, where they had stood on its decks…in that spot could now be seen only churning black seawater, flotsam popping up. Flotsam and Drammune sailors, who now swam for their lives.

Then the Firefish returned to the surface, sleek and subtle, and snapped them up.

CHAPTER 13

Bloodstained

The *Trophy Chase* sailed east, easily outdistancing an Armada that suddenly had no flagship, no supreme commander, and no desire to pursue. As the western horizon swallowed up their enemies, the crew hailed Packer Throme without reserve, and without bounds. Every last one of them, including the pirates late of the *Seventh Seal*, held him in the highest possible esteem, feeling to the bottom of their hearts that he was the finest example of a sailor to ever set to sea, of a warrior to ever wage war, of a man to ever manage the taming of a beast. They pounded him on the back, they shook his marred hand, they picked him up and paraded him around the decks.

He had shown them, once and for all, that he did indeed have the favor of God. And now they believed they had it, too. He was a hero, a saint, and a warrior. As were they all.

And so it did not take Packer long to become—perhaps inevitably—completely and utterly miserable. Somewhere between the two-hundredth and three-hundredth chorus of "Death from the Vast," while he was grinning modestly at the thankful, almost worshipful sailors who simply had to come by to pat him on the back one more time and say the most wonderful things they could dredge up from their hearts and souls about his swordsmanship and his bravery and his humanity, offering the highest praises their limited verbal skills could muster—things like "Heavin' good with a sword, you are," and "How about starin' that devil-blasted Fish right in the eye, eh?"—somewhere in the midst of this earthy celebration, while he was dutifully if not very effectively mopping up blood and stray pieces of dismembered flesh, it hit him.

Fully half, and maybe more than half, of the dead Drammune sailors who were now being merrily stripped of their armor and chucked into piles were dead because of his sword. The blood under his feet, on his mop, and in his bucket suddenly turned bright red. He could smell it; it reeked like the back alley behind the butcher shop in Mann. His hands were sticky with it. He looked down at himself. His white uniform was crimson in great patches where the blood had gushed, speckled red where it had spattered, pink in places where it had mingled with sweat, and white only in small, isolated patches that had remained, somehow, unspotted. He had a sudden vision of his clothes not as clothes at all, but as his very soul, soiled and spoiled in almost every way, innocence gone forever, a purity lost that never, ever would return. The soul of a butcher, long gone from Eden.

He reached up to his face, felt the stickiness, and then felt the clumping and cracking of dried blood in his hair. He recalled the way Scatter Wilkins had looked after the great Achawuk battle, and knew he looked the same.

Men killing other men with every ounce of strength they have.

Packer Throme killing men with every ounce of strength he had. And worse, praying to God for the strength to do it.

What had happened? God had granted his request. Yes, God had answered his prayer. But still, Packer had descended from the rigging into the fray. He had unsheathed his sword. He had joined in. He had not just joined in; he had exceeded all others. He was Levi with a sword, Samson with a jawbone. And when it was done he not only joined in the guttural, visceral celebrations around him, he accepted his companions' praise as though he deserved it, as though he had accomplished some great feat by his own strength, his own might, his own great power.

He began to shake. A dark cloud engulfed his spirit. What had he just done? Yes, God had answered his prayer. Yes, absolutely—Packer had prayed for the strength to fight, and God had granted it in enormous measure. But did that mean it was good? Because it came from God, did that mean God was pleased? And in the end, didn't He give Samson power to kill himself? The Almighty visited a spirit of oppression on Saul. And didn't He send Israel a king because they asked, even though He was angry with them for it?

And then Packer knew: He had asked for the wrong thing. God had sent the Firefish to achieve the destruction of the *Rahk Thanu*. Packer could have asked for anything. Anything at all. He could have asked God to fight this battle. He could have asked for a Jericho. But he had not. He had wanted to fight it himself. He had wanted this, wanted exactly what had in fact come to pass. He had wanted his sword and his own swordsmanship to win the day, to justify forever the path he had chosen when his opportunity for the priesthood was taken away. And God had granted it! But Packer was quite sure He didn't like it.

This answered prayer was a curse.

And then, as if to confirm his worst fears, the next three sailors to approach him found no higher praise than to compare him to the archenemy of his soul.

"I never thought I'd see anyone as bloody as Talon, but you are. Maybe bloodier!" With a big, affirming nod.

"Not even the Witch could kill that many that fast!" A hard, respectful slap on the back.

"You move like her, catlike, you know? Like I was watching Talon all over again." Big grin, more gum than teeth. Smith Delaney.

Packer grabbed his arm. "I don't want to be like her, Delaney! Don't tell me I'm like her. I don't want to be good at killing."

Delaney looked confused. "Little late for that, I'm thinkin'."

Packer's eyes were wild. "What have I done, Delaney?"

The sailor scratched his head. "What've you done? Well, you saved us all, for one. And second, if not for you we'd all be dead. You'd rather that?"

"No." Packer let go of Delaney's arm.

"'Cause we would be," Delaney said earnestly, rubbing his arm. "We all know that. Look at 'em." Packer looked at the gleeful crew, many still chanting "Death from the Vast" in a foreign tongue, apparently oblivious to the death and destruction of friend and foe alike who lay at their feet. "Every livin', festerin' soul aboard knows those Drammune bulldogs would be stripping our reekin' flesh right now, rolling us to the beasties, 'stead of the other way round, except for what you done to save us. What *you* done."

Packer now watched the process with glassy eyes, Drammune bodies, arms limp, heads hung and tongues lolling, manhandled into piles against shattered rails. "Yes. I did it."

Delaney continued. "It's them and not us 'cause you got a gift from God."

"A gift?" Packer looked him with astonishment. "Didn't you see the Firefish? That was the gift! God could have defeated that ship without anyone drawing a sword. Why didn't He?"

Delaney shrugged. "He didn't want to?"

"Because no one asked Him to! Instead, I asked to fight! That thing could have destroyed the ship before a shot was even fired."

The old sailor squinted. "Didn't think a' that."

Packer's heart fell further. The memory of all he'd done now came back to him, not like a memory but like a waking nightmare, jumbled and chaotic, images of his blade slicing in and out, blood spattering. Eyes wide and fearful. Cries of pain.

How would he ever escape this?

And then the stench of blood and death and burned black powder rose up into his nostrils and went deep into his head, and began to choke him. He looked again at his hands, his arms, and understood that the blood that covered him was the life of men. He had scattered his enemies across the decks. Like a pirate.

He wanted to vomit.

And then he realized that he would, in fact, vomit, that he had little choice in the matter. "I'm going to be sick."

"Well, don't let the boys see ye." Delaney grabbed Packer's mop bucket and threw the reddened water back onto the decking. He then handed the pail to Packer, putting a firm hand on his friend's shoulder. "Come on, let's get you down the hold and find a nice quiet spot." He maneuvered him toward the main hatch, the celebrated warrior clutching a pail in both hands and breathing heavily, trying to keep his stomach down. His hands and feet tingled; he felt the breeze through every hair on his sweaty, bloody scalp.

He fairly ran the last few steps, flew down the companionway, banging his bucket against it as he went, and barely got to the bottom before he was emptying out his guts. And then, when his stomach had nothing left, he began emptying out his soul.

When he finally finished, he looked around him. He was in the dark, alone. The hatch above him was closed. Delaney was gone. No

The Hand That Bears the Sword

chanting could be heard. He thanked God for that. He sat a long time, head pounding, until he felt fairly sure he could make it to his bunk without being sick again.

Packer left the bucket where it was, apologizing silently to whatever poor sailor found it. His hands were shaking like a dog's hind leg as he followed a companionway astern. He felt weak, thin, transparent. It was an effort to take air into his lungs. His legs were numb. He shivered like it was midwinter. He did not want to go above, and so he felt his way through dark and unfamiliar companionways.

He turned a corner into a cargo hold, saw a lantern lit, resting on the floor. He tried to ignore it, tried to fight off the meaning, the memory. But it stopped him anyway. The crates here. The bench there. This was the place where Talon had interrogated him...so long ago.

And suddenly he knew he wasn't alone. A chill raced up his spine as he wheeled to his right, drawing his sword as he did. Fen Abbaka Mux sat in chains, his beard caked with blood, his hair wild, his eyes closed as if asleep. Packer's ears rang with a pounding din. Mux was not asleep. His lips were moving.

Packer looked at the sword in his hand and felt ashamed. He sheathed it. He did not want to appear to this man like Talon had appeared to him. He turned to leave, was leaving as Mux spoke.

"Packer Throme." The voice was a rasp, but the rolling R's reminded him of Talon. Another chill ran down his spine.

Packer turned slowly, met the commander's eye. It was dark, and far away, brooding. "How do you know my name?" he asked.

Even if Fen Abbaka Mux had understood the boy's question, he would have had no interest in answering. He had his own message to deliver. His voice was deep and ragged, and utterly assured. "Rahk thanu anachtai aziz. Eyneg anachtai aziz."

Packer did not understand all the words, but the meaning was clear enough. He spoke of the Law of the Drammune, and of death. The supreme commander did not believe he was yet beaten, did not believe the Vast would prevail.

Packer dropped his eyes, saw a bucket of water on the floor at Mux's feet. He remembered how terribly thirsty he had been when he had occupied that bench. He picked the pail up, smelled it, took a sip. Then he walked it to Mux. "It's water," he said softly. His hands shook as he raised the bucket. He felt no fear, but he felt weak to his very soul.

Mux looked at Packer suspiciously, surprised by the calm in the one blue eye he saw illuminated by the lantern. But he watched the boy with disdain, as though Packer were a small spider that needed crushing. Packer held the bucket close to the commander's face. Mux did not look into it, or smell it. He did not acknowledge it at all until he spit in it.

Packer nodded, with a trace of smile. He wondered what it felt like to have so much pride, so much strength. How simple life would be if one never dwelt on one's own weaknesses, if pride and hardness of heart were not sins, but values to be cherished and built up. He envied this man. He set the bucket down and walked away.

"Rahk thanu anachtai aziz," Mux repeated, calling after him. "Eyneg anachtai aziz."

The fist of the Law will kill you. I will kill you.

Packer made his way back to his bunk, head aching, body wrung, back to the tiny cabin Scat Wilkins had given him after he had managed not to kill Delaney those many months ago. He grabbed a blanket and climbed into his hammock. He lay there shivering. He wanted oblivion; he wanted sleep so endless he would never wake up.

When his heart finally slowed, when some warmth returned to his body, when the pounding in his head eased, his mind finally began to flow smoothly again.

And then the whole battle unfolded before his eyes, not in bits and pieces this time, but in its totality, beginning to end. He was standing at the rail, and he tried to ram his sword into the lumbering warrior. He saw his own sword bend, recoil. Then he watched every fluid motion of every cut, every thrust, every puncture, every death, every injury with equal attention to every detail. He watched it like a man watching some disaster unfold, some horror about which he could do nothing…watching his barn burn with his livestock inside, watching a landslide take his home and his family with it, watching a ship blown onto the rocks with all his loved ones and all his possessions aboard. He could not stop it, but neither could he turn away from it.

The Hand That Bears the Sword

His swordsmanship was almost perfect, and where it wasn't, it was more than sufficient.

When it was over, when the battle finally stopped and his sword was poised an inch from the Drammune commander's throat, Packer finally turned away from the vision. His back and shoulders were as tense as steel. His brain was an anvil pounded by the hammer of his heart. He had counted as he went. The count was seventy-nine, either brought down directly by his sword or by a crewman after Packer had slashed open a wound.

Seventy-nine men who had lived and breathed as the sun came up on the world this morning were dead now, and would be dead forever, because of his sword.

Will Seline had little trouble learning which upper corner was known as the Tower. The palace was, roughly, a huge rectangle. With its grounds it took up about a quarter of the space within the old Rampart of the city. The oldest part of the building, which dated back about four hundred years, was a square. The new kitchen and the new ballroom, along with servant's quarters and a half-dozen formal sitting rooms, had been added only about a hundred-and-fifty years ago.

Above this new addition, as though resting on top of it, was an even newer suite of rooms, only eighty years old, designed for the royal family to use in the summer as an alternative to fleeing the city entirely. The theory had been that the coolness of the mountains could be accessed without the long and difficult trip, if only the suite were built on the highest part of the house. But the engineers who designed it hadn't bothered to check on whether an additional forty feet of altitude would actually create any measurable climatic difference. And of course, it did not. So in the summer the rooms broiled under the sun and were all but unusable, and in the winter they were drafty and hard to heat, and hardly worth the climb. Only in the spring and the fall were they actually livable, but since all the rest of the house was equally livable during those delightful seasons, the suite was barely used at all.

When it was, it was most often as a place to send the royal children when they had misbehaved badly enough to warrant confining.

It was they—Prince Mather, his younger brother, Ward, and their elder sister, Jacqalyn—who had named it "the Tower." Jacq had actually come up with the term.

But now it was spring, and the place was quite pleasant. Draftiness felt like openness, remoteness felt like safety. The view of the city, particularly from the large porch built on the northeast corner, was superb. On clear days Panna could see all the way to the Vast Sea.

But it was still a prison, and it worked well in that capacity. Any thought of escaping from the Tower except through the one, main door left Panna's head quickly, and with a surge of vertigo. A wide rim of roof blocked her view to the ground, but the few city streets she could make out below the porch balcony were at least a hundred feet down. With a long enough rope, escape was perhaps possible. But she would need to be far more desperate than she was now. And of course, she would need a rope.

The streets were almost invisible from the Tower, but not quite. Will Seline managed to find a street corner, some three hundred feet from the palace as the crow flies, from which he could see two open windows with white curtains fluttering in the breeze. The Tower. And there Will stood, hour after hour, on the doorstep of a pawnshop, hoping Panna would come to the window.

"What you lookin' at?" the shop's proprietor said, finally baffled enough to come out and ask. She was a frumpy woman, who sagged in almost every way it was possible to sag. She smoked a small cigar, and looked cross enough that Will Seline was quite sure few had ever asked her how she'd picked up the habit.

"My daughter is being held in the palace. I'm trying to get a look at her."

The woman stood next to Will and squinted in the direction he pointed. "I don't see nothin'."

"Those two windows, right at the top. Just between the trees."

"What, she run away from home?"

"No," Will said in a tone that suggested the thought was an absurdity. Then he thought better of it. "At least, not this time."

"Girlfriend of Prince Ward, is she? He has lots of girlfriends."

"Perhaps, but she is not one of them."

She shrugged. "Just what I hear. I know what you need," she

said matter-of-factly, and disappeared. She returned, after some loud rummaging, with a telescope. It was badly tarnished, badly dented, and the lens was cracked. But it worked.

"That's great!" He tested it. "Thank you very much." He could see the windows quite clearly now, enough to recognize that the curtains were cream-colored lace. He would be able to see Panna perfectly if she ever came to the window.

"Ten cents!" the frumpy woman accused.

"Oh. Of course." He handed it back. "I'm sorry. I don't have that to spare."

"Make me an offer!" she demanded in the same accusing tone.

"One penny."

"Sold!" She put out a hand, palm up.

Will fished in his pockets and completed the transaction.

"And don't think about selling it back, cause I ain't buyin'. Been tryin' to move that piece a' junk for years."

Will wished her well, glad for the telescope but equally glad to be shed of the woman.

But he did not see Panna that day. That evening, he went to the gatehouse as he always did, but Chunk was not there. He gave the man who was there yet another letter, but this one addressed directly to the prince.

The next day, after only an hour of his vigil on the pawnshop stoop, the proprietor came out to see him again. She was wearing the same dress and smoking, or so it seemed to Will, the same cigar.

"You can't stand there anymore," she announced.

"Excuse me?"

"You're runnin' off business."

"How am I doing that?"

"By being a priest. People come here because they're in trouble. You make 'em feel guilty." She narrowed her eyes. "You gotta go."

Will pondered that. "Perhaps they feel guilty because they've spent their rent money on things they should not have been buying, and have come here to sell things they really should be keeping."

She squinted. "What's your point?

"Perhaps I'm advancing the Lord's business."

Her eyes grew harder. "I'm helpin' people here. All you're doin'

is sending 'em down the street to old man Hooper's, and he's takin' away my money."

Will pondered her. Perhaps she could be persuaded to look at it philosophically. "The Lord giveth, and the Lord taketh away."

"Yeah? Well, I buyeth, and I selleth. You gotta leave."

Will sighed. "I have a right to stand in the street."

"So stand in the street."

Will took one large step off the porch. She scowled and went back into her establishment. She closed the door, locked it, and put a *Closed* sign in the window. Then she put on her shawl, and left through the back.

A few hours later, a member of the Royal Dragoons rode up on a very large roan horse. He was a calm, mustachioed man with graying hair.

"Afternoon, Father."

"Hello." Will glanced toward the window of the pawnshop, saw the smoking woman peering out at him from behind a ragged curtain.

"You want to tell me what you're doing here?"

"I'm trying to see my daughter. The prince has her stowed away in one of those upper rooms."

The dragoon nodded. "You're going to need to come with me."

Will was surprised. "Am I breaking some law? Or did you come here because this woman complained I was hurting her business?"

He shook his head. "Report I got was of a Drammune spy, dressed up like a priest."

Will was impressed. He looked over at the woman, who closed the curtain quickly. "Very creative."

"These are dangerous times."

"I understand that. But my daughter is Panna Throme, wife of Packer Throme."

He nodded again. "If that's the case, I'm sure it will all work out. But you'll have to come with me."

"Gladly," he said with the utmost sincerity. "Gladly."

Delaney knocked and got no answer, so he pushed on the door, peered into the shadows as it creaked open. "Packer?" He could see his friend now, lying in the hammock. A scarred, bloodstained right hand hung over the edge. A fly walked around on his palm, in no particular hurry.

Marcus Pile peered in from behind Delaney. "Is he there?"

Delaney didn't answer. "Packer?"

The fly buzzed, circled, and landed again on Packer's hand. Then the smell hit Delaney. Dried blood and sweat and vomit. "Whew! Marcus, go get a bucket of water with plenty of lye. Someone here needs a bath."

"Aye, aye."

Delaney entered, and as his eyes adjusted to the dim light, he could see Packer looking at him. The young man didn't move. His eyes seemed distant, unconcerned.

"Oh, so you're awake."

No answer.

"Admiral wants you. I told Mr. Haas you're sick. He told admiral that."

Packer's expression didn't change. His eyes looked at Delaney with a calm sadness, a listless unconcern that worried the old sailor. "You're still frettin' about what you done, eh?"

Packer closed his eyes.

Delaney sighed. "What you done was for your country. It was for us all. You didn't start the fight."

Packer looked at him, knowing better. "I started the whole war."

Delaney grew grim. "That bein' the case, then you're right to finish it."

Packer's eyes sagged closed.

Delaney sighed. He knew he needed to take a different tack. He rubbed his head, then his chin. He sat on Packer's locker. When he spoke again, his voice was gentle. "I'm not much a' one for preachin'. So I won't. But I'll tell you something that happened to me. Maybe it'll help, maybe not." He sniffed. His voice dropped.

"One time I was up in the rigging. Morning it was, no clouds anywhere but on the eastern horizon. Chill was already burnin' off with a warm breeze, and the sun was hoverin' just over the sea where the water and the sky are all kind of runnin' together, you know, so you can't tell which is which. And I remember thinkin' that the sun looked like a great bird, with wings of clouds stretchin' all out along the horizon, north to south. And then I remember thinkin' that was what an angel of God would look like. Not the kind that sings and plays a harp, now, but the kind that comes and pours God's own wrath right down on the world, like out of one of them judgment bowls in the Book of Revelations. Like what was on the front of the *Seventh Seal*." He pondered a moment. "Only that one was kinda sickly compared.

"Anyways, while I was thinkin' it, I was thinkin' I was proud to know the God who could do that. Who could create a sunrise that looked like an angel. Who could create an angel that could pour down wrath to fix a earth that had got all skewed around, away from what it was suppose to be."

Delaney got very thoughtful. "'Cause this old world sure ain't what she's suppose to be. And I got this feelin'." Delaney paused, and his voice softened further. "More than a feelin'. It was a knowin'. Aye. I got this knowin' that God was there, and He was sayin', 'Just for you. Just for you this morning, Delaney. I did this just for you.'"

Delaney dabbed an eye. "Well, those weren't in actual words, and now I say it out loud, maybe it sounds a lot smaller than it was. But it wasn't, not then. It was big, as big as the sea itself. And I just wanted to stay right there in that spot, hangin' out over that ocean just forever, lookin' at what God made just for me."

Delaney sighed, and smiled at the memory. "Couldn't do it, a' course." He sniffed, rubbed his nose vigorously. "Had to reef the mizzen four points. And then Jonas Deal starts to screamin' up at me like I'm doin' nothing but wastin' his own precious time. I tell you, I sure ain't sorry that rat badger got killed off." Delaney pondered another moment, then returned to the subject at hand. "Anyway, you ever had a time like that?"

Packer smiled. He was quite sure there was no man on earth he loved so much as Smith Delaney. "Yeah. Yeah, I've had a time or two like that." He thought of the cliff, of the sunrise he'd returned to today. And then he thought of Panna, of his own little cottage, and the Eden he'd been given there. Yes, he'd had that moment.

Delaney was happy to hear Packer's voice, and to sense a softness in it. He sounded like the regular Packer. "Well, my point is that there are other times, after that, when I've done something bad, you know? Things I had to confess. I'm talking about bad things. No need to get into the details now—unless you want to hear 'em?"

"No need."

"Right. The point is, bad as I felt, I still remembered that time in the rigging. And I remembered God talkin' to me, to little Smith Delaney, because He knew me. He knew all I ever did, and you know what else? He knew all I'd ever do. And though I felt low about the sin, it was good to know He didn't hold back from makin' that sunrise for me, knowin' later I'd skew it all up again. It's like, He just wants me. Near Him. Listenin'."

Delaney waited, but Packer didn't speak again. He was still thinking of Panna and the Garden.

"So," Delaney continued, "you have to know that everything He gave you then, He gave you knowin' all about today. All about the Drammune and the killin' and the Firefish crackin' open the hull of that ship. He knew what you were gonna pray for before you prayed it. And even if it was wrong, He still loves you now anyways. Just as much as He ever loved you before."

Packer was deep in thought.

Delaney felt like he had failed. "I don't guess I did a good job of explainin'," he said glumly. "But anyways…"

"You did a very good job of explaining," Packer said gently. "Thank you."

Delaney cheered up immediately, a bright glint in his eye.

Marcus returned with a bucket of cold, soapy water. It took that bucket and three more to get all the blood off Packer, and to wash out his blood-soaked clothes. But Packer refused to put his uniform on again, preferring his loose-fitting peasant shirt and breeches. Delaney reminded him of the admiral's orders, but Packer was adamant.

Then Marcus suggested a prayer. Packer hung his head, not sure he was ready for another one of those. Delaney and Marcus both misread the gesture and simply followed suit.

Marcus spoke. "Dear Father of us all in heaven, help out our brother Packer here. He has slewn our enemies, and has saved us from their mighty swords by his even mightier sword. We know he is saddened that he killed so many of those fearsome Drammune, even though no one else aboard is anything but fairly thrilled about it. But he's thinkin' Thou had rather a' done it with the Firefish. Anyways, we're all thankful no matter how Thou didst do it because Thou saved us to live on here for Thy reasons, and for Thy reasons Thou killed off a whole bunch of the others. For reasons which we can't dream of knowin' why. Like usual.

"But as Thy Son said, he that heareth My word and believeth on Him that sent Me is passed from death right on into life. And by that we know that we start out this life dead even though we may not look it, and then we come to life when we meet up with Thee, even though we may not look no different. So I figure, Thou couldn't care less about whose heart is still beatin' in his chest, but Thou carest a whole lot more about whose soul comes to life, whether or not he be actually alive or dead. I mean on earth." Marcus paused for a moment. "Thou knowest what I mean.

"So take us from this world or keep us here, but make us all three of us to know Thee, and the others aboard as well. So we ask for Thy peace and wisdom whether You set our hands to the sword, or to... some other thing that ain't the sword."

"Ploughshare," Delaney whispered.

"Good, right—the ploughshare. Or the windlass or the chainplates or the ship's wheel, as the case may be. Thanks be to God. Oh, and thanks for sending a Firefish that is more friend than enemy, may that sort of thing last a long time and help us out. Amen."

"Amen!" Delaney grinned at Marcus. "You know, I'll tell you what. You can pray at my funeral any day."

Marcus was moved by the offer. "Why thanks, Delaney. That'd make me real happy."

CHAPTER 14

Power

The news of the death of the Hezzan, and the sudden shift in power that followed it, swept through the Kingdom of Drammun like a hurricane. The assassination, the jailing of the Twelve, and the dark rumor of the rise of the Hezzan's wife under the protection of the Hezzan Guard, unleashed chaos.

The traditional mourning period for the passing of an emperor was three months, during which solemn ceremony followed solemn ceremony, and black-garbed officials snaked their way through the cities and the countryside with the funeral bier, followed by agonizing masses of mourners who loudly proclaimed their grief and undying loyalty. Then, the next three months saw formal and informal celebrations led by red-garbed officials who paraded the new Hezzan throughout the cities and the countryside, followed by teeming throngs who loudly proclaimed their joy and their undying loyalty.

But without the Twelve to duly appoint and swear in the new Hezzan, without officials to plan the processions and wear the garb and direct the mourning and the celebration, without a new Hezzan or even, seemingly, the possibility of a new Hezzan, the streets erupted in violence. The riots were led, of course, by the Zealots, who were confident that the end of all morality and the fall of the kingdom had come upon them all, and therefore the palace should be stormed, the Unworthy ones who were holed up within it dragged into the streets to be dismembered and hanged, and the government taken for themselves, they having proven beyond any doubt their own fitness for rule in the process.

The Zealots were unsuccessful, however. They were stopped at the palace gates by Vasla Vor and his grim Hezzan Guard, who killed twoscore of them in a matter of minutes before the leaders of the uprising, the Quarto, called a retreat. They then determined that restoring the moral rectitude of the kingdom might require just a bit more planning.

But no arms or gates could stop the rumors that flew like flashes of lightning in a summer storm. The Hezzan wasn't really dead, he had gone into hiding. The Hezzan was being held in prison, in secret. The Hezzan had been kidnapped by the Vast. The Hezzan had gone mad and killed himself. The Twelve were all actually Zealots and had killed the Hezzan for marrying a warrior. The Twelve weren't really in prison but had gone into hiding. The Warrior Wife, Talon, had gone mad and killed the Hezzan and the Twelve. Talon wasn't Drammune at all, but a Vast spy, and Drammun was now being governed by King Reynard. And—inevitably—Talon was a witch with unspeakable powers, bent on taking the throne for herself.

Talon stood at the window of the Hezzan's bedroom and looked out over what was now, in effect, her city. Fires burned in a dozen places; dark smoke rose into the summer sky. People chanted at the palace gates, calling for her death. But she looked past this. Beyond the city was her country, peaceful in the evening twilight, and beyond that, the sea. This present turmoil seemed to her rather predictable, given the ignorance of the people and the biases of men. As long as the guard could hold the gates, calm would eventually be restored. The Zealots would keep the fires stoked as long as they could, of course; and as yet she had no plan for them. But she would find one. One would come to her.

Before she could make any plan, small or great, she had a crucial decision to make, one on which all other plans would hang. She could either make Vasla Vor into the next Hezzan and rule by proxy, or she could make herself the first female Hezzan. She didn't really care which path she took, so long as it was the direction that gave her the best chance of finishing her husband's work: defeating the Vast and making Drammun the most powerful nation in history.

Either path had its difficulties.

Ruling through Vasla Vor would be the simplest move now, but would become more and more difficult as time passed. Once she convinced him to become the Hezzan, which would require much flattery and unending appeals to duty, he would be a willing puppet, uncomfortable with his own authority, in need of approval, unwilling to compare himself to his glorious predecessors. But over time, she knew, this would change. The natural vanity of men would change him. He would eventually come to believe he was chosen by fate, and utterly capable in his own right. And then Talon's influence would fade. He would one day find her not only unnecessary, but an embarrassment. He would see his former dependence on her as a black mark in the history of his otherwise glorious rule, a blotch on his record that he would just as soon forget. Or erase.

To take over the government and to sit on the throne herself was by far the more difficult route, in the short run. The nation was not prepared to be led by a woman, and the Zealots would never stand for it. They would need to be co-opted or crushed at the outset. The military would likely need to be fully engaged, and that presented a problem when a good portion of it was somewhere in the middle of an ocean. And when it returned, Fen Abbaka Mux would need either to be won, or beaten. But if the Quarto could be dealt with now somehow, and peace and confidence restored before the armies and the navy returned, she would be very hard to unseat, even by Mux.

Talon might have opted for the easy course, trusting that she could accomplish her ends before her own influence eroded, if it were not for another significant piece of the Hezzan's legacy, another player with a role to consider. What if her child was a boy? Vasla Vor had sons of his own. As Talon's influence waned and her boy grew, he would come to be seen as a threat to the crown.

And what if the child was a girl? She might well grow to be a woman with great skills, better able to lead than any man. Yet she would be opposed then just as Talon was opposed now. And this same struggle would need to be played out then, under circumstances Talon could not foresee. Today, Talon knew precisely who the players were, and where they were. The Twelve were in prison. The Glorious Drammune Military was halfway across the world. And the General Commander of the Hezzan Guard was in the palm of her hand. Only the Quarto remained to be overcome.

No, the difficult path was the right path.

Her decision made, Talon spent no more time deliberating. She took Vasla Vor under her wing, giving him the constant attention he needed in order to keep him focused, in order to weave the broken threads of his devotion to the Hezzan into the fabric of a new devotion to her. The rest of her time she spent interrogating the Twelve.

She sent for each of them, one at a time, several times, to learn who they were and where their darkened hearts and minds might lead them. If she could salvage but one or two, she could institute a new government, could devise a transition of power, with at least a semblance of continuity. She needed an ally from among them.

She found one in the least likely place. Sool Kron was slippery as an eel, as crafty as a pack of foxes. He was dangerous, and she had outwitted him once in front of his peers, which made him doubly dangerous. But he was no Zealot. He was a practical man of great pride, who was quite old and did not want to end his career or his life powerless and in prison. He understood what the others did not, that these interviews with the Warrior Wife in the Hezzan's chambers were not in fact interrogations, or even tests of the will. They were negotiations.

"It would take but one member of the Twelve," he told her, "not just any member, perhaps—but one member of the Twelve to turn the tide in your favor."

"Why would one of the Twelve turn against his brethren?"

He shook his head, stroked his matted beard. His body ached; he dearly wanted a bath and a bed. But his mind was crisply focused. " 'Brethren.' Ah, that is a strong word for an assembly handpicked by a single man and thrown together come what may. You may learn that at least one of us finds the future of the nation more important than a charade of solidarity."

"The others already believe you have betrayed them."

"Do they? Still?"

"And why wouldn't they? I have told each of them you are in fact already free, and advising me."

He smiled ruefully. "I have underestimated you."

"You are not the first. Nor are you the first to suffer for it."

"I will not make the same mistake again. Since we are speaking frankly, may I ask how you knew of the plot? And how you lured the Hezzan to your chambers?"

She did not answer. Sool Kron grew nervous, and then frightened at the dark look that grew in her eyes and then suddenly vanished, like the shadow of a wolf passing between a dozing man and his campfire.

Talon spoke carefully, not wanting to betray the emotion within her. "Now you overestimate me. I knew nothing. He came to me of his own accord. He died of his own accord..." she struggled with the next words, but finally said them, "...in my arms."

Kron nodded. "My apologies. I did not know." So she was truly a wife to him. And more interestingly, she wanted Kron to know it, to understand her devotion to him, even though that devotion betrayed her weakness. She was but a woman, after all. This was useful information. "Let us assume that you have found a member of the Twelve who will support you."

"That is a very large assumption to make for the sake of argument."

He smiled at her. "You leave me few choices. You have in fact found an ally in the Chief Minister of State."

She nodded. "I thank you. And the Hezzan thanks you."

"And may the two soon be the same."

Now, finally, she smiled. "Go on."

"All the pieces are in place for you to carry on the work of your husband. All the pieces but one."

"The Quarto."

He nodded. "How well do you know the Rahk-Taa?"

"I am Drammune."

"Then you know the Kar Ixthano," Kron said, with an air of certainty.

"It goes without saying." Her heartbeat increased. Did he believe he had already found a way to co-opt the Quarto? "If a man kills a Pawn in war, he takes that man's earthly dominion for his own."

"That is the base of it. But there is more." Sool Kron splayed his bony fingers on the wooden table before him. He had thought about this at length, Talon now knew, and was laying out before her his plan, every word rehearsed. Perhaps she had underestimated him as well.

"In the Kar Ixthano, the Rahk-Taa does not speak directly of war, nor even of those who are Drammune by birth and those who are not. It states simply that the Worthy displace the Unworthy, in order to rule. The Worthy are, of course, defined as those who most closely follow the teachings of the Rahk-Taa."

"Very handy."

He grinned. He appreciated the disrespect she was willing to show to the great book of Law; it meant she was someone who could discuss these things rationally. "Yes, indeed. Three principles are given. They function as examples in the text, but the Zealots take them literally. They call these the 'Three Laws of Kar Ixthano.' The First Law is the one you have stated. It is generally understood to be about war, but the Zealots do not limit it. It forms the philosophical basis of the riots now occurring in our streets. The Zealots are the Worthy, attempting to displace the Unworthy...you. They seek to kill you and take your dominion."

Her eyes narrowed.

He shrugged. It was their belief, not his. "The Second Law is that one who is not Worthy may martyr himself for one who is, and then the Unworthy becomes Worthy in death, and his family and his line are then elevated by this act. Let me quote. 'By freely giving his life and dominion to save and protect the Worthy, the Unworthy earns the status of a Worthy one.' Simplicity itself. And thus hordes of ignorant peasants are sent by their leaders to die. You will see this in action, if the Vast ever land on our soil, when wave upon wave of human shields die unarmed, simply to protect their Zealot masters."

"Again, very handy for the Zealots. But I see no help here. What is the Third Law?"

Sool Kron seemed disappointed. "Hmm. Well, the last is that any Unworthy who takes the life of a Worthy One is to be hanged, dismembered, and cursed. In practice, the Zealots have been known to execute it in the reverse order. But it is in fact the Second Law that may come to our aid. If you were to become a Zealot."

She watched his eyes, his expression. He seemed to be serious. "You are suggesting that I go the Quarto, put myself under their authority, and claim that the Hezzan was Unworthy? You would have me argue that he knew I was more Worthy, and therefore granted me his dominion through martyrdom?"

He nodded, pleased that she was keeping up. "The Quarto does not demand that he be wicked, mind you. Simply less Worthy than you. He did die in your place. That, I believe, we can prove. And he was no Zealot. If you are a Zealot, or can convincingly present yourself as one, they will see their opportunity."

She said nothing, but studied him and his proposition.

"He did die in your place?" Kron asked, needing confirmation. "He knew the danger?"

"He took arrows meant for me. He heard the assassins, and took my place at the window."

He saw the emotion in her again, and was pleased. "Perfect." His voice was compassionate. "They will hear your story, and your claim, and their greed for power will blind them to all else. You will need only to signal them prior to making the request that you have room for them in your new Court of Twelve. They will recognize themselves to be one small ruling away from achieving their great ambition. And not incidentally, all will know of the Hezzan's dedication to you." He smiled as warmly as he knew how.

Her expression did not change. "Why will they confer on me the title of Hezzan, when they might claim it for one of their own?"

Sool Kron smiled, held up his hands. "It is the way of the world. You already have his power. You already command his armies. Unseating you would be a long and bloody affair. You grant them a seat of power, and they make your power legitimate. A stroke of the pen, and their power is increased a hundredfold. And you, the Hezzan, are beholden to them for it."

"That sword has two edges."

"Most swords do."

Panna was awakened in the middle of the night by two very insistent dragoons, ones she had never seen before. They told her she was required to come with them, but would not say where. "Mather," she breathed out angrily, but secretly she was quite worried about what this might mean.

They waited while she dressed; she was not going to walk through the palace again in her robe. But they did not take her to the prince. Instead they escorted her down several long flights of stairs, through a great door they unlocked with a huge iron key, into a basement, then through a cold, wet tunnel carved through what seemed to be bedrock, which opened directly into the main passageway of a prison.

Now she was frightened. Was she being placed behind bars? Had he decided to punish her for striking him, after all?

The place reeked of human waste. The prison cells were illuminated only by greasy lanterns hanging over the wide corridor, which was lined with emaciated faces, men who pled through bars with their eyes, most of them too tired or weak or hopeless to speak. A few begged for help; one called her "Princess." Behind them in the matted, filthy straw, were bodies, whether living or dead she couldn't tell.

The dragoons took her to the last cell on the right. Here the floor was covered with fresh straw. Lying face down in it was a big man in a gray priest's robe.

Panna felt dizzy. "Daddy?"

He rolled over, and when he saw her he beamed with joy. "Panna!"

"Oh, Daddy! What have you done?"

He came to the bars laughing, straw clinging to his beard, his great girth shaking merrily. He reached through and held her, pulling her against his belly and the bars all at once. Fortunately for Panna, a good bit of his flesh was soft enough to protrude through and provide some padding. "Are you all right, little one?"

"I'm fine. But what about you? You've been arrested!"

"Yes. I have in fact been arrested. For trying to see you."

"But, why didn't you just ask? Didn't you get my letter? I'm sure the prince..." but she trailed off as he shook his head. "You never got it, did you?"

"I haven't been home in a while. But I have sent you a message every day, through the dragoons at the gate." He gestured at the two who had escorted Panna here, and now chatted with the two regular prison guards.

Panna glanced at the four men. "I never got any notes. Why did they arrest you?"

"I heard you were being held in the upper rooms, in the Tower, and so I was trying to get a look. The proprietor of a fine used-merchandise emporium reported me as a spy."

Now Panna laughed.

"What's so funny?"

"You, a spy. You would be horrible at it."

"Hey!" he protested, but he was smiling. Then he grew serious.

"I've been very worried about you. I was afraid something awful was happening."

"It's not good. But it's not the worst. I can handle the prince."

Will spoke softly, so as not to be overheard. "What has he done to you? Has he hurt you?"

"No. Well, he tried once to...He tried, but I hit him. He hasn't tried since." She smiled ruefully.

He shook his head, but there was admiration in his eyes. "Has he said why he won't let you leave? Does he give a reason?"

"At first he thought I'd tell everyone what I know about the war, and the Fleet."

He looked quizzical. "And what do you know?"

She gave him a look that said he had just asked about the dumbest question she could imagine.

"Sorry. Right. You can't tell me."

"I don't know anything, really, just guesses. But now he's more worried I'll tell people who he really is, and what he did to me. Frankly, I'm not sure why he cares. He has a horrible reputation in the palace anyway."

Will Seline sneezed.

"Daddy, are you all right? Are you getting sick?"

"No. Something in this straw isn't doing me well, that's all."

"This is a terrible place. I'll talk to the prince. I can appeal to his better instincts. But you have to promise me you'll go home and quit worrying. Pray, Daddy. That's what you do best." She smiled.

He beamed. "I'm just so glad you're all right."

"I love you, Daddy."

"I love you, too."

He sneezed again as Panna turned toward the dragoons. Now she was all business. "Take me to the prince."

The dragoons did indeed take Panna to the prince. Or at least, most of the way. They walked her up to the large double doors that led into his private chambers, and then stepped aside. They did not announce her, nor did they make any move that made her believe they would.

Feeling this was odd, Panna knocked. But the doors were huge, and her knuckles were small, and the rapping was barely audible. She looked at the dragoons. Still they offered no help. Panna took one of the large iron door handles in both hands, and pulled it open. She stepped inside.

The prince's private sitting room was large, paneled in dark oak and pine, and trimmed with walnut. The floors were dark, polished mahogany, shiny as glass. Directly in front of her, across the huge room, a large fire burned in an enormous fireplace. The reflection of its flames were long tongues of fire reaching out toward her. Candles glowed from elegant stands all along the walls, illuminating paintings and mirrors and a few old documents framed behind glass. An ornate piano near her and a large sofa facing the fire filled the room to her left, while a fully provisioned bar, made of polished mahogany, gleamed to her right. The room gave her the sense of being set just so, as though someone were expected. But it was the middle of the night.

"Come in," said the prince, in what would have been his oiliest, most congenial tone, were it not for the nasal stoppage. Even so, it made her shiver.

"Where are you?" she asked tentatively.

He stood, turned to her, already smiling. He had been sitting on the couch, which was angled away from her toward the fireplace. Its high back had concealed his head. He was holding a glass of wine, or port, and he was wearing a silk bathrobe. "Panna! To what do I owe this honor?" She was quite sure he knew exactly why she was here. He had sent the dragoons to take her to her father. When she did not answer, he said, "I apologize for not being dressed. But I'm sure you understand that I mean absolutely nothing by it."

Anger rose in her. But when she walked over to him, she was careful to keep the back of the sofa between them. "My father is in your prison."

"Really. What has he done?" He sipped his port.

"He's done nothing. He's only tried to speak to me. He's been sending notes to me daily, through the guards, notes that never reached me."

"Really. I will have to speak to the Captain of the Guard about that."

Panna didn't like this version of the prince. His eyes were colder than the last time she'd seen him; he was clearly enjoying himself, but his smile was insincere. He was perhaps slightly drunk. She began to fear what might have gone on in his head since she'd last spoken with him. She expressed herself carefully. "I would like you to release my father. He is no threat to anyone."

"Interesting request. Please, sit down. Let's chat about it."

"I'd rather not sit."

"Again with the sitting! Well, this time, I'd really rather you did." He smiled, but it was a cold and insistent smile.

"This is about my father. It is not about..." She trailed off.

"About what? About you? About me? Heaven forbid anything should be about *me*. Or were you going to say, about *us?*"

A chill ran down her spine. "Mather."

" 'Mather'? Now that Daddy is in trouble, I'm finally Mather?"

Fear rose. "Don't do this."

His face grew colder. "Sit down."

"And if I don't?" She couldn't keep her voice from quavering.

His jaw went taut. "Always getting to the point. Would you like to see your father out of jail?"

"Of course."

"Then...sit...down."

She did, quickly skirting the sofa and sitting on the very corner of it. The prince sat at the other end, angled toward her. He crossed his ankles out in front of him, striking a relaxed pose.

"There. That wasn't so painful, was it?"

She waited.

"Port?"

"No. Thank you."

He looked at her, swirling his port. She was much more willing to listen to him now. He smiled again. "I don't know why I have taken such a liking to you, but I have, and there's nothing to be done about it. I erred at dinner, but that does not mean I will act on my feelings again. They are more pure than you know."

Her eyes widened just slightly, and he saw it.

"Fine, mock me. But you don't know what you mock."

"I was not mocking you."

"Don't lie to me!"

She cringed.

He took a deep breath, controlling himself. "You think you know me, but you do not. Nothing will ever happen between us. I know that, and I'm sorry I ever gave you reason to believe otherwise. My intentions are good."

"So why is my father in prison?"

"Because I cannot, I can *not* have you wandering about casting aspersions on my character. I don't want you locked away any more than you want to be locked away. I just need your word. I need your promise. I need you to tell me that whatever transpired between us is a secret, and will stay that way forever. Your father's imprisonment is just a small incentive to help you see reason. That's all. That's it. Promise me you will be silent, treat me as your prince, not some child who needs to be taught a Scripture lesson, and you go free. Your father goes free. It's over."

Panna's eyes were black ice. "And if I refuse?"

He smiled, shaking his head. "Why on earth would you refuse? This is easy. Make a promise, and I'll believe it. You are an upright young woman. I know you won't lie; I know you'll keep your word. Just promise me silence, and it's over."

"Then I can go home?"

He stared hard at her for a moment, then turned away. "Yes," he said at last.

She was not sure she believed him. He was saying he wanted to be treated like a prince, but he was saying it as he threatened to keep her father in prison. Was that how a prince behaved? Of what was he capable, really? "And if I refuse, what happens?"

He closed his eyes. He opened them again and leaned forward, pleading with her. "Panna. You do understand the nature of power, do you not? I have it. You don't. I do not want to use it in this way. You simply leave me no choice."

"No choice? You have no other choice but to keep my father and me locked up until I swear I will never tell anyone about your attempt to assault me?"

He shook his head. "That is your description, not mine."

"And if I don't play along, how long will you keep us captive? Months? Years? Forever?"

"Panna, you struck me in the face. He is accused of spying. I've had people jailed for years for far less. No one will question it."

She searched his eyes. He would do it. She looked at the fireplace, and a large log fell into the flames, glowing red, burned right through the middle. A shower of sparks fled upward. When she spoke again, her voice was flat. "You want me to swear that I will tell no one. Not even my husband."

The Hand That Bears the Sword

"Especially not your husband. This is the bargain. He cannot know who his benefactor has been, nor can he know anything else that transpired between us at dinner. No one can know about any of it, including this little arrangement and the reason for your silence. Everything shall be expunged from the record. It's a very simple request. It never happened."

Panna's heart felt as heavy as an anchor. Who was this man? She was sorely tempted to give in, to take the bargain. But it felt so very, very wrong. She would be proving to him that this was, in fact, how to use power. That this was an effective way to run a nation. "Mather," she now pled, "you were going to read Scripture. You were going to learn what repentance really means."

Mather stood and strolled calmly away from her. She was weakening, and that felt good. It felt good to turn his back on her, to be in control. "I thought about what you said. I thought long and hard. And I decided you were right. I am selfish. But then I realized, that's exactly what drives me to do the things I do. It drives me to get what I want. My selfishness drives me to rule this nation, to win this war, to be a great king one day. And I realized that reading Matthew or Mark, or whichever one it was, could only change me. And that would mean I might not get what I want." He turned on her. "And I want what I want."

"And so to get what you want, to your other crimes you now add blackmail."

His lips tightened, went pale. "You have a very nasty habit of putting horrific labels on my conduct."

She shook her head sadly. "You make me ashamed of my country."

He shrugged. "I'm sorry you feel that way. But you are naïve. All kingdoms on earth are run by people like myself. It is the nature of politics. It is the nature of power."

She closed her eyes, praying that was not true. And yet it might be true. It could be true, if everyone allowed men like Mather to get away with "bargains" like this one. She opened her eyes. "If that's all, you can ask your dragoons to return me to the Tower."

"What?"

She stood. "Is that all? Your Highness?"

"You are *refusing* my offer?"

"Yes. Now and forever. I am refusing to be begged, bought, or blackmailed into hiding your crimes."

"Why, you little hypocrite."

"What are you talking about?"

"You have committed crimes yourself for which you did not pay. I have delivered you from the consequences of your own indiscretions. Now you refuse to do the same for me?"

She laughed once, shaking her head. "Everyone in the kingdom knows what I did to Riley Odoms. I am not proud of it. But it is known, and public, and I have apologized and done all I can to make it right to that poor, sweet man. It was your choice to protect me from justice, justice I would have accepted because I deserved it. But you are trying to *hide* your shameful behavior, to *avoid* what you deserve."

He ground his teeth. "What happened to forgiveness?"

"Forgiveness comes after repentance."

"Again with repentance. I am trying to save us both a lot of trouble."

"It is still my choice to make. And I choose not to accept your bargain. May I go?"

"You will regret this."

"No, you will regret it. Packer will return. And then what will you do? What will you tell him? How will you keep him quiet?"

He fought back rage. "Do not threaten me, Panna." He hesitated, then decided to play his final card. He would show her what power could do. "Your father will be denied food and water until you accept my bargain. My physicians say he can last four or five days. I suggest you change your mind before that time goes by."

She thought he couldn't shock her, but this did. "You wouldn't."

"I already have. The orders have been given. He will not eat or drink again until you see reason."

She held her head up, turned away from him, then walked with head high toward the huge wooden doors. She held back the sob that threatened to undo her show of strength.

CHAPTER 15

Sacrifice

"Packer? How you feeling, son?"

Packer was lying face down on the floor of his cabin, wearing his civilian clothes. John Hand had decided to visit the young man to determine for himself why the hero of the hour wasn't coming up on deck. Packer hadn't answered his knock, so the admiral now stood in the open doorway.

Packer finished his prayer, then raised his head. He sat up, put his back against the wall and his arms around his knees. He didn't salute. He didn't speak.

"Delaney says you're sick. That true?"

"I was, yes."

"Feeling better, then?"

Packer looked him in the eye.

"I want to talk to you about what you did today, Throme. You did good."

After a pause, Packer spoke calmly. "Killing men, no matter how well it's done, is not something I would call 'good.' Sir."

"May I come in?"

Packer shrugged. John Hand entered, left the door open behind him. Packer saw that he had brought with him a large, leather-covered book of the Scriptures. He sat on Packer's footlocker.

Packer watched him suspiciously.

"You wanted to be a priest at one time, is that right?"

Packer's suspicion grew. "That's right. Sir."

"Let me read you something." The admiral ran his thumb down the page. "I assume you know who Samuel was?"

Packer nodded.

"He was a prophet."

Packer waited.

"Man of God. Holy man. No question he did the right thing most all the time."

Packer waited.

"From One Samuel, chapter fifteen. 'And Samuel said, As thy sword hath made women childless, so shall thy mother be childless among women. And Samuel hewed Agag in pieces before the Lord in Gilgal.' I ask you, Packer, did Samuel do good?"

Packer's jaw clenched. He knew now that the admiral had spoken to Delaney, and Delaney had spilled everything, all of Packer's doubts. He was sorry Delaney had done it, but he couldn't blame him; he was a man under orders, and a man who would obey orders. Delaney's world was an easy one in which to live.

"You understand my point?"

Packer nodded. "Whatever God commands, that's what we should do."

Hand pretended not to hear. "These Drammune, Packer. They've already made a whole lot of God-fearing Vast mothers childless, and good women husbandless, and innocent children fatherless. The ones you 'hewed' today were on their way to do more of the same. You stopped them. *You.*" Hand watched Packer's darkened expression, puzzled. "Speak freely, son."

"I notice you didn't choose to read from the Ten Command-ments. Or Matthew, chapter twenty-six."

Hand didn't pause and didn't blink. " 'Thou shalt not kill.' 'And Jesus said, put up your sword, for all who live by the sword die by the sword.' "

Packer nodded, waited.

"It's an imperfect world. There are no perfect choices. You've made yours, Packer. You are not a priest. You are a swordsman, and a great one. You're going to have to live with that calling."

" 'Greater love hath no man than this, that he lay down his life for his friends.' "

"Exactly." Hand leaned in. "Your friends are here aboard this ship, and at home in Nearing Vast."

Now it was Packer's turn to be puzzled. "Begging your pardon, admiral. But I didn't lay down anything. Unless I'm missing something, taking away someone else's life is a very far cry from laying down one's own."

"But surely you would fight to save your mother's life. Or Panna's. Would you let them die at the hands of the Drammune? Because that's exactly what it means, if you choose not to fight them here."

Packer felt a pain shoot from his heart into his hand. He looked at the claw at the end of his arm, the hideous curved thing that had been melted to fit a sword's hilt. "You say fight. But you mean *kill*."

"Yes. I mean *kill*. Kill them here and now."

" 'For ye are not your own, ye were bought with a price.' " Packer's voice was flat, resigned. "I can choose to kill or not to kill. But I don't get to choose what happens after that. I don't get to decide the results of my actions." And at that moment, as he stared at the mark of ownership that was his right hand, he realized that faith was defined by doing the right thing now, in the moment, and trusting God with the outcome, no matter what it might be, no matter how bad the outcome seemed. Faith didn't look into the future the way John Hand did, trying to sort it all out in advance.

And at that moment Packer decided he would not kill again.

Hand rubbed his beard. He turned pages in the big book. "First Corinthians. Very good, that's exactly what it says. And then it says this: 'Therefore glorify God in your body, and in your spirit, which are God's.' There's the command, Packer. Glorify God. Look around you. The men know God is at work through you. They know it's not just you. They see His power in you."

A sharp tear threatened one eye. Packer wiped it away harshly. "Do they?"

"Yes. I see it, too."

"But you don't believe it's God at work."

Hand looked at him for a moment. "Perhaps. But I believe it's something. And whatever it is, Packer, I will use it. I will use your sword and God's power to beat the Drammune. If I possibly can."

Packer felt only resignation. "But I'm through killing."

Now Hand spoke with anger. "You are under my authority. Put

here by God, and by the prince. The apostle tells us that the prince does not bear the sword in vain."

Packer closed his eyes, spoke softly. "But I notice that the prince does not bear the sword himself, either. The hand that bears the sword bears responsibility as well."

"So who fights the Drammune if all are so righteous? No one?"

"God does. If He chooses."

Hand grimaced. "With thunderbolts? Or with men?"

Packer knew his argument sounded weak. "I'm not saying He doesn't call people to fight, or to kill. I know He has. I'm sure He still does. But not me. I can't do it, Admiral. I can't trust myself with a sword in my hand. God sent the Firefish to work His will. I got in the way. God may well have won that battle for us without any loss of life to our side."

John Hand rubbed his entire face. He sighed deeply. "Every man of conscience has doubts after his first battle."

"I don't know about every man."

"All right." Hand set his jaw. "Stay here; you're confined to quarters until I figure out what to do with you. Speak to no one." He picked up his book of the Scriptures, slapped it shut. He stood. "If you change your mind, if you get any further enlightenment from above, don't wait for me to come get you. Just come on out; there's work to be done. I won't say a word about this, nor will I ever, if you just come back around to help us."

Packer felt grateful. "Thank you, sir." He felt proud to serve under a man of such understanding. "What will you tell the men?"

The admiral paused, looked down at the young man. "I'll tell them you're still sick. I'll say you may have something contagious. And trust me, I do hope that whatever you've got, it isn't."

The Glorious Drammune Military was not built to fall apart because one cog went missing, even if it was a cog the size and shape of Fen Abbaka Mux. The *Kaza Fahn* was captained by Huk Tuth, the Commander of the Drammune Navy, second in command of the expeditionary force, who now assumed charge of the entire operation. He had signaled the rest of the Armada, now his Armada, not to give chase to the Vast ship. Rather, they were to turn for Nearing Vast, to wreak their vengeance on the City of Mann. In the process, they were to fan out even further north and south.

At all costs, the *Trophy Chase* was not to reach Mann before the Armada. Huk Tuth could not let the *Chase,* with all the information it possessed about the Drammune Armada, arrive in time to warn the Vast. He would force her to sail for days to try to flank him, or else take the risk again of running through his ranks. Tuth did not relish another engagement with the Vast ship, or with that demon beast now traveling with her. But he would fight them both together rather than let them reach the Vast capital first.

"Admiral wants to know if any of us have the ability to do what Packer did. Movin' in and out like what he did, you know, while the rest fight 'em head on." Delaney's voice was thin, his demeanor several notches below confident.

The eyes of the sailors gathered around him on the main deck went distant, as though they must not have heard him correctly. "But that was God did that. Right?" Marcus asked. "You said so, that the Spirit of God was movin' him around like that."

Delaney sniffed. "I know what I said, Marcus. But I know what the admiral's orders are, too. So anyways, who wants to give it a try?"

Arms crossed. "Where's Packer?" Mutter Cabe asked. "How come he's not here? He's the one knows it all."

"Yeah, what's wrong with him?" asked another.

"Told you, he's sick!" Delaney barked. "Don't wanna hear no more about it. Now come on, someone! We got to figure this out. Admiral wants one of these new kind of fighters for every five or six regular ones. Gotta have a dozen volunteers."

All eyes studied the decking, or scanned the seas.

"Marcus, it's you, then. Let me show you what I saw him do, and we'll just see."

The boy nodded dutifully, and stepped into the middle of the ring of sailors.

The past three days had been torment. Panna had heard nothing more from the prince. She careened within from hope to despair to brutal anger to hope and back again to despair. What remained consistent was her opinion of Prince Mather. Who would do such things, say such things, then leave her alone for days on end? Mather did not deserve to be called a man, much less a prince.

Had he really cut off a man's food, his water? Was there no bottom to Mather's wickedness? She couldn't stand to think of her father lying there in that filthy cell with the rats, sick and getting sicker, hungry, thirsty, cold, nothing for comfort but a bed of straw that might well be his deathbed. And where was Mather all this time? Was he waiting for her to call to him, to change her mind and beg him, tell him she'd do anything, anything to save her father? But if she did that, Mather might ask her to do anything, anything at all. If he would starve a man to get his way, why wouldn't he change the terms of his agreement, go back on his word, do something worse? What would keep him from assaulting her again if he thought he could get away with it?

Then grim thoughts, dark images would run through her mind, as she envisioned the prince entering her rooms with evil intent and winding up lying on the floor at her feet once more—this time lifeless. If he was willing to kill a priest, then why should she be unwilling to kill a prince? If that was how he chose to run his kingdom, with brutal power, so be it. She would show him the results of such choices.

She hunted around her rooms for a weapon, her thoughts straying into the realm of plans. She had been an outlaw once, she could certainly be one again. She found herself almost hoping he would come back here, this time alone, so she could face him again. But Mather had done a thorough job of removing anything sharp enough to accomplish the work, or anything heavy enough to deliver a blow but still light enough to wield. She had a small hairbrush, but no combs, no scissors. Her food came with a wooden spoon, but no forks, no knives. She even upended and tried to take apart the small table, and then to break apart one of the heavy chairs, so she could wield a stick of wood, sharp or blunt. But she had no success.

Frustrated, she threw herself across the bed. What was she doing? She was planning to kill the prince. That thought dragged her deeper into despair. She tried to pray. She couldn't eat, couldn't drink. She felt sick and weak, just when she needed to feel strong. Finally, exhausted, she climbed into her bed fully clothed.

But what she found was not sleep in any real sense of the word. She would drift into unconsciousness, only to find cruel fates awaiting her: She was running from danger, fighting off people with fists and swords and chair legs, watching people she loved die, starved and stabbed. Everyone was vulnerable, overwhelmed by the worst odds, and her savage efforts to help were too meager to matter, leaving her exhausted and defeated. Packer was helpless, so was her father. So was the Fleet. The palace was burning, the prince was leering from its upper windows, stoking fires with draperies, paintings, chairs and tables, books, all the emblems and accoutrements of civilized society, then sending dragoons out into the darkness to do evil, to seek her and her family. She found that when she prayed inside one these dreams, she would wake up; and then she would be thankful for a moment, until she remembered the full ugliness of her waking reality.

She prayed for her father, but found no comfort. She could not get around the rage she felt, the desire to hurt Mather, to stop him forever. But then she would come around to realize that all she needed to do was give in, accept his bargain. Keep his secrets. How bad was that, really? It was the lesser of two evils, far less evil than death and murder, and what was so terrible about that? How bad would it be to take such secrets to her grave? She felt hope then. All she needed to do was cave in, let him wield his power in these ugly ways, and be done with it. But in her heart she could not trust him. She couldn't believe he would keep his side of the bargain. She did not, ultimately, believe he would let her go. This was false hope.

Eventually, she blamed herself. She didn't want to; she wanted to blame only the prince. But she couldn't avoid forever the thought that she might have prevented all this if she had just treated the prince with more respect. She had been careless with his perception of her, and then careless with his affections. His accusations at dinner, that she had made him believe she was available, made her shiver with regret and with shame. She hadn't meant to convey any such thing. But if not, she asked herself, what on earth had she been thinking, running to him in a bathrobe? What else could someone like him conclude about someone like her?

She thought of Packer often, looking for hope there. She had spoken confidently to the prince, but she couldn't know whether Packer was alive or dead. She only knew he was far, far distant. She tried to pray for him, too, and these prayers sometimes broke through, sometimes seemed to reach all the way to God in heaven. She could lose herself within them. But even so she had a hard time believing he would return soon, if at all. And if something happened to Packer, if something befell him, what might the prince do then? Only Packer's return, she felt, could force the prince to change his mind and let her go. Only the promise of her husband's return could keep Mather from doing something rash.

She did try to pray for Mather, for his better angels to win the day. She pled with God that the prince would turn, would think again about this thing he was doing, this judgment he was bringing on himself and his kingdom. That he would repent. But such a prayer seemed to require faith not only in God, but in Mather Sennett. And in him she had none.

There were a few clearer moments, when sunlight peeked through the roiling thunderclouds overhead. Now and then she realized that, in fact, nothing had happened yet. Her father was still alive. She was untouched. God could still provide a way out. He was still in heaven. He still had all the power in the universe, and all was not lost. Certainly, He would do something. He cared about these things. He would set it right somehow. He would change Mather from within, or compel him from without.

It was during one of these hopeful moments that she remembered Mather mentioning secret passageways. Ward used them to get in and out of the palace. Why hadn't she thought of this before? She worked her way through the apartments, running her hands along walls, looking under rugs, behind furniture, searching for something, some hollow wall or mechanism that might open a secret door. She ended up on the balcony, looking for some contrivance, some possibility she had missed. But there was nothing. This was the new part of the palace, and those tunnels were ancient. Despair rose again like a specter. Then the cycle began anew.

Panna was considering giving in again, just pleading with the prince to let her accept his bargain, when he returned. It was late in the morning and Panna was in bed, though fully clothed, when she heard the footfalls in the hall outside. She sat up panicked, clutching the comforter around her. Low voices outside the entranceway. She scrambled out of bed and threw the covers back up over the sheets, straightening it with trembling hands. She heard the sound of a key in the lock, then footsteps in the entrance hall just outside her bedroom, coming toward her room. "Panna?" A cautious voice.

The prince entered her bedroom without knocking. He was composed, groomed, perfectly dressed, appearing to be his previous unctuous self, except that the bandage was gone from his nose and blotchy makeup now covered the discoloring. Two dragoons stood at the doorway to her bedroom, just behind him. Mather turned, shooed them back, and they disappeared from view. But they did not go far.

He looked at Panna with a rather sad smile. "Say, you look a mess."

"What do you want?" She snarled, standing with arms crossed in front of her bed.

Now she sensed an air of regret that hung about him, a sense of inner turmoil that immediately gave her some hope. Perhaps he had come to his senses.

"How is my father?" Her voice was accusing.

He blanched, as though the question were unexpected. "Oh, still well. A bit hungry. A bit thirsty."

Her anger rose. "Do you not know how wrong this is?"

He turned away, saw the heavy chair by the dresser, still over-turned. He walked to it, set it right without saying a word. But when he looked back to Panna, he seemed more troubled yet. He sat in the chair, leaned forward. "I don't like it, either. I want this to end."

"Then end it."

"You haven't slept well. Neither have I."

"Then do the right thing. Let my father go. Let me go."

"Panna, I have news."

She waited, heart pounding.

"Three ships sailed. Only one has returned."

Hope and fear warred within her.

"It is the *Marchessa*."

Her face fell, then went pale. "And Packer?"

"Nothing known for sure. But the *Trophy Chase* was last seen on a fading horizon, surrounded by more than fifty enemy warships. Perhaps as many as a hundred. I'm sorry, Panna."

She shook her head. "No. He's still alive."

He was surprised by her adamant tone.

So was she. But she suddenly felt sure to her bones that he lived.

"It's good to hope," he said.

The Hand That Bears the Sword

"I am not a widow!"

He nodded, studying her. "No, of course not. But even the *Trophy Chase* cannot stop all those Drammune warships. They are coming. They will arrive here within days."

Now Panna realized how much she had been preoccupied with herself, and with her father, and how little she had thought about the war. But it was now upon them. The City of Mann would be attacked. That would change everything. Everything.

"The *Chase*'s mission has failed," the prince continued. "We have nothing to stop the Drammune Armada but our aging Army and our ragtag new recruits. The secret of the Fleet will be out soon enough. So, considering the circumstances, I am prepared to free your father, and to free you."

She did not let her heart believe it. "When?"

"In the morning. I just need one thing from you first. One small thing."

She watched him, fearing what might be coming next.

But he said, "I want to dine with you one more time. I want to do it right this time. I want to be a gentleman. I want you to remember me that way."

Panna's insides went cold.

"You look like I just sentenced you to death."

"The answer is no."

He was dumbfounded. "Is dining with me such a bad alternative? Is it so horrible?"

"You're still bargaining with my father's life."

"But it's an easy bargain. How can you refuse?"

She wasn't sure she could explain it. Finally she asked, "I dine with you tonight, or else what? Or what, Mather?"

He narrowed his eyes. Anger grew within him. "Panna, you still don't understand power. I will come here tonight, and we will eat together, out on the balcony. My servants will cater it all." His eyes were cold. "Just so long as you treat me well, you and your father may leave in the morning. I want to know what it feels like to be... cared for. Loved. By you. And that is what will happen. Is anything about that unclear to you?"

She seethed.

"I apologize for the method, but really, it's the choice you left me."

She started to speak. He held up a finger. "Make me believe you are happy to have dinner with me. Enjoy my company, just once. And then all will be well."

She stared at him for a moment. "There is one other way."

"And what is that?"

"Let my father go. Let me go. Then ask me to dinner."

"And if I do, will you dine with me?"

"You can only know that when I have the freedom to choose."

He pondered it. Then he shook his head. "You want me to be powerless. But I am not, and while I have power, I will use it." He stood and walked to the door of her room. He leaned on the doorpost. "It's over, Panna, don't you see that? Everything's over. Packer's gone. The end of the kingdom is at hand. Life under the Drammune will either be short, or so brutal we'll wish it was. I have one desire left, one bit of comfort I'd like to take, and while I still have the power, I will make that one thing happen."

Her insides felt like ice. "I want to see my father."

He squinted at her. "Why?"

"How do I know he's still alive?"

"Panna, I am not a monster."

"You are. And a bully. I want to see him."

"And then you will dine with me?"

"You truly don't know your own heart." She spoke the words with utter certainty. "You will attack me again."

"No. I won't."

She lowered her eyes. "I wish that were true."

"I won't touch you. I promise you that." But she had planted a doubt in his mind.

She looked at him again. "I want to see my father."

"Do you promise you will dine with me here tonight?"

She paused. She said the word with her eyes closed. "Yes."

He smiled. "Good. Go see your father. And then get dressed. It will be a formal dinner, nine o'clock sharp. I'll send servants to prepare the table."

He left. She heard him whistling as he went.

The big dragoon hung back as Panna ran to the last cell on the right. She found him exactly where she had found him before, face down in the straw. The straw, however, was no longer fresh. The smell of urine and feces was strong. When he sat up this time, his face was haggard and pale, his eyes sunken. His hair was matted, and his beard was speckled with dirt and straw, his lips cracked and dry. But his smile was the same. "Panna!" He coughed, a rough and haggard sound, and he rose with difficulty, and when he hugged her through the bars, she felt more steel than she had just a few days ago.

He tried to straighten her hair. His hands shook. "Panna, you've been crying. Are you all right?"

She shook her head.

"Tell me what he's done." His mouth was dry and his words had a croaking tone, but this was a father's command, not to be questioned—but spoken in a tone as tender as she ever remembered him using.

"He...he ordered you to be starved because of me."

Will nodded. He had guessed as much. "Tell me everything."

Now her tears came in a torrent. He was her father asking for the truth, but he was also her priest, asking for a confession. And she gave it. She hadn't planned to, but it all came out. She told him everything that had happened since she had seen him last, how the prince tried to blackmail her into silence, how she'd believed she had somehow led him on, how he had come to her just now and she had agreed to dine with him again, alone. And she told him that the prince had said that Packer was dead.

She wiped at her tears. "And now it's all led to this. Look at you..."

His heart felt like shattered glass in his chest. "Panna. Don't give up hope for Packer."

"I wanted to sail with him, to go with him. That's all. That's why I went to see the prince, to ask him, to beg him. Now I have to spend the evening with him again. I don't know what he'll do."

"Panna," he said, "listen to me. Are you listening?"

She nodded up at him.

"This is simple. Do not dine with him."

She shook her head. "I already said I would."

"He is a dangerous man. Do not do it. God will find a way. Trust Him."

But she went hard inside instead. "I could kill him. He wants to dine on the balcony. I think I can push him over. Or if I just had a weapon..." She looked around the prison as though one might appear.

He shook his head. "No. No, Panna. There is another way. There is a third choice. There is always a third choice. And it's always the same choice, to trust God."

She squeezed her eyes shut. That seemed to her like no choice at all. That seemed to her like doing nothing but pacing and hoping and fearing, all the things she'd already been doing for three days.

"But Daddy, you're sick!"

"You can't worry about me. Once you give in to blackmail, there's no end to it. Not until you stand up to it."

"You're hungry and thirsty—"

"Yes, and tired and flea-bitten and filthy." He seemed to think all this was humorous. "But I love you, more than anything in this world. And I know you love me. You want to make a sacrifice for my sake, but little girl, hear me now. It's not you who is being called to make a sacrifice. This is not your sacrifice to make. It's mine. You need to protect your honor, and love your husband, and your God. Do what's right. The rest is up to Him."

She closed her eyes, shook her head, and when she looked at him again, fears from far back in her past, deep in her heart, flickered in her eyes. "But you can't die!" she pleaded.

"There are worse things." He knew she wouldn't see it that way. She still carried wounds from the loss of her mother all those years ago. He remembered Panna's eyes, then her questions, over and over it seemed, asking about when Momma was coming back home. That's what drove her to chase Packer so recklessly last summer. She was afraid that God would always take those she loved. He sighed. "Who knows what God may do? He opens prison doors, closes lions' mouths, rescues His people from the bellies of whales. All we need to do is trust Him. And do the right thing."

She looked away. God did all that, yes. But a long time ago, and for people she didn't know. God had spared Packer. Once. But then God had taken him away again, and now the prince said he was dead. God let people die. And now her father was dying.

"If it does come to that," Will continued, "then that's His business. I would be honored to make that sacrifice. For you. For Packer. Do you understand me?"

She wouldn't look at him. He was trying to build up her resolve, but it was crumbling instead.

He sighed. "Panna. Your mother is waiting for me."

The Hand That Bears the Sword

Now she looked up at him. She saw his pain and sadness deep inside him, and she remembered. When she was young, and her parents were all the world to her, she remembered that same hurt as he told her, so long ago but so present, that her mother had gone to heaven and would never return.

He took her head gently between his hands. "I haven't seen my Tamma in so many, many years. And I miss her. You do the right thing, Panna. You do the good thing. God will take care of the rest. It will all work out."

Her thoughts were her own, deep inside her. She looked at him from far away.

He smiled. "This a trial, that's all it is." He said it as though it were the most obvious, most welcome thing in the world. "God is testing us. He wants us to make the right choice. He wants us to pass this test." Will Seline again wiped tears away from the cheek of his only child. "To be faithful until the end, that was His command. Yes?"

"Yes. But Daddy. Do not die."

Behind her tears he now saw the familiar fires crackling within her. His Panna. "I am so proud of you," he said gently. And he embraced her one last time.

The dragoon walked up to them. "Ready to go, Mrs. Throme?" he asked in his high-pitched voice. Panna turned to look up at him, and blanched. Were those tears in his eyes too?

"How are you, Chunk?" Will Seline asked. "I didn't recognize you there!"

"'Lo, Pastor." His chin definitely quivered, and he wiped an eye. He had heard the whole exchange. "I'm sorry about all this."

"You just take care of my little girl, and all will be well."

"I'll try, sir. I sure will try."

Panna turned to her father, her questioning look bordering on shock.

"Panna, this is Stave Deroy. His friends call him Chunk."

"His friends..." She couldn't finish the question. She had gotten to know several of the servants, but it never once occurred to her that she might introduce herself to the hulking dragoons who imposed the prince's will. And yet all this time, this one knew her father. He was a real person with a name. And, apparently, a heart. "Well hello, Chunk," she smiled. "I'm very, very pleased to meet you." And she

The Hand That Bears the Sword

shook his hand. It was wet. To Panna, it felt like hope. There might be another way. There might be a third choice.

"Ma'am." He wiped his eyes again. "And now we best get goin'."

As Panna and Chunk walked away, the two prison guards looked at one another and shook their heads. They hadn't overheard the conversations, but whatever was going on here, it couldn't lead to anything good.

The prince had a spring in his step as he bounced up the stairs, then down the hallway toward Panna's rooms. He carried a bouquet of fresh daisies in his hand, and had a boyish smile on his face. He wore his best dress uniform, the one he'd worn to send off the *Trophy Chase*. He was followed by an armed dragoon, who carried a pike.

When he reached Panna's door, Chunk saluted. The young guard tried not to look like he had something to hide.

"Listen, men," the prince said, leaning in to speak to both of them quietly. They could smell the cologne, the hair oil, the mouth freshener; he had overdone all three. They could also see the patchy makeup that mostly covered the bruising around his nose. "If I call out to you, come in immediately. That young woman can be dangerous."

"Yes, sir," they both replied dutifully. Chunk's jaw went tight.

The prince looked the two over carefully. "There'll be a steward up in a minute, and then several courses brought by the dinner crew. Each is to knock. No one is to come in or out unless I say. Do you understand?" They nodded. "No one in or out without my orders." He looked into their eyes until he was sure they understood him. The prince straightened his hair, the cords of his jacket, the epaulets, then checked the bouquet in his hand. He fished the key from his pocket, and unlocked the door. He smiled broadly, and pushed it open.

The lamps burned brightly, and to his amazement, Panna stood waiting for him.

Amazement melted into adoration as he absorbed the vision before him. She was dressed not in her own finery, but in one of the dresses he had sent to her; and in not just any one of them, but his favorite. It was a cream-colored, sequined ball gown cut just off the shoulder. She had put her hair up, wrapped and pinned it, revealing a graceful, perfect neck that flowed down to angular shoulders. The light-colored gown contrasted with her dark eyes and hair, and brought out the color in her cheeks. She held a bottle of wine in her hands, the rare bottle Prince Mather had personally selected and sent up to share with her. She held it delicately, as though thankful, appreciating its worth. But more amazingly, she beamed confidence and warmth.

She was, in a word, dazzling.

Whatever had happened, however she had done it, she was now transformed. Gone was any hint of the sleepless, tormented girl he had left here earlier in the day. More incredibly, she looked at him not as a monster, not as an object of hatred, but as though she were truly happy to see him. She had hope in her, light and life. This was not feigned…how could it be? And yet how could it *not* be? He didn't know, but he was not in the mood or the mind to question it. He had arranged everything so it would work exactly this way. And it was working. Perfectly.

"Panna," he said, his voice catching in his throat. "You are an angel."

She lowered her eyes shyly.

He stepped inside the room and closed the door behind him. He leaned back against it for support. He reached back and, without taking his eyes off her, fumbled the key into the lock and turned it. Then he took a deep breath.

As he looked at her, he knew, absolutely, that he could never give her up. Not now. Not after he'd seen this, felt this. He didn't care what he'd said, what he'd promised. He didn't care if Packer were alive or dead. Now that she showed him herself in her glory, with this obvious affection pouring from her, now that he knew what it felt like, he could never let her go.

And then she walked toward him, slowly and purposefully.

He was utterly, totally smitten. She would be queen! She was destined for that. Hang the Drammune; he would find a way to make it happen. And so he told her.

"You will be my queen," he said simply.

She stopped an arm's length away. Her head cocked just slightly, as though she hadn't quite heard him.

His chin quivered. He held the flowers up, giving them to her. As he did, he felt his stuffed head open. He took a sharp breath in through his nose. He smelled the flowers. Finally, for the first time since she had hit him, he could breathe! He could smell. And those daisies…they were ridiculously fragrant. Intoxicatingly sweet, unbelievably wholesome. He brought the flowers up, buried his face in them, and breathed them in. They were life, and comfort, and wonder. A bright light flashed, the world went white, then all went black.

Panna looked at the prince, crumpled at her feet, and then at the bottle she still held in her hands. She was thankful it had not broken. She was equally thankful he had finally sent a weapon up to her rooms.

CHAPTER 16

Escape

He had called her an angel in that adoring, worshipful voice, and that's when Panna's eyes were opened. She suddenly realized that not only did Mather not know himself, he didn't know her, either. He had no idea who Panna was. He wasn't looking at her. He had never looked at her, never seen her. He saw in her a light, but it was not her light. It came from beyond her, or perhaps from within him.

She felt for him at that moment, but it was far more pity than it was affection. He was a small puppy with very sharp teeth, miserable and alone, with no one who cared for him, no one who cared enough to teach him to behave. He was, in fact, looking for help. He needed, he wanted to be overwhelmed by something greater, stronger, better, purer, and more powerful than himself. He was looking for something above and beyond, and in his own dark world, Panna had become that something. But he did have sharp teeth, and he did need to learn to behave.

His queen. It would have been laughable if not for all the things such a statement revealed about him, and assumed about her, and implied about Packer. Prince Mather had sealed his own fate with that promise. He was completely untrustworthy, and she could not take a chance on the sort of thing he was capable of attempting, here in her rooms with doors locked. She needed to protect her honor, and love her husband, as her father had instructed. For once she intended to follow his advice. She fully intended to escape tonight, so she had put this dress on, put her hair up as a disguise, knowing she would not be recognized on the palace ground in this unfamiliar finery, at least not immediately, at least not from a distance. She had also suspected, perhaps even hoped, that this outfit would lower Mather's guard and provide her an opening for her escape. He'd reacted a bit more emotionally than she had expected, but even that had turned out to the good.

He thought she was an angel—fine. Angels cannot save men's souls. Angels are messengers of God. They execute God's judgment. So when the opening came, she took it. He put his face into the flowers. Here was the third way her father told her to look for, presented to her in a bouquet of daisies.

But even as she felled him, swung the bottle with her two hands as if she were beating the dirt from a stubborn rug, as his head jerked backward and slammed hard into the door behind him, as he slumped down to the floor, even then she hoped he would think better of his actions, and would one day come to understand how love truly behaved.

It was a fortunate thing, really, that he had banged his head on the door. The crack of his head on the stout wood behind him doubled the force of her blow and turned his legs to jelly. So everything had worked out quite nicely, and now the second most powerful man in the kingdom lay prostrate at her feet, again, this time with a contented smile plastered across his face and dozens of little white and yellow flowers scattered over and around him.

Now came a sharp knock. The dragoon! She believed that only Chunk stood on the other side of the door, so she turned the key and opened the door a crack, then froze. It wasn't Chunk. Chunk stood to one side, eyes wide. The man before her was just as big as Chunk, but ten years older, gruff and grim and suspicious. She did not want to pit Chunk against this man. "Yes?" she asked. She tried to sound sweet, but the question had a decidedly testy edge.

"Beg pardon, ma'am. Is everything all right?" He looked at the wine bottle still in her hands, then strained to look past her, but could see nothing around her. The prince was obscured by her puffy skirts.

"Everything is fine," Panna told him. That came out a little sweeter.

There was nothing to be seen without pushing her physically out of the way. "Heard something hit the door," he said.

"But all is well."

The dragoon was not convinced. Chunk looked over at his partner. "I didn't hear him call for us, did you?"

"No. But something hit that door."

She smiled and held up the bottle. "Clumsy of me."

He thought a moment, then said, "Please stand aside, ma'am."

Panna could think of nothing to say, and so she stood firm and looked the man square in the eye.

The dragoon turned to his partner for help.

Chunk shook his head thoughtfully. "His Highness's orders were, no one in or out unless he said. And I didn't hear him say. Did you?"

As the suspicious dragoon hesitated, Panna looked away, back into her apartment, smiled at something only she could see, then turned back and said calmly, "I'm sorry, but the prince can't come to the door right now. I'm sure he'll be very pleased that you asked about him. And that you obeyed his orders."

The dragoon's face knotted up. "So you're telling me he's fine."

"The prince?" She turned away to look at Mather again, the smile still on his face where he lay. She turned back. "Blissful."

The guard was weighing the consequences of believing her when something amiss caught his eye. He stared hard at her shoulder, his brow furrowing. She glanced down, fearing she would see a blood-stain on her dress. But it was a daisy, clinging to a stray wisp of hair. She smiled, plucked it up, and handed it to him.

He smiled back, surprised. "Why, thank you, ma'am."

"You're welcome."

He caught himself, grew serious again. "You're sure all is well?"

Her response was light. "All is well."

"All right then." He nodded. "If you're sure."

"Very." She smiled and waved.

He waggled his fingers at her. She closed the door. It clicked shut. She heard the dragoons discussing the situation. She turned the key.

She took a deep breath, feeling secure for the moment. Then she looked down at the prince. "Well, Prince Mather Sennett, Crown Prince of Nearing Vast. Do you think I understand the nature of power yet?" But she didn't feel that the answer was any too obvious.

She pondered. The Tower balcony was not more than twenty feet away. She could drag him to the rail, wrestle him over it, and the world would be rid of him. She could say he had attacked her, and she hit him, and he fell. All that would be true. Her father would then live. She might go to prison, but she might not. Either way, her father would be free. And the nation would be free of Mather Sennett. He would never be king. All this would be good.

She closed her eyes. But Pastor Will Seline would know. She could lie to him, but in the end he would know. She couldn't hide something like this from him for long. He would be crushed. He would try to convince her to confess. He might even turn her in. And if she didn't confess, how would she be any different than Mather? She had lectured him on exactly this point. No, she couldn't get away with it. And God would know, regardless.

She sighed. The third choice had led very quickly to something of a dead end.

And then Mather groaned.

Panna looked at him, then up the ceiling. "Well? What now?" The question was urgent, even angry. She couldn't have Mather coming around. But there was no time to make a plan, no time to pray, no time even to think. He groaned again. His brow furrowed and his head turned to the side. First his shoulder, then his hand twitched. Then his whole body writhed.

She knelt beside his head, shushing him gently. She set the bottle down, then took his hair in her hands, knotted it between the fingers of her fists, raised his head high, and slammed it back down onto the oak floor, hard. He whimpered. Then she did it again. "Now be quiet," she said urgently. He seemed content to oblige. She felt both relief and nausea. This was a horror.

Knuckles rapped at the door. "Everything okay in there?" the gruff dragoon called through the door.

"Just fine!" she sang out. But her own head pounded, and she put a hand to her forehead. What, precisely, was her plan here? To bang his head on the floor every couple of minutes? She looked out the doorway at the porch rail, tempted once again. If she just threw him over, she could walk to the dragoons, surrender, and let the chips fall where they may. She hung her head. *I could really use some help.* Then it occurred to her. She didn't need to be rid of him. She only needed to keep him still, and quiet.

Panna had been but a child, and certainly had not seen any-thing, nor had she been told very much when Mr. Sopwash was found trussed and gagged after being robbed near Inbenigh. Lack of knowledge hadn't bothered the children of the village, however, who faithfully bound and gagged one another for weeks afterward, the technique becoming an instant requisite for every game of Sher-iffs and Brigands, remaining so until worried mothers put a stop to it. But Panna knew how to play that game. She had no rope now, but she had bedsheets, and she quickly tore a long strip from one of them. She certainly knew how to work with cloth. And one thing every child in every fishing village learned, male or female, was how to tie a good, tight knot.

When she was finished, she checked her handiwork. One strip bound the prince's feet, another his hands behind his back. He would not wriggle free. Panna had less confidence in the gag. The knot would hold, but would it keep him quiet? She studied his breathing. He seemed to be having no difficulty. She looked at the large area at his hairline that was swelling, turning crimson. A few drops of blood oozed. He would live.

Satisfied, she grabbed the Crown Prince of Nearing Vast by the ankles and dragged him, face down, into her bedroom. She took him straight to her closet. She rolled him in, leaving him face up on and among the shoes he'd bought for her, that she had never worn, under the gowns and dresses she would never wear. She closed the heavy doors and piled the comforter up around them, hoping it would help muffle his inevitable cries for help.

She walked to the balcony, past the table set here under the stars, where two wine glasses sat empty, two candles sat unlit—the white linen setting where a dark royal ambition would never come to pass. She looked down on the lamplit streets far below. She looked up to the black sky, a billion pinpoints glowing bright. She took a deep breath and offered up a quick prayer.

Then she screamed.

And then she screamed again.

There was a banging on the door. "Ma'am! Open up!"

She screamed again.

The door cracked, splintered. Chunk was by her side. "Are you all right, ma'am?"

"Where's the prince?" the older one demanded, looking around with deep alarm.

She shook her head and pointed down into the darkness over the railing. "I hit him."

"What?"

"I hit him. And he fell." She didn't look at either one of them.

"Dear God," the older man said, looking ill. "He fell?"

The two dragoons stared at one another. "We have to get down there and find him," Chunk said, stating the obvious.

The elder one's eyes narrowed. Panna closed her own eyes, praying silently that Mather would stay unconscious. "Ma'am," he accused her, "if you hit him here, why are the flowers all on the floor in there?"

Panna looked where he pointed. The wine bottle still sat on the floor among the daisies. She turned now to look at her accuser. She had no answer. She raised her chin.

The dragoon saw only an admission of guilt in this, and his lips pursed in anger. Panna glanced over at Chunk, whose mouth dropped open. She tried to tell him silently that all was indeed well, that it would be all right. But he just shook his head, unbelieving. She felt badly for him.

The older one grabbed her roughly by the elbow. "You're coming with us."

Chunk ran ahead to find the Captain of the Guard, to report what would surely become the news of the century. The elder one, taking Panna through the winding stairways and hallways down to the ground floor, had visions of inquests and testimony and, ultimately, prison for himself and his young partner. Maybe hanging. He hoped upon hope that the young woman had a good story and some very, very good friends.

Panna's mind raced. Would this really work? She didn't know. It seemed to be working so far. She had neither given in to Mather nor had she killed. This was the plan that had popped into her head when she'd asked God for help. Did that mean He'd given it to her? Or was it just her own mind, churning and desperate?

In a few minutes the prince would recover. Someone would find him, and everyone would know. He would be furious. Who knows what he might do? But at least everyone would know. Perhaps someone would care.

The main stairway at the end of her trek was a huge, ornate cascade of steps that flowed down to the main hall, the one used for the most fabulous of fabulous events. As she descended it, Panna saw another opportunity.

The constant state of fabulous perfection that was Princess Jacqalyn streamed across the marble floor below.

"Princess!" Panna called out. "Princess, please help. It's the prince!"

Jacqalyn turned and looked up. She sighed. The girl had gotten herself into trouble after all, in spite of her warnings. She hoped Panna didn't expect her to support some claim against Mather. "What is it, dear?" she asked as Panna flowed breathlessly down the stairs, having wrenched her elbow from the grip of the dragoon.

"I don't know how to say it."

Jacqalyn looked at Panna's captor, hustling to keep up with her. He wore an expression of fear, something Jacq never saw in a dragoon except when Mather was drilling into one over some perceived offense. "Well, someone had better say it."

The dragoon grimaced. "Begging your pardon, ma'am. Seems the prince took a tumble. From the balcony."

Jacqalyn's eyes went wide. "The Tower balcony?"

The fear in the dragoon only grew. "Yes, Your Highness."

Jacqalyn turned on Panna, her face twisting into a rabid scowl. "You have no idea what you've done, you stupid little—" She spun on the dragoon. "Where's your captain? You'll hang for this."

He nodded glumly. "Yes, ma'am."

"Go get the surgeon! And get every servant and every guard in the building out onto the grounds. We need to find whatever's left of my dear brother before some guest stumbles upon...whatever's left of my dear brother." The dragoon stood still, not wanting to leave Panna behind. "Go!" Jacq ordered. "I'll watch this..." But she trailed off again, thinking better of each of the many descriptive words for Panna that popped into her mind in a staccato cadence of impropriety.

The dragoon ran off at a sprint. Jacqalyn immediately grabbed Panna hard, by the upper arm, her fingernails digging in painfully. "*Fell* from the balcony indeed. *Pushed* is what you mean. And I believed your innocent little girl act." The princess sighed and then said, "Let's just go take a look at your handiwork."

The two women went out to join the dragoons, servants, household physicians, and almost every other resident and guest of the palace in the search for the prince. Dragoons searched bushes, servants pointed upward, discussions were held about where, precisely, one might stand to be underneath the railings of the Tower. Many glances were thrown Panna's way, all suitable for the occasion.

The prince was nowhere to be found, of course, which led to a call for torches and lanterns to light the underside of the trees. Surely he had been caught in one of them. Guards and servants were sent to the rooms facing the gardens, to the windows and lower balconies, to see if Mather's body might be wedged, living or dead, in a crook of some dark oak.

Panna, of course, searched only for a chance, one chance when no one was looking, when all eyes were upward, when she might slip away. And finally, one came. Everyone strained upward, following a call from a guest to the effect that he could see, or thought he could see, something caught in the tree above. "There, right there!"

"Where? I don't see anything!"

"Look, that dark spot right there."

"It's a squirrel's nest. Isn't it?"

"Too big for that. See that, that's a foot."

Gasps could be heard.

"We'll need more light," the Captain of the Guard announced grimly. "And bring a ladder, and some rope."

Within minutes, the crowd had all gathered in this one spot, many holding lanterns and torches, all staring up with craned necks at a dark shape, in truth nothing more than leaves and shadows and a bit of dead tree branch, but now transformed before their earnest eyes and ignited imaginations into a body: the head here, the feet just there, and a ghastly bit of brokenness in the middle part.

At this moment Prince Ward arrived, sauntering up to his sister. "What's up?" he asked, adding his to the array of upturned faces. He carried a tumbler of brandy in his hand, several more on his breath.

"Your brother, the prince," Jacqalyn answered.

"Ooh. That can't be healthy."

"Seems the hero's wife pushed him over the edge."

He grimaced, squinting into the dark. "I take it we are not speaking metaphorically."

"He'd have given her half the kingdom," Jacqalyn said bitterly, still peering upward. A moment later, seething, she tossed back toward Panna, "I hope your little fits of monogamy are worth all this." But when she turned to give the vapid girl the full brunt of her royal, withering scorn, Panna had vanished.

Prince Mather tried to put a hand to his throbbing head, but found he could not. It took him a long while to regain his senses, to understand his predicament, to remember, to piece it together. But eventually he succeeded: He was trussed up like a turkey for basting. By Panna, no doubt.

He remembered the vision of beauty that had met him at the door. He remembered thinking this was the most wonderful moment of his life. His eyes were welling up with tears. Yes, he remembered that. And the flowers! He could smell the flowers. Even now, he could smell them. The pure sweetness of them was astonishing. He had put his face into them.

He couldn't help himself. He drifted off into their joyous ether again.

He squinted and blinked. He regathered his thoughts. Then he burned with embarrassment. She had hit him at that moment. Hit him from within the daisies. Then she had tied him up and left him here in the dark. He felt around with his hands. Shoes. He was in a closet. She'd left him in the closet!

His head pounded furiously. But now, even in his pain, he felt again the warmth of that moment at the door. He teetered in his anger. The light of her smile, the vision of her, walking toward him, joy in her eyes. He could feel her; he could smell her. He could smell the flowers...

No. This time he stopped himself. He couldn't keep drifting off into the flowers. He squeezed his eyes shut. His head pounded. She had hurt him badly this time, he knew. His mind wasn't working right. He kept losing consciousness. He shook his head, felt the throbbing pain. He cursed himself for it, but he couldn't hate Panna. He knew that she had in fact given him what he wanted. He now knew what it felt like to be loved by her.

And worse, he knew she was right to do what she'd done. He

would not have kept his bargain. He had determined already, in that one brief moment at the door, that he could not let her go, that he would break every promise, every law, every principle of good behavior, just to prevent her from leaving him. She had been right. He might have done anything.

He struggled against his bonds. But she had done a thorough job. How would an innocent like Panna Throme learn to tie and gag a man? The answer was, she was not at all what she seemed to be. She only feigned all that sweetness and piety. But he knew this notion was not true. She was indeed what she'd seemed when she'd approached him at the door. The light on her shoulders, the gown, her hair up just so, and that smile. Those flowers…the smell of them…

When he pulled himself together again, he knew he had to get up, get out. "Guards!" he tried to call through the gag. His voice sounded ragged and desperate in his own ears, like the cry of some wounded animal. He listened for footsteps. But there was nothing. All was quiet.

With a great effort, Mather managed to roll himself out of the closet, pushing the doors open. With significant further difficulty he was able to free himself from both the comforter and the lavender gown that had come off its hanger, determined to entangle him in a permanent embrace. He made it to his knees, and then to his feet.

He hopped to Panna's bed and sat. He was breathing heavily through his nose now. It hurt him. His whole face hurt him. His head pounded. If he could just get his hands free. Or get this gag off. But all the knots were tight, and each one seemed to pull tighter as he struggled against it.

He cursed silently, looking around the room for anything sharp, anything he might use to cut through these cords. But he had banished all sharp implements from her quarters. He had doomed himself to this fate. He hopped over to the dresser. Hairbrush, ribbons. No help.

Would he have to hop all the way downstairs? He closed his eyes as his anger rose, then turned to embarrassment, then to shame. Then it turned to resignation.

He took a deep breath. So be it.

And he hopped to the door.

Four dragoons were holding a ladder against a tree while a fifth stood at its top, perhaps twenty feet above the ground. He had a long pole in his hand, which he used to jab at the dark spot in the leaves. Lamps lit the branches. It was slow going because he got only one or two pokes in before losing his balance and hugging the tree trunk again, trying to regain his nerve.

"I don't think there's nothin'," he called down.

Prince Mather stood in the doorframe of the palace entrance, gagged, bound, and sweating from his long and clumsy descent. He watched, confused. What on earth were they doing? For a moment he couldn't get the thought out of his head that they were looking for Panna, that Panna had somehow climbed down the trees. Then it occurred to him that he might be the missing one. His confusion turned to rage. The stupidity!

He hopped down to where his brother and his sister stood.

Princess Jacqalyn turned to look at him. She blanched. Her eyes roved up and down him. She covered her mouth, stifling laughter. Finally she spoke. "Gracious, Mather, you always did know how to make an entrance."

Prince Ward turned now, registered shock just briefly, then smiled warmly. He clapped his brother on the shoulder. "I am so glad to see you alive, if not particularly well. Say, you could probably use some help there."

By now, the crowd was buzzing and gathering around their prince. The guests and dragoons were wide-eyed, at once delighted that their prince had not died and yet fearful of his wrath. The dragoon on top of the ladder called out for help, hugging the tree in a panic as those bracing the ladder abandoned their posts. But they did not return; he was left to descend the shaky thing on his own.

Jacqalyn couldn't stop laughing. To her, Mather looked like some dimwitted fish: His mouth was pulled downward by the gag, which accentuated his small chin; his eyes were wide and listless; his arms were pinned behind him, his hands like little dorsal fins; even his feet were bound together like a tail. A purplish lump swelled beside his left eye, at the hairline.

But it wasn't just his appearance she found humorous, but the thought that he had been outwitted, outmaneuvered, and apparently overpowered by the sweet little hero's bride, who had now, finally and with great panache, escaped from his amorous schemes. The great Prince Mather, taking the reins of the state, remaking the halls of power, dismissing as incapable his own father the king, commanding the war himself...this same man stood here in his fine dress best, bound and bruised, as thoroughly humiliated as any man could be. Before God and everyone.

This she found endlessly entertaining.

Panna had made it out of the palace grounds, but she was far from safe.

She had needed to make her way through a good deal of shrubbery in order to stay out of sight, but fortunately, she knew these grounds as well as anyone. She had gotten past the guardhouse just before the alarm was shouted. Why the two gatemen there had simply let her walk out, she couldn't say. But she had put her head high once again, ignoring the fact that her hair was a mess and her dress askew from her scrambles through the brambles. She had apparently made them believe she had every right to be where she was, doing what she was doing.

She was still within the Rampart, within the Old City. The great city wall now loomed before her—three, maybe four blocks away. As she neared she saw that a military checkpoint had been established at the Old Gate, under the stone arch that cut through the wall. She could see soldiers milling about, musket barrels pointed to the sky. They were preparing defenses against the Drammune.

The wall of the Old City, known simply as the Rampart, was over forty feet high. She followed it with her eyes to her left, northward as it rose and fell, its stonework visible wherever the yellow street lamps illuminated it. Guards patrolled along the top, shielded on occasion as they walked past a thick parapet. From these walls they could command much of the entire city, both within and without.

She saw where the Rampart turned, angling west. The ground sloped down from her toward that corner, but in the corner it rose up again slightly, revealing a small clump of buildings that looked familiar to her. But how could they be familiar? She had only been in the city twice before. Once was when Talon led her here, and the other was when she was very young, visiting with her father...

Panna's heart skipped a beat. She turned left at the next street corner, headed for those buildings in the corner of the Old City. She did recognize them. That was the Seminary of Mann. She would find priests there, people who knew Packer, friends of her father. The Church was there, and would rescue her from the State.

Panna found the Seminary ringed by a low iron fence, painted black. The iron posts were pointed, but being only three feet in height and set at three-foot intervals, they were not much of a deterrent. But security was not their purpose; they were designed only to protect grass and gardens from the feet of wayward pedestrians.

Inside the fence were six small cottages and three large, square schoolhouses that also served as dormitories. A chapel stood prominently among them, but was not much bigger than her father's little church in Hangman's Cliffs. Robed seminary students wandered in the gardens, walking in no hurry from building to building to chapel. Panna sighed. All of them were male. Of course. They would have no facilities to take care of a young woman arriving at night without her husband.

She shook her head in disillusioned anger at her country, her people, and their leadership. How did it happen that only men seemed to run anything? And the kind of men in power, in authority...Scat Wilkins in business, Mather Sennett in government. Who headed the Church? Harlowen Stanson, the man they called "Hap," the one who'd given Packer a sword and treated it as though it were a cross. She could only hope he was a better man than the other two.

And then she considered the possibility that at least some of the priests who taught here must be married. The wooden cottage nearest her had a low roof, reaching down almost to eye level. She couldn't decide if its slightly ramshackle look was relaxed or just lazy, inviting her or warning her away. Before she could make up her mind, an elderly priest, dressed in a full, dark-gray robe, stepped out the front door. He was quite wrinkled. As he approached she could see that the skin of his face was very loose, so that it pulled down on his eyes, showing a red half-moon beneath each one. The whites of his eyes seemed oddly yellow, but his pupils were sharp and focused, and they danced as he looked at her. He seemed kind. "Hello," he said gently. "You look as if you've lost your way."

"In a manner of speaking, I suppose I have," she said. "I could use a little help."

He put gentle, wrinkled hands on the black iron fence between them. "We don't get many young ladies in need here. But help is what we do."

"I would very much appreciate a small measure of it."

He looked at her for a moment. "Come, follow me."

"Thank you." She was thankful he didn't ask the hard questions about who she was and why she was out alone at night. They would be difficult to answer right here, in the open, in the dark.

As he turned to lead her to the gate, he glanced quickly around him, as though scanning the area for someone. She followed his gaze, saw only the students milling in the distance. She took another look at the cottage, the warm lights coming from within. Then her eyes caught the small sign on the postal box by the door, dimly lit but quite readable: *Fr. Usher Fell.*

The name held no meaning for her. No one had ever told Panna the name of the priest whose actions here had once caused Packer to lash out in a burst of anger—a response that had led to his expulsion from the Seminary.

CHAPTER 17

Protected

Packer was asleep in his hammock when the knock came. Delaney didn't wait, but stuck his head in and whispered hoarsely. "Packer! Can I come in?" But he was already in, closing the door.

"Sure." Packer sat up and scratched his head. He had been having unsettling dreams, but thankfully they had not been bloody. "What time is it?"

"Middle of the night," he said, lighting Packer's small lamp.

"What's going on? You're not supposed to be here."

"Don't I know that? But I got something you should see." Packer rubbed the sleep from his eyes as Delaney held a bit of cloth up to his face.

"What is it?"

"You tell me."

Packer took it in his hands. It was an odd material, thin and flexible, but firm to the touch. It felt like chain mail, but was much lighter. He tried to unfold it. It was cup-shaped. "Looks like a hat."

"It's what covers them Drammune helmets."

Packer felt a chill as he squinted at it. Now he could tell that it was indeed the crimson color of the Drammune chain mail. The coloring had rubbed off, or had been scratched off, in a couple of places, showing the metallic sheen underneath. This was an article of clothing from a man Packer had killed, no doubt. A heavy curtain dropped down within him. "Why did you want me to see this?"

Delaney took the thing back and pulled it onto his own head. "Hit me."

"What?"

"Hit me in the head." Delaney stood stock still, crossed his arms, squeezed his eyes tight shut. "Careful you don't hurt yourself." He awaited Packer's blow.

Packer was tempted to laugh. "I'm not going to hit you, Delaney," he said gently.

Delaney's eyes popped open. He was disappointed. "Well, fine then. Looky here." Delaney balled his own hand into a fist and struck himself in the head with his knuckles. It knocked like the sound of wood on wood. "See that?"

"Yes. You hit yourself in the head."

Delaney pulled the cap off his head in frustration. "No! This is armor! The helmet it came off was nothin' more than a thick piece a leather. It's this little thing what made their heads into iron skillets. Watch now!" He held out his left hand, palm up, with his fingers spread open so that they formed a cup. Then he put the cap over his hand, covering it. With his right index finger he slowly pushed down on the center of the small expanse of unsupported cloth, pushing the material down to his palm. "Just a piece a' cloth," he said.

"I see that," Packer said, still amused.

"But watch now!" He did the same, but instead of slowly pushing with his finger, he hit the unsupported cloth with his right fist. His knuckles bounced off it, as though it were hard as a steel plate. Now he had Packer's full attention. "See, it's the impact does it," Delaney said with glee. "Stays soft until you strike. Then somehow it all tenses up, like."

Packer took the cap back and studied it. He punched it, felt it harden instantly under his knuckles. He turned it inside out. The back of it was soft like kid. He could see it had been sewn together with thick thread. He looked more closely at the mesh. Now he saw small interlocking plates, in no discernable pattern. A chill went through him. "These are scales."

"It's Firefish hide, and no lie! They colored it all up somehow, but it's the same stuff what's hangin' on our hull."

Packer could only shake his head. It couldn't be. "But they're

Drammune." How would they... "You're saying all their armor is made of this?"

Delaney nodded. "Admiral's got us practicin' to fight like you. He's callin' us 'little Packers'—you know, those who move in and out, like you done. Point is, he gave us their armor, what we took off the dead ones. Next time we fight, he says we'll be protected with this. Just like they were."

The two men stared at each other for a long, quiet moment. Then Packer looked back at the armored cap in his hand. "The only way the Drummune would have this," Packer said simply, "is if Scat Wilkins sold it to them. If John Hand sold it to them."

"Maybe the Drammune figured out how to do it, too. They're a clever lot, you know."

Packer shook his head. Scat had protected his monopoly. "You sailed on this ship a long time."

Delaney felt awkward, then downright uncomfortable as those blue eyes seemed to be searching him. He rubbed his chin thoughtfully. "Well. We sold the meat in a lot a' ports. Leastways, I always thought it was meat. I wouldn'ta knowed if it was other than that. Captain was always secret about it, you know."

"Did you stop in Hezarow Kyne? Anywhere in Drammun?"

"Once. In their big city, what you called it, the Hedgerow Kind. No one but Captain Wilkins and Captain Hand ever went ashore, that I knew anything about. I didn't think we ever even delivered nothin' to 'em. Not even meat. But now I wonder."

All along, Packer thought, *John Hand knew.* He knew the Drammune had this. The whole Firefish industry was suddenly suspect in Packer's mind. Why hadn't he seen it before? But now it was so obvious. "It was never about the meat."

"What?"

"It was never about the meat. That was just the story. To cover the real product." Packer was utterly sure now. No meat, no matter how legendary, could provide the kind of money that might be made by draping an army in invincibility. It all fit now. That would be why Scat was so greedy, and so secretive, why he wanted no fishermen aboard, no ports of call for his crew. He wanted only pirates, who knew better than to ask questions, and who, if they did ask questions, could disappear with no inquests or courts. Scat wanted men like Delaney, who were accustomed to obeying without question.

"Can I borrow this?" Packer asked.

Delaney nodded. "Sure. Anything you want. But what are you going to do with it?"

"I'm going to ask the captain of the *Camadan*, the commander of the *Trophy Chase*, and the Admiral of the Fleet of Nearing Vast just how it is that common sailors in the enemy Armada end up with painted Firefish hides on their hats."

"We obeyed you, sir. And we believed Mrs. Throme," Chunk said proudly, almost defiantly. "If that deserves prison, then so be it." He was so relieved that Panna hadn't killed the prince, he was almost glad to face punishment.

Prince Mather was seated in a velvet-covered chair in the Great Hallway of the Palace just outside the Blue Rooms, his left eye shut, a cold cloth on his temple. "It does deserve prison. Because either you were deceived by her then, or you're trying to deceive me now. And frankly, right now I don't care which. Captain, take them both away." He fluttered his hand about in a gesture of dismissal.

The Captain of the Guard motioned, and two other dragoons stepped forward. Glaring looks from the new prisoners were returned with sympathy by their comrades. But not so much sympathy as to allow any doubt about how this would go. "Hand over your arms," the captain said firmly. He was a solid man, a bit rounder than his uniform was comfortable covering, a bit grayer than he had been when his uniform was tailored, but careful and dutiful and quite comfortable with his long-held, unquestioned authority. He watched as Chunk and his partner handed their pikes and swords to their captors. Then the four guards left the prince's presence.

As they did, a clattering of footsteps approached. "Your Highness!" said a breathless dragoon as he burst through the front door into the hall.

"Yes, what?" Mather asked testily.

"Please your Highness, two gateman saw her leave."

The prince's receding jaw tightened. He stood. "Where are they?"

"Right behind me, sir."

In a moment two guards appeared before their prince, looking as miserable as any two schoolchildren ever summoned before a schoolmaster.

"Well?" Mather asked. "Where is she?"

They stole glances at one another. The older one of the two spoke for them both. "Not sure, sir. We was just changing places, bein' at the end of the shift. She walked by, and we didn't know her. But we now believe it was Panna Throme leavin'."

"Which way did she go?"

"Straight down the street, then turned left before she reached the Old Wall."

"She stayed inside the Rampart?"

"Yes, sir."

The prince turned to the captain. "She was spooked by the checkpoints. Make sure every guard unit at every gate of the Old City knows no young women are to pass through. Then search house-to-house if you have to. I want her back in the palace before dawn." The captain hurried off to make it so.

The prince turned back to the two offenders. "And why didn't you stop her? Were you unaware of the standing orders regarding Mrs. Throme?"

The younger one now spoke up. He was technically the one on duty. "No, sir, we were aware."

"So why did you let her go?"

"We didn't know it was her, sir."

"And who did you think it was? The Queen Mother?"

Agonized silence. They had in fact believed she was a woman of uncertain affiliation, one of Prince Ward's girlfriends, a type they had seen leaving the palace on foot before. The prince was working himself into a state of molten anger when the Captain of the Guard returned, having given orders sufficient, he believed, to ensure Panna's capture. The prince transferred his anger immediately. "I suggest you take two more of your imbeciles to the dungeon," he ordered.

The captain looked surprised.

The Prince stared hard at the two miscreants. "Royal Dragoons indeed." The bitterness in Mather's voice seemed to have been wrung up from his intestines. He spoke as if he believed every ill in the world could be traced directly to the men before him. "How do you find your recruits, Captain? Do you scour the countryside until you've found every village idiot in the kingdom? And how do men who couldn't possibly find their own mouths with a spoon grow so very big? Do you just feed them out of troughs? And how do you keep them from slobbering on their fine uniforms?" Now he screamed at the Captain of the Guard. "Get them out of my sight before I order them all hanged!"

The two guards and their captain all looked as though they'd been kicked in the stomach. They left in a hurry.

Panna turned into the iron gate, at the beckoning of the old priest. He put a hand on her arm. She shuddered involuntarily.

"It's all right, young lady. You're safe here."

She smiled at him. "I just got a little chill, is all." But she pulled her arm away. This was not right. Packer had spoken to her about his departure from the Seminary nearly four years earlier, but only in the broadest terms. Her father had also shielded her from the ugly realities of what had happened here. Those efforts to protect her sensibilities now put her in jeopardy.

But Usher Fell's eyes were warm. "Let's just talk inside."

He escorted her to his cottage. As he opened the door for her and stepped aside to allow her to enter, she stopped, a catch in her spirit. He hadn't even asked her name, hadn't asked the nature of her trouble. A moment ago she had been thankful for it; now that he was inviting her into his cottage it seemed quite odd. He had no idea who she was, and yet he was willing to take her in. She studied his smiling face, searching for some clue. "Is your wife at home?"

"I'm not married, child."

Just then, a friendly voice called out from behind them. "Hello, Father Fell." Panna and the priest both turned to find its source. Panna felt immediate relief.

A smallish priest, round in a robust sort of way, stood looking at them, grinning broadly. He carried a hoe in a gloved hand, and mud was spattered around the hem of his robe where the toes of muddy boots peeked out. His gloves were far too big for him. His face was round and flat but very pleasant. His eyes were naturally puffy, enough so that when he smiled, as he did now, they were little more than slits. But those slits were pleasantly angled half circles, and a sparkle of good humor, or perhaps sharp wit, seemed to leap from them.

Panna laughed. She immediately put a hand to her mouth, realizing this was not nearly the most polite response possible, but then she was not laughing at him, precisely, but because of him. The word that popped into her head was *delight*. He seemed utterly delighted to see them, and so she felt the same in return. The sudden appearance of such an emotion in her was so incongruous with the darkness she had been enduring for days on end, that it simply overcame her inhibition. "I'm sorry," she said, without any elaboration, or any possibility of elaboration.

He seemed completely unfazed by her faux pas, accepting it as though it were a normal response to his presence. "And who is your lovely companion?" he asked Usher Fell. "Won't you introduce me?"

The old priest continued to smile, put his hands together, and looked to Panna. "Ah...actually, we just met. We were about to get further acquainted. The young lady is in some trouble, and so I felt it best to get her off the street and into a...safer place."

"Quite so." Now the little man did not look at Usher Fell, but put a gloved and muddy hand out to Panna. "I'm Father Bran Mooring. And you are...?"

Panna beamed. "Father Mooring! I'm so pleased to meet you!" She reached out to the muddy glove, but he finally realized his own error and fumbled with it, quickly pulling the glove off. She grasped his warm hand with two of hers. "Sorry," he said, "I was trying to get to my cultivating all day and just finally got it done."

"My husband has told me such wonderful things about your teaching," she said. "Wonderful things."

"Really? That's so nice to hear. And who is your husband?"

"Packer Throme."

Father Mooring glanced happily at Usher Fell, who seemed to take a large step backward, though his feet never actually moved. Bran Mooring's sense of delight only grew.

"Ah, Packer! I certainly enjoyed him. Wonderful mind for the things of God. A great spirit. He's done large things in the greater world of late. We're all so proud here. Aren't we, Father Fell?"

"So very proud," Fell managed.

Panna beamed.

"I think of him often," Bran continued, "particularly when I'm looking for examples of those who 'hunger and thirst after righteousness.' I always felt he was like that, you know, someone who simply wanted everything to be right, and good. He struggled so with the burden of evil in the world. So he always struck me, at least."

"Yes. He struck me also," said Usher Fell grimly, rubbing his jaw. "You know, I'm just thinking. You two seem to have so much in common, and so much to talk about. Father Mooring, I wonder if you would be so kind as to take a bit of time to find out about Mrs. Throme's current difficulties."

"Well, of course I will! If that's all right with you, Mrs. Throme? Or may I call you Panna?"

"Why, yes. Panna is fine. But how do you know my name?" she asked, already following along as he led her away from Usher Fell.

"Well, it would have been quite difficult to know Packer Throme for any length of time without knowing something about Panna Seline, the girl back home. And I must say, you are every bit as beautiful and charming as he led us all to believe."

Packer. Tears stung Panna's eyes as she followed the small man's muddy footsteps to the doorway of his cottage.

"And how is your father, Will Seline?"

"You know him?"

"Why, of course. We're not close, but there are a limited number of priests in this kingdom, and only one Seminary. Will Seline has a great heart. A great heart. I've said before that if God were to answer only one man's prayers on this whole earth, I believe it would be his."

"He does have his good points." She wiped a tear away, trying not to let her voice break. She looked up to heaven and paused just before she entered the priest's home. Stars shone brightly, and the moon reflected the hidden glory of the sun. She was thankful to the God of the Universe, to the core of her being. All was working out, just as her father had predicted.

She felt safe.

The priest's small cottage was a wonderland of knickknacks and bric-a-brac and artwork, large and small. Every inch of every wall, it seemed, was covered with parchments or paintings or framed squares of line drawings, or handwritten thank-you notes, poems, and every other type of memorabilia. The floor, except for the one deep, thickly-woven rug before the fireplace, and a few pathways to and from it, was stacked with books and statuettes and paintings and sketches lacking frames, frames lacking paintings, and a host of odd implements of every description, from farming, fishing, shoemaking, haberdashery, and many other trades. A cluttered desk against one wall was stacked with papers and books. Four chairs faced one another at the four corners of the rug, each draped with not one but two or three blankets, knitted, crocheted, or quilted, so that the chairs themselves were barely recognizable as chairs.

After removing his boots and gloves, Father Mooring trimmed several lamps. Panna closed the heavy curtains of his sitting room and bolted the door shut behind them. The priest noted her actions without comment, then went to the fireplace and began to stir it. "I'll put on a pot of tea," he suggested as he fanned the flames. "Do you like tea? I could make coffee."

"Tea would be wonderful. But about the trouble I'm in. I'm afraid I may..." she hated to bring such ugly realities into such a pleasant place, but she knew she must, "...pursued."

He paused and looked at her. "Are you running away from the law, or are you running toward it?"

She set her jaw. He didn't seem to suggest he'd mind either way. But it was hard to form the words. "Away, I suppose. But I have done nothing illegal. At least, nothing that wasn't justified." She knew how weak that sounded.

He looked back into the flames, seemed satisfied with the job he'd done. "I have some nice jasmine tea, from the East. Actually, it's Drammune, but I won't tell if you won't."

"I won't."

He smiled at her and went into the kitchen, busying himself loudly with the banging of pots and the clattering of cabinet doors and an incomprehensible screech of metal or two. "My house is always full of people, you see!" he sang out from the kitchen, "even when I'm home alone. I started collecting little items from my students years ago. It's gotten rather out of hand, I'm afraid. Now they send me things from their travels. Their work. I have students' children sending me things now. Trouble is, I can't seem to throw a thing away."

"All of these are gifts?"

"Most of them," he said, coming back into the room with a large teapot and a bright, proud smile. "Some are items I simply kept to remind me."

"And how long have you been teaching?"

"Oh, heavens. Forever. I don't know, twenty-five years? No, more than that now." He put the teapot on an iron hook over the flames. "There. It will be ready in just a few moments." He saw Panna scanning the walls and floors, as though looking for something.

He walked to the wall opposite the one she searched, and took a framed sketch from it. "This is what you're looking for, I believe." He handed it to her. It was a line drawing of a sea monster, very much like the one above Cap Hillis's pub. "By a young student named Packer Throme."

She smiled. "Firefish."

"His father's interest back then, I believe."

She handed it back to him, sadness growing in her. "His now."

"Ah yes, quite famously so. But we haven't talked about your trouble." His voice was gentle as he took the frame, returned it to its place. "Please, sit by the fire."

She did, and he sat down in the other lumpy chair by the hearth.

"I don't know where to begin," she said truthfully. "There's so much."

"We will have time enough. Perhaps we should start with why you are out by yourself tonight after dark in the Old City, a young bride from Hangman's Cliffs."

She took a deep breath. "I have escaped from the palace, where the prince has been holding me against my will."

She was afraid he would be startled by such news, but if he was, he didn't show it. "The prince. Mather Sennett, or his brother, Ward?"

"Mather. I hit him in order to escape. He won't stop looking for me until he finds me, I'm afraid."

The priest's dancing eyes looked into hers for quite a while. "You and Packer are a pair, I see."

"I suppose so. But my father's still in danger."

"Your father?"

"Yes, he was arrested, and the prince is holding him to get me to...comply."

Now Father Mooring's eyebrows went up. "Serious indeed."

"It's not as bad as it could be. But it's plenty bad. And now I've brought my troubles on you."

"Oh, I am happy to share your troubles! I have so few of my own."

She looked at him blankly, expecting some evidence that this was a joke, but she quickly realized he was perfectly serious. He was stating what to him was a simple fact. The thought of a life with few troubles was refreshing, like a warm sea breeze coming off the surf. And the thought of someone willing to take her burdens as his own was like the sun rising over that same pristine beach.

" 'In this world you will have trouble,' " he quoted abruptly. " 'But fear not, for I have overcome the world.' Do you believe that? "

"Which part?" she asked glumly.

He laughed, a bubbling thing. "Why, both parts."

"Yes, I suppose I do. But I'm ready for a little more of the overcoming part."

"It has ever been so." The teapot whistled. "Well, let's have tea!" He hurried off to the kitchen and returned with two cups and a tea strainer full of small, chopped leaves. Panna kept glancing at the door as he poured, sure there would be an urgent knock any moment.

When they were both seated again by the warm fire with cups of hot tea in their hands, he looked at her and smiled again. "Are you afraid? Of the prince?" The way he asked it, without scolding, made it easy to answer.

"Yes. I'm very afraid. And not just for me, but for my father."

"Hmm. You don't seem a fearful person at all." He sipped. "I love jasmine."

She sipped, too, and tried to pay attention to the taste. It was strong, rich, and sweet, and it smelled of far away places. But she could not give in to it. "Maybe I'm not fearful. But I'm plenty worried." She glanced at the door again.

"The prince will not harm you. Not while you're here."

"I don't think you know the prince very well."

"If you're here, God has led you here. If the prince comes here, he'll find out who he should fear, soon enough." The bold words seemed quite incongruous with the tone in which they were spoken. He smiled warmly. "Tell me everything."

Panna nodded. She didn't really believe he could help, one little priest in a cottage full of memories. But she didn't know who he might know, or how he might be connected. And he certainly seemed comfortable with the idea that he could protect her. Or rather, that

God could. And since he was apparently the help God had sent her, she could hardly turn him down.

She had gotten through most of the tale, all but the escape through the hedges, when there was a loud banging on the door. Panna jumped; it was a harsh and brutal noise.

"Open up! Royal Dragoons! We have orders to search!"

Outside, the Captain of the Guard himself stood in front of the door, having decided the prince's mood required him to take personal charge of the search. He was flanked by two other guards, one with a pike in his hand, the other with a battle-axe.

Standing in the dark behind the three of them was Father Usher Fell.

Panna jumped to her feet, reproaching herself silently. Why had she been sitting here, having tea, allowing herself to be charmed by this priest, when she could have been running?

"There, there," Father Mooring said in a whisper. "All shall be well."

"Do you have a back door?" she asked.

"I'm afraid not. And even if I did, it wouldn't help. They'd have men posted there." He smiled, then very deliberately stood up.

"Father Mooring! We know the fugitive woman is in there. Do not make us break down this door!"

"I'm coming!" Bran called. Then he sighed, and whispered to Panna. "You'll be fine, really."

"You meant for me to be caught!" she accused him, in a hoarse whisper. Her eyes were aflame. "You're on *his* side. I'm so stupid, drinking tea with a silly old—"

"Shhh! Now don't be hasty," he whispered back, holding up one hand, balancing his teacup in the other. "Or you'll say something you'll regret." He smiled. "Follow me." He said it in an encouraging tone, and since he walked into his kitchen rather than toward his front door, she followed.

Loud banging on the door continued. "Open up! We'll be breaking this door down in ten seconds! This is your last warning."

"One moment!" Bran calmly put his teacup in among a stack of dirty dishes. "Over there, my dear," he said gently, pointing toward the floor on the far side of the small stove. "I hope you don't mind tight spaces. It's a bit dank, but it will only be for a short while, I hope."

The axe hit the front door.

"What?" she asked.

The priest gestured again, this time with an open palm, toward the floor at his feet. Now she saw the square hole, not much wider than her shoulders. A wooden ladder led downward. She immediately sat at the edge of it, gathered her gown around her, and started down.

The axe slammed the door again.

"Stay on the ladder," he instructed.

"Watch your head now," he said calmly. As her head cleared the plane of the floor, the priest slid the oven back over the top of her, with the same scraping sound she had heard when he was busy making tea. And then she was in darkness.

"Goodness, what a racket!" the priest shouted as he walked to his front door. "I'm coming! My, can't a man have a quiet moment in his own home?" He opened the door and immediately examined the axe marks in it. Then he smiled up at the guard. "You'll need a good woodsman's axe if you're going to chop through solid oak."

"Out of the way," the Captain of the Guard said gruffly, "or he'll be chopping something much softer."

"My." Bran Mooring stepped aside.

The cottage was tiny. There were three rooms: living, bed, kitchen. A toolshed stood outside. And that was it. The eaves followed the roofline, so there was no attic. There were no stairs to any sort of cellar. It took the guards no more than twenty seconds to search the entire place. Then the captain turned on Usher Fell.

"You said she was here."

Usher Fell shriveled, shrugged, pointed at Father Mooring. "She came in here with Father Mooring, that's all I know."

Father Mooring stood serenely by his fireplace, drinking tea from Panna's cup. The captain turned his haggard gaze on him. "She was here, wasn't she?"

"Who?"

"Panna Throme."

"Ah, the wife of our national hero."

"Yes, and wanted for assaulting a member of the royal family. Was she here or was she not? I want the truth."

"You don't want the truth."

"Of course I do!"

"No—no you don't. But I'll tell it anyway."

"And you'll tell it now!"

"Very well. The truth is this: Panna Throme was here in this room tonight. She was here because Prince Mather, whose bidding you are now doing, has abused his privileges with her. Anything she did to protect herself is fully justifiable, whereas the prince's actions are not. If you find her and take her back to him, he will continue his shameful conduct, and you will be as guilty as he."

The captain's eyes went wide. "That is none of your business!"

"The truth is my business." He gestured at his robes. "But as I said, it's really not what you want to hear."

The captain stepped closer, put a finger in Bran Mooring's face. "If you think you're safe from me because you're wearing a robe, you're sadly mistaken."

Bran looked him in the eye. "I am sad, but I am not mistaken. And you should not be mistaken, either. You can do no more to me than God allows."

"I am willing to test that limit."

"And I am willing," the priest said with great determination, and in a tone that sounded like a threat, "to submit to whatever test God allows you to bring me!"

The captain looked perplexed. The attitude was there, but the words were anything but intimidating. He shook his head, unwilling to follow Father Mooring's moral logic, whatever it was. "Where did she go?"

"Into hiding."

"Where?"

"That I cannot say."

"Don't play games with me. Did she tell you where she was going or not?"

"She did not."

"Would you tell me if she did?"

The priest's intensity turned soft, and he smiled. "Now, my dear Captain. Why ask me a question like that? If I would lie to you about what she told me, would I not lie about whether I would lie?"

The captain grabbed the priest's robe at the throat. His teacup hit the floor and broke in half. "What is it you know that you aren't saying?"

"Well, quite a few things, I would guess. But pertinent to the moment, I know this: While you attempt to wrench information from me that I would not give you even if I did know it, time melts away. If she's not here, I would suggest you search for her somewhere else." He nodded at the doorway.

"She's not here," the captain said to his men as he released the priest. "Go find her." But after they left the room, he turned on Bran Mooring one more time. "If you've lied to me, you'll go to prison."

"The fact is, I have not lied to you. But the truth is, the facts will not keep me out of prison if you determine I should go."

The captain looked quizzical. "You think you're the only one with a moral obligation or a shred of conscience. But you're not."

"I'm glad to hear that."

"If she's innocent, I will do all in my power to keep her safe."

Father Mooring's look turned compassionate. "But dear Captain—how much power is in your power? Can you keep her safe from the prince?"

The captain said nothing. After a moment, he turned and left the priest's home.

The priest locked the door behind him, then peered out from behind the curtains for some time. When he was finally satisfied he was in no imminent danger of their return, he picked up his broken teacup, examining it as he walked back to his kitchen. He dropped both halves into the pile of dirty dishes, and slid the stove away.

Panna climbed out. She was covered in dirt and dust, but otherwise she was fine. "Thank you," she said. "I'm so sorry for what I said."

He looked confused. "About what?"

"I doubted you."

He beamed. "Not at all! I am in fact quite a foolish old man, you know. But fortunately, God in His grace intervenes on my behalf quite regularly. In most cases, that more than makes up for my own shortcomings."

"Why do you have a hiding place like this in your kitchen?"

"For hiding you, of course! I just didn't know it until tonight. Up until now I've thought it was for hiding onions and potatoes, storing butter, and saving up a little bit of beer."

"That's not why you built it."

"I didn't build it at all. It's ages older than me. The Old City is full of secrets, and since we are not fifty feet from the Rampart, I can only assume that at one time some passageway led to the tunnels within it." He waved a hand. "Ancient history now. But your dress is ruined, I'm afraid."

She looked at the dark dirt and dust on her hands and arms and down the front of her dress. Her wide, starched skirts had functioned like a chimney brush. "It certainly needs a good cleaning."

"May I make a suggestion?"

"Please."

"I have several robes. You're a bit taller than me, not so round, but I'm sure one of them would be a comfortable fit. And you will be far less noticeable around these grounds in a hooded robe."

"That would be very kind."

"I'll just pour you some hot water so you can bathe off some of that grime."

"Thank you." She followed him to the living room, where he pulled the teapot from the fire with a heavy rag. "Is there anything you can do for my father?"

"Well. He was put in prison by the prince. Not many powers in the land can undo that."

"I was hoping, perhaps the Seminary could appeal directly to the king?"

He nodded, carrying the teapot into the kitchen. She followed, watching as he set it on the stove and found a large bowl, and blew dust out of it. "The dean of our Seminary is the head of the Church. The High Holy Reverend and Supreme Elder, Father Harlowen Stanson."

"Hap." She fought disappointment, though she didn't know why.

"Hap. He has the ear of the prince. But I would be hesitant to seek his help in this matter." Panna stared in silence as he poured some of the hot water into the bowl, then tapped the surface with a finger. "Needs some water to cool it just a bit."

"But why?" Panna asked. "He has power. He should be able to use it."

"Ah, he has power, and he is certainly able to use it." The little priest picked up a brown jug and glugged a cup or so of cool water into the bowl. "But I am sorry to report to you that he does not always choose to use his power as you or I might hope, or expect, from the highest cleric in the land." He tapped the water with his finger again, then settled a hand into it. "There. That's better."

He looked up at Panna with a smile, which melted as he saw her stricken look. "Yes...well, you see, in every heart there is good and there is evil. I wish it were that only good would be allowed in the hearts of those who enter the work of the Church. But it is not so. Men everywhere are free to choose. Even after they become priests."

"You're saying Father Stanson is an evil man?"

Father Mooring held up a hand. "All of us are evil, except to the extent that God makes our hard hearts soft. But like your Prince Mather—"

"He's not mine."

Father Mooring smiled sadly. "Like our Prince Mather, he has made choices. Not all of them have been wise."

"I know all about the prince's choices. What about Father Stanson?"

Bran Mooring looked quite empathetic. "He has made the choice to align himself with, and befriend, and draw power from, the king. And Prince Mather."

Panna was crestfallen. "He'd turn me over to the prince."

"I believe he might."

"So what can be done?"

"We can pray."

Panna sighed.

"God has His designs. We can ask Him to release your father, and set things right. He's far more interested in justice and mercy than we are."

"Well, I know He's interested in mercy. But I sometimes wonder about justice."

"I do not wish God's justice upon anyone, even my worst enemy." The priest shivered at the thought. Then he brightened and said, "I'll get you that robe."

The priest did own a hairbrush. He was quite sure of this, though his certainty was not accompanied by any actual evidence, at least not for the several minutes during which he contemplated, scratched his nearly bald head, looked in cupboards and cabinets, then contemplated with furrowed brow once again, then searched an old knapsack and a duffel bag. Finally he looked deeply into a lower shelf in the kitchen, behind an ancient tin of brown shoe polish, and produced a flattened, matted bristle brush. "Dried boot paste," he said glumly, poking the offending substance hardened among the bristles. "I knew I hadn't thrown it away."

"I can go without a hairbrush," Panna said cheerfully. "Really."

But he kept thinking. Her hair was a mess, as she had needed to wash it in order to get the dirt out of it, and even as she protested, she couldn't quit running her fingers through it, trying to remove the tangles.

"Wait!" He returned to his living room and cleared a path through the knickknacks and whatnots until he found a small, shiny black box, just about big enough for a child's pair of shoes. He opened it and took out a small brush, the head of which was no bigger than two gold coins laid end to end. "It's Urlish," he said proudly, holding it up. "Sent to me by a student who went abroad as a missionary. I believe it's actually a doll's brush." He handed it to her. "The Urlah have quite an extravagant culture when it comes to their children. At least, in the upper classes."

She held it delicately. It was quite ornate, made of silver inlaid with mother-of-pearl. "It's beautiful. Are you sure you want me to use this? It was a gift."

"Dear Panna," Bran said with a smile. "It sat in that box for more than ten years. Once you're gone, it will sit in there for ten more, if God wills. I would be pleased if you would put it to use once in the middle."

"Well, then, if you're sure."

"I am, quite."

She began brushing her hair. After a while, looking into the fire, she asked, "Father Mooring, why is it that men are so wicked?"

He looked up from his book. "Are you asking about mankind, or men as a sex?"

She thought a moment. "I suppose it's the same thing, isn't it? No offense meant to you, but isn't it always men who ruin everything with their greed and their lusts?"

"I would only remind you of Talon, who started this current war."

Panna thought again. "She seems like an exception."

"She certainly was exceptional. But I believe that men and women are equally lost. So the Scriptures say. It's just that the evil in our hearts shows itself in different ways."

She stopped brushing and looked at him. "Different how?"

"Well, I think men are quicker to accept their own wickedness. They will give up on goodness, and consciously embrace evil, for any number of reasons. For a gain in the short term, for power in the long, for some passion or some ambition, as in the case of the prince. Women, however, when they give up on goodness, tend more often to justify their actions to themselves. They will try to convince themselves and others that what they are doing, no matter how vile, is actually a good thing. Or at least, that it's making the very best of a bad situation."

"So you think women are more often deceived, while men more often commit evil with eyes wide open. Like in Eden."

He smiled. "You are a quick student as well. But it is complicated, and certainly it doesn't hold true in every case."

"But wouldn't that make a woman's sins less bad? Isn't it better to do wickedness believing it's good, even telling yourself it's good, than to do it purposefully, knowing it's wicked?"

Father Mooring smiled somewhat bashfully. "Ah, well. There is the heart of the matter. If I am correct, then you and I might never come to agreement on that point."

With their conversation wound to a comfortable halt, Father Mooring sat in his chair, working on his lessons. But he glanced up on occasion, as Panna brushed her hair out, sitting before the blazing fireplace.

And then, glancing up once more, he realized he had misspoken. That little brush would never go back into its black box. She would take it with her. Or, if she left it behind, it would sit out on one of his side tables, or perhaps even find a place of honor on a wall. Then, when he was by himself again, as he most often was, and when he started to feel lonely, as he too often did, he would be able to look at it, as he did all his precious things, and remember.

And he knew exactly what he would remember. He would recall their conversations, of course, and how God had protected her from the dragoons. But what he would remember most fondly was this very moment—when God allowed the fine, troubled young wife of one of his dearest, most remarkable students, in spite of all her dire circumstances, to sit in front of his warm fire, wearing his own brown priest's robe, and unselfconsciously brush out her long, dark hair.

And he would be thankful.

CHAPTER 18

The Quarto

Talon was cloaked in her warrior's robes, hood up, head down. It was impossible to recognize her as a woman, much less the infamous wife of the Hezzan. She stood outside a small building in a humble part of the city, where all the buildings were built of clay bricks, and the wooden and tin roofs were painted red to look like the more expensive tiles in neighborhoods further up the hillsides. Beside Talon stood Sool Kron, also dressed in informal robes. They awaited an invitation to enter.

"You have sent a message that you are willing to bring the Zealots into your Court of Twelve?" Sool Kron asked.

"Yes," she answered. "They understand what is at stake for them."

"You are a brave woman. You are taking a great risk to come here," he said.

"I have taken greater," she said easily. The fact that heavily armed members of the Hezzan Guard blocked all four streets with access to this building gave weight to her words. The fact that, at each hip, she had a long knife she could have in her hands within seconds, further bolstered her claim. But she knew she was about to put herself, her future, and her child at the mercy of the Zealots. And mercy was not their strong suit.

A gruff man, poorly dressed and unkempt, opened the door. "You may enter now," he said.

Once inside the doorway, the humble building grew humbler yet. The vestibule in which they stood was unpainted, the floorboards filthy. Two men with swords drawn stood watch as two others began searching Kron and Talon to ensure they were unarmed. All four were dressed poorly, barely above the level of rags. This was a particular vanity of the Zealots: the appearance of poverty. In truth, the order owned nearly half the city.

One man patted Kron, but the other stood with his hands out, unmoving, suddenly realizing he could not fulfill his duty. If he touched Talon, a woman who was not his wife, he would be guilty of a criminal act, according to the Rahk-Taa.

She smiled at him, arms open. "Have you no women you trust for such duty?"

"I will vouch for her," Kron said, before any of them could answer.

She nodded her thanks as they were ushered from the vestibule into a wide, circular room. It was dark except for two floor lamps on either side of a long table. Behind the table sat the four men who had risen to the pinnacle of Worthiness, who oversaw the resurgence of the true nature of Drammun and the purifying of their homeland. They used no names, having given up their individual identities to the service of Rahk, the Law. They were the Quarto.

Talon studied them. Three were young, in their twenties or early thirties. The fourth was in his forties. It was known that three of them had killed their predecessors and the fourth had aided the other three. She guessed correctly that it was the elder who had engineered the coup. All, however, were grim-faced, dour, with hair and beards uncut.

As her eyes adjusted to the light, she realized that all along the walls men were seated; a silent gallery, perhaps forty Zealots, here to witness these proceedings. Every one of them had a sword at his hip. She flicked her eyes over to Kron, wondering if this was a surprise to the old politician also. But either he was unconcerned about it, or pretended to be.

"What is it you require of the Quarto?" asked the eldest bluntly. He was seated second from the right as Talon faced them.

"Please Your Worthiness," Sool Kron cooed, "the woman Talon requests permission to speak on her own behalf."

The gruff elder answered, "She may speak." Talon stepped forward and removed her hood, displaying hair cropped, but grown long enough now to cover most of the scarring. Sool Kron noticed for the first time that she wore the triple golden earring that signified a wife of the Hezzan. He was quite sure he had never seen her wear it before. Talon opened her mouth, but before she could speak, the elder began to question her.

"Do you place yourself under the jurisdiction of this body?"

"I do."

"And do you swear before the Quarto and the Law that the decisions made here by this body will bind you in life unto death?"

A chill went through her. "I do, according to the Law."

"And in turn this body swears to make the Worthy judgment, according to the Rahk-Taa, witnessed by the Worthies here present. Speak."

"I have come to claim the Kar Ixthano," she said, "to claim rights, titles, and property according to the Rahk-Taa."

The elder nodded. At this, Sool Kron stepped away from Talon so that he stood off to her left at a right angle between her and the Quarto. Talon's honed instincts for battle lit up within her. He was leaving her side, leaving her to her own devices. Treachery walked in those small footsteps. She now saw it in Kron's eyes, felt it in the room. He had spoken to them already! But how?

"Make your claim," the leader commanded.

Talon raised her chin with a look of defiance. "Before I do, Your Worthiness, I would like clarification regarding the laws that govern my claim. If I may."

There was some slight shifting in chairs, and the leader glanced at Sool Kron. But now Kron did not take his eyes off Talon.

"Ask," the elder allowed.

"Only the Quarto may grant the Ixthano. Is this correct?"

"Yes," the elder answered proudly.

"And does the Rahk-Taa allow for a mere woman to claim the Ixthano?"

The elder looked to the Quarto member seated to his left, a bookish, bespectacled man, and nodded at him.

"Only at the request of her husband," the other said, as he put his left hand on the ancient, leather-bound volume before him. He was the legal expert in these matters.

The room filled with whispers. Talon looked at Kron. He shrugged, as if to say he couldn't have known about this. But behind his eyes was that same gloating victory she had seen at her wedding. She was surrounded by enemies, none of whom expected her to leave this place alive.

When quiet returned, Talon spoke evenly. "I am a warrior. Are there no exceptions for the Mortach Demal?"

The younger one gained another slight nod of permission from the elder. "Only on the field of battle," he said.

"Single combat, or armies joined in battle?"

He looked at his fellow members, then shrugged. "Either."

She nodded. "Are there no other exceptions?"

"There are others," admitted the younger man. "In the case of—"

The elder cut in. "The Quarto is not here to educate you on the Rahk-Taa. Make your claim, and accept our judgment as you have sworn to do."

She looked at Sool Kron. He met her gaze with the merest trace of a raised eyebrow. It was barely a twitch, but it told her he wanted her to know what he had done, and that he had outwitted her. Talon spoke while looking directly at Kron. "Then I will make my claim as having been won in single combat."

The whispers returned. Each man in the Quarto nodded, glanced at the others. They were surprised, but not displeased, that she would continue this brazen attempt to take the Hezzan's kingdom for herself. They had in fact been in touch with Sool Kron, through a sympathetic Hezzan guardsman. All four members understood that by making the claim for the Right of Transfer, Talon would jeopardize herself. First, she would put herself under their jurisdiction; and then she would claim the Hezzan was an Unworthy who had died willingly for his own wife, a mere woman, yet who was somehow more Worthy than he. When this preposterous claim was denied on the basis of her gender, she would be accountable for attempting to steal his lands and titles and thus make herself emperor. These were offenses punishable by death. They would execute that punishment where she stood. Kron would become Hezzan, and the Quarto would lead the Twelve.

The Quarto was therefore greatly relieved to learn that Talon, while apparently astute enough to have uncovered the gender trap, was prepared to make her situation worse, if possible, and their ruling more just yet. Rather than claim the Second Law, she would claim the First: that the Hezzan was an Unworthy whom she had killed in single combat. This was an offense far greater than plotting to steal his throne. It would be impossible for her to prove he was Unworthy, especially with the countering testimony of Sool Kron. When she failed, she would die. Kron would become Hezzan, and the Quarto would, again, lead the Twelve.

But as the Quarto's confidence swelled, Kron's faltered. He was worried. He believed Talon had courage enough to stand up to anyone, including these four self-inflated ministers of supreme justice. But to claim to have murdered the Hezzan? She was not so stupid. His mind raced; she must have some other design.

"Make your claim," the elder repeated.

Kron opened his mouth to plead for more time, but Talon spoke first. Her voice showed no emotion. "I claim the First Law of Kar Ixthano, for an Unworthy enemy of Rahk, killed by my hand in single combat."

Kron closed his eyes. In a flash of realization, he knew. Of course! He had been blind to it. "Your Worthiness, if I may—" he tried.

"Silence!" the leader roared. "You may not. Woman, state your claim."

Talon smiled at the Quarto's hunger, their greediness for her demise. Then she turned to Kron, savoring the moment. Now she raised her eyebrow almost imperceptibly. Kron gritted his teeth.

"The enemy of Rahk, the Unworthy I have slain," she said, turning back to the Quarto, "is the Traitor, Senslar Zendoda."

The room erupted. The Quarto looked over at Kron in a single movement, as though their heads were yoked to a swivel. But he smiled. Suddenly, he seemed not at all perturbed; he looked at Talon and nodded, letting her know how impressed he was with her. And he was, in fact, very impressed. He had said he would not underestimate her again, but he had, and for the same reason as before: her sex.

"What does the Rahk-Taa require from you in judgment?" Talon asked, as soon as it was possible to be heard. "Have I earned the Kar Ixthano for this deed?"

The Quarto conferred briefly, but the decision was foregone. The story was well-known. She had been celebrated by the Hezzan himself for this act. The Hezzan had many times referred to the slaying as single combat, and he had publicly claimed not to have ordered it done. It was her glory alone. And the Quarto had brought all these witnesses.

After a moment, the elder spoke. His voice was lower than it had been, but no less gruff. "The Kar Ixthano is granted, in duty to Rahk."

The instant the words were out of his mouth, Talon spoke again. "As the owner of the dominion of Senslar Zendoda, including all his rights and privileges as a man of noble birth in Drammun," she put a slight but noticeable emphasis on the word *man*, "I now claim the Second Law of Kar Ixthano, pertaining to an Unworthy man who gave his life willingly in exchange for mine, taking arrows meant for me." She paused. They waited. "I claim the dominion of the Hezzan Shul Dramm."

The room roared with shouts and oaths, men crying out for justice, then died down just as quickly as all waited for the judgment of the Quarto. The elder looked shaken; he was unable to speak. Finally, the young man to his right, silent until now, stood. He was agitated. He looked sour and peevish. "And so you claim to be more Worthy than the Hezzan."

"I do."

"On what basis?"

"On the basis of the Rahk, as laid forth in the Rahk-Taa."

"What right do you have to interpret the Rahk?" the elder steamed.

"Let her speak," the peevish one said, quite certain she would hang herself.

"Please Your Worthiness, I cannot speak with authority on these matters, and have only my perceptions to bring. I require your ruling." Talon said it calmly, submissively. She nodded at them, and continued. "My belief is that the Hezzan defied the Rahk-Taa by marrying a warrior. He defied it again by decreeing that she should be both warrior and wife. He defied it a third time, and defied all that is Worthy, by elevating his wife above the status of the Council of Twelve. These are the three offenses on which I base my claim."

Shocked silence reigned. Her list was appalling. She stated the very accusations that the Quarto had hurled at the Hezzan for weeks now, in the exact language they had used. She was quoting the Quarto.

The elder now burned with rage. She had trapped them. He glared at Sool Kron. He had done this to them! He spit a molten-hot question at her: "And you dare to accuse the Hezzan of crimes of which you are equally guilty?"

Talon bowed her head. "I am but a woman. I have obeyed my Hezzan, and my husband, even against my own wishes. If that is a crime, then I am guilty."

The silence in the room only deepened. A chair in the gallery creaked. Every man present knew that the Quarto was caught fast in their own beliefs, strung up by their own dogma. They were flies in her web. Without abandoning all pretext of basing their rulings on the Rahk-Taa, or without reversing their public position entirely, they could not execute any judgment against her. She was a dutiful, obedient wife, precisely what they taught every woman should be. And when she wasn't, she was destroying the Unworthy, on the basis of the very charges the Quarto had voiced.

The peevish one, still standing, spoke again. "Can you prove he martyred himself for you? Where are your witnesses?" It was a weak question, and he knew it.

"I can state that he did so," Talon answered humbly. "By the rights of Senslar Zendoda, and his nobleman's title, I need no witnesses. Rather, you must prove—"

"Do not tell us what we must prove!" The elder banged his fist on the table. "Zendoda was a traitor! You have a traitor's dominion," he screamed. Then he leaned in, conferring in harsh whispers with the others. The peevish one leaned down, listened, but kept shaking his head. He waved off the discussion, faced Talon again. "No crimes of an enemy combatant can be transferred in the Ixthano. Zendoda's dominion, not his crimes, have been transferred to you. However, to claim the Kar Ixthano, the arrows that killed the Hezzan must have been meant for you, and he must have taken them willingly in your place."

"Yes, Your Worthiness. He knew my life was in danger, and he swept me aside from where I stood and stepped to the window himself, to be killed in my place."

"We must accept your account of his intentions, but—"

"We must do nothing of the sort!" the elder fairly shouted.

The peevish one glared at him, then turned back to Talon. "According to the Rahk-Taa, as you have the rights of a nobleman, we must accept your statement of his intentions," he repeated. "But we will need time to find witnesses who may counter your claim that those arrows were meant for you."

The elder still threw off fire, but now he aimed it solely at his fellow council member. "How dare you speak for this Quarto!" Every man in the gallery shifted uncomfortably. The elder glared at each of the three younger members in turn.

"If I may," Sool Kron purred. And now he stepped back to stand beside Talon. He stroked his beard. All looked at him, hoping for a solution. This time, they would hear him out. "Please Your Worthinesses. The Council of Twelve, against my will and my best arguments, did seek to kill the woman Talon, with arrows, at her window that night. This was their plot. They admitted such in the presence of Vasla Vor, General Commander of the Hezzan Guard. Without my consent, the other eleven plotted the murder of Talon. It was never their intention to kill the Hezzan. He died saving his wife. These men are, I might add, justly imprisoned now for these Unworthy acts."

"Do you swear to this as Chief Minister of State of the Kingdom of Drammun?" asked the peevish one.

"I do."

The elder opened his mouth but found no words.

The peevish one nodded, looking decidedly less peevish now. "Very well." He looked at Talon. "Have you stated all your proofs of the Hezzan's unrighteousness?"

"There is one more," Talon answered.

"State it."

What she was about to say had not been part of her plan. Rather, it had come to her as she watched these fools force all of reality through the sieve of their pride-driven belief system. The Hezzan was a good man, a better person than Talon. This was apparent to any who knew them both. Talon had killed in hatred, had despised God and man. But the Hezzan had cared deeply for his nation, his people, and for Talon, and he had seen in her what others had not. He had raised her out of her selfish anger, and given her a more noble view of the world, and of the people in it. And because he had cared for her, he had chosen, in a moment, to risk everything to protect her. It was that simple. But the Quarto did not understand, nor want to understand, the true and powerful motivation for the self-sacrifice at the heart of his actions. So she would force them to address it.

"He died for me," she said simply.

"This is a proof of his Unworthiness?"

"You must decide, of course. But the Rahk-Taa does not speak to any reason that a Worthy man would ever choose to die in the place of the Unworthy. Therefore if he chose to die for me, he must have known, or believed, that I was Worthy of such a sacrifice."

The silence of the room was now the silence of a bent bow. With a single statement she had gone beyond using the words of the Quarto against them. She was using the very heart of the teachings of the Rahk-Taa.

She was correct, of course. The Three Laws of Kar Ixthano did not account for a good man who would die for someone who was not. Such was absurdity. If the good, the noble, the Worthy were to die for the evil, the ignoble, the Unworthy, how could the Worthy ever rule? If the highest calling was, as taught in the Vast religion, to lay down one's life for others, regardless of their Worthiness, then the best of all men on earth would always be dead, or dying. And dead men cannot rule. Only the miserable, maddening teachings of the Vast and their Jesus dared claim honor in such foolishness.

But Talon now understood the nature of God's power—that it came in through a window, or a back door, and rarely came announced. She had fled all her life from a doctrine that demanded, that elevated as the highest principle, self-sacrifice. She had denied it, and despised it. But then she had been crushed by it in the arms of her father, burned by it in the flames of the *Camadan,* engulfed by it in the arms of the Hezzan. It was the Hezzan's sacrifice for her, displayed in that simple act, that had granted her all his power, all his dominion. Not the Quarto. Not the Rahk-Taa. But these fools could not see it. The greatest Law of Transfer remained unmentioned and unaddressed in the teachings of the great book of Law. And the greatest Transfer was this: the Worthy who died for the Unworthy, and thus passed to them his title and his dominion.

If the Quarto had been enmeshed in her web by her first three proofs, this last one found a drawstring and yanked it tight. They could not argue. They had no way to counter these claims, nor could they question the authoritative testimony of Sool Kron. So the very core of their beliefs now stood as Talon's pathway to the throne. One word of agreement, and the kingdom was hers.

Finally, Sool Kron broke the silence. "We await the judgment of the Rahk-Taa." He purposefully did not say, "the judgment of the Quarto." Talon noticed this.

So did the Quarto. "And you shall have it," the peevish one said. He looked at his compatriots. Two of them nodded. The elder shook his head. He looked back at Talon. "Your proofs are sufficient."

"No!" shouted the elder. He stood, nose to nose now with the peevish one. "We need more than the words of a mere woman and this old snake!"

The peevish leader glared back. Then he spoke quietly. "We have conferred on her the Kar Ixthano for the death of Senslar Zendoda. Her claims are just, according to the Rahk-Taa."

The elder wanted to shout out that he didn't care, that it wasn't right, but he held his tongue.

"She has in fact followed the Law," said the bookish one, his finger running along lines written in the Rahk-Taa, which was open before him.

The elder could not hold back now. "Don't you see? We have been tricked!"

"Tricked? By the Rahk-Taa?" the fourth one asked as he stood. He was a solid-looking young man who had been seated silently at the end of the table. He was the most heavily armed of the three, with a pistol in his belt and a long sword at his hip.

The elder did not back down. He pointed at Talon. "Don't you see? If we grant her the Kar Ixthano, we lose the kingdom! Are you mad? What will the people think of us? They are with us now! They will turn against us!"

"Since when is the will of the people a reason to abandon the teachings of the Rahk-Taa?" asked the bookish young man sedately, not looking up from his reading.

The elder spun, turning on him, spittle flying. "I'm talking about what's right for the kingdom! It's not right to let a woman rule! We all know this!"

"The Rahk-Taa determines what is right for the kingdom. And only the Rahk-Taa."

The elder's face was crimson, his frustration extreme. "This path

The Hand That Bears the Sword

is wrong. You think for this she will give us seats at the Council, but she is treacherous! This is a grave mistake!"

"She may do as she likes. The Quarto has ruled," the peevish one said quietly, but he smiled at Talon.

"Then we must rule again!" He drew his knife. "We agreed to this! She must die!" He pointed his knife at Talon.

The other three grew alarmed now. The solid young man drew his sword. "Are you now revealing your own Unworthiness?"

Breaths were held. He had asked the question softly, almost gently, but it hit the room like the death sentence it was.

"No," said the elder, not backing down. "This Quarto has a duty to stop her. Don't you understand what she's doing?"

He looked around the room at the faces of the other men, the witnesses. They were blank. "Don't you see it? Speak up, or she'll take the kingdom! She's tricked us, used our own Law against us! The kingdom should be ours! It should belong to the Quarto, to the Zealots! This weasel and this witch have conspired together! They killed the Hezzan, and now you're going to let them steal his kingdom?"

Now the bookish one stood as well, so that all the Quarto were on their feet. The peevish man turned to face his elder, and looked stonily at him. "It is not stealing to gain dominion through Kar Ixthano. It is Worthy. The commands of the Rahk-Taa are to place the upright in power. She has proven her Worthiness according to the Rahk-Taa. You, however, have profaned the Kar Ixthano. You have profaned the Rahk-Taa. You have proven your Unworthiness to serve here. You are an Unworthy."

"No, don't you see—"

But he never finished the sentence. The bookish one had drawn his own knife and now plunged it into his elder's back.

The elder cried out and sank to his knees, never taking his eyes off the peevish one, who looked down on him without mercy—in fact, with very little interest. The elder trembled violently. "I put you in power!" he whimpered. "And you betray me?"

"Our own Worthiness put us in power."

The elder fell to the ground, his own knife now clattering to the floor. The peevish one picked it up and, as the elder struggled for his final breaths, drove the blade point through his ribs.

He ceased struggling. A pall of death lay over the room.

The three remaining Quarto members returned to their seats. "The Kar Ixthano is granted," said the peevish one to Talon, with all the emotion of a government official issuing a license to fish. "The Quarto has granted you the dominion of the Hezzan."

CHAPTER 19

Prayer

John Hand was prepared to fight again, but he did not want to fight again. The difference this time was that he now had the Drammune Supreme Commander in his keep, and a box full of Drammune battle plans in his cabin. He also had his best fighter, his leader, his hero, pining away in his cabin in a fit of religious mercy, unwilling to fight, or lead, or otherwise be the least bit helpful. Getting back to Mann was now a priority that exceeded any other.

Hand kept the Drammune ships in sight on the western horizon, watched them spread across the sea, and guessed their strategy. The ships were sailing away from him, toward Mann, apparently ignoring him. But they were not sailing in alignment. They alternated front and back, so anywhere the *Chase* tried to make a run between two of them, she would be headed straight for a third. When she turned to avoid the third, one of the first two would be there to gain her from behind.

Their commander had seen the *Chase* at full gallop, knew her top speed, and had done an admirable job spacing his ships. It was possible to run them, John Hand figured, but a slight miscalculation and those grappling lines would be pulling on his sails once again. But if he chose not to go through them, he would need to sail behind the Drammune line for a good long while, perhaps days, spread out as they now were. It was an elegant trap, well-laid.

John Hand needed to deliver his winnings and associated warnings to the prince, and he needed to do it days ahead of the Drammune if the city's defenses were to be adjusted to counter the enemy's plan of attack. It seemed unlikely he could succeed; the whole Armada was but days from Mann. So it was a race to Mann, and a fight only if the *Trophy Chase* tried to win the race. The new Drammune commander, whoever he was, had the Vast admiral's respect. The set of this battle was against him.

Hand needed a new plan, a surprise, some way to take advantage of his assets. And what were his assets? Speed, obviously. Mystery, certainly, thanks to the unexpected appearance of the Firefish, apparently on the side of the Vast. Fear, maybe. The Drammune sailors, if not their masters, would certainly feel a healthy dose of terror at the prospect of facing down the *Trophy Chase* and the Firefish. These were not insignificant assets, with or without Packer Throme.

After a few more minutes' consideration, and then several notations in the ship's log, the admiral called his first mate to his cabin. "I need your crews to work in tight rhythm tonight," he told Andrew Haas. "If we can make this work, we may scoot through without a fight. But it all depends on the men knowing their orders, and following them precisely on command. Not a moment too soon, or too late."

"Aye, sir," Haas answered, a bit hurt. "They always have obeyed, haven't they?"

"I promise you, they have never been asked to follow orders quite like these."

Packer worked the Drammune headgear through his fingers absently, deep in thought, as though some of its protective power might rub off onto his hands. He had already scraped the crimson paint from it as best he could, using the edge of his sword. Now its gray metallic sheen nearly matched the hulls of the *Trophy Chase*.

It was near dawn. It had to be, Packer thought, though he hadn't heard the ship's bell in hours. He had to speak to the admiral. He had been pondering this all night, and he couldn't ponder it any more. Packer remembered with great clarity the elation he'd felt at the prow of the *Chase*, riding a moment into history. Whom would God favor? That was the question then, and was still the question now. But behind it was now another question, the one that kept him awake. What kind of nation did he serve? Who was John Hand? He had seen this admiral serve the greed of Scat Wilkins. He knew the man to be essentially amoral, committed to no particular ethics, no stated principles, just to riding out the tides of history. He would use Scripture, use Packer, use God, as he himself had admitted, to work his ends. Had Hand sold armor to the enemies of the Crown? Scat certainly had. And if Scat had, then John Hand had. If John Hand had, what of Prince Mather?

Packer stood. He clenched the Firefish cap in his right fist. He looked at his sword, where it lay sheathed on the floor at the end of his hammock. It would stay there. He looked at his own book of Scriptures, where it now lay on top of his footlocker, open to the passage from Corinthians. *Ye are bought with a price.* It would stay there as well. Then he walked unarmed out his door, in search of the admiral, and in violation of his direct orders.

The ship was deathly still, and dark. For a moment, Packer was disoriented—this was the *Camadan,* as he roamed the darkness in search of Talon. But no, it was the *Chase,* heeled to starboard, her rails down, sails full, at hull speed. Packer stood in the shadows outside the companionway that led to the main deck. He could see men in the rigging, but they were motionless. He could hear the prow slice the waves, hear the slap of water against the hull. Masts creaked, but not a single canvas popped or flapped. All held full. It was as though this moment were hung in time, not frozen, but caught while in motion, as though they would sail like this endlessly under a pale sliver of a silver moon.

Packer felt that the *Chase* was fully poised at the edge of something immense. He climbed the stairway to the quarterdeck. John Hand stood still, his telescope to his eye, straining to see ahead into the darkness. Beside him was Andrew Haas, grim as death, staring forward. The helmsman matched them both, in silence and in focused determination. Not one of them turned, not one acknowledged his presence in any way.

Packer looked out ahead. A Drammune warship sailed less than two points off the port bow, less than a thousand yards away. Another sailed the same distance off the starboard bow. Both were on the same heading as the *Chase.* A third ship could be seen dead ahead, but farther off, maybe fifteen hundred yards away.

"They're starting to squeeze us," Admiral Hand said. "We are known to them now. Are your men ready?"

"Aye, sir. Ready as they'll ever be."

Packer waited, but nothing happened. "Sir," he said aloud.

John Hand jerked his head toward Packer as though he were an apparition. He stared hard a moment, then his face relaxed. He looked through his telescope again. "Feeling better, are we?"

"Aye, sir. I need to speak to you."

"As you may have noticed, now is not a particularly good time for a conversation. If you're well, your place is at the prow. If you are not well, you may return to your cabin."

"Admiral, I—"

"Those are my orders!" he barked, without bothering to look again at his confused and wayward ensign.

Andrew Haas looked at Packer quizzically, but then looked quickly away, back toward the enemy ships.

Packer watched the Drammune ships ahead for just a moment. Then he pulled the hat onto his head and descended the stairway to the main deck, toward the foredeck and the forecastle.

He was still on the main deck when the admiral gave his orders. "Now, Mr. Haas."

"Light 'em, ye blaggards!" Andrew Haas boomed.

Packer heard flint wheels scrape, matches scratch, and he saw sparks fall from above. Flames followed, and yellow light glowed. Packer craned his neck. Every lamp the *Trophy Chase* carried, it seemed, was up in the rigging, held by a sailor. Within seconds all were lit, and every bit of arched canvas glowed yellow, each sail illumined like the sunrise had caught it with a single ray.

"Feeding time!" Haas called.

On the main deck a small team of sailors started throwing Drammune corpses, still piled by the shattered rails, overboard.

"NochTAH VastCHA!" John Hand started. "Knock-TAH Vast-CHAH!" the crew began to chant, the chorus growing steadily.

Lightning flashed in the sea just behind the *Chase*. Packer ran to the port rail, saw the brilliant yellow streak of the Firefish below the surface.

"Not so fast!" Hand called to the men rolling the Drammune overboard. "One at a time boys! Make 'em last!"

Then the admiral looked at Packer, pointed at him, and swept a finger toward the forecastle. "To the prow, son," he said evenly.

Packer couldn't hear the words, but read the meaning easily. He obeyed, unthinking, wanting to see from that particular vantage point what reaction the Drammune might have to this strange show. As he walked, as sailors saw him, they started whooping. Amid the chants could be heard, "Packer!" and "Look, Packer Throme!" And the chanting grew more intense. It took on an air of eerie joy.

Packer climbed up on the base of the bowsprit, holding the guy wires for support. The Drammune ships were not five hundred yards away; the *Chase* was gaining on them like they were standing still. They were turning now, not toward the *Chase,* to pinch her and cut off her path forward, but away from her, to give her room. To let her pass.

"They're runnin' scared now!" shouted a sailor in the rigging.

Packer turned backward, craning his neck to look at the spectacle that was now the *Chase.* It was an impressive, almost fearful sight to him—the sails on fire above, the sea on fire below. If it scared him, what must it be doing to the Drammune?

Huk Tuth was no Abbaka Mux. Where Mux was sturdy, strong, a passionate leader in his prime, Tuth was bent, gnarled, and old. No one in his command remembered the last time Commander Tuth had shown the least trace of an emotion, any emotion. But he betrayed one now.

There, coming up behind the *Kaza Fahn,* was the *Trophy Chase,* illumined like the royal palace during the Feast of Fire. Her sails glowed in both moonlight and lamplight, billow upon billow. The great cat was heeled at an angle that would capsize any ship in his Armada, but she seemed in no danger at all. Rather, she was flying like a ball from the muzzle of a gun.

And that was not nearly all. Below the surface of the water, lightning flashed. A yellow flash, then another, and then darkness. And then, rising to the surface, a glowing yellow streak. That beast again, the Devilfish, traveling alongside the *Chase,* still traveling with that ship, snaking through the water like an eel! Like an escort. Like some protecting demon.

Huk Tuth felt the cold breath of terror. His knees wobbled; his mouth dropped open. What could create such an apparition? Surely it was a dream. Surely it was not real. But then, as the glowing ship approached at impossible speed, he heard the chant. He recognized the cadence, the nasal attempt at the Drammune tongue, well before he could distinguish the words. "NochTA VastCHA!"

Tuth grimaced, as though in pain. "Enahai!" he called out. His men's heads turned toward him as though they were guns and he was their target. *Retreat?* But how could they retreat? To where would they run? They were making the best time they could already.

Tuth realized his mistake. "Enka! Enkato charnak!" *Load! Load and prepare to fire!*

But the helmsman had heard the first command and had already obeyed. The ship began turning away from the *Chase*. The captain of the *Karda Zolt*, opposite them, saw the maneuver and followed suit, giving the Vast ship way.

The warriors of the *Kaza Fahn* moved quickly into position, but every hand shook and every nerve danced.

Who were these people?

What was this ship?

And what was that Devilfish with them?

The men aboard the *Trophy Chase* were drunk on their own emotion. None of them had slept more than an hour or two, but none of them felt anything but the ecstasy of the moment. All any man needed to do was to look around to gain a full measure of courage and inspiration.

John Hand was in command on the quarterdeck. Just looking at him, no man could doubt he was the most courageous, confident, brilliant commander ever to sail a ship to war. Packer Throme was at the prow. He held no sword, no weapon at all. He simply watched, calm as a freshwater spring, as the nightmare beast rose from the sea. He removed his hat, held it up to the beast in salute. He was totally vulnerable. His shirt billowed in the breeze, his hair wild behind him. Any man who did not take courage from such a sight had no heart beating behind his ribs.

On deck behind Packer now massed the fighting men of the *Chase,* sailors who had fought Drammune and prevailed, and would do it again. Behind them were seven handpicked Vast sailors—one Delaney, another Marcus Pile, three of them pirates from the *Seventh*

Seal, and two others—all wearing the full armor of the Drammune, the hauberk and the helmet, but each with a blue bandana tied around his neck to mark him. Each carried a sword in one hand and a long knife in the other. These were the "Packers." These men would ensure victory.

And the Firefish! That Packer Throme had some otherworldly connection to them, that he could call them, that they would obey him…no one could deny it now. No one.

John Hand's plan worked. It worked even better than John Hand had planned it. Not only did the Drammune believe that the *Chase* was an apparition, impossible to fight, much less to defeat, not only were they letting her pass without firing a shot, but a good portion of the *Chase*'s own crew now believed it as well.

Below the waves, the Firefish was as energized as any man above. It had filled its belly on the slow one, then followed Deep Fin, elated, sated, anxious for nothing. Deep Fin was great and terrible, wondrous, supreme above all creatures. The Firefish circled far below all day as Deep Fin roamed the surface. The beast understood this; Deep Fin was eyeing the edge of the pack, watching, waiting for a straggler, waiting for a moment to pounce on some poor prey. As Deep Fin hunted, the beast followed, all night, its hunger and its appreciation both growing. Deep Fin was as patient a predator as any Firefish.

And then, before the great light broke forth above the waves, Deep Fin attacked. It ran not for the closest prey, but for one far off. This was troubling to the beast. Two slow, fat ones closed in on it. How could even Deep Fin kill three storm creatures?

But then, something astounding! Deep Fin began to glow. Yes, yes, the familiar glow, the Firefish glow, the glow of a creature that was Firefish, and yet not Firefish. A creature that was Firefish, and yet more than Firefish. Deep Fin burned in the air as a Firefish burned in the sea. And the fat ones ran! They turned away, fearful, recognizing a predator that would kill, and eat.

The Firefish swam alongside Deep Fin, its scales ablaze, and then…a meaty morsel! Dropped from the side of Deep Fin! The Firefish had no explanation for this, but gobbled the morsel greedily, thankfully, trusting Deep Fin wholly. The great storm creature swam on at high speed. The Firefish ate, then ate again, its jaws engulfing one morsel after another, sending each to its gullet as its lightning flashed through the sea.

These morsels were not fresh meat…they were cold. And then it knew…it knew. The beast understood that this was the flesh of the slow one! Somehow, after Deep Fin had done battle, after it had taken the slow one's flesh, it had held it—it had not eaten but instead had held these morsels. And now it released them to the sea. And not just to the sea…to the beast below the sea.

Deep Fin fed these morsels to the Firefish.

For a wild creature to be fed by the hand of man and not to distrust, something must turn it, something must soften it. And something did. Something remote and distant, something from beyond history, from the creation of earth itself, found its way into the beast's brain. An ancient door opened on a primal pathway to a time, a place long, long ago, when the world was new, before the world was cursed, when beasts obeyed, happily obeyed the greatness of the Great Creatures, whose fearsome, powerful love was that of the Great Creator Himself.

The lone predator, having found in Deep Fin a greater being, now also found in that being a link to that time in those ages past. The spirit of Deep Fin was the spirit of Mankind, and in the spirit of Mankind was the Spirit of the Creator. The love, the attention that Deep Fin now showed for such a vicious, scarred, and scattered beast, the love Deep Fin showered freely by offering these morsels—this was a renewal, a rebirth of that most ancient kinship. Deep Fin gave its own food, its own hard-won meat.

And that spirit made the Firefish dance.

It raced through the waters, looking for more morsels, excited and energized, a wild and playful wolf pup, and those morsels came raining down!

The wolf had turned. For this moment, for this time, by the hand of man, by the hand of God, the beast was the tamed animal, the trained lion. Deep Fin was the Master! And the Firefish loved the Master.

And so it leaped.

Its leap was a great, circling arc across the prow, high over Packer Throme's head, over his upraised arms. The glistening yellow scales caught the lamplight; the sea spray flew like liquid fire.

Coming up out of the water from Packer's right, the beast's jaw dropped open, revealing its mass of jagged teeth. Its eyes were glued on Packer as its head loomed above him, as the long cylinder of its huge body snaked up through the air until it was a soundless, mesmerizing, dazzling, perfect half circle of power and might and miracle, streaming overhead, flowing, ringing the *Chase*'s prow like a halo, like an archway into eternity.

The *Kaza Fahn* and all its men cowered. No signals went out from the Drammune lead ship to its cohorts. Their captains and crews loaded weapons and waited, wanting and not wanting to see what this shining light, this spirit from out of the darkness would do to them all.

Admiral John Hand laughed merrily, and steered a course straight for the third ship. "We have to survive this, boys," he said aloud to no one in particular. "The world needs to know about this!"

The captain of the *Nochto Vare*, a name which could be roughly translated as *Sudden Death*, could not move his ship. His stern was to the devil ship, and he was calling out orders to turn, turn, turn, but he was standing moveless on the afterdeck with his helmsman and the rest of his crew while the ship's wheel was abandoned. He could no more take his eyes off the blazing thing that drove at him than his crew could.

The *Trophy Chase* was on a collision course, a mere three hundred yards away.

Packer Throme prayed. He knew now that God had brought him here, called him up from his cabin not to confront John Hand as he had planned, but to stand here at the prow as God had planned, to witness the leap of the great Fish. The admiral's plan had been honored by God and by the Firefish, for reasons known but to Him, and the *Chase* had sailed past the *Kaza Fahn* and the *Karda Zolt* without a single weapon fired on either side.

But such would not be the case with this third ship, dead ahead. John Hand believed it would run, apparently, and so he kept a steady course. But the enemy wasn't running. John Hand believed the *Chase* would fly past it, apparently, and so she yet might, but in Packer's mind a fight loomed. Surely that warship had grappling guns. Surely the Drammune would recover their senses, remember their commander, now captive aboard the *Chase,* and fire those hooks into the *Chase*'s rigging.

And then the killing would begin again.

Packer had erred before. He had prayed for a fight. He would not do so again. He stood still and erect, watching the ship ahead grow larger and larger, and he prayed. What he offered up was more cry of pain than petition, more rending of soul than intercession, but the heart of it was a plea that God would find another way. That God would send the Firefish this time to fight instead of, not in addition to, the bloody combat. Before, not after.

Packer did not believe he had the faith to summon the beast to him. He did not believe the beast came, or would come, because of his faith. He didn't think he could command this living mountain to be thrown from the sea into his foe. He did, however, believe—without doubt, without question—that his prayer should be what it was: that God, and God alone, would win this battle.

He prayed for a battle such as Joshua fought at Jericho. He prayed for a battle such as Jehoshaphat fought at Tekoa. And he knew, absolutely, that God could do such a thing, could lay waste to the walls, could win against a superior enemy without a sword drawn or a shot fired. If He willed it. Packer felt, deep within, that this was the right prayer, the good prayer, the best prayer, the only prayer he could pray.

And as he prayed, the head of the beast rose once more from the water at his right hand.

The prince was brooding in his quarters, sitting on his high-backed couch in front of his enormous fireplace, delicately touching his purplish, swollen forehead. He tried not to think of Panna, but he could only dam his thoughts or channel them in another direction for so long, and then they flowed to her like a torrent down a drainpipe. That beauty, that radiant smile…those flowers…

He knew he was a fool. He shook his head. He feared he was losing his grip on reality.

"The Captain of the Guard, my liege," said Stebbins, the ancient valet.

"Send him in."

The prince stood up and asked, "Any news?" before the captain had taken two steps on the polished wooden floors.

"No, Your Highness. We're still searching."

The prince flashed his anger. "How could she just disappear? Has no one seen her? I thought your men knew how to conduct a search!"

"They are on her trail, sir. A couple of priests spoke with her, at the Seminary. She was seen entering a cottage. But she seems not to have stayed long, and we lost her trail there."

This gave Prince Mather pause. The Seminary. Of course. She would be spreading news about her father among those she thought might help. Smart move. If she could create an uproar in the Church, they could demand the release of Will Seline, and everything would be out. Well, he too had allies in the Church. He had to speak with Hap Stanson, try to counter this, get out in front of it. The prelate would help.

The prince dismissed his visitor. But before the captain left the room, Mather had another thought.

"Wait."

The captain turned back. Before Mather spoke with the head of the Church, perhaps he should release the priest. Or, at least, come to some sort of understanding. "Bring me the priest, Will Seline."

The captain flinched. "But Your Highness…"

"You have a problem with that?"

"No, sir, not at all. It's just that he's…"

The prince fought back fury. Was there no competence anywhere in this kingdom? "Speak, man! He's what?"

"I believe he may be dead, sir."

The words hit Prince Mather like another punch to the nose. "What? How?"

"He took a turn in the night, I'm told. Just took ill."

The prince felt sick, and put a hand to his stomach. "Are you sure?"

"The prison detail reported it this morning. Surgeon said there was nothing more he could do."

"But you don't know for sure. He may be alive."

"I…apparently, no one could wake him. It was only a matter of time."

"Well, feed him! Force some water into him! No, never mind, I'll do it myself!"

The Hand That Bears the Sword

The prince rushed through the halls of the palace, down the cellar stairs, followed by the two dragoons dispatched by the captain. Mather cursed out loud. He had fully expected to be letting the man go this morning, or soon anyway, and hadn't really thought about him actually dying. He thought about the language Panna had used, the way she'd made everything he did sound worse than it was. *Murder,* that's what she would call it if her father died. And now she was gone, beyond his control, spreading her stories like a disease.

He needed to find a way to keep that man alive.

The Firefish looked Packer Throme in the eye. It had risen slowly, its great, misshapen head dripping water in the lamplight, each of its eyes as big as Packer. What Packer saw there, was quite sure he saw there, was a question. But it was more than a question. It was a longing. It was a look Packer recognized, a powerful desire to know what its duty was, what command it should obey. And so Packer looked to heaven, asking God the same.

And then he looked back to the beast. Its scales glistened. Fire grew in its eyes, yellow fanning out, quickly coloring its whole body. But Packer did not feel then that he was in any danger whatever, though afterward he could never explain why. There was something present, was all he could say, something waiting. In some way the thing seemed almost joyful, if that could be. Regardless, neither then nor later did he believe that the beast intended to devour him or the *Trophy Chase.* And after a moment, he felt he knew what it wanted.

"Okay then," he said to it with a sigh, acquiescing to its desires. "Go." And he looked toward, and pointed toward, the *Nochto Vare.*

The massive, dripping beast turned. Its jaw dropped; its teeth glistened; its eyes shone like fire. Here, no doubt, was delight. And then its head went down, down into the water as its finned back stayed high, almost even with Packer, an arc of glowing yellow scales whirring like a windlass, like a wheel, rolling away toward the doomed ship.

The Master had commanded. The beast would obey.

The storm creature would die.

The Firefish did not attack from below, but from above. It rose as it approached, its head cutting through the water, its body snaking yellow behind it, its jaws open. It struck the *Nochto Vare* amidships, just fore of its beam. It was a direct hit, an impact that opened a hole from port to starboard, clean through the vessel. Screams were heard. Planking flew. Masts and muskets cracked. On the other side, the beast turned to strike again.

There would be no survivors.

Huk Tuth and the Drammune aboard the *Kaza Fahn,* aboard the *Karda Zolt,* watched in horror. Instead of looking for a way to destroy the *Trophy Chase,* the commander now hoped only that the Vast ship would keep sailing, keep flying at hull speed, and would not turn back toward him to fight.

He was relieved to see this hope fulfilled.

The Drammune commander then flashed orders to his Armada that they were to resume the trek to Nearing Vast, to fulfill their glorious destinies. Then he went below deck to his cabin, took a piece of parchment, and wrote out in short, plain words all he had witnessed this day. He put the scroll into a leather pouch and lashed the pouch to the foot of his falcon, a bird not as large but faster than that of Fen Abbaka Mux. He walked his messenger to the afterdeck and set it free. He watched it until it was a small black dot, and then he watched the dot disappear on the horizon.

Will Seline had been praying when he took ill. In the days leading up to Panna's visit, he had slept off and on, drifting from prayer into sleep and from sleep into prayer. He was praying when Panna came to see him the first time, and started praying again when she left. The same was true of her second visit.

After she told him her story, he found an image on which to hang his prayers. It was an image he at first believed was simply a helpful picture from the Scriptures that focused his mind and heart. But the more he prayed, the more be came to believe that the image was real, in fact more real than the matted straw beneath him and the grimy stones that surrounded him.

The image was of an altar. Not the altar of the Vast churches, covered in white and blue satin, where pristine women and spotlessly clad men said vows of fidelity, or where bread was passed on gleaming platters and wine was sipped from ornate chalices. It was the altar of the Old Testament, square, over seven feet across and four feet high, a cooking grill, with a mesh grate across the top and a fire burning perpetually below. It was the altar where the bodies of animals, having had their throats slit and their blood drained away by priests, were laid to burn before the Lord.

This image had come to Will's mind as he contemplated the Apostle Paul's yearning request that believers offer themselves as living sacrifices, holy and acceptable to God. Will imagined…as he lay dying slowly, fevered, his mouth caked and his tongue swollen, his body racked with pain…he imagined that those who read the words for the first time, fresh from the pen of the apostle, understood completely the meaning of a burnt offering. It was an awful, entirely physical reality: to lay a freshly killed animal on a flaming grill and watch, listen, and smell it as it cooked, then burned.

Will Seline was just such an offering. That was the image he held on to. He was not an animal carcass but a breathing human, a living sacrifice. Still, this was a burnt offering, destined to stay on that altar until there was nothing left upon this earth.

He felt the spiritual flames entering his soul, illuminating and then burning away his self-righteousness, his self-pity, his selfishness, all his sins of pride and of gluttony, all the desire to be loved and admired by people rather than by God, to hold onto rather than to give away. And he realized these flames were very real. These were the same tongues of fire that danced on the heads of the disciples at Pentecost, the same fire that burned the burning bush, that rose in a column in the desert to lead the children of Israel. This was the flame of the Spirit, more real by far than the prison walls around him.

And then he remembered another altar, not in the Old Testament but in the New. The altar in the Book of Revelation, the altar in heaven, from which burning coals were hurled to earth, and under which the martyrs gathered in the flames. This was the true altar, after which all other altars were patterned. And when he, Will Seline, in this filthy cell, laid himself in spirit upon that altar, that act became more than image. It was not symbolic. It was no longer imagination. Though it was not happening physically, it was happening in truth.

And so he stayed there, in those flames. He did not want to leave. He wanted to be burned up, made holy, purified for the sake of the love and the glory of God.

He stayed in those flames as he lay dying, joyful, tearful, protected and safe, safe in a way he had never been before.

And Will remembered Daniel's three friends in the fiery furnace, remembered how they walked and spoke with God in the flames, and Will knew they were content to be there, that they were utterly safe inside that furnace, that all was well there, and he understood why they did not want to come out. They did not want to go back to the world of men, the world that people had abused and God had cursed, where goodness was always crushed and holiness always stained and love always torn and marred. Yet those three had been called out by a king of that world who needed to know why the men were not dead, and needed to know who the fourth man was. King Nebuchadnezzar needed to know God. And so the three friends had left the flame to help him.

Father Seline. Will Seline! Can you hear me?

The words came through to the priest's mind, and he realized he too was being called out of the flames, by the prince of this realm.

With great difficulty and greater reluctance he struggled back to a place where he might open his eyes once more in the darkness, before the eternal light swallowed him forever. And the flames receded, and he was greeted roughly by the sounds and smells and sights of the bleak, dank world, the rustle of straw, the smell of urine, the face of the prince.

But this physical reality was not ugly and cold and barren, as he expected it would be, rather it carried with it and in it a joy that was buried deep somehow, covered over, but that could not be quenched. The very character of God, the reflection of the flame, was in these things, and Will now knew he had never seen the flame in them before only because he had not known how to look.

"Thank God you're alive," the prince said. "Here, take some water." He tried to pour water into Will's mouth, but the priest gagged and coughed. It tasted of vinegar. He spit it out.

"Do not die, Father Seline. We will make you well again." The prince's face was pleading. Will felt pity.

"You can do nothing…" Will said in a dry voice that surprised him with its resonance and assurance. He felt he had no strength, his lips were cracked and his tongue was coated, and yet his vocal cords worked easily, smoothly, as though oiled. "…unless it is granted to you from above."

The Hand That Bears the Sword

"It was not my intention for you to die."

Will looked at the sorrowful, pained face of the prince. "But was your intention to commit adultery with my daughter?" Will asked without malice. He simply spoke truth, with a deep desire for the prince to agree, and accept, and repent.

Mather shook his head. "No...I would never have..." But he trailed off, unsure suddenly of precisely what his intentions were.

And then words came to Will Seline, thoughts he had not summoned. But he knew where they came from. He knew why he must say them. "Your kingdom groans under the misdeeds of your family. It will be taken away," he said. "It will be given to one who is worthy."

The prince's chin trembled. *The Worthy.* "The Drammune? Is this a prophecy? Are you a prophet? Or can I yet change this?"

"It is decided. But you may choose the manner."

The prince felt panic. "What does that mean? Can I be forgiven?"

But the fat old priest went silent. Rage rose within the prince; he wanted to shake him, scream at him, hit him, make him talk. But instead he crumbled within. "Explain it to me. Please, please," he begged. "Explain it to me."

But the priest was gone.

CHAPTER 20

Harbor

"Get rid of the body," the prince told the guards. "Bury him in the Pauper's Plot. Keep it quiet."

The guard nodded dutifully, and went to organize the detail.

Mather turned slowly for the palace, his mind far away. It was all coming down now. Everything he had built was crashing down around him. He had worked so hard to take the reins. He was going to build the future, recapture former glories. But none of that would happen. Prince Mather walked back through the grim, lamp-lit corridor underground to the palace.

Why did the priest have to die? It had not yet been four days he was without water. He had a weak heart or something; it wasn't Mather's fault. And what was the prophecy? Did the priest speak the inevitable? Or was it just ranting, madness brought on by hunger and thirst?

As he topped the stairs and entered the polished hallway, he saw his younger brother, Prince Ward, waiting for him. Lanky, loose-limbed, and tall, he leaned on the stairway banister, arms crossed.

"What are you doing awake?" Mather asked with his customary reflexive scorn. "It's barely noon."

Prince Ward smiled. "Excellent, you're in a good mood. Father wants to see us."

"Oh, he's awake too? A banner day in the palace." Then Mather caught the meaning. "Us?"

"You and me and Jacq."

"How lovely. A family gathering. We haven't had one of those since what, Christmas?" But it made Mather wonder.

The king of the realm had gathered his children around him at his table. He sat at the head, and the queen, his wife, the mother of these three royal children, sat at the foot.

"I've asked your mother to join us here," the monarch began, "because I want her to hear this. It pertains to you all."

There was a reason he felt the need to explain why she was present. Madam the Queen Maeveline loved her children, but she knew her place, which was, essentially, to provide the king with heirs. She had fulfilled her obligation more than two decades ago. She had no illusions of power; hers was a subservient role. Of this she was reminded, through circumstances, constantly.

She had managed to provide a bond of love early in her children's lives, as was deemed necessary to their upbringing, but the raising of royal children was not to be left to the whims and emotions of any one woman, regardless of her bloodlines. She did nothing to get in the king's way, or to point out his failings, and in exchange she lived a fine and pampered life.

As one of the servants brought food, the king began to eat. In the pause, his daughter spoke. "So how is the hero's wife?" Jacq asked Mather, her voice a pointed instrument.

"I wouldn't know," Mather said, honestly enough.

"Funny. I hear you know little else these days, brother dear." She smiled. "No potatoes," she said to the servant, who pulled back the serving spoon immediately. "As always." Jacq was eight years Mather's senior, more like Mather than like Ward, and like him, had never wandered very deeply into her own feelings. She recognized the minefields that lay buried there, and stayed at the boundaries where she could mock them.

"Escaped from the Tower," Ward said nonchalantly, as the servant heaped mashed potatoes on his plate. "Rather dramatic, the whole thing."

"Yes, how very fairy-tale," Jacq jibed. "But wait, something's

The Hand That Bears the Sword

amiss. In the fairy tales, aren't they maidens? And aren't they rescued? And isn't it generally the prince who rescues them?"

Mather shot her a glance but was silent.

"But I'm being callous. It is, of course, very troubling for you that she's gone." Jacq pouted. "Poor Mather will need to find another hero's wife to dote upon."

"Or another way to woo a woman," Ward added breezily. "Shackles and blackmail never worked very well for me." He smiled. "Not that I haven't tried." Then he looked around the tabletop. "Will there be meat of any kind?"

"Coming, sir," the servant said.

They ignored their father, who ignored them in return as he ate greedily all that was put in front of him.

"Well, I do hope your next hero's wife packs a little less power in her punches," Jacq quipped. "This one would have been the death of you, eventually."

"You know nothing," Mather said, finally unable to hide his sour spirit.

"Nothing about love, you mean? Ah yes, that is what you meant, I can see it your eyes!"

"Your left eye in particular." Ward winked.

"Well, well, Mather is in love." Jacq now poured it on. "Ah, what a wondrous thing it must be! Tripping all over oneself, putting oneself in harm's way, embarrassing oneself in front of servants and guests and God knows who else, breaking one's nose once or twice! Or was it more? I may have lost count."

"Only once," Mather said, perversely allowing his sister to revel in his misery.

"How gloriously romantic to come so completely untethered while the nation hovers on the brink of destruction by an enemy force. I would only hope that everyone in the Army and the Navy, the whole kingdom for that matter, could know what it feels like to become such a blithering, foolish, idiotic, shameful—"

"That's enough," the king said dryly, picking up his wine glass and drinking deeply.

"Well hello, Daddy," Jacqalyn purred. "I had almost forgotten you were there. Why, I was just talking about the wonders of love. But I suppose you and Mommy could tell us all about that, couldn't you?"

"Leave Mother out of it," Ward said, his spirit suddenly darkened. "She doesn't deserve it."

The only one of her three children to show the queen continued kindness and respect was Ward. He was more profligate than the other two combined, but in spite of that, or perhaps in some way because of it, he continued to hold her in high regard and watch out for her welfare, her comfort, and her feelings.

"And the rest of us do deserve it?" Jacqalyn asked. "Well, I'm sure you're right, Ward, whatever 'it' is. Sorry, Mother dear. Now, where were we? Oh yes, love…"

"No, no," the king said, swallowing the last of his wine and studying his empty plate with a frown. "I brought you here to talk about something else."

"Excellent. I can't wait." Jacq smiled pleasantly. She held up her empty glass with the calm assurance that it would be refilled. It was.

"No sense beating around the bush," the king said. "The fact of the matter is that I have made the decision to step down, and turn the throne over to Mather."

There was silence. Jacq and Ward looked at Mather, who lowered his fork and looked askance at his father.

"You don't seem pleased, brother dear," said Jacq. "I would think you would leap for joy at such news. King at last."

"Now is not the time," Mather said, eyeing his father sideways.

King Reynard reached into a basket, found a roll, slathered butter onto it as he spoke. "While I am king, that is a decision I will make." He bit into the roll.

"When?" Mather couldn't hide his anger.

"Soon." He shrugged. "It just needs to be arranged."

"Why? And why now? We're at war. Father, we've talked about this." Mather did not want a change in power at this critical moment. And, when Nearing Vast lost to the Drammune, which seemed more inevitable every day, he would much rather be a mere prince than the king.

"I'm an appendage in this war. You know that. I'm long past my usefulness, as was proved in the small, unfortunate incident regarding the Fleet. I'm sure you recall it."

"It rings a bell. But father, you *must* wait," Mather entreated. "A few more days at least."

The king sighed. He looked old. "If you insist. But I don't want to wait long. I want to retire."

"And you will. You deserve to."

"Either way, I'm going to the Mountain House."

Mather grew alarmed. "When?"

"Leaving tonight."

"Tonight?" Mather studied him. "You're fleeing. You're fleeing the city. What news do you have that you haven't shared? Have the Drammune landed?"

"Not yet. But the *Trophy Chase* has returned."

"What?"

"Hooray!" said Jacqalyn, raising her glass with genuine glee. "The Hero returns to claim his bride! Oh, this will be sweet." She drank.

"And what news does she bring?"

"The hero's wife?" the king asked, baffled.

"No," Mather said irritably. "The ship." Why hadn't anyone told Mather about this? But he knew the answer. It was because of Panna. Because people thought he'd lost his mind, and were worried about what he might do to himself, or to Packer. Mather's world was growing darker by the moment.

The king spoke through a large bite of his roll. "Well, unless the wind changes dramatically, the Drammune Armada will likely arrive on our shores by morning, day after tomorrow."

This poured cold water on even Jacqalyn's spirits. "Oh, dear. Say, Daddy, would you have room for an extra passenger on your trip?"

"Of course. Ward, will you come along as well?"

"You're taking Mother," Ward answered, "right?"

There was a long pause. Then the king said, "What about it, Maeveline? Would you care to come with me?" He asked it with a rather sad smile.

She looked him in the eye, but didn't answer.

"Mother, you have to go," Ward insisted gently.

"Very well, then," she said. But her desolation was complete. She was an appendage to an appendage.

"Good. And I'll stay and help big brother fight the war," Ward declared, grinning. He turned to Mather. "What can I do to help?"

Mather looked at him with a bitter half-smile. "You could ply the attacking hordes with the king's rum. That might slow them a bit."

"I'm glad to see that our kingdom's imminent destruction has not lessened your wit." Ward held up a glass. "It's been a good ride, then, but it's over. Here's my last drink. I will remain sober until I celebrate victory, or die attempting it." He threw the wine into his mouth and swallowed.

Jacq smirked. "Do you mean, die attempting victory? Or attempting to remain sober?"

"And my sister's wit remains keen as well." Ward turned to Mather. "Well, brother, what shall we do? Inspect the troops?"

"If you're serious, say so."

Ward looked him squarely in the eye. "If I can help motivate our men to kill rather than be killed, I will gladly do so. Yes. I am serious."

Mather studied him. Ward had a strange edge to him that had all the characteristics of determination. And Ward did know most of the generals and commanders, or at least had gone out drinking with them. "Well. I'm sure a visit from their prince would hearten the troops. Especially on the eve of battle."

"Then I'm your man."

"Touching," Jacq offered. "But what about your woman, Mather? And your woman's man? Surely Packer Throme will come looking for his innocent young wife."

"I'll tell you what, Jacq," Mather said icily. "Why don't I worry about that while you go pack your bags and run away. How does that sound to you?"

She smiled and held up her empty wine glass. "It sounds…inevitable." The servant dutifully poured.

The two guards stood in the cell looking down at the body of the big priest. One had two shovels, one carried two poles with a piece of canvas sewn between them. A stretcher. They shared a discomfort that kept them quiet, and at the moment, immobile.

"Don't seem right to bury him without a priest," said the first. He had a sallow face, and the physical appearance of a man who had once been powerfully built, but who had not kept himself fit as he aged.

The second guard was younger, stronger, but wore a permanent, jaw-clenching frown. "He's a priest already. Don't that count?"

The first took it as a fair question. "Not if he's dead, it don't."

The second man shrugged. "But the prince said keep it quiet."

"Who's quieter than a priest?"

"A dead priest."

"Let's just get him out of here."

The *Trophy Chase* attracted a crowd almost immediately. Her rails and cabinets and cabins were splintered and battered—in many places gone, in others almost so. Her boats were shot full of holes. Cannon placements were blown up or blown away, with cannon cracked, askew, or missing. Her sails were shredded in places, her masts had large chunks gouged from them, splinters spreading like thistles. A few small grappling hooks still clung high up in yards and sailcloth, trailing their fine woven lines, waving in the breeze. Far above all these battle scars, the flag of Nearing Vast flew proudly from her mainmast.

But it was her hull that had everyone talking. The gray sheen of an odd material clung tightly to it, wrapping it, covering the wood. Underneath, the boards seemed undamaged, even pristine.

Not that the citizens who came by to gaze understood what they were looking at. "That's western hardwood," one grandfather told his small grandson as he pointed up from the dock. "Comes from the Farther Forest, where my own grandparents lived." He spoke with pride. "You just can't knock a hole in it. You can hardly see the grain there." He pointed. "That's how you can tell."

The crew were not granted any leave. The Drammune were not far behind, and so only the most urgent repairs to cannon and gunwales, ship's boats, sails and lines, were undertaken. The *Chase* would need to ship out at a moment's notice. But leave or no, they were not sworn to secrecy, and so the crewmen spoke to anyone who wandered near. The stories spread from almost the moment the ship's mooring lines hit the docks.

And the stories were marvelous.

Packer Throme alone had killed hundreds of Drammune warriors with his sword. John Hand had captured the enemy's admiral, a man who stopped musket balls with his forehead. The Vast sailors had stormed the very flagship of the Drammune Armada, just before a Firefish ate it. Then Packer had tamed the monster so it swam alongside the ship, laughing like a porpoise. Then he'd trained it to attack on command. The *Trophy Chase* herself had become part Firefish, and was now pretty much unbeatable.

Of course, few were willing to believe any of this, at least at first, but here was some evidence: the battle damage to the decks of the *Chase*. And before too long, the chained figure of a Drammune officer, being taken from ship to shore to palace. So whether confirmed news or tall tale, the stories were heard, repeated, and passed along in the pubs and inns along the docks, through the ancient and honored channels, wives and barbers and old men on stoops, and also through the new network of raw military personnel that now spread through the city like a nervous system. And the system was plenty nervous, fearful of the impending attack, so the stories of the *Trophy Chase* energized the people and gave them hope, precisely as the Drammune commanders had feared.

Surely, the people thought, this would be a short war after all, and a great triumph for Nearing Vast.

Packer had seen nothing but the inside of his small cabin since the brutal demise of the *Nochto Vare*. He had watched it from the prow, of course, a clearer view than any man needed of that scene. The Firefish had ripped the warship to flotsam.

The eerily glowing beast struck not once, not twice, but three times before the craft sank forever beneath the waves. The cheering of the *Chase*'s crew, the roar of the cat, turned to an unnatural whimper, then to a horrified silence in the face of the sheer carnivorous energy meted out against the floundering ship. It was as though the beast, having been sent on a mission, was determined to prove its destructive bona fides. It lunged, it tore, it crushed, it lunged again, it whipped its body around, thrashing the offending warship, it lunged a third time, then thrashed at the fragments, then the fragments of the fragments, all the while devouring all the Drammune it could devour, electrified jaws clamping down again and again.

As the seas claimed the last of the *Nochto Vare*, as the flat pool of boiling waters, calming now as the men watched, receded into the distance, Packer stood silent at the base of the bowsprit, wondering at the meaning of it. God had saved them from battle. A prayer answered. God had spared the *Chase*. But what of the enemy? They were utterly destroyed. Packer took no joy in this; instead he felt a deep sorrow he could not name. What did such a thing signify? Why did God send the Firefish to Packer so that he might command it? Why did God not command the Firefish Himself? Packer wished that He had; the ache within him was keen, like an arrow, like a knife's blade.

As he had pondered these things, the crew on deck, one by one, had turned back to look at him. Their eyes were full of questions. And fear. Packer looked around at the faces. He had seen this kind of fear once before, after Talon had revived him with the witch's breath—so some of the crew had said—back when the men did not know who, or what, he was. Whatever they thought of him now, he would not be paraded around on their shoulders this tme. And yet, he couldn't help but feel that this time, such a spontaneous outburst would be more appropriate than the last.

"God did it," he told them, when all eyes were on him. "He sent the Firefish." It was a confession, an acknowledgment.

Packer looked from face to face, but saw little evidence they believed him. Or even heard him. Delaney managed a nod and a ghost of a smile, but even he looked worried. Then Packer met Marcus Pile's eye. Here was one, at least, aglow with the fire of God, with the thrill of a battle won by the very hand of God. Packer smiled warmly at him. Marcus.

The men parted as Packer walked across the decks. They gave way, allowing him plenty of room. Packer felt sadness grow in him. They did not want to touch him now. As a fellow warrior, as a fellow pirate who ranged the bloody decks of this world with a sword in his hand, he was sung and praised and hoisted to the skies. Now that he had made the harder choice his faith demanded and let God determine the outcome, they gave him wide berth.

He walked silently to his cabin. Only when he'd reached out to open the door had he noticed that he still had the Drammune war cap clutched tightly in his scarred right hand.

Now the door creaked open, interrupting Packer's thoughts.

"Prince Mather needs a debrief," John Hand announced, sticking his head in. "We're going to give it to him, and deliver these." He stepped in, displaying for Packer a leather-covered wooden strongbox, the hard-won battle plans. The Skull of Drammune had been tooled into it.

Packer sat up, then hopped down from the hammock. "We?"

"He asked for you specifically. He sent us a coach; we're to take the prisoner and go straight to the palace."

Cheers rose as Packer walked down the gangway. He scanned the docks, squinting, his eyes still adjusting to the bright sunlight. Hands reached out to him, citizens trying to touch him. But with John Hand in front and a beefy dragoon on either side and behind him, no one could get close. Packer felt more prisoner than hero.

He kept looking for Panna, and every face that wasn't hers was a disappointment to him. Of course, she would have no way to know that he was coming home. It might take days for news to get to Hangman's Cliffs. But at his last return, she'd been here, magically, miraculously, standing on the dock waiting for him. Packer couldn't help but hope for some small, similar miracle.

He was put into a carriage much like the one in which Panna had ridden off, and at this very dock. The crowds were smaller now than they had been then; no proclamation invited the citizens this time. But those who'd come were plenty boisterous and excited.

The carriage sat for several minutes here, and then Fen Abbaka Mux joined them, his shaggy head and scowling face popping suddenly into the carriage, followed by a thick body in deep crimson, the Drammune naval uniform. He was chained hand and foot, his wrists manacled to a belt fashioned of iron. The crowd behind him booed and shouted catcalls, hurled apple cores and chicken bones that bounced off his back before the door was closed. If Mux noticed them, he didn't show it.

Once they left the docks it was evident the city was bracing for attack. It reminded Packer of the hurricane preparations he had witnessed twice in these streets. Windows were boarded or shuttered, sandbagged walls placed at the foot of major streets. But more than high winds and water were on the way this time: Cannon placements lined these strategic posts, and men of the new Army dug and filled while uniformed soldiers, the regular Army, patrolled.

Packer tried not to look at Fen Abbaka Mux, who was seated across from him. The man's glower was truly extraordinary; Packer believed he could see death in those eyes, and felt quite sure it was his own. Mux was a broad, strong man, and though he was thoroughly bound, he was still dangerous. It occurred to Packer that this man might at any moment simply lower his head and ram his skull through Packer's chest before anyone else in the carriage could look twice, much less make a move to stop him.

The dragoon sitting next to Mux had a short sword at his belt, but it was sheathed. A pistol was similarly holstered on his belt. He sat like a lump, paying little attention to his prisoner, assuming the chains would be enough. Packer felt a strong desire to have his sword in his hand. But he did not have it with him. He would not carry it again.

"You feeling all right?" John Hand asked Packer. "You look a little pale."

Packer didn't look at him. "I'll be fine."

Panna turned away from the window, letting the curtain fall back into place. She crossed her arms. Everything she wanted to do was deemed unwise by someone, and it was always some man in a position of authority. She was no longer a prisoner in the palace, but now she was a prisoner in this little cottage. Anger and frustration mounted.

The priest was compassionate. "It was just one man shouting in the street. He wasn't a crier, or a herald. It's a rumor, Panna. Perhaps the *Trophy Chase* has returned, perhaps not. But fairly or unfairly, you are a wanted criminal. You must hide. I will go learn what I can."

"Where? How?"

"I'll go to the palace."

"But you can't get inside."

"I'm not sure what God may allow. But I will again trust His grace."

She waited. "That's your whole plan?"

"Well, I've had worse. But there are priests who serve within the palace. Perhaps I will find one. You would be amazed at the intricate little network we maintain."

She sighed. "Okay, fine." She looked at him, earnest and tender but somehow strong as steel. "Good luck, then."

He unlocked the door, opened it. He looked around the yard, and past it onto the streets. "Panna, I hope you understand now that I operate with something far more effective than luck." Then he turned back to Panna and shrugged, smiling. "Unfortunately, the outcomes are equally difficult to predict."

And he was gone.

Dog Blestoe straightened up as the carriage went by, and caught a glimpse of Packer Throme within it, his arm resting casually on the window sill as he chatted with some white-suited muckety-muck. Dog scowled, then grunted as he slammed a sandbag into place next to its neighbor.

He picked up the next sandbag and slammed it into place as well. Life in the military had been much like this for Dog, just as it had been for most of the farmers and fishermen and cobblers and cart-wrights who'd brought their dreams of martial glory into the City of Mann. The real soldiers stood around and smoked, wearing their fine uniforms, while the new recruits did all the digging and filling and lifting and hauling, wearing not much more than rags.

Dog hated his lot, but mostly he hated that he was stuck in the Army. The Navy needed him, he knew, and every day he was more sure that they, at least, were preparing for a proper war. But the little green and blue ribbons had turned out to mean precisely nothing. Some old general, or maybe it was a colonel, had come by on the first day of muster and sorted the men out, sending some this way and some that, regardless of where they'd signed up or what color their bits of cloth were. At the time, Dog hadn't been able to figure any logic in it, but now he was convinced the officer had simply ear-marked the strongest-looking men for manual labor, to build the city's fortifications. So Dog had spent his Army career to date man-handling a shovel and several tons of sand.

Not that there weren't military moments. The recruits drilled on the parade ground twice a day, once at dawn and once at dusk. They were pretty good now at marching in a line. And they had instruc-tion in small arms once a week. They were not allowed to fire their weapons, of course, as they needed to conserve ammunition. And once or twice a week they had practice using a sword, or a pike, or a stick, whatever it was they actually owned. But that was as much time as could be spared from digging and stacking, apparently. They had to build these fortifications around the Rampart. How sand could fortify stone remained a mystery to Dog.

This morning at drills, they had been told the Drammune were arriving tomorrow, maybe the next day. Everyone shouted "Death to Drammun!" six or eight times, and then they marched in neat rows for an extra ten minutes. Then, however, they were allowed to fire live ammunition, one round each at a practice target. This presented a small host of complex problems to be solved, including the misplacement of powder, ammunition, and practice targets, and there was general confusion regarding which weapons could fire which size shot. But after only an hour or two, most of these difficulties had been worked out. It was a good thing, too, because that's when the not-quite-ubiquitous figure of Bench Urmand had ridden up on his pale white steed, galloping at the head of a small contingent, four of his fiercest fighting men, to proudly oversee the actual shooting portion of the drill. He saw, in fact, some marksmanship of excellent quality. Convinced all was well, he'd congratulated the officers and ridden off.

The gunnery crews were more efficient, thanks in large part to the fact that the cannon were already placed in the streets of Mann, and so firing live ammunition was not practical. The artillerymen were quite accustomed to firing charges without shot and, if powder was short, pantomiming the entire process. So these drills had gone off pretty much without a hitch.

But none of that appeased Dog's simmering sense of injury. And now to add searing insult, some breathless idiot runs up saying that Packer Throme has taught Firefish to eat Drammune warships. And then Himself rides by in a shiny white carriage pulled by two brilliant white horses, chatting away like nothing whatever was of concern in the world. If the fate of the kingdom hinged on such men as Packer Throme, Dog thought, they were all doomed to die bloody deaths.

He sneered, then slammed another sandbag into place as the carriage disappeared from view. Everything always came so easy for that boy.

As quickly as the carriage moved, with the hooves of its twin white horses clattering at a fast trot through the city streets, it still could not outrun the rumors. When the coach stopped at the guarded gate leading into the palace, a small crowd of people cheered. They pushed up around the carriage, wanting to put their hands on it, wanting to reach it, to touch Packer and the dashing Admiral John Hand. Guards and soldiers saluted, men waved, old women reached up to touch them, mothers held children up, young women blew kisses.

"God bless you, Packer Throme!" they said, and, "Thank you, Admiral!" and "Tamed the Firefish, did you?" and "We'll win this thing yet!" Many said, "God bless Nearing Vast," and one even called out, "We got their commander—good work!"

"We should let *these* people debrief the prince," John Hand suggested as the carriage jolted forward again.

From half a block away, a small priest watched. He grimaced, then looked up to heaven. He turned and walked away.

Father Mooring did not go straight back to the Seminary, back to Panna with the news that Packer had returned. Instead, he walked the length of the palace fence, then turned left, following it around toward the far northwest corner of the compound, where the fence around the Green met the Rampart wall. There a gritty, rusted iron gate with an enormous padlock fronted a huge wooden door, large enough for three horses to pass through abreast. On the other side of that door was a ramp that led down into the palace prison.

The little priest was not sure why he went there, other than that he felt some deep misgivings that prompted him. But he was quickly thankful that he did. He found a guard holding the old gate open as a wagon drawn by a single, swayback old mare groaned out onto the street. As the guard closed the huge wooden door and padlocked the iron gate, Father Mooring wandered up to the side of the wagon and peered in over its side. He looked up at the driver with piercing eyes.

"Anyone I know?"

The driver looked like he had been caught stealing. Father Mooring studied his sallow face and blinking eyes for a moment, then turned to the gateman, who stood frozen in place, padlock in his hands, frown drawn down to his chin. Then the two guards looked at one another.

The driver looked back at the priest. "Can you keep quiet?"

"As the grave," Father Mooring promised.

"Ah, Admiral Hand and Packer Throme!" Jacqalyn Sennett gushed as they entered the main hallway of the palace. Packer was watching a contingent of dragoons walk the Drammune prisoner, plodding and jangling, to the stairway, headed down. He felt a heavy load lifted; he hadn't realize how tense he had been until he relaxed. Now he turned to Princess Jacqalyn, and saw her hold out a hand for the admiral to kiss. Hand obliged, with practiced grace and warmth.

"Welcome back, Admiral," she said in a voice smooth as oil. I understand you had quite the adventures."

"Yes, actually," John Hand began. But she wasn't interested in him.

"And the heroic Packer Throme," she cooed, holding out her hand limply. "I'm Princess Jacqalyn. I've heard so very much about you."

"Pleased to meet you." Packer took her hand and kissed it clumsily, he felt, in a poor imitation of the admiral.

"Oh, but you are a handsome boy," she said, thinking how drab and common he looked, pockmarks and unruly hair and all. Not anywhere near the dashing swordsman she had imagined. "And the pity is, you just missed seeing your wife."

He looked, and felt, as if he had just come wide awake from a deep sleep. "Panna? She was here? When?"

"Why, I thought you knew," the princess purred. "She never left. Until just last night, oddly enough, when she escaped. Oops. I mean, left unexpectedly. But I'm sure Prince Mather will explain it all. His business, not mine."

Packer's heart felt like it had been ransacked. First it was filled to the brim, thinking Panna was near, then it was punctured with the thought she had been in the palace all this time, then it spilled open suddenly with that single word. *Escaped.* All of his senses were now attuned to danger. Hair bristled at the back of his neck.

Jacqalyn laughed at the utter transparency of the boy. A good match for Panna—the same lack of guile, and undoubtedly the same moral backbone. Probably the same pugilistic style. Perhaps they had even learned to box together. "I'd love to join you in your discussions with Prince Mather. Really I would. Really. But I must be off! Bye-bye now!" And she sashayed away.

Packer looked at John Hand accusingly.

"Easy, Packer," the admiral said. "I'm sure the prince was just keeping her safe."

"From what?"

"I said easy, son. That's an order. Let him explain."

Packer had little time to deal with his emotions, or to prepare himself to be careful and proper with the Prince of the Realm. He had a deep, empty, sullen spot where his stomach should have been as the prince walked briskly up to them, a broad smile on his face.

Neither Packer nor John Hand could possibly have been prepared for the changes that had come over, or more precisely, had overcome, Mather Sennett. His face was a blotch of makeup, and where it wasn't makeup, it was bruised purple and yellow and black, and where it wasn't either, it was pallid white. His nose was misshapen. A knot bulged at his left temple. His perfect hair was not perfect, but looked as though he had been running his hands through it, or had been pulling on it, and had just now hastily put it back in place with his fingers. His eyes were red and blank. His smile was forced.

"Gentlemen! Welcome back."

"Good Lord, Mather, what's happened to you?" John Hand asked bluntly.

"Me? Oh, little bit of trouble here and there. But I'm sure it's nothing compared to what you've been through! Come in, sit down." But the prince didn't guide them into his quarters. He stood rooted to the spot, looking at Packer, smiling thinly. He didn't mean to, but he couldn't help it. Once he had caught Packer's eye, he could not pull his own away. The young man's expression was completely open, a window into a turbulent, accusing soul. The look penetrated through the prince's dark secrets and left him stunned and vulnerable.

"Where is Panna?" Packer demanded.

The prince straightened up, and took a step back. "Panna?"

"We just ran into the princess," John Hand explained.

The prince recovered somewhat, and smiled again. "Ah. Dearest Jacqalyn. She is such a one for making up stories—"

"What happened to Panna?" Packer asked urgently.

"Packer," John Hand said, putting a very firm hand on the young man's shoulder. "Let me handle this."

Packer didn't budge, and didn't take his eyes off the prince. John Hand stepped into his line of sight. "Walk away, Ensign Throme. Wait for me at the end of the hall."

Only when the admiral broke Packer's focus did he understand the danger he was putting himself in. "Sir?" he asked, his intensity unaltered.

"Step away. That is an order."

Packer turned and walked down the hall, his ears filled with a loud buzzing, his hands tingling.

Mather and John Hand chatted for a few moments, and then the

The Hand That Bears the Sword

prince motioned to a dragoon. "Guard, take Mr. Throme to the Blue Rooms," he instructed quietly. "And once you put him in, do not let him out."

The wagon groaned, and the swayback mare plodded with heavy hooves on the cobblestones. Bran Mooring raised his head, having finished his prayer, feeling deeply saddened, but confident now about what must be done. He was seated inside the wagon facing backward, at Will Seline's left shoulder. He pulled back his hood and looked at the driver's profile. The man's eyes were narrowed and focused.

"Of course," Father Mooring said with a smile, "you're taking him to the church for preparation first."

The driver's brow drooped further, obscuring his eyes completely. "Church?" he asked without turning.

"You're burying a priest."

The two guards looked at one another, deep concern mirrored in their faces. "Or else what happens if he don't go to a church?" asked the driver.

"What happens?" Bran asked right back, as though amazed by the question. "My good man, this is a priest of God." He emphasized the last word. And he said no more.

The driver swallowed. "How long would such preparations take?"

"No more than a few hours. Usually."

"Hours?"

"Overnight at the longest."

The man jerked his head around and stared wild-eyed at Father Mooring. "We can't do that!"

"Ah, that is unfortunate, then." And Bran Mooring turned away, facing backward. He bowed his head.

The wagon drew to a halt. The driver turned in his seat and stared hard at the two priests in the back of his wagon. He wasn't sure which would cause him more trouble now, the live one or the dead one. "Look, we can't wait around at a church for you to do your... whatever. We gotta bury him and get back. We got orders."

"Maybe you could do it in a few minutes?" the younger one asked. "Sort of a rush job?"

Bran Mooring looked him in the eye. "A rush job?"

The younger one hung his head. The driver looked at him like he'd suggested treason. The silence deepened. Then deepened further. Finally, Bran Mooring decided to take a risk.

"You could always leave him at the chapel with me," he offered. "We'll bury him quietly. We do take care of our own."

"Why couldn't we do that?" the younger one asked his partner plaintively.

"I will promise," the priest added, "that no one but priests will know of his burial. And you two gentlemen," now he summoned an extra dose of solemnity, "will be remembered in our daily prayers for a long time."

"How long a time?" the younger one asked.

Bran nodded, stroked his chin. "Two weeks."

The two guards looked at one another. The younger one shrugged. It seemed like a bargain.

"Three," the driver countered.

"Done."

Once Will Seline's big body was laid out on the floor within the nave of the Seminary chapel, covered with the single grimy sheet from the prison, Bran Mooring put a hand on each guard's shoulder. Several other priests had gathered by this time. All managed to refrain from asking Brother Bran what in the world he was doing. They were in fact a very quiet bunch, which put the two guards at ease.

"Thank you," Bran told them. "You have made the good choice, even though it was the hard choice. You will be remembered in our prayers. Let this be the beginning of a new page in your lives. Go in peace, and seek the things of God."

They both smiled as they turned away. Their deep sense of satisfaction would last almost all the way back to the prison, when they would begin to worry that they had just left a dead man unburied, against the orders of a prince.

As soon as the two were out of earshot, Bran Mooring knelt and pulled the sheet away. He turned his face up toward his fellows. "This is Will Seline, father of Panna Throme. He died in Prince Mather's prison for the crime of trying to learn his daughter's fate."

"And do we yet know her fate?" one of them asked, alarmed. They had all heard by now of the dragoons who had taken an axe to Father Mooring's door.

Bran looked from face to face. He found Usher Fell's and spoke directly to it. "Thankfully, she has escaped Prince Mather's machinations alive. But my brothers, this is the evil done within the palace walls, even as the Drammune are poised to sack the city. Let us pray that God may show mercy on us all."

Usher Fell was as impassive as stone. "Yes," he said, as the others looked at him. He did not break eye contact with Father Mooring. "Let us pray indeed."

CHAPTER 21

The Siege

Within a few hours, the euphoria created by the stories of the glorious exploits of the *Trophy Chase* had vanished. The tail of the tale, like a scorpion's sting, struck home. It was this: The Drammune Armada was but hours away, thousands upon thousands of troops bent on vengeance for the awful things the *Trophy Chase* had done to them, for the way Packer Throme and Admiral John Hand had humiliated them. A hundred ships, a thousand ships, more, all on the warpath, just over the horizon, in the Bay of Mann. And then the grim rumor spread, the darkest of all, as impossible to verify as any other, but more insidious for its being true: The Vast Fleet had already been destroyed. Only the *Trophy Chase* and a handful of merchant vessels remained.

By nightfall, the panic had begun. Someone heard that the king had fled. Someone else heard someone say that the Drammune were already here, had already arrived. Warriors would be pouring into the City in the darkness. Someone packed up his family, and someone else decided to send his family away, and then someone decided to take her children to safety, and then several someones saw whole families leaving, and decided the time had come for them as well, and all those someones began hurrying so as not to be left behind, and many others in turn saw their haste, and in it detected fear, and soon the streets were filled with people and carts and dogs and bags and wagons filled with cherished possessions, all heading out of the City in a great emotional frenzy. And the filled streets filled even more, grew glutted, and the movement slowed to a stop. And that's when the panic set in. They would surely be killed where they stood! So the push began for the Old City, to get inside the Rampart, where they all would be safe.

When the soldiers saw the size of the crowds and began to refuse people entry to the Old City, the panic turned to terror, and then to anger, and the trouble began. Punches were thrown, rocks were thrown. Gunshots were heard.

Packer was awakened by the sounds, went to the porch as he shook dark dreams from his head. Across the landscaped serenity of the palace grounds, the Old City was in turmoil; citizens hurled stones, fought with dragoons, swore at one another. He heard the crack of a pistol, then the sound of muskets. He rushed to the door, opened it, and found it blocked by a dragoon who immediately turned to face him. He held his pike up as though to ward Packer off.

"There's trouble in the City," Packer told him calmly. "I wanted to tell…someone."

"My orders are to keep you here, sir. I'm sorry."

"Well, get someone else, then!"

"I'll do that, sir. Now please, step back inside and close the door."

Packer shook his head in disbelief, but he did as he was told. What kind of nonsense was this, to confine him to quarters as though he were dangerous? And how silly was it to post but one guard, if he were in fact dangerous? What was the prince up to?

And what on earth had happened to Panna?

Bench Urmand rode the streets as long as he could, trying to calm the citizens, trying to help organize the military. He succeeded at neither.

When he had shouted himself hoarse to no noticeable effect, and begun to fear that he himself might soon be caught and unable to move, he turned his horse toward the Old City, toward the palace, and ran at an angry gallop.

Up until this moment, his plans had been going quite well. He had been reasonably satisfied with the work on the defenses of the City. He was working through a well-designed communications plan,

The Hand That Bears the Sword

a series of proclamations that would result in a well-defended city, evacuated of women and children. The first was read two days ago, with instructions on fortifications for homes and businesses, and how to begin making preparations to send noncombatants away. But the proclamation that was to be read this very evening was the one with key instructions for an orderly evacuation.

Bench had moved as fast as he reasonably could, he thought, without inciting panic. But the *Trophy Chase* had arrived with her news one day too early. He had made all the plans, but they were useless now, dust and vapor. The city was in an uproar, and it was beyond his means to contain it. He could only pray that the rumors of an imminent attack were not true, and that this furor would calm down overnight. He needed to redraft his proclamation and get it out to the people as soon as he possibly could. He needed to get to the palace, and to the king's heralds, so they could get to the people.

The Armada, now led by Commander Huk Tuth on the Drammune warship *Kaza Fahn,* furled sails just over the horizon from Nearing Vast. It was approaching sundown when nearly a hundred warships, three fewer than had set out from Drammun, all hove to and awaited orders to land their cargo of warriors on the shores of Nearing Vast, near the City of Mann.

Admiral John Hand entered Packer's quarters. Packer stood. He had been seated by the open doorway to the patio, with the night breezes blowing in. The violence in the streets had calmed somewhat, but the turmoil within him had not. He wanted only for all things to be right, and all things, it seemed, were wrong.

John Hand looked into the eyes of the young man and recognized something new there, a dead calm that was something like the distant, watchful look Packer had worn when walking from the prow of the *Chase* back to his cabin, after the Firefish had destroyed the *Nochto Vare.* But this was calmer, stiller, more composed. There was no trace of the torn and tormented soul that had set sail with him but days ago, or even the angry, confused young man who had learned an hour ago that his wife had been held captive by his prince.

"I'm taking the *Chase* and the new Fleet, such as it is," Hand announced, "out to open waters."

"When?"

"Now. We sail tonight."

Packer's jaw tightened. "I can't go with you."

John Hand smiled. "Well, you don't have a choice in the matter. But as it turns out, you're staying here."

Packer nodded, but now he wondered. "On your orders? Or his?"

"His."

Packer's expression did not change. "What do you know about Panna?"

John Hand met his gaze. "More than I will tell you."

"Did she hit him?"

Hand was silent.

"Was it Panna who hit the prince?"

John Hand was silent again. And Packer knew the answer.

"What did he do to her?"

"He is the Prince of Nearing Vast, Packer. And I am the Admiral of the Fleet. You do not get to ask all the questions."

"Because I'm just an ensign. That's what matters here, isn't it? Power? Power to take what you want, to abuse those who have no power, for whatever purpose seems good at the moment?"

"Are you talking about the prince? Or about me?"

"I'm talking about the prince." Packer reached into his shirt and pulled out the Drammune cap. He held it out to the admiral. "If I were talking about you, I'd be talking about greed."

John Hand, without missing a beat, slapped Packer hard, backhanded, across his right cheek. Packer's eyes widened, but he took it. Then he stuck out his chin and pointed to his left cheek. "Don't forget this one."

Now John Hand smiled. It was a cruel smile. "I was an honest businessman, doing honest business for king and country. The Drammune bought, and we sold. And they paid a reasonable price."

"I'll bet they did."

"The king got his taxes. It was no secret to the Crown. But that's over now. Times have changed. There's a war to fight. It's not the prince's war. It's not my war. You may not like everything that I've done, or that he's done. You may have good reason for that. But it's your country under attack. It's our war, Packer. It's yours just as much as mine. And your country needs you. Will you fight for your king? Your prince? Your kingdom?"

Packer dropped the cap on the floor. "That's why you came in here, to find out if I'm still loyal? What do you want, a promise that I'll keep your secrets? His secrets? No matter what you've done to your country, or what he's done to my wife, I should swear allegiance and keep my mouth shut?"

"Yes."

"Why?"

"Because anything else is treason."

Packer waited a long while before answering. But during that time John Hand saw no faltering in the hardness of Packer's blue eyes. Finally, Packer said, "I am not the betrayer here. I am the betrayed. This nation has been betrayed."

John Hand just laughed. "Bravo. Nice performance. Son, your ethics are well-honed. You would do well, however, to sharpen them to a more practical edge."

"I'll leave that to you. You seem to be good at it."

"It's called strategy. And I'm *very* good at it." And with that, Hand walked away. But he paused at the door and turned back to Packer. He simply could not leave on that note, with those words hanging in the air.

"Packer, I don't believe what you believe. If there is a God, I don't think He cares who wins wars. If He's there, I would hope He's bigger than to send Firefish to fight for one side over another. I don't really know what happened out at sea, why that dumb beast did what it did. And neither do you. If you want to let others believe it was because God favors you, that's your business. But when you start believing it yourself, start putting yourself above your country, then that's *my* business. The simple fact is, you can't be trusted. For you to turn against your kingdom, on the eve of war on our city streets? It would be a crushing blow. It would hurt us more than anything you've done so far has helped us. The people need to take heart, not lose it. But don't worry, you've got one chance left to help your country. Heroes make the very best martyrs."

Packer sighed, ignoring the threat. "You don't see it, Admiral." Now he spoke more gently, now that the parting was done, now that the cards were all on the table. He felt no need for anger. Sides had been taken, decisions made. So be it. "But there truly is a Kingdom that matters more than this one."

"Ah, the Kingdom of God." Hand smiled a crooked smile. "And that's your allegiance, is it? Well and good. But wait and see what happens to that Kingdom, to all its churches and its choirs and its little lambs, all its humble believers, once the Drammune get hold of this one."

Packer remained silent.

John Hand's look softened. Despite his best efforts to the contrary, he couldn't help but like Packer Throme. "I'm glad I knew you, Packer. I mean that. Truth is, I would be happy if this world were actually the one you think it is. But unfortunately, it's just not."

"Goodbye, Admiral."

As the Admiral left, he nodded to the dragoons who waited outside the Blue Rooms. They entered, four of them, heavily armed, brandishing swords and pikes.

Packer was escorted with respect to his new quarters. The dragoons bade him well, apologized for doing their duty. The door clanked. The straw was fresh, but the smell was not. It was the same dank cell that had last seen Father Will Seline.

The two prison guards watched the dragoons leave, then turned to look at one another. The sallow one's raised eyebrow and the frowning one's pursed lips said the same thing. A prince who would jail a sick priest and then Packer Throme had something to hide. So maybe all the rumors were true.

As the dragoons walked away, Packer looked across the aisle at a stony-faced, shaggy prisoner in the opposite cell. This man showed little surprise, but felt a significant amount of it just the same.

"Afternoon, Commander," Packer said to him grimly.

Abbaka Mux said nothing.

By nightfall, the crowded streets were still packed, but at least they were moving: a teeming mass of citizens putting as much distance between themselves and the Drammune as they could. Dog Blestoe and his fellow citizen-soldiers had finally ceased their toils. Most had been given a musket or a pistol or at least a decent saber, several rounds of ammunition, and were placed inside the sandbagged redoubts that peppered the streets. It was just possible, Dog thought with some satisfaction, that he would finally have a chance to prove his mettle. When the shooting started, he would show these fat, lazy regulars what ferocity looked like.

But right now he, like them, simply watched the thick river of humanity flow by. He checked his musket's flint once more. Satisfied, he relit his pipe.

If it was true that the Drammune were coming tonight, this would be a night to remember. Dog Blestoe would make it memorable for a few Drammune, anyway.

Candles lit the inside of the chapel, surrounding the coffin that lay on the floor before the altar, under a wooden cross. A young woman in priest's robes entered from the nave, and stopped at the back of the tiny sanctuary. She looked behind her at the smallish priest who had brought her here. His glistening eyes could not contain his sadness, which now rolled down his round and ruddy cheeks. She turned away, and looked again at the rough pine coffin, open where it lay, a gray-robed figure within it. She looked up at the altar, glowing with thick white candles, their flames in a gentle, silent dance, and then she looked up at the cross. Moving slowly at first, so as not to stumble, feeling transparent and ethereal, weightless, as though any small breeze might take her away, she walked toward the altar. Halfway there she broke into a run, and fell upon the gray form, burying her face in his robes, her body racked and trembling. There she knelt, sobbing, embracing him, feeling the coldness, the stillness in the great girth that should be shaking with laughter and drawing her close, or rising and falling with deep, sonorous snores. All this was wrong, everything was askew and twisted, all was now hope crushed, and ruin.

Words unformed and unspoken fell within her tears and soaked into the cloth of her father's robes. *Why, why cannot all be well? Why must this dark world never cease to hurt and maim and kill? Why does joy lead to grief, and why do hopes live like tenuous candle flames within so deep a valley of shadows? And when, when will You put all this to rights?*

And then a touch on her shoulder brought her back. "We must go," Father Mooring implored her. "You must not be found here."

She looked at her father one more time, his face peaceful in the flickering light. He was not here, she knew suddenly. He had gone away, and would never return. He was with her mother now. He was with his Tamma. She said goodbye, and kissed his forehead.

The streets were a river of people fleeing, and the uncertainty of war did not allow for planning, nor for waiting, not even for one day. Messages to, and then from, the High Holy Reverend Father, dean of the Seminary and head of this order, were succinct. FR. Will Seline was to be buried tonight, immediately, and in an unmarked grave on the Seminary grounds. A more suitable resting place might well be found when safety and security reigned in the City once more, but only the days ahead could tell.

And so a phalanx of priests carried the big coffin to the very corner of the Seminary, where the two great walls of the Rampart met. Guards looked down from the parapet in puzzlement, watching as the pine box was set deep beneath the earth, buried alongside the cornerstone of the City's earthly fortifications.

Whether this rite and the death it commemorated would secure the City's foundation or undermine it, Bran Mooring thought, only the days ahead would tell.

By eleven, the stream of evacuees had become a trickle, and the streets had attained something close to their usual level of quiet. But the scene itself was not usual in many regards. Not only had most of the citizens left for the countryside, Vast troops—such as they were—patrolled casually, or watched groggily, or dozed openly at their posts. Among the customary characters of the night, the inebriated and those who would steal from them one way or another, were a dozen men dressed in garb typical of those around them, except that they appeared far less dangerous than the brigands who flitted from shadow to shadow, following drunks home. These were Drammune scouts, a dozen spies who spoke perfect Vast, had lived in the City for long stretches in the past, and who now spread out through the City, noting every cannon placement, every earthen barrier, every posted guard.

By midnight, a common coach pulled by four plodding draft horses had left the palace gates, curtains drawn tight. On top, rough hemp ropes tied down a soiled canvas that covered bulky trunks and bags. Inside the carriage were four occupants accustomed to somewhat higher standards of travel: Princess Jacqalyn, Queen Maeveline,

King Reynard, and the High Holy Reverend Father and Supreme Elder Harlowen "Hap" Stanson.

Following this coach was another, equally common. Inside it rode two garrulous household maidservants, an elderly valet already fast asleep, and a very wide, exceptionally grumpy herald. Before and behind the two coaches rode a contingent of armed horsemen, dragoons in civilian dress, protecting the advance, the rear, and the flanks of the royal family.

Also by midnight, the spies had reached their rendezvous point, reporting their information to Huk Tuth himself, who, surrounded by his generals, consulted maps and drew up new battle plans, dashing out orders and sending them back in small, dark boats to tall, dark ships that had moved silently into position and stood in blackout at anchor near the Vast shoreline, but outside the Bay of Mann. Then nearly a hundred ships began lowering hundreds of boats, packed with men and gear. The great troop ships unloaded bloodthirsty warriors into enormous tenders built to ferry thousands to shore. They disgorged their cargo as efficiently and as effectively as the great Drammune fishing boats caught and ingested theirs.

By five in the morning, fifty thousand Drammune troops were on the ground, all moving silently toward the City like a seeping, steady flood. With the information gathered by their spies they quickly, silently, and mercilessly overran the outermost guard posts and watches, small squads stationed here to provide early warning, to prevent precisely what was now happening.

These Vast outposts were completely surprised by the attack. They had been told that the Drammune would likely not move in the night, but would gain a beachhead in darkness, in a single spot to the north of the Bay of Mann, perhaps as far away as Split Rock, massing their troops for a daylight march and then a prolonged onslaught. The assault was expected to take days. These, in fact, were the battle plans captured by John Hand.

But Huk Tuth had made no small adjustment, assuming his commander's strongbox had fallen into enemy hands. He changed everything. He landed his boats in a hundred different spots. Then he used his spies to guide his officers. He was particularly concerned about the cavalry. He recognized that as fierce as a man on horse was in battle, his greatest value was in reconnaissance. A single horseman could gain knowledge of his enemy's position while in full stride and take that news to his commanders with enough speed to turn a battle. Or a war.

So the Vast cavalry went next. Surrounded where they bivouacked, none escaped. The Drammune commanders took the mounts for themselves. And then they led the Drammune troops, a crimson flood, moving quickly with small arms but with a very large and visceral desire to avenge their losses at sea.

By six in the morning that flood had reached the outskirts of the City, maps and orders and muskets and swords in hand, waiting for the moment they would overflow the banks, storm over the walls, and top the crumbling levee that was the Vast Army.

Huk Tuth was satisfied. Messages from his Armada told him all was quiet at sea. A contingent of Vast merchant vessels had left the harbor yesterday, a dozen or so ships that had set sail around nightfall, skirting the coast, avoiding the strength of the Drammune as if they knew what lurked over the horizon. Tuth was happy to let them go. He cared about the Vast Navy, not a few ragtag merchant ships. The Fleet, and he still believed there were at least fifty warships remaining to the Vast, was not in the harbor at the Bay of Mann. So far, they had not appeared at sea, either. But they could not be far off.

The commander did receive one report that the great *Trophy Chase* was among the merchant vessels that had escaped, but this was unconfirmed, and Huk Tuth was loathe to believe it. That particular ship would be leading the entire Vast Fleet in defense of the kingdom, not running for its life with a flotilla of merchant boats.

And besides, Tuth's troops were safely ashore. The *Trophy Chase* and all the Devilfish in the sea couldn't stop the Kingdom of Nearing Vast from falling now.

At the first light of dawn, it began. Trained and disciplined troops began to move, each one wearing an impenetrable hauberk and helmet, each equipped with musket, pistol, short sword, powder, and ammunition, each rested, fed, and focused on a single objective: taking for themselves and their Hezzan the dominion of the Vast.

With scouts and outposts—the outermost defenses that should have sent messages down the line—already destroyed, the Drammune rolled over the Vast forces before most of them even understood they were under attack. Of the five thousand Vast troops stationed on the outer perimeter, less than five hundred were able to fire a single shot in defense. A handful managed two rounds. But not a single placement, not a single battery fought tenaciously enough to slow the onslaught. Not a single Drammune warrior even stopped to take cover. They reloaded on the run.

The career Vast soldiers and the officers were no more proficient than the raw recruits, except in one regard. Many who had seen battle before, however long ago or far away, recognized it in the air; the silence grew thick, the hair on the napes of their necks stood on end, and the smell of the air became tinged with death. And so, thanks to these instincts, many of them survived. They ran sooner and faster than their greener compatriots.

The second line of defense heard gunfire, and were thus more prepared. Twenty thousand men along the second line, the primary defenders of the city, all of whom were ensconced in fortified positions behind sandbag redoubts in narrow streets and broad highways, readied themselves, palms sweaty, breaths coming short. What they saw, however, surprised them as much and left them as defenseless as their counterparts on the perimeter. They saw uniformed Vast regulars, hundreds of them, running toward them, fleeing for their lives. At first, it was all they saw, but very quickly Drammune horsemen appeared among them, cutting them down with flashing swords, and then came Drammune foot soldiers behind them, thousands upon thousands, a solid mass of muskets and swords and blood-red anger.

Though there were more Vast soldiers here, fewer of them in the second line of defense were killed or injured. This was because a far greater number of them turned and ran, and did it far sooner. The few who stayed, who fought bravely, who fired and reloaded and attempted to fire again, did not live to fight another day. While the blood of the ferocious seeped into the soil, the feet of the fearful saved their finely uniformed posteriors.

The inner ring of defense, stationed around the Old City at the Rampart, another ten thousand regular troops, heard little gunfire. What they heard instead was an eerie sound, like a rumble of thunder and a rush of wind combined. Dog looked over at his fellow soldiers, who were just as perplexed as he was.

"What on earth is that?" he asked.

But within minutes, they all knew. It was the sound of men running, the Vast armies fleeing for their lives up cobblestone streets, chased by horsemen and by thousands of roaring, mocking warriors from the Kingdom of Drammun. The sight was shocking, and utterly unnerving. Dog's mouth dropped open. But when he looked back at his comrades, he was alone. The eight men who had been stationed behind the sandbags with him were simply gone, having joined up with the fearful Vast horde, having without word or vote, unanimously disappeared. Or, almost unanimously.

Dog cursed. He couldn't run. Not because he didn't want to, but because he was too old. His feet were bad. If he'd been the first out, maybe he could have gotten somewhere. But now it was too late. The Drammune were within range. He'd be shot in the back, or stabbed from behind.

He swore again. Then he took aim at a horseman, a particularly big, burly one, and fired. The man just kept coming. He didn't even slow. Dog was stunned. He looked at his musket. Had he forgotten the musket ball? No, he had checked it a dozen times. And it had fired; he felt the kick. But as he looked back up, a Drammune sword slashed him across the chest, from left armpit to right shoulder.

The Drammune horseman had meant to take the gray-haired Vast soldier's head, but Dog had looked up, straightening at the last moment, and the blow struck low. The warrior kept his horse at a gallop, sure he had taken the dominion of one more salamander. His blade had bitten deep, and the force of the blow had knocked the old man backward to the ground. Surely, he was dead.

Dog lay on his back, putting frantic hands to his chest. Blood pumped from him. He rolled over, groaning, both hands still on the wound, attempting to hold it shut. He didn't feel pain from the gash yet, only from the bone-jarring blow of the impact. He knew he had to stop the bleeding. He shoved earth, clay, sand, whatever his clumsy, uncooperative hands could sweep up around him, into the gaping wound. Then he lay still, squeezing the wound, fearing it was mortal.

He cursed once more. He was helpless. A helpless old man, unable to defend himself or his country or his king. His countrymen had turned and run, and left him to fight alone. Now he would die alone.

Half the Drammune horde gave chase, keeping the Vast on the run, while the other half, following carefully prepared orders, overwhelmed the defenses at the Rampart gates and streamed into the Old City.

Here, finally, the Vast army displayed its mettle.

There were fewer than twenty-five-hundred dragoons here, but they fought.

They fired from the Rampart; they fired from the redoubts. They fired face-to-face with the Drammune. They stopped only those warriors who took a musket ball to the face, or the neck, or the leg, or a lucky shot to the ribs at the armpit, but these Vast warriors did not pause to wonder why. The dragoons simply went for their swords and pikes and halberds, battle axes and maces. They fought brilliantly, they fought maniacally. They fought in the tradition of their forebears, and they lived up to an ancient standard of martial merit, a standard set high in action and then raised higher in the telling and retelling. Still, they met that standard.

Had their numbers been even, or close to even, the dragoons would have won the day.

But the numbers were far from even.

Prince Mather stood in the shadows of his balcony, watching. He hadn't seen the cowardice of his main troops, but he knew they had put up little resistance. He had received the breathless reports that they had been overrun quickly, shamefully. The Captain of the Guard had insisted that Mather flee through the tunnels underground, but Mather would not. He dismissed the captain, and then his own bodyguards, sending them out to join the fight.

And the Royal Dragoons fought as he watched. They were cornered badgers, rabid dogs. They fought where they stood, and they fought where they fell, sweeping with their swords as they dropped to their knees, reaching for hidden pistols, the derringer each had tucked into a belt or a boot, the one they liked to call their "grave surprise." They fired as they lay on their backs with mortal wounds, pikes and swords already driven through them. They showed the prince the true spirit of his Army.

But Mather took no satisfaction in their show of mettle. He was witnessing the end of everything, just as he had feared. The last trace of the glory of Nearing Vast, the extinguishing of the flame. Here was the last paragraph of the last page of a wondrous tale of valor that began long, long ago, with the Brothers Mann. It was ending here, before his eyes. Under his command.

Mann had fallen. And thus the whole of Nearing Vast had fallen. The kingdom was being taken from him, just as the priest had predicted. His rule was vanishing before his eyes. His people would no longer be his people. His power and his authority, gone like a wisp of smoke. He would be remembered, if he was remembered at all, in the same breath as the demise of a great nation. And why? Because of his sins. Because of his father's sins. That's what the priest said. *It is decided.*

Mather Sennett cursed the priest and his prophecy. He had foretold this end. But Panna, whom he had watched from this very porch while she sat in these very gardens, on a lawn now littered with the bodies of his soldiers, by that pool now red with their blood...Yes, the priest had predicted this end, but Panna had revealed to him the reasons for it. You will attack me again, she had promised. *You truly do not know your own heart.* So who was he? Certainly not the leader, the great king he had envisioned, the next King Fram the Fifth. A bully. That was her view of his character, his power. Now he had to consider that she was right on all counts. And what was left him? One choice. *You may choose the manner.*

If it was his duty to turn the kingdom over to the Drammune, then he would do it. He took a deep breath, which caught in his throat. He went to his bookshelf, his hands tingling with pinpricks as though they had fallen asleep, and he pulled out a thick, dark volume. His hands shook as he read the words "Rahk-Taa" tooled into its leather cover, in the bold strokes of the Drammune alphabet.

What he felt now, deep in every pore, was fear. The engraved leather radiated it; his fingertips absorbed it; his blood carried it to his heart and to his mind. He was powerless against it, against this book, against this people. And he loathed being afraid.

But in his hands he held the keys to power, raw power, greater than any he had ever wielded or known, the naked, brutal power that ruled the earth by force, that had always ruled the earth by crushing foes and destroying enemies. Mather had never been brutal enough to amass power like that. Mather was a bully, and King Reynard a fool, but Fen Abbaka Mux and his commanders were different, they led from a different level of brutality. They understood domination.

The Hezzan was an absolute monarch, a dictator, an emperor who ruled with iron. And here in this book was the power that would rule from this very palace before the sun rose again over the Vast sea.

Mather began reading, refreshing his memory, absorbing. He already knew this book as well as he did his own nation's Scriptures. In fact he knew it better, since it contained Drammune law and not simply philosophy or belief systems. He had studied it dutifully through his youth, never imagining it might save his life one day.

Nearing Vast might be finished, but Mather Sennett was not.

The fighting Panna heard outside the priest's little cottage was brutal, cries and shrieks, guttural roars of pain and anger, swords clashing, bodies thudding to the earth or into one another or against the wooden walls, shaking the entire cottage. Father Mooring had brought her back to this cottage after she had said her goodbyes to her father, then he had left her alone. He had not returned. She had slept little, sitting by a cold fireplace, wrung out and defeated. Her mother and father were together. That was good. But she was now alone. She wanted Packer, she wanted to see him, she needed to be with him. The shaft that led down to safety stood open, and it beckoned her. But Panna was not willing to go hide just yet. The fighting had begun, and Packer might be out there.

That there was fighting here, inside the Rampart, on the grounds of the Seminary so near the palace, struck her as a very bad sign. She remembered Packer's warning, that this war would be short. But still, it was certainly possible that the Drammune would be stopped here, and turned back. Wasn't it? If the Vast had the better swordsmen? She wondered how she could help. Perhaps there was a role for her.

She had Father Mooring's largest kitchen knife in her hand as she moved silently to the front window. She put her face close to the curtain, then parted it ever so slightly, one eye peeking out onto the grounds. What she saw shocked her. She had expected to see duels, men paired up evenly, fighting nobly, bleeding sparingly as they sunk to their knees in defeat. But what she saw was quite different. Bodies flew, steel flashed and sang, blood spattered and poured, men rammed heads into walls, skewered one another on fence-posts, gouged and bit and stabbed and cursed, all in a jumble of activity so chaotic and frenetic that it was impossible for her to discern any pattern. Everyone was bloody, everyone was maniacal.

She couldn't determine which side might be winning. She could hardly tell which side was which. It looked to her like a single pack of rabid dogs destroying one another. The image came to her of the Firefish at the feeding waters, as Packer had described it, tearing one another to bits.

Just then a helmetless head slammed against the glass right in front of her, then slid downward, leaving a trail of blood. Panna took a deep breath in, an audible gasp. A Drammune warrior stood before her, not four feet away, his battle axe dripping blood. But then he looked down, grunted once, and kicked the lifeless body at his feet. Apparently satisfied with his handiwork, he turned back to the fray. Panna closed her eyes in a silent prayer of thanks. The darkness inside the house had kept her hidden; he had seen only his own reflection.

Panna decided she needn't part the curtains again. Instead, she went to the kitchen and found an oil lamp. She lit it, tucked the knife into the braided cord that was the belt of her robe, and climbed down the ladder. Leaving the lantern at the bottom, she climbed back up and, with a great effort, managed to pull the stove over on top of her.

She climbed to the bottom again, twelve feet down, and sat on the cold stone, waiting there among the priest's stock of onions and potatoes and jars of preserves, for she knew not what.

"I'm joining the Army," Prince Ward announced. He wasn't quite in the room, his head and torso only, his right hand flat against the wall as he leaned in. His eyes were alert, afire. Almost merry.

Mather looked up from his book, trying to make sense of the statement. It couldn't have seemed more ridiculous if his brother had announced he was running off to join the circus. "Where?" he asked, finally.

"Wherever I find them. Do you know where they are?"

"No. You're assuming there's an Army left to find."

"Yes, I am assuming that. Say, where's your guard?"

"I sent them all down to fight." Mather didn't look at Ward as he said it. He controlled the fear within him; he would not let his brother see a trace of it.

"Oh. Pity about that. You're leaving, aren't you?"

"I'm not." Mather said it curtly. Ward was so at ease, it was maddening.

Ward nodded, but did not move. The silence grew. Then a thought occurred to him. "I heard you put the Throme boy in prison."

Mather's fear turned to anger. "Yes, what of it?"

"Just wondered on what charge?"

"None whatsoever!" Mather turned to glare at his brother. "I'm holding him there for my own protection." He turned back, scanned the page in front of him with his finger.

Ward nodded. "Don't suppose I could get him out? He might be helpful."

"Drammune are already there, I'm sure. They'll want their supreme commander back."

"Oh. Tough going, then."

A pause. "Was there something else you wanted?" Mather asked, hardly able to control his irritation.

Ward shrugged, but took no offense. This was hard for Mather. "Do you plan to surrender?"

"Call it what you will. I intend to negotiate the fair treatment of our soldiers and our citizens. And yes, myself to boot."

"The Drammune aren't known for any of that."

Mather turned and stared hard at him. "If you'll excuse me. I'm busy here."

Ward nodded, frowning in a knowing way. Mather had always wanted to be a great king. As much animosity as there had been between them, Ward had always believed Mather would become just that. He found it sad now that it would never be. He wanted to be encouraging, but it seemed far too late for that. "Well, good luck to you, big brother."

Mather looked him in the eye. Ward had never called him that before. He softened a little. "Thank you. And to you."

And then Prince Ward was gone. Mather looked back down to the book before him, read a line or two, and then put his head in his hands.

Prince Ward could hear them. The booms, the groans of the palace doors under pressure from whatever ramming device the attackers were using. Then he heard the crash of glass, the halberds and swords clearing window frames.

He kept moving. He felt his way along the stonework of the passageway in darkness until he was far enough from the library above him that he could hear nothing. Then he stopped and lit a match. He put it to the small oil lantern in his hand. His position now illuminated, he squinted in the darkness ahead, saw where the walls took a sharp right turn, thirty feet or so in front of him.

He turned the corner, then traveled within the narrow passageway for another hundred yards, through two more iron doors that required the key he had in his pocket, and then past three intersections with other passageways, making turns at two of them. Finally, he came to the end, a heavy iron door that appeared to have been rusting here, unused, for decades. It was covered with cobwebs. Three iron bars as big around as Ward's forearm served as deadbolts. He felt in his pocket for the key, and inserted the small, tarnished brass thing—not into the rusted padlock that hung there, but rather, into a small, covered opening just at knee level. This hidden lock freed the iron bars. He heard the click and slid the bars away. He pulled on the handle, and the door swung open toward him.

A moment later, he stood inside a cell within the palace's prison.

CHAPTER 22

The Fall

"The city is ours, Supreme Commander," the warrior told him, falling to one knee, placing his forehead on the floor.

Once the Drammune had stormed the palace, they found and took the prison easily, shooting the two guards where they stood. The older one, the one with the sallow face, had a key ring on his belt. Before the gun smoke cleared, the cell door of Fen Abbaka Mux swung open. Mux stepped out, immediately and fully in charge. The warrior in submission before him was Huk Tuth, Commander of the Glorious Drammune Navy.

"Rise. And their troops?"

Tuth stood. "Fled like cowards."

Mux nodded.

Then the gnarled old commander added, "Most of them."

Mux cut his eyes toward him. "How many have we killed?"

"No count yet. We shot many in the back as they ran, but many more escaped. They ran like rabbits. Their blue warriors, however, fought very well inside the palace grounds."

Mux looked surprised. Commander Tuth did not hand out praise lightly. "The dragoons?"

"Yes, sir."

Mux knew the report he had just been given was not nearly so good as it might have sounded to the other soldiers listening. The

348

Drammune armies had taken the city quickly, but many more Vast soldiers had escaped than had been killed. Worse, those who had stood and fought had taken a toll on his own troops.

"And their king?"

"Fled also. Of the royal family, only a prince remains."

Mux grimaced. Their king was alive, their armies intact. "How easily did we rout them?"

"Quite easily, sir, except within the stone walls here."

"They didn't stand and fight?"

"Only inside the walls."

Now Mux's great brow furrowed. "And how many officers did we capture?"

"None alive."

"None?"

"None alive, sir."

"Are our troops pursuing theirs?"

"Yes, sir."

"Stop them. Immediately."

"Sir?"

"Call a halt to our advance; all troops are to camp where they stand, and await orders."

"But sir—"

"Do it now!" Mux roared.

"Yes, sir!" And Tuth hobbled off to find a horseman.

The supreme commander sighed. Maybe they *had* routed the Vast soldiers that easily. But Vast leaders were wily, and loved deception more than battle. It was likely a trap. This war was far from over.

He looked up and down the putrid cells.

"Shall we kill these Pawns now, sir?" a soldier asked, clearly hopeful.

"No. We are inside the palace grounds. These are political prisoners, trouble to the Crown one way or another. Some might be useful. We will sort them out later."

He walked over to the cell containing Packer Throme, who was seated cross-legged in the center of his straw bedding, watching. Mux pointed a finger. "This one, I know. I do not know why he is imprisoned, but I know he is a hero to the Vast. He has killed many Drammune. We will hang him publicly tomorrow."

"Yes, sir."

Packer did not know what all the words spoken by Abbaka Mux meant, though he was able to pick out "Vastcha," "nochtay" and of course, "Drammune." Packer also understood that he held a special place in the supreme commander's plans, and that it was not a particularly pleasant place.

Just to be sure Packer didn't miss his message, though, Mux grasped the bars with his thick fingers. He put his face in close, so that his beard jutted inside the cell. He was but six feet from Packer. "Nochtai Packer Throme," he said evenly, looking down on him. Then he waited. "Where is your chant now?" he asked in Drammune. "Where is your Devilfish now?" He waited several more seconds, then asked, "Where is your God now?"

Satisfied the yellow-haired warrior knew who had won, he turned his back, faced his own subordinate. The man was holding a bucket of water with a ladle. "What's that?" Mux asked.

"Water, sir. Thought you might be thirsty."

Mux shook his head, then changed his mind. "Give it." He took the bucket, ignored the ladle, and took a deep drink. Then he held it up toward Packer, spit in it, and poured the rest out on the ground.

He turned back to his subordinate. "Now take me to this prince."

Prince Ward closed the heavy door, and slid the iron deadbolts back into place. He had heard it all. He was sweating now, and his whole body seemed to shake. He put his forehead on the cold iron.

The cell on the other side of this door, where he had been standing a moment ago, was used for torture. It had no bars, but rather solid wooden walls that were lined with manacles and chains. The single oaken door that led out to the prison hallway locked only from the inside. Dark stains covered the floor. From within that chamber, Ward had been able to make out most of Mux's conversations. Ward's skills with the Drammune language weren't strong, but they were good enough to understand that Packer Throme would be hung in the morning.

But all Ward could think, and it was a thought he couldn't get past, was that Mather was plenty smart enough to have planned this ahead of time. Why had he not sent Packer away with the *Trophy Chase?* Why had he not sent him out to fight the Drammune? Why had he put Packer behind bars? Was it really about that girl? Or was there something else?

For my own protection, Mather had said. And now Ward couldn't shake one thought: What was the one offering a man like Fen Abbaka Mux might accept as evidence of Mather's goodwill toward Drammun? Who was the one sacrifice that might protect dear Mather?

Ward Sennett felt the need for a good, strong drink.

When Mux arrived in the prince's suite of rooms, Mather was seated at his desk, reading the Rahk-Taa. He was flanked by two Drammune warriors who guarded him with battle-axes. Several other warriors stood by, on watch, swords unsheathed. The show of force seemed all out of proportion for one slightly built, unarmed, beat-up young man intent on his studies.

As soon as he saw the supreme commander enter the room, Mather slid from his chair to his knees, and placed both hands and his forehead on the polished floor. "I submit to your will, and to the ruling of the Law," he said in Drammune, his voice quavering.

Mux narrowed his eyes, taking in this show. He looked from guard to guard, read the amusement in their eyes. "As is right," Mux said at last. "Rise."

When the prince stood, Mux saw clearly the fear within him. He also saw for the first time his damaged face. "You are a prince of this land?"

"I am Mather Reynard Mason Sennett, first son of Reynard Redcliff Odolf Sennett."

Mux looked him up and down. He noted the signet ring on his right forefinger. "Give it."

Mather took it off, held it out. Mux held his hand underneath it. The prince was careful not to offend the supreme commander by touching him as he dropped the signet into the thick, calloused palm. Satisfied that the blue opal was set within the royal crest, he tossed it back to Mather, who caught it with two hands.

"Who did this to your face?" he asked.

"My brother," he lied.

"Why?"

"I have turned against my own people." He said it with a forced smile. "I have worked tirelessly for this day. I welcome you, and all the Drammune."

Mux snorted. He could read a coward easily enough, and this

so-called noble was certainly that. His chin actually quivered. "You know you are a dead man. This ruse will not save you."

Mather's eyes grew wide. His conversion was very recent, true, but it was not in any way, by any means, feigned. Sitting alone in this room, one of his own rooms, surrounded by enemy soldiers who were spattered with Vast blood, who smelled of death, who would relish the opportunity to be spattered with royal blood and to smell like royal death, was an experience that invited just the sort of reflection in which he had already begun to engage.

Mather swallowed hard, trying not to appear as fearful as he felt, knowing the Drammune respected only strength. "You have slain many of the Unworthy," he said, nodding. "You have taken their dominion." He had to remind himself to quit nodding. He had to tell himself to breathe. "It is now my honor to serve you." He fell again into a position of prostration. He hoped his body's quaking wasn't too noticeable.

Mux looked at his soldiers again, who were trying not to laugh. Mux motioned them to be silent. Then he boomed, "Why should I believe this pretense?"

The prince's thin voice all but squeaked, as it rose up from his prostrate position. "I have delivered the nation's hero, Packer Throme, into your hands."

Now Mux scratched his beard. This, at least, was true. "Why?"

Mather spoke into the floor, chills going through him. "I thought you would like to kill him yourself, Your Worthiness. His dominion is not in titles or lands, but in the leading and inspiring of his people. That dominion should be yours by all rights."

"Stand before me." Mather obeyed. Mux tried to look past the abject terror, to see what kind of man hid within, and what his motives might be. "You speak excellent Drammune. And you know the Kar Ixthano."

He started nodding again. "Yes. I know it. I have undermined the strength of Nearing Vast, that you might arrive here as you have."

Now Mux hesitated. *Could it be true?* "Why?"

Mather breathed. He quit nodding. "I did not know why until now," he said honestly. "But I have studied the Rahk-Taa from childhood. I now understand where true power lies. I know for a fact it does not lie here in this land. We are weak. We are vile. I have contributed greatly to our downfall. This land is Unworthy. I have been Unworthy. But I now welcome the Worthy, who are destined to rule."

"So you will renounce your loyalty to your own kingdom?"

"I will," he said without hesitation. "If that is what you ask. I would rule it for you, however, under your Worthy guidance. I know these people. I have knowledge of our secrets. That is, their secrets. The Vast."

Mux stared hard at him. "You would become Drammune?"

"Oh, yes. Yes, sir. I would welcome that honor."

The soldiers glanced at one another. This weakling could never pass for royalty in Drammun. And yet, Mux thought, he could be extremely helpful. If, that is, he was truly in earnest.

"Do you renounce the God of your land?"

"Yes," Mather said instantly. He felt a twinge of conscience as he did, but he pushed it back to its source, wherever that was. No moral qualm could compete with the fear that sat like cold iron in the middle of his chest, like boiling liquid in his stomach. "With your permission, I now serve Fen Abbaka Mux."

One side of Mux's upper lip rose to reveal a broken tooth. "We shall see."

Dog never quite lost consciousness, though he drifted close several times. After waves of Drammune soldiers rushed by, he lay in the bloody dirt and sand for quite some time, expecting he would die. But after a while he didn't, and then after another while he thought maybe he wouldn't. This left his situation considerably improved, but also considerably more complex. He was very badly wounded, a Vast soldier lying in a sandbag redoubt in a city now taken by the Drammune. He was behind enemy lines.

So after another while, he realized he had to do something, and so he rolled over. His chest roared its unhappiness. It felt like it had been sliced clean through to his spine.

But it hadn't been. With great effort, and more excruciating pain yet, he sat up. His arms didn't work quite right, and when he looked at his chest, he knew why. He saw sand and rocks and dirt and caked blood filling a huge, straight gash across him, right through his shirt and skin and deep into the muscle.

He now heard footsteps, hobnailed sandals, soldiers speaking in a harsh foreign tongue. He put his head back against the sandbags. He was facing away from the street, toward the Rampart wall; there was a chance they wouldn't see him. He pulled his feet up toward him, which caused him almost as much pain as sitting up had. But it did the job. The soldiers passed by.

After several more whiles, during which he couldn't come up with a better plan than to stay hidden, a head popped over the top of the sandbags. "Are you all right?" it asked. This was the face of a well-meaning, smiling man, with merry slits for eyes.

"Fine," Dog answered bitterly. "Couldn't be better."

"Excellent," it said, and the face was gone.

Dog's anger rose, then was quickly replaced with a whimper of regret. He did need help. He wanted help. He simply had too much pride, even here at death's door, to admit it. He closed his eyes. He was a foolish, arrogant old man, and he would die here alone now from sheer orneriness.

But the face popped back up over the sandbags. "Just sit still. I'll bring help."

Tears of thankfulness stung his eyes.

Soon, three or four citizens were removing sandbags. An older gentleman had a light jacket that he took off, and without pausing in his efforts, threw it over Dog's shoulders. The smiling face, Dog now saw, belonged to a priest.

" 'In the world ye shall have tribulation,' " he quoted gently. " 'But be of good cheer; I have overcome the world.' " These words were a great comfort to Dog. He wasn't a very pious man, but the thought that anyone, ever, would have so much confidence as to speak words as bold as those was itself comforting.

"Can you stand?" the little priest asked in a whisper as he tugged at a sandbag.

Pain seemed to rack Dog's entire body, but when he looked at his legs he saw nothing wrong with them. "I think so."

"We'll have to make it look like you've been working. When I say so, stand up and walk."

"Should I take up my bed too?" Dog asked through gritted teeth.

The little priest smiled. It was a very tough man who could attempt humor at this moment. "I'll help you."

A moment later, three other men, all older than Dog, one appearing to be as old as Dog and Father Mooring combined, were working on the sandbags nearby.

"All right…stand up!" the priest said in a whisper. He and the coatless man helped Dog to his feet. Dog's face went white with the effort not to cry out. The priest hummed a hymn.

Standing, Dog could see that the work crew had been carrying bodies to the center of an intersection, stacking them there on wooden debris and straw, making an unceremonious funeral pyre of Vast soldiers. The conscripted Vast citizens were mostly old, infirm, female or, like Father Mooring, otherwise considered no threat to the Drammune soldiers who oversaw the effort. Dog was concerned that the jacket didn't cover the bloody gash across his chest. But before he could worry about it, someone standing by the pyre shouted to the Drammune.

"Hey! This one's still alive!" But he wasn't talking about Dog, he was pointing at a dead dragoon. The priest and Dog stood side by side, watching, their backs to the two Drammune overseers, who now came running to understand what the Vast salamander was yelling about.

"Ana nocht," Bran said to them as they passed.

The Drammune soldier kicked the dragoon, then calmly drew his sword and plunged it with two hands down through the dead man's back. "Nocht," he said confidently. "Charna," he ordered. And then he watched as the men put the dragoon's body onto the pyre. Kerosene was poured, and then the fire was lit.

A few minutes later, as the Drammune warriors watched the black smoke rise from the center of the intersection, it occurred to one of them that the little priest had spoken to him in Drammune. He looked around, but the priest had disappeared.

Bran Mooring was by then sitting in the back room of a small, boarded-up inn off a nearby alley, tending to Dog's wounds.

It was almost noon before Father Mooring set out for his own cottage again. His muscles ached, and his heart beat furiously as he picked his way carefully through the city streets. Makeshift funeral pyres were now burning at almost every intersection. The conscripted workers tried to be silent, tried to obey their conquerors, who had ordered silence, but they were exhausted, and so as they watched through tears and terror, an involuntary whimper, or groan, or sob provided a counterpoint to the roar and crackle of flame.

More than one citizen knelt and retched, overcome by the smoke

The Hand That Bears the Sword

and the stench of burning flesh, the sight of mangled bodies, the ruin it entailed, and the deeper darkness it promised. Other citizens, those who had not fled and who were not volunteered by the Drammune for this detail, stayed indoors and watched. Weeping could be heard from behind shuttered windows.

The Drammune warriors wrapped the bodies of their own fallen comrades in sheets and bedclothes taken from Vast homes, and loaded them carefully, even tenderly, into carts, to be taken to the shores of the Vast Sea, where they would be cremated in a far more ceremonial fashion.

Bran Mooring moved quickly, purposefully, along the edges of these streets, hugging the walls and windows of the closed shops and looted stores, staying in the deepest shadows. An occasional Drammune warrior would look at him, assess him, and let him pass. The priest did not understand this. Certainly he was a marked man, wearing the most visible badge of a God foreign to these people. But he thanked that God, and kept moving.

But it was no great mystery. With blood staining his hands, blood and sweat drenching his robes, he seemed to the Drammune both purposeful and pitiful. Since he had so obviously been put to work already, they assumed he had been sent on some errand. He did not appear to have the backbone to disobey.

When he saw his own cottage, Bran stopped and put a hand to his chest, trying to calm his heart. The front windows were broken in, and the door hung ajar. Heart still racing, he walked up to it, and gingerly stepped in.

A tornado had blown through. Every item in his living room had been displaced, overturned, broken, or stolen. He felt as though his very memory had been violated. He feared as he stood there that he would never be able to recall his students again. There at his feet was the little silver hairbrush. He picked it up, wiped glass shards from its bristles.

Still holding the brush in his hand, he crunched on broken glass toward the kitchen. But he stopped short. He heard snoring. He glanced into his bedroom, and then caught his breath. Hobnail sandals on grimy feet, protruding from the end of his bed. He stood still a moment, listening, then tiptoed closer. Two beefy warriors were sound asleep on top of his bedding, fully armed, their Drammune uniforms and crimson armor bathed in blood. The rest of the room was in total disarray, with all drawers and closets emptied onto the floor.

Father Mooring walked gingerly back into his kitchen. His stores of food were gone, his larger pots and pans missing, his shelves pillaged. His teapot had disappeared. The stove, however, had not been touched. He thought, not for the first time, how brilliant the idea was to hide a secret passageway below a stove. Men of violence might overturn everything in a house if they were searching for something of value, but a potbellied stove they would leave unmolested. Even the most ruthless of men had been children somewhere, and unless they'd been raised by wolves they had a mother or a grandmother or an aunt or some sort of guardian, someone who cooked meals on just such an implement. The bed was a place of deep mystery, of extremes, of dreams and terrors, pleasures and pains. The table was a place of exchange, of conflict and resolution, of argument and anger, commerce and camaraderie, lies and love. A chair was a seat at the table, representing authority, membership, rest, or reward; to have a chair was to belong, not to have a chair was to have no place. Drawers and shelves and closets were for hiding things, holding things in abeyance, planning for uncertain futures, and organizing unruly pasts. All these could be ruthlessly attacked, rifled, overturned, discarded, and for violent and unfulfilled men, all might be done with a deep sense of satisfaction, justified by the value that they held, that they might still greedily withhold.

But a stove? No, a stove could hold no deception; it had no ambiguity. It promised, and what it promised, it delivered. And no matter how bad a bad man's home life had been, how hated he was or starved for attention, the stove was still the producer of comfort, the hedge against hunger, the generator of warmth and light and sustenance. What need was there for, or what pleasure could be taken in, ransacking a stove?

Father Mooring let these thoughts slide quickly through his mind as he prayed that Panna was safe at the bottom of a twelve-foot shaft, that she was at this moment protected by such ordinary miracles.

Bran Mooring left his cottage with the small brush in his pocket, and saw a gathering of Drammune soldiers talking among themselves. He put an earnest look on his face and padded up to the group, as though continuing on his diligent mission. He bowed to them, and spoke in broken Drammune: "Two Worthies, dead in house," he said. "Many sorrows."

One scowled at him, then barked out curt orders. Another grabbed him by his hood, bunched it at the nape of his neck, and marched him back toward his own cottage. Three others drew swords and ran ahead. Bran Mooring was a study in smallness, a wisp of nothing, soft and round, surrounded by, propelled forward by, enormous, rock-solid, armed, dangerous men.

When two beefy, sleepy warriors came out of the cottage blinking and scratching, the others roared in laughter. They looked at the priest's wide eyes and laughed louder yet. Bran smiled sheepishly, bowed several times. "Sorrows for trouble," he said in broken Drammune. "Happy not dead." And when they let him go he padded off up the street, their laughter fading behind him.

Father Mooring turned the corner, and as soon as he was out of sight, he stopped, leaned back against the wall of a tobacco shop, and took a deep breath. He peeked back again. The gaggle of soldiers was now drifting away from his cottage, away from him. He looked up and down the street. Then he turned to look at the tobacco shop behind him. The front windows were broken in. The entire store had been looted by the Drammune, property claimed through the Right of Transfer, no doubt. A solitary cigar lay among the shards, just inside the window.

Bran felt a powerful desire to find some dark spot, some little haven, maybe even his own ruined home, and enjoy what might be his last simple pleasure for a very long time. He reached for the cigar, but before he touched it, his hand stopped. It wasn't his. It belonged to Bing Hamman, the proprietor. Some other day, when times were right again, he would pay for it, and he and Bing would smoke together. He pulled his hand back. He looked around the corner again. The Drammune were gone. He glanced up and down the street, then hurried back to his cottage.

All that day, the cleanup continued. The Drammune had complete control of the city, taking over the redoubts and fortifications that Dog and his comrades had built. The Drammune commanders were quite impressed with the planning that had gone into these positions. From them, the flow of traffic in the entire city could be controlled. The defenses had been well designed. The rings of defenders, if they had held, would have been formidable. "Brains but no heart" became the watchword among the Drammune. Another way to translate that would be *schemes without courage.*

As bodies burned, the gallows rose. Lumber had been found, men conscripted. It would not be a towering edifice, as was traditional among the Vast, but it would do the job. When finished, its deck would stand ten feet above the ground, and it would be large enough for nine men to stand across it, four on either side of the condemned.

The stairway, being the most time-consuming item to build, would be borrowed. A suitable staircase was found outside one of the finer homes, leading up to a second-story porch. It was ripped away, hastily cut to fit, and nailed to the gallows.

By late afternoon the nature of the structure was obvious, and fear-filled rumors began circulating throughout the City. The Drammune would hang the king. They would hang the prince. The entire royal family. They were going to hang one prisoner of war every hour, round the clock, until their demands were met. This rumor did not explain what their demands might be. The one rumor that did not circulate was that they had caught, and would now hang, Packer Throme. Whenever this was suggested, the speaker was immediately castigated. Everyone knew the *Trophy Chase* had sailed. Packer Throme had sailed with her, of course. The *Trophy Chase* and Packer Throme were practically the same. The *Chase* was gone, and therefore so was Packer.

Packer and the *Trophy Chase* were their hope. He and that ship were all but unbeatable. And standing with them was the Fleet, which was still out there, somewhere. The glory of Nearing Vast was alive and well, out at sea, in the natural habitat of the Vast, the one place where all others would fall short. It was only a matter of time before white sails filled the horizon, blue smoke filled the air, and red sails were driven back where they belonged.

One item that was not a rumor was the time of the execution. Handbills were posted. At ten in the morning, justice would be served. All citizens within the city were expected to gather inside the Rampart to witness it.

Prince Ward saw no handbills. He was deep underground, making his way through the tunnels. He knew the farthest ends of the passageways, and could navigate most of these routes blindfolded or, more to the point, blind drunk. He knew the route that would take him out into the countryside north of the city, in the direction that his armies had fled. He was confident he could bypass the Drammune, find a way to his countrymen, let some solid military man know about the hanging, someone who could form a raiding party. Then Ward could lead them back to rescue Packer. Four or five raiders, even if they started at first light, could move in, and with surprise on their side overcome the prison guards, release Packer, and be back in the safety of the underground tunnels before anyone knew what had happened.

But Prince Ward did not follow the path out of the city. Instead, he turned down a well-traveled passage that led to a small iron door. He unlocked it, swung it toward him. He stepped into a roughhewn but neatly kept wine cellar. He closed the door behind him. Where he had entered, now only a simple, plastered wall could be seen. He climbed the stairs out of the cellar.

He stood for a moment, surveying the familiar room. It was daylight outside, and though the inn had been shuttered and barred, sunlight streamed through several cracks, illuminating walls covered with the implements of war. A huge mahogany bar with rows of ale barrels behind it filled the wall to his left. He turned to his right and walked confidently to a display case that featured several ancient swords. He knelt in front of it. He pulled on a large drawer at its base, but it didn't open. He pushed it in, then reached up under the lip, found the latch, and opened the drawer.

He held his lantern over the contents: a large, long canvas bag, fastened with brass buckles. He pulled the bag from the drawer, and laid it on the floor. He opened it, and held the lamp above it. Inside were three oiled and sheathed swords with belts, three holstered pistols, with musket balls and powder charges, several long knives, and two short battle axes. All the latest manufacture, the best quality. The rest of the displays here were artifacts. But these were, in truth, the king's arms, kept for the use of dragoons who gathered in this tavern. Just in case.

Ward knew all about this stash. He had emptied many a mug of ale in this place. He had contributed to the right sort of drunkenness for many a Dragoon. He quickly loaded two of the pistols. He strapped a sword around his waist, tucked two pistols in his belt. Then he packed the rest back into the bag and returned it to its hiding place.

Armed and ready, he went to the bar. He looked for several minutes at the ales, the taps, the mugs hanging in front of him. Just a quick one, he thought. His throat was dry as a down thistle. Just one mug of that cool amber liquid, to see him on his way. *How could that hurt?* It couldn't. And it would help immensely. It would calm his nerves, end this shaking in his hands. He would feel better; he would be ready for anything, instead of feeling thin and stretched and sickly as he did now. Just one. To taper off.

But as he selected a mug, he knew exactly how it could hurt. As he walked behind the bar and put the mug under a spigot, turned it, watched the fluid fill the cup, smelled it as it filled his nostrils, he knew how it would hurt. The same way it had always hurt. Just one drink would make it easy to have just one more, and harder to go do what he must go do.

As he took his first large gulp, as the cool fluid poured down his throat to warm his belly, he knew without a doubt that if he had a second mug, he would be asking himself just who he thought he was. A rescuer? He was Prince Ward, a drunk. And after his third, he would be unable to face himself. He had sworn he would drink no more, and had meant it. But here he would be, having a fourth, and then a fifth, by himself, in the dark. And if he couldn't face himself, how could he face his own Army? And if he couldn't face his own Army, how could he face the Drammune?

He looked at a wall clock, its pendulum swinging slowly, ticking gently. Just after one. Tomorrow was a long way off. And perhaps, he thought, looking at the promise of relief offered by all those oaken barrels, perhaps this was all he really wanted to be. His eyes focused on the mirror's image of himself on the wall behind the bar, a dashing figure without backbone. Every time an opportunity to rise to his duty came, he wasted it. He treated every obligation like it was a mountain to be climbed, and every temptation like it was a gift from the dark gods, a way of escape, an opening into some cave or crevasse where climbing mountains was unnecessary.

It was a weakness of the Sennett line, he thought. That's what it was. His father was the same, though the temptations differed. His sister was given over to whatever whim struck her fancy. His brother, he had thought, was different. But Panna had proved otherwise to all and sundry. At root, the Sennetts were all the same. Surely, they were the weakest royal family that had ever pretended to nobility. And now they had together ruined their nation.

That fact begged for another drink.

So here was his gift from the dark gods. Rows of barrels of ale, all his. Bottles of rum. A cellar full of choice wine. For no one but Prince Ward Sennett. He took another long pull and wiped his mouth. It tasted so very, very good.

He was quite sure this was the best ale he'd ever had the pleasure of consuming.

"Mr. Throme?"

The words called him from a deep, dreamless sleep. "Who is it?" Packer squinted. He could see nothing.

"Stave Deroy. Royal Dragoons."

"Where are you?"

"Two cells down."

Packer squinted into the dark. He could see a big man's silhouette.

Chunk waved a hand in salute.

"You're a dragoon?"

"Yes, sir."

"And a prisoner?"

"Yeah."

"Why?"

"I let Mrs. Throme escape."

Packer thought about that. "Thank you."

"Only I didn't mean to do it. Prince Mather got angry, like I planned it. But I'm glad she did get away, though."

After a pause, Packer asked, "Do you know what happened to her?"

"What Prince Mather did, you mean?"

"Yes. What Prince Mather did to her."

"Yeah. I think. Most of it."

"And will you tell me?"

"Yeah. And there's more."

"More?"

"Her father."

"Will Seline? The priest?"

"Yeah."

"What about him?"

"He was here when I got here. Where you are now."

"Here? In prison?"

No response.

"What happened to him?"

"I'll tell you."

And Chunk told Packer all he knew.

The morning dawned hot and merciless, the first summer day of the season. The air was thick with the rain that had fallen all night in an angry argument between earth and sky. The elements had fought with lightning and thunder, rain and wind, and when their battle was done, and the ground strewn with wet leaves, twigs, and branches, the sky had cleared. Now the sun rose through the humid air like a glaring eye, its heat and light boring through the upper palace windows, then slowly working down its walls, down the western wall of the Rampart, then falling across the timbers of the gallows. When it reached the base, its rays then fired the grassy expanse of the open square. The Green was the large area just north of the palace, within the palace compound, appointed for great public gatherings, feasts, concerts, national celebrations, and public executions.

The handbills had done their job. Citizens began arriving early to claim a spot with a good view, as they always did for hangings. But it was a different kind of crowd today. Where usually there were families, parents bringing children to teach them the ultimate object lesson about the end of a lawless life, much of this crowd was made up of the lawless themselves, those who had stayed behind for dishonest gain, or because they cared little who held power in the palace. Dirk Menafee was here, he of the grizzled beard who had once attempted to rob Senslar Zendoda, along with a few of his fellow highwaymen and bounty hunters. So was Croc-Eyed Sam, with a handful of his regulars, old cutthroats who for whatever reason did not sail on Scat Wilkins' latest, and last, voyage. And here too was the proprietor of Will Seline's favorite used-merchandise emporium, already smoking her cigar. The rest were the ragtag remnant who for motives known best to them neither fought nor fled. Many still had the sullen looks, the sunken eyes gained from yesterday's grim labors. Filling out their numbers were the elderly, the marginally sane, the beggars. And of course, the priests.

The prince looked out from the north balcony window, over the amphitheater that was the heart of the Green. All gates into the palace grounds had been opened early, and the gentle bowl that rose up and away from him, away from the gallows in the foreground, was slowly filling with these dregs, the last of the Vast in Mann.

"Not our best face, I must say," the prince said, noting the disdain in his new master's expression.

"Hmm." Fen Abbaka Mux wrinkled his nose as if he smelled something foul. "The best face of your people…would that be your soldiers, hiding in the countryside? Those who ran like cowards?"

Mather smiled thinly. "You have a point."

"Or would it be your women and children, who fled first, knowing their warrior husbands could not protect them?"

He nodded glumly. "Another point."

"You think these brigands, these drunks, these doddering old men and women are not representative of your people? And yet, they are here. They have not fled in terror."

"No. Nor have the priests."

Mux spat over the rail. "Your *priests*. The most unworthy of all. The greatest shall serve the least, and the weakest shall be the strongest? Great fools teaching lesser fools to be greater fools yet. I should line them up and hang them all, one after the other."

Mather did not need to try very hard to see these robed characters from Mux's perspective. The Drammune were strong and the Vast were weak, with the inevitable results here lately. Could a Will Seline stop a Fen Abbaka Mux? Could anyone? The answer was apparent.

"And perhaps we should not stop with the priests. We should hang every last Vast native who attends this morning, for the dishonor they have displayed by not dying more nobly yesterday." The thought gave Mux some satisfaction, particularly as he imagined his new lapdog, their glorious prince, pulling the lever again and again until his hands blistered.

Mather smiled wanly.

The Vast were all miserable. Mux let Mather worry, but of course he couldn't possibly indulge such a plan against the general citizenry without the Hezzan's direct approval. Today's festivities were to be a message, loud and clear and public, that the rule of the Vast was over, the rule of the Drammune had begun. It was about the Hezzan Shul Dramm replacing their king. It was about Fen Abbaka Mux subjugating their prince. It was about revenge for the defeat of the *Rahk Thanu* and the *Nochto Vare*. It was about proving the weakness of their government, their people, and the falseness of their religion.

But mostly, today was about killing Packer Throme.

Mather had told Mux all he knew, and this included all the heroic deeds Packer was supposed to have achieved against the Achawuk, and against the Firefish. Mux asked and Mather related all that was told him by John Hand, word for word, of the demise of the *Rahk Thanu* and the *Nochto Vare,* how the crew had believed that their God sent the Firefish, and that Packer was chosen to command these creatures. Such tales were being told even now on the Green below, Mux knew, stories of the yellow-haired warrior who fought like a hornet and had defeated Fen Abbaka Mux and the Drammune through miracles sent by God. Such was the sewage that flooded the streets of this vile city.

But this morning, the Vast hero would die, and with him, these false hopes, these fictitious dreams. Mux couldn't remember when he had wanted to kill a man as much he wanted to kill Packer Throme.

"I want a speech from you today," he said to Mather.

"My lord?"

Mux took a folded scrap of parchment from his vest. "I want you to praise the Rahk-Taa and welcome the rule of the Drammune. This is the purpose for which I have made you a citizen." He handed the parchment to Mather.

The prince took it, began reading. He would stand before his own people and admit his treachery, his treason. "As you wish," he said dutifully. The power had shifted, and he had shifted with it. That was all.

"You will of course speak them in the Vast tongue."

"Yes, Your Worthiness."

Huk Tuth had counseled Mux against this course, arguing that a prince of Nearing Vast could not be trusted. But Mux knew men. And he knew Mather was not one. This weakling was terrified, and would do precisely what he was told to do, nothing more, nothing less. And thus Mux would rub all Vast noses in their own soil.

The Hand That Bears the Sword

Prince Ward awoke in the half light of an alcoholic haze. He was sitting up, his back against something hard and uncomfortable. He looked around him. A candle on a clay dish had burned down to a nub. His head felt like someone had put an axe into it. He reached up to touch it, just to be sure that was not actually the case.

He saw bottles and mugs and dishrags in front of him. He was seated on the floor, on hard wooden slats. He was behind a bar. He looked up. A spigot was directly above his head. He reached up, touched it. Yes, that's why he was here. From this spot he could refill his mug without needing to stand. He looked around on the floor, saw a mug lying on its side. He picked it up, looked into it. Empty. He started to reach up to fill it. Then he remembered that he was supposed to be doing something.

He sat up straight. A sledgehammer hit him in the back of the head. He let the pain pass, then stood, wiping drool from his chin. He was in the King's Arms. He squinted around, saw the two pistols and the sword, still where he had left them on the bar. A memory crept back.

Packer! The self-recriminations rolled over him like high waves at high tide. He put a hand to his forehead. What time must it be? He looked at the clock. Just after one. He stared at it for a long time. Just after one? He had come here at one in the afternoon. Light was shining through the shutters now, but it was indirect, gloomy. It was still one o'clock. Nothing connected. How could it be...But wait, the pendulum wasn't moving. The clock had stopped at one in the morning.

It must be dawn.

Ward laid into himself with a stream of whispered invective. Packer would be hung in a matter of hours, and here was his rescuer, recovering from a drunken stupor. He put the sword belt around his waist, fastened it, then picked up a pistol. He looked down at the wavering barrel, considered putting it to his temple. But no, that would be stupid. He'd just miss and make a mess, and the end result would be one more self-inflicted delay. He considered going back to the prison, trying to free Packer himself. But that was also foolish. He didn't mind trying, certainly didn't mind dying, but if he couldn't hit his own temple, how could he hit someone else's? No, he had to find some soldiers.

Maybe there was still time, if he hurried.

The Hand That Bears the Sword

He cursed himself three more times in rapid succession. Feeling better for it, he staggered for the stairway. At the top, he paused and cursed the Sennett line. On the way down, he cursed the time he had wasted. At the bottom, he cursed the life he had misspent, that would now cost the life of Packer Throme, a young man as noble as Ward was not. He managed to get his key into the secret lock, and pushed wide the door to the passage that would lead him out of the city. He closed the door behind him, slid the bars across, locking it.

He took a deep breath of the dank air.

It smelled good. It smelled right. It smelled of getting on with it.

CHAPTER 23

The Gallows

Ten o'clock approached. The sun had not grown any more merciful, though dark clouds now threatened on the horizon to the south. The promise of more rain could be felt in the humid air. The people gathered, a large, sweltering crowd that still didn't know who the Drammune planned to hang. Their trauma, their fatigue, the bitterness of their defeat, and the uncertainty of the moment had coalesced over the last few hours into an edgy impatience that showed itself in a growing carelessness, a disregard for their status as the newly subjugated. Voices rose and fell. Shouts came from nowhere—"Hang the Drammune!" and similar.

The Drammune troops surrounding the Green did not enter the heart of the crowd to investigate the source of each impudent outburst, but they silently grew impatient themselves. Firefish armor was many things, but cool and breezy it was not.

"Let's get this over with," was pretty much the theme of the morning.

Then suddenly, there was the condemned. Without announcement or fanfare, he stepped into the sunlight from the dark arched doorway set into the Rampart, guided by two guards. The crowd went silent.

To him, the people filling the huge square felt like part of the sodden heat that now blasted his senses. He could hear them breathing in the humid air. He could feel them; he could smell their sweat and last night's ale and this morning's coffee and the frayed nerves and the bitterness that bound them all together.

He could not see them, however. He was blindfolded. Nor could he reach out to them; his hands were manacled behind him. Nor could he run; his feet were chained together. The crowd went silent, stood shocked, until the rhythmic jangle of his shackles was the only sound in the Green. They watched as he walked to the gallows.

Then a murmur grew, like a wave. His name was spoken, overheard, then repeated, spoken again, building, swelling through the crowd.

At first the name was a question. Is it Packer Throme? How could it be Packer? Isn't he at sea? The *Trophy Chase...*? But as the repeated name built to a crescendo, it became an exclamation. It is him; it's Packer Throme! They caught him! And then it fell away, withdrawing, the name turned to lament. They're hanging Packer Throme! Then the name, the murmur, and the wave died away into a whimper, draining down into the sands of the inevitable, into silence once again, a silence thick with one stark thought:

Packer Throme, the best of us, conquered like the rest of us. Now we must watch him die.

Packer felt a hollow dread. He felt a sharp, pointed sorrow. But he felt no fear. Death was an open gate, and he walked toward it quietly and quite willingly. He'd been here before. How many times? And how many times had he been turned away? But this was different. This time he was brought here by the world, for crimes against the nature of the world, for choosing something that was not of the fabric of the world.

He had made a stand; he had laid down his arms. That choice had led him from a hero's welcome to a prince's prison to a conqueror's gallows with almost stunning speed. Was that sequence a coincidence? He had thought about it all night, and he thought not. He thought it highly remarkable, the power of the world to thwart anyone who countered its blind blood oath of mutiny. There were many varieties of mutiny, perhaps as many as there were people on the earth, he had concluded. So there were many ways to drop the sword. Some men, perhaps many, could wield a weapon and trust God at the same time. Samuel did it; so did David, and Joshua.

The Hand That Bears the Sword

Senslar Zendoda, certainly. Marcus and Delaney, most probably. But Packer's own mutiny was sheathed in the darkness of a scabbard. He had picked this weapon to redeem himself and his name, and his father's name. He had chosen this form of piracy.

Perhaps, he thought, as his feet reached the gallows, as he felt for the step and faltered, as the two guards caught him, held him, and propelled him upward, perhaps it's impossible for us to see the world for what it is, and ourselves for who we are, until we are prepared to die. That's how blind we are, how devoted to ourselves and our own ways. We cannot bear the meaning of it all, so we avoid Him, invent luck, fight with one another and alongside one another, agreeing in the darkest places of our hearts that we will believe lies.

And why? Because we cannot bear the meaning. Anything is preferable to the weight of a life lived entirely at the doorstep of the Kingdom of Heaven, where everything matters, where every gesture, every thought is eternally significant, and yet where we are also all too keenly aware of our inability to measure up to the lowest standards of the humblest doorkeeper within its gates, let alone the standards of the King Himself. We cannot bear the light that shines on us here, mere inches from Eden, just a hairsbreadth from the patient and invisible Gardener, who waits, all powerful but entirely humble, always watching, refusing to force Himself on us, wanting instead that we would drop our arms and raise our heads. We maneuver ourselves into dead ends; He sends us there Himself so that we might finally accept our own brokenness and our uselessness, and simply cry out to Him, for rescue.

But when we do cry out, we prefer to do it as angry, wounded animals, rather than as fearful, helpless infants. And yet, true power can only be found in infancy, in tears, in the acknowledgment of our own powerlessness.

And Packer was through being angry. He was through fighting. His own mutiny was at an end. God would now do as He pleased with Packer Throme.

Packer climbed to the top of the stairs, a Drammune warrior on either side of him. No drums beat; no fife played. Once on the platform he stood still, his shoulders squared to the crowd. Abbaka Mux took his place on Packer's left. The prince took his place on Packer's right. Next to the supreme commander was a translator, a Drammune guard who would take Mux's low, rumbling, foreign words

The Hand That Bears the Sword

and bellow them as pronouncements to the Vast, and who would take the prince's proclaimed words and whisper them in Drammune to the supreme commander. Next to the prince stood one Drammune guard. Packer's two escorts took their places behind him. All together, seven men stood on the platform: four Drammune guards, Mux, and the two Vast natives.

In front of Packer was a trap door; at the edge of the platform on his left, by the stairs, was the wooden lever that would open it. Above him hung the noose, coils draped over the crossbar like a sleeping snake.

The supreme commander looked out over the audience, sniffed once, and said in a low monotone, "Haraka rolhoi Nearing Vast."

"Here is the hero of Nearing Vast!" the translator bellowed.

"Nochter harakar karchezz nocht."

"His death is the death of your nation!"

"Kai rayn nochtor ar."

"Your hope dies with him!"

"Hezz Drammun, hezz Hezzan."

"The Drammune now rule! The Hezzan now rules!"

"Kai hezzo ak Drammun. Hezzo taa."

"Your prince has become a citizen of Drammun! The prince will now speak!"

The prince took a step forward. Murmurs, then hisses could be heard. Prince Mather, a citizen of Drammun? Certainly they had heard wrong. But the crowd saw a miserable little man, hair plastered in rivulets of dripping sweat, a blackened eye dark and uncovered, makeup blistered and running down onto his white jacket and ruffled shirt front. Though he wore a look of grim defiance, the fear within him was legible; the way he stood, the way his eyes darted. He seemed hunched and small next to Mux, next to Packer, next to the guards.

Mather looked out over the crowd. They questioned; they narrowed their eyes, waiting for the proof he was about to give them, the stench of his disloyalty already showing on their faces. He glanced at Mux, whose slitted eyes were a warning. The Drammune guard beside him drew his dagger.

Mather shook his head at this unnecessary show of force. He had never known such fear as the Drammune commander engendered in him; he had no strength within him to counter that power. As Mather stood on the platform, prepared to become the most despicable character in the long history of his country, he realized he had no power whatsoever, and never had. And he still didn't. He had always had position, and now he had it again. But power? No, he had nothing within him that would allow him to stand for one moment against the true, stark, ominous strength wielded by a Fen Abbaka Mux. He was quite as repugnant to himself as he was to the crowd before him.

Mux cleared his throat, impatient.

Mather swallowed, then raised his hand. He would obey, just as Mux supposed he would. He could do nothing else. "By authority of Fen Abbaka Mux," the prince's voice was thin, and it quavered, "Supreme Commander of the Glorious Drammune Military, and the government of Drammun now in power here, I have been made a full citizen of the Kingdom of Drammun!"

A sick pall fell over the crowd. The translator repeated the words in a low tone in Drammune to the supreme commander, assuring him that Mather was following his script.

Mather closed his eyes tightly, remembering the words. Then he opened them. "I am now revealed to you as a follower of the Rahk-Taa, the great and true book of the Law of these, the Worthy Ones."

Grumbling and catcalls from the crowd. With their doubts now answered, their contempt was undisguised.

"Silence!" roared Mux. The crowd went quiet, obeying but not bowing.

The prince sniffed once, then continued. "I am but the least Worthy of the Worthies. My errors are many. Here on this platform with me, however, is one of the great Worthy Ones, one who will rule in power in my father's place, and take his dominion for the Emperor of Drammun." The prince paused again as the translator droned. He looked out over the crowd. They were a rough and ragged group, and their hatred of this moment, of the Drammune, and of him, was etched into every face, manifest in whispers and gritted teeth and hard, hard eyes. His beloved subjects.

Mux nodded, quite satisfied.

"And so," the prince continued, his stomach now wrenched and burning, "as a Prince of the Kingdom of Nearing Vast..." he paused once more, then fell to silence. The prince's text was prepared. He had now only to tell all here gathered that he would give the Kingdom to the Drammune, and then that he would gladly, symbolically, and dutifully pull the lever that would hang Packer Throme for his many crimes against the state.

But he never said those words.

Prince Ward's mission had been one misstep after another. Finding the Army of Nearing Vast was not the problem; in fact, that had proven far too easy. Ward arose from under ground far outside the city, well past the main encampments of the Drammune. He needed to evade only a few patrols to get to the countryside. But once there, he was helped by every citizen he met. In fact, the disheartening fact was that while no one knew who he was, everyone knew the exact location of the Army, details about its poor condition and its wretched morale, and all were more than happy to reveal it. They told everything they knew to a stranger who reeked of ale and who had clearly slept in his rumpled clothes. His people, he realized, simply did not know how to keep a secret.

He found the Army, such as it was, encamped on farmland several miles from the city. Ward was immediately appalled by what he saw. It was just after dawn when he arrived there, but campfires burned everywhere. Men sat and slept around them, fully visible from miles away. They talked as though in no danger greater than perhaps the accidental disturbance of a random anthill. Here and there loud talking, laughing, even a pistol shot—men who had not slept at all, women, too, even children. Ward's spirit burned within him. He was angry; but what right did he have to be angry, when he was guilty of the same? And yet he had to fight back rage.

"Where is Bench Urmand?" he asked a soldier who stood casual guard at the edge of the encampment.

The man, hardly more than a boy, seemed taken aback by Ward's harsh tone. "Who?"

"Take me to your commanding officer."

"He's dead, I think. They was mostly all killed or injured, they say."

"Well, who is in charge?"

The boy thought hard, sure he would be blamed for something. "I don't guess I know." He was afraid. Afraid of Ward Sennett, whom he recognized not in the least. The prince felt his anger wither and his scorn falter, like a chock kicked out from in front of a wagon wheel. "Can you at least suggest where I might look?"

"Well, General Millian is here. But I know he's injured. He's in the 'firmary, which is that white tent right over there. With the bright lights on inside it? But I don't think he's in charge."

Ward walked away without another word.

General Mack Millian, brought out of retirement for the occasion of the inglorious Invasion of Mann, was certainly not in charge. He was not conscious. Bench Urmand was not in charge, either, though he was at least conscious. He lay on a stained bedsheet that had been spread over the hard ground just a few feet from the general. He was sweating out a fever.

"We need to evacuate in an orderly manner," Bench told the prince with dark and troubled conviction as he grabbed the kneeling prince's sleeve, almost pulling Ward down on top of him. Beads of sweat streamed down from his forehead; his hair was matted with it, his eyes wide with intensity.

"Yes," Ward answered him gently, "I agree. A very good idea. I'll handle it."

Bench looked at him urgently, wanting to believe it. "You will?"

"Certainly. Now get some rest. We'll be needing you."

"Yes. Rest. Thank you." And Bench relented. He lay his head back on the hard ground and closed his eyes, instantly unconscious.

"Is he badly injured?" Ward asked the surgeon on duty.

"Musket ball to the calf is all," the man answered. The surgeon was twenty-five years old, but carried himself with the air of someone half that age. "Hard to get it out, but I did it. Really had to dig around, and—"

"I understand. What's his prognosis?"

"His what?"

A pause. "What are his prospects?" A short wait. "Will he recover, do you think?"

"Oh, that. Well." The young man thought long and hard, looking at his patient while chewing his lip. "I think he should be fine. Provided the calf heals up. And so long as the fever or the gangrene don't kill him first."

Prince Ward squinted, nodding thoughtfully. "You've been most helpful."

The surgeon grinned.

Prince Ward was rubbing his throbbing head, when a breathless young soldier burst into the tent. "Your Highness!"

"Yes?"

"Someone said you was here. There's a row about what to do next. Can you help?"

"What to do next?"

"Yes, sir. Colonel Bird and a Lt. Colonel Somebody, just a goin' at it."

Ah, leadership at last. "I'll follow you."

Prince Ward knew Colonel Bird. He was the same old man who had told him swaggering stories at the King's Arms a few days back. He looked sallow and pinched now, though, not ruddy and beaming as he had been when in his cups.

Ward didn't recognize the other man, the lieutenant colonel. He was much younger than his antagonist, maybe thirty-five, square-featured without being handsome, and very calm. The two stood face-to-face by a campfire with a small crowd of soldiers in witness. The lieutenant colonel stood with feet wide apart, hands behind his back, unmoving as the colonel laid into him.

"I'll have you whipped, do you hear me?" The colonel pointed a bony finger at the younger man's nose to emphasize each phrase. "Court-martialed, disgraced, relieved of command. And whipped!"

"Colonel, with all due respect, I'll be happy to be whipped, and whatever else you please. But unless we get the men out of these pastures, you won't live long enough to do it."

"Are you threatening me?"

"Not at all, sir, I'm speaking of the next wave of attack by the Drammune."

"We have outposts, scouts. We have time to organize!"

"We had outposts and scouts yesterday. The Drammune overwhelmed them."

"And so we wisely called a retreat!"

"Retreat? Sir, with all due respect, that was a rout."

"It was a retreat, sir!"

"Then where was the delaying action? Where was the rear cover? We were routed, sir, and you know it. We need to stand and fight next time, not turn and run. But to do that, we need a defensive position. The forest will provide cover, and we'll have the high ground."

"You are impudent, sir! And as of this moment you are relieved—"

The Hand That Bears the Sword

375

"May I be of assistance?" Ward interjected, stepping too close to be ignored.

The old colonel turned on him. "Who the blazes are you?"

Prince Ward smiled. "Ward Sennett. Sir."

The colonel's hard gaze melted into a prunish smile. "Ah, many apologies, Your Highness. I did not recognize you."

He took Ward by the arm and walked him away from the group, speaking warmly. "Highness, I appreciate your offer, but this is a military matter involving both discipline and battle tactics. I will gladly brief you." He raised a bony finger. "Give me but a moment to conclude here, would you?" His tone was paternal, and dismissive.

Ward nodded, and the colonel left him to return to the campfire.

The prince looked at the ground, kicked a rock. He was tempted to walk away. It was what he had always done. Instead, to his own surprise, he followed the colonel back to the campfire and spoke first, before either man could pick up the conversation. He spoke evenly, calmly, and with a confidence that amazed even himself. "Excuse me again. But we are going to move these men out of this farmland. The lieutenant colonel is right. There are forests not ten miles from here that are easily defensible."

"Your Highness," Colonel Bird protested. "The defensibility of an army's position is not a matter of state. I appreciate your desire to—"

"You are going to do this, Colonel," Ward said calmly. "And you're going to do it now, on my orders. And should you wonder, yes, I am speaking in the name of the king. Is anything about that unclear to you?"

Colonel Bird was astounded. "Your Highness. Forgive me. If I have offended you in any way, why, I offer my apology."

"I don't want your apology. I want these men moved. And I want the women gone, the children gone, the ale cut off."

"You want the ale cut off...?" He smiled at all those gathered around. Then he chuckled. "With all due respect, you have no authority to countermand my orders. I am a member of the military with a rank of—"

"And I am your prince, and while I might not have the authority to countermand your orders, I do have the power, in the absence of the king, to take away your commission." Ward said it easily, firmly.

Even diplomatically. "And sir, that is what I am forced to do. As of this moment, you are relieved of your command."

"You speak on behalf of the king?" the colonel was shocked. "That is only possible in wartime, and if the king is—"

"Deposed or indisposed or decomposed or some such, I don't remember exactly, but yes, I know," Ward said. "It is wartime. The king is one of those words, you pick. Regardless, I can assure you the king will be unavailable for any appeal for the remainder of the day, as will be the crown prince. So thank you for services, that will be all." Then he turned his back on the wide-eyed old man, and faced the lieutenant colonel. "What's your name, sir?"

"Jameson, sir." He saluted. "Lt. Colonel Zander Jameson."

Ward returned the salute casually. "You have a plan for moving this Army?"

"Yes, sir. I've already moved my troops to the Hollow Forest. Little over nine miles from here. I've come back to get the rest of the men, but I'm having trouble as they aren't under my command."

"They are now. You're a brevet colonel. Get it done."

"Sir, even a colonel can't move this Army. Only a general can issue the orders to—"

"Fine, now you're a general."

"Sir?"

"You've been promoted. Get used to it, and get the task done, General Jameson. Did you not hear me? Why are you still standing there?"

"Yes, sir!" He turned away with a bright determination lighting his face.

"Wait!"

The new general turned back.

"Do you know where I might find a raiding party? Bench Urmand was known to lead a fairly gallant bunch, but he's a bit under the weather."

"Yes, sir. His horsemen are ranging the area. But I think we may be able to find some of them. I saw a few up in those rocks." He pointed uphill. The area was dark, under a stand of trees.

Ward smiled. He was sure he would find them quite well-armed, and at least some of them wide awake. "We won't be needing the horses. But I believe those will be precisely the men. I'll see to it myself."

The Hand That Bears the Sword

The raiding party was not, however, ready immediately. Bench's horsemen were accustomed to taking orders from Bench and only Bench, and though they were eager to fight, they were not eager to leave either their leader or their current assignments. With Ward's permission, one of them went to ascertain Bench's opinion. Ward wished him luck.

But when they were finally organized and ready for the journey, there were six of them: four of Bench Urmand's best fighters, Prince Ward and, in a late addition, Bench Urmand himself. His fever had broken, and neither the surgeon nor Prince Ward was able or willing to keep him lying down on a bedsheet when there was work to be done. He was a bit weak and quite pale, and he limped badly, but he was coherent and appeared to be almost as capable as he claimed to be.

"You are the minister of defense," Prince Ward suggested over the hardtack and jerky that was breakfast, likely lunch, and maybe dinner. "Moving our armies to defensible ground would seem a higher calling."

Bench looked around at the slow movement of troops across the ploughed fields, heads hung down as they gathered up weapons and what little else they had under the tongue-lashing of their newest general, and began a trudge that would take most of the day. Bench's moustache drooped and his skin was pasty, but his neck was bulled and his hard eyes were ablaze. "I will not send a prince of this realm into danger, nor will I let a national hero hang, so that I may watch over yet another evacuation."

Ward got the feeling Bench had had quite enough of bureaucracy. And while he didn't know much about the military, he knew better than to tell a leader that he could not lead.

But Ward's troubles were far from over. First there was Bench's injury. The spirit was willing, but it turned out the calf was weak. Bench's limp quickly grew worse, and he was forced to use the walking crutch Ward brought along for him. He refused to slow the team, however, and so he pushed himself, not only to keep up, but to stay in the lead with Ward. His calf was wrapped tolerably well, but it turned deep red, the cloth soaked through before they had even reached the tunnel entrance. The toll that this effort was taking on the indomitable former sheriff was obvious to all, with the possible exception of the former sheriff.

Then there were the Drammune who blocked their way. The entrance Ward sought was a trapdoor inside an old smithy. But two heavily armed Drammune scouting parties had met there just moments before the raiding party arrived, at this precise location, and had stopped to smoke and trade war stories. They sat and stood on the smithy's front stoop.

Ward and company sat in frustrated silence, hidden behind an ivy-covered fence just across the street, watching and waiting impatiently for, it turned out, more than an hour. It was one of those maddening decisions; of course there were other entrances to the tunnels—one was less than thirty minutes away—but they would take a chance of being caught if they moved. And these soldiers seemed again and again to be saying their goodbyes, only to strike up some new line of discussion or tell some just-remembered joke. As time dragged on, the idea of fighting through them seemed a more and more positive alternative, at least to Bench's men. But it was out of the question. They were outnumbered, and even if they hadn't been, they needed to save ammunition for their objective, the prison at the palace.

Then when the Drammune finally moved on and the raiding party was safely underground, their movement back toward the palace was painfully slow. This was due not only, or even mainly, to Bench's injury. Rather, it was the layout of the tunnels themselves. Each door was quite obvious to any traveler headed away from the city, but as these were designed as escape routes, every door headed toward town was heavily camouflaged. Ward didn't know these doors nearly as well as he did those closer in, so finding the door, and then the hidden keyhole, took time.

Bench grew impatient and irritable. A glance at his sweat-soaked shirt told Ward that the minister was rapidly growing weaker, anxious to press on because he feared his stamina was nearing an end.

And then, in what would be the second-worst development of their journey, Prince Ward got the party lost. The others looked at him in stunned silence. He sheepishly admitted that he was most familiar with passages that allowed him to move freely between the palace and the pubs.

"I have wandered on unsteady legs through many of these dark

The Hand That Bears the Sword

hallways, escorting once or twice women of less-than-stellar reputation. I have even awakened, groggy and disoriented, at a crossroads that had proved too much for my sodden brain the night before. But I never did memorize the pathway to the prison. For some reason, that route did not catch my fancy."

Bench and his men seemed to appreciate the prince's honesty and good humor, if not his compass. Moral or otherwise.

Ward eventually found his way. But then came the worst setback. They were nearly back to the familiar passageways around the palace when their one small lamp ran out of oil. The next door they reached took all their matches, and still Ward could not find the keyhole. Nothing remained but for the prince to leave the party in the dark and feel his way backward toward an exit where he could surface to find some kerosene. And some more matches.

So when they finally entered the small torture chamber of the palace prison, it was nearly ten o'clock. What had taken Ward hardly more than an hour going one way had taken closer to three hours coming back. Bench was white and pale, his lips blue, his clothing drenched, his hands trembling. But they had arrived.

The six men now stood in the enclosed space, listening. Bench leaned hard on the crutch, propping himself up between it and the wall, his head down, breathing hard. They all heard voices in the corridor: the guttural vowels and rolling R's of the Drammune. Prince Ward crept near the door and listened intently, the only one among them who knew the language.

"The hero of Nearing Vast," one of the guards was saying. "He looked soft to me."

"I saw no fear in him, though. And why do you suppose he was locked up in here?"

Ward sighed. "Past tense," he whispered. "They're talking like he's gone already."

"How many are there?" asked Bench, his voice surprisingly strong. Ward saw fire in his eyes. But it was a gritty, almost frantic fire. His bandage now dripped blood.

"Hard to tell. Two at least."

"Well, open the door, and let's find out." Bench pulled his pistol from his belt. "And let's see what they're made of."

"Are you sure you're well?" Ward asked.

Bench straightened, handed Ward his crutch. He pulled a second pistol from his belt. "I'm well enough. You'll want to wait here, Highness." His men followed his lead, bringing out their own pistols and squaring themselves to the task at hand. Just that quickly, the raiding party was ready to deal out death.

Ward believed. "Remember the armor," he said.

"What armor?" Bench asked.

Ward closed his eyes. Did Bench not know? Had Mather not told even Bench Urmand? "They wear armor. Your pistols won't penetrate it."

The five looked at one another in surprise. "Really?"

Ward smiled sadly. "Really. Vest and helmet. Shoot anywhere else."

"Good to know," Bench said matter-of-factly. "All right, then. Let's do this."

It was over instantly, and silently. There were four guards, and they were surprised to the point of shock. They threw their hands up and surrendered.

But the cell at the end of the row was empty. Packer was gone.

Then the minister of defense all but collapsed. He struggled to the nearest cell, held onto the bars, his body betraying his will. "Now what?" he asked Ward.

The prince was shocked that Bench would ask that question of him. The faces around him all looked to Ward for leadership. But his mind was blank. He had made no plans past getting Packer and getting out. He cursed himself silently. He should have been thinking about this. Mather was always thinking of what next, and what if. And Ward was always sitting back and letting him.

He rubbed his chin, then his neck. A drink, just a quick snort, and his brain would work better. "I don't know," he admitted. "We don't even know how long he's been gone."

"About five minutes," came the answer from a nearby cell. Ward now noticed, for the first time, the emaciated faces that peered out from the cells, watching listlessly. But one of them wasn't emaciated. Not nearly. It was Chunk, still in his dragoon uniform, leaning on the bars, his broad face pressed up between them.

"Where did they take him?" Ward asked.

"Took him to hang."

"Where?"

"Don't know. Don't speak Drammune. Probably on the Green."

"What are you in here for?" Bench asked suspiciously.

"Helping Panna Throme escape."

Ward smiled. "A friend of the cause! Where are the keys? Let's get you out of there."

"Whoa," Bench said. "How do we know he's telling the truth?"

Ward grew irritable. But he had no answer for that. "Look, you question him." Ward tried to suck some moisture into his mouth. He couldn't stand this indecision. "I need to do a little scouting. You just stay here until I get back. And don't close that door behind me, or you'll be stuck here."

"Wait!" Bench called, but the prince was gone, practically at a run. The raiding party looked at one another.

They had been led to the prison, and then left.

Prince Ward fought demons. They were in his head, and in his throat. They were in his chest, and in his belly. They wanted him to go back to the King's Arms. They pulled on him. They taunted. They pleaded. They wanted to buy him a drink. And he very much wanted that drink.

What was he doing? Who did he think he was? Surely Packer was dead already, hung for the world to see. Surely the war was lost. The Vast Army couldn't stop the Drammune. The only thing the average Vast soldier could stop was a musket ball. And then only if he couldn't outrun it.

Leave the raiding party in the prison. They'll be fine. Just as well they stay there as die out on some battlefield. Prison is safe. Bench can't fight anyway. He needs a doctor. Just leave him. Leave them all. Have that drink. Have several. What does it matter? Drink a whole barrel. Why not? Let them find you passed out, dead drunk. The Drammune will put you in prison, or kill you. Probably both. Serve you right. No more than you deserve.

Ward moved as quickly as he could without running. This mission was over.

Bench tried to summon his strength. He had to think through what he must do; he had to command his troops. But he couldn't. He was weak, and sick, and the chills had returned. He had depleted all his remaining strength. Now he staggered back into the chamber that led to the passageway. It was cool in here. He would feel better in here, in just a moment. He leaned against the wall. And then he lowered himself slowly to the ground. He would have to rest. He looked up. His men were gathered around him. They looked worried.

"What?" he asked them, and his eyes closed of their own accord.

CHAPTER 24

The Hangman

From where she stood in the crowd beside Father Mooring, not fifteen feet from the platform, Panna could see everything. She had seen everything. She had watched Packer climb the stairs to die. She had paid little attention to Mather, not until this very moment. Until the prince paused, and looked at her, she could see only Packer.

But she couldn't see Packer clearly. She saw him partly in life, partly in memory, and partly in a dream. The life, the memory, and the dream were nearly identical, and now they were so intertwined she had trouble separating one from the other. In life, she saw him standing on a gallows. In memory, he stood on a dais on the deck of a ship. In the dream, he was at the edge of a cliff. In one a king stood beside him, in the other two a prince. In the dream, Packer was pushed from the cliff; in memory he was pushed out to sea, lauded to the heavens. And in life...which? What? Would he fall through that trapdoor? Would he sail off again, leaving her behind? Or would he be cast off the cliff, trailing a rope that Panna could not catch in her hands, that would burn her forever and yet not save Packer? Or, would he somehow walk back down those stairs and embrace her again?

Panna closed her eyes and prayed, prayed, prayed that God would stop this, that He would step in, that He would change this reality, awaken her from the dream, free her from the memory. She prayed,

prayed, and prayed that He would glorify His own name for all the Drammune to see, for all the Vast to see, and show Himself to be God.

She prayed that He would somehow, in so doing, save Packer. She prayed that she was not praying selfishly, that it was not the pain of losing her father, that she wasn't demanding or sulking, but asking for others, for Packer, for posterity, for all who would know and repeat the story. She prayed as her father prayed, understanding now why he prayed, honoring him in her heart, feeling in her spirit his spirit, his yielded humility, knowing now that nothing and no one could change outcomes such as this, that no one could alter the inevitable, no one but God alone.

If He would but grant her this one request now, here, and at this moment. If He would...

Then she opened her eyes, and that was the moment Mather saw her. But what he saw was far more than a helpless woman in a poor disguise, powerless against the machinery of death that ground away at her, that had been sent to her from the cold, hard center of the world to kill her father and then her husband. He saw instead something shockingly earnest and innocent, painfully vulnerable, but undeniably, unquenchably powerful. In her was something strong enough to stand against all the kingdoms of earth, against any Abbaka Mux and every Hezzan and every state and fate and all the tides of time and history. She would never cease striving. The power within her would never crumble. And what was it? A simple, aching desire for goodness, for rightness, for love. Because God was there within it. Here was the power of weakness that could overcome the world.

"Taa!" Mux demanded of the Prince. *Speak!*

Mather opened his mouth. But only one thought entered his mind, just one solitary thought. It careened through him like waters roaring through the cataracts of a mountain river. It cleared out all the debris before it, washed away all his plans and schemes and desires and fears, all his wickedness and pride and foolishness. And then suddenly he reached the bottom of the chasm.

He was in the center of a glassy lake. His mind was perfectly focused, clear in a way he had never known clarity, as though a cacophony of voices had been silenced, voices that had roared and chattered and accused within him, unnoticed until they were gone. And the idea, the still and silent idea that was left, was one he knew had been given to him here, now, for a reason. It had been set down within him, and it seemed to him right, even perfect. All he needed to do was give in to it.

And giving in was the one skill he was confident he had mastered.

He nodded, acquiescing not to Mux, not to Panna, but to something else. He now understood the message he had been given.

You may choose the manner.

Mather knew his path now. He almost laughed. This was easy, and far better than any plan he had ever made or could have ever made. And to act on it, he needed only to let it happen. He felt almost giddy. Perhaps, he thought, he had just lost his mind. Perhaps he was lost again in the flowers, asleep and dreaming amid the daisies. But if so, what a relief it was to finally give in to it.

Mather spoke, and when he did, he strayed quite far from his appointed script. He wandered off the page entirely. His voice boomed, too, a voice that had been a thin sheet of tin whining in a strong wind was suddenly a cannon from an approaching warship. This surprised Mux, the people, Packer, even himself.

And after he spoke, the crowd joined him on the crystal lake. They went utterly still, pondering what he said. He felt as though the finger of God had let peace fall onto him, a single drop of cool, clear water, and that peace had then rippled outward, riding on these words, calming the people, too.

The translator droned. As the meaning was conveyed in a ragged whisper, Mux's eyes widened.

But Mather did not see Mux. He saw Panna, saw her shining eyes aglow, saw her mouth drop open as if to sing, and stay there, as if she held a long, single, pure note. He saw his people stare in wonder, amazed. And in those words, his words, given to him, flowing from him, he now knew for the first time what power really felt like. True power, from above. All his failures had turned in a moment into something that would never fail.

His words were these:

"By the authority of the Rahk-Taa, and as a full citizen of Drammun, I hereby claim the Second Law of Transfer. I claim the right to die in place of a Worthy One, one far more Worthy than I: Packer Throme."

He took a deep breath. Yes, he would take up a simple cross that was given to him by God Himself, carry it but a very short distance, two short steps to the hangman's noose, and then he would lay it down. This death, dying like this, would be freedom. Mux couldn't touch him. Failure could no longer reach him. Fear couldn't rule him. Absolute freedom.

Mather spoke again, just as the translator finished, repeating in Drammune and in a tone that relayed his own amazement: "Meht ema Kar Ixthano, anochter Packer Throme!"

Now all the Drammune guards reacted at once, reflexively, defensively, raising muskets and pikes as if to ward off the words. And as they did, the crowd came alive. What did this mean? Did the prince really mean to die for Packer? Why would he do that? Wasn't he Drammune now? Had the Prince just surprised them? Would that be allowed? Would Packer live after all?

At the first sign of Mux's anger, a Drammune guard grabbed the prince from behind and put the edge of his dagger against Mather's throat. He looked to his supreme commander for a sign, the slightest sign, that he might bleed the royal salamander to death here before all the eyes of Nearing Vast.

But Mux did not give the sign. Instead, he raged at the prince. "No! You cannot claim the Ixthano!"

The crowd's questioning grew into an amazed glee as the great conqueror bellowed out his rage. Look how it angered him! And to the crowd, the superiority of Nearing Vast over Drammun was proven instantly, shown in the sacrifice that a prince of their land would make to save a hero.

The prince spoke carefully, attempting not to move his throat into the razor that was the guard's blade. But his voice was serene. He was in the eye of the hurricane now—let the storm winds whip around him. He had nothing left to lose, and this fact gave him power. He reveled in the peace he felt, in the sudden energy that had gripped his people. The idea that he had just done, was now doing, something heroic did not cross his mind. But it did revitalize his soul.

He spoke with complete assurance. "I am a Drammune citizen, my lord. You yourself have declared me such. And as such, I have this right. Do I not?"

The supreme commander's anger was a furnace door flung open. The conniving prince had planned this all along, had feigned a conversion, just to make a mockery of this proceeding!

This would not stand.

The Drammune guards who ringed the lip of the amphitheater and who stood upon the Rampart walls all looked to one another, questioning. Abbaka Mux was a Zealot, and thereby honor-bound to honor Mather's request. But Mux was also a warrior. He would massacre the entire lot of these miserable people without a second thought if he thought it right. They hoped he thought it right. The guards did not like what they now saw growing in this rabble.

Mux still focused only on Mather. "Admit that your conversion was false-hearted!"

"It was not," Mather said, more in confession than argument. "I freely offered you my allegiance."

Mux pointed at Packer. "He is a Pawn, an Unworthy! You are Drammune! You are a Worthy One! There can be no question!"

But Mather looked at Mux steadily. Then he spoke words that he knew, even as he said them, would seal the decision. These were words the conqueror could not evade, and Mather was thankful to have been given them. "Do you have the authority to decide that I am the Worthier man?"

"Silence!" Mux bared his teeth. The prince indeed had him. As the Supreme Commander of the Glorious Drammune Military, he could kill one or both or neither. As a Zealot, however, he had but two choices: He could allow a citizen to define his own Ixthano, or he could get a ruling from the Quarto. And the Quarto's decision would be weeks, perhaps months away.

And then Packer spoke. "Please. Let me die."

"Silence!" Mux raged, not understanding the words.

"No, Packer," the prince warned, aghast at the thought. "Don't."

Mux's eyes lit up as the translator spoke into his ear. "Yes, tell the yellow-hair he may deny the Ixthano! Tell him to speak freely!"

But as the translator spoke these words to Packer, a voice rose from the crowd before them.

"Oh, Packer!"

It was the same voice, saying the same words that had broken his will once before, when he stood beside her above the bunting that ringed the deck of the *Chase*. But this time he didn't hear the rushing sigh of a broken heart. He heard instead the heart's protest of the woman with whom he had become one flesh. His wife.

Packer's knees betrayed him. Still blindfolded, he felt disoriented. He lost his bearings. The guard beside him caught him by the elbow, stood him roughly back upright.

Panna. She was here, right in front of him, an eyewitness to everything.

"Do you reject the Ixthano?" Mux demanded of Packer. "Speak now, or your prince's blood will be on your hands!"

What in heaven's name was Packer thinking? This was the best he could manage after all his heroic deeds, all his slaying of Achawuk and Drammune and Firefish?

"Let me die"?

Panna had been praying fervently. And then, miraculously, the prince had said this amazing thing; he'd made this outlandish, unexpected, inconceivable demand, that he die in Packer's place. And it was, of course, a miracle. It was of God, and from God. Such an exchange made all the sense in the world to her, proving God's presence here, answering prayers not just for Packer but for the prince. Mather had, in the very end, listened to the word from above. He had triumphed. Tears stung her eyes. All would be well.

But then suddenly Packer, counter to all that God was doing, in opposition to all that was good and right, rebelling against the obvious intervention of God here in this place, against all wisdom and all justice—Packer himself spoke up to stop it! He wanted to die! The world, and the heavens above the world, crashed down like a hammer through a stained-glass window.

Fen Abbaka Mux scanned the crowd, looking for the woman who dared speak up now, to stop the yellow-hair from his appointed fate. At first he saw no likely candidates…his mother? No, a mother's cry would be more plaintive. It had to be his wife. Such interference from wives was not tolerated in Drammun. At least, not in public. But here, anything was possible. And then his eyes lit on the young woman in the priest's robes, her eyes still red from tears. This was she, surely.

Packer knew for a fact that somehow again, the doors of heaven were closing. He stood outside the Garden, his head hung down. Once again, and once more for Panna's sake, he would stay on this side of the veil. But it did not escape him that the prince had done something unselfish, and remarkably so. Here beside him was a man who had only and always taken whatever he wanted, whether it was money from the Drammune, or power from the king, or Panna from him, but who now laid it all down, gave it all up. Packer nodded slowly and spoke softly, unwilling to counter the apparent will of God. Or the quite obvious will of his wife.

"I will accept."

Mux shook his head in disgust. Here was Nearing Vast in all its degenerate glory, wrapped up in this moment. A man of the royal family, prince of the realm, deals falsely in matters of honor. A young woman, disguised as a man, and as a priest no less, speaks out in public uninvited, muddling a situation in which men needed to think clearly and act reasonably. A warrior who is a coward and is thus, of course, held in highest esteem by his countrymen, swoons like a schoolgirl, and is then persuaded against his better judgment by the meddling of his wife. Yes, here was the very best of Nearing Vast, on full display.

They were all dishonorable. They were all beneath contempt.

But Fen Abbaka Mux was not one to let the failures of others lower his own standards. The Vast might debase themselves, but this would only strengthen his conviction to abide by his own higher principles. Great strength could be found in all things Drammune. Strength of character. Integrity. Power to rule, to die with honor, and to make worthy decisions. No, Fen Abbaka Mux would not abandon the teachings of the Rahk-Taa the first time they were tested on Vast soil by shallow deceivers.

Besides, hanging a prince was not such a bad alternative. And with this thought, Mux now embraced the choice. With one decision he would obey his Hezzan, submit to the Quarto, and hang the prince. Not bad. Packer Throme could die some other day. Feeling better, Mux removed Packer's blindfold himself.

Packer, sweat now running down into his eyes, searched the crowd, blinking against the brutally bright sun. There she was. Wearing a priest's robe, eyes locked on his with some incalculable mixture of gratefulness and relief and pride, and a lingering trace of fear. He smiled. And Panna smiled back.

The prince watched the exchange between Packer and Panna, the exchange he had just engineered. He almost smiled. Theirs was a love that ran deep, but now he saw it would also run through the usual dry stretches and rocky patches and thorny underbrush of any marriage. The sharp blade of jealousy did not slice him within. That familiar, raging, ragged pain was gone. He felt instead a sense of pleasure at being the facilitator of such a moment. He was pleased to give them, if not endless bliss, then at least peace, and the opportunity for a normal life. This unselfishness was new to him. He found he liked the feeling very much.

He looked up at the sky, and breathed the air. It was warm and humid, and the sky was blue. It surprised him just how blue. Had it always been this way, and had he simply never noticed? What a shame, if that were so. But it was wonderful to see now. Just then the wind kicked up, and he felt the cool of a thunderstorm coming in from behind him, from the south. He glanced back at the dark clouds. Even they were glorious. It was a memorable day.

Then he looked back at the crowd, across this sea of faces, all waiting, watching. There was respect here. Hope. There was concern as well. He felt a lump in his throat. He had let them all down, in almost every way. He hoped they would forgive him.

Mather took a breath and stepped in front of Packer onto the trapdoor, gingerly, but without hesitating. Why was it, he thought, that only now, only as he gave up all his rights and titles, as he gave up his nobility, that he now felt noble? And he did feel noble, for the first time in his life.

Mather looked up at the noose above his head. The supreme commander reached up and pulled it down, its coils falling free from the crossbar where they had rested. Mux put the loop around Mather's neck, positioned the knot behind his head, then pulled the coarse hemp tight against his throat. "Die, then," he said in Drammune.

"May I first speak the Ixthano?" the prince asked, also in Drammune.

Mux nodded and grumbled, "Taa." *Speak.*

When the prince turned toward him, Packer felt like he had never seen this face before. The bruises faded into insignificance, the makeup was an artifact of some distant reality. It was as though the mask that had hid Mather Sennett, Crown Prince of Nearing Vast, had been taken off and cast away. Whoever this was now spoke without polish and without airs. He spoke in a strong voice, easily audible, but he spoke to Packer and didn't care whether anyone else heard, or what they thought.

"My crimes are great, Packer Throne. I am sorry for them all." His eyes trailed downward, as he recalled his actions. "Only if God is absurdly merciful do I have any hope."

"He is," Packer said immediately.

The prince looked up quickly. Packer truly believed this. Perhaps it was true. Yes, of course. Mather had been given this idea and those words because of God's mercy. It wasn't just for Packer or Panna or even Nearing Vast, but a gift from God to Mather. And then a genuine affection for Packer shone through him.

Mather now felt as though he was seeing Packer for the first time—not a tool for the furthering of the war, not an opportunity to persuade the people, not a rival for Panna's love. Just a firm, fine young man, upright in a way Prince Mather was quite sure he himself was not and now would never be.

The prince's voice grew warm. "You are the hero of Nearing Vast." He took the signet ring from his right index finger and held it out on his left palm. "Here is the sign and seal of all that is mine. I give it to you freely."

Packer, of course, could not take it. He was still chained.

The prince looked at the supreme commander with steady eyes. "Ixthano?" he asked. It was a bold request, really. But the prince waited, sure that Mux's sense of duty would win out. And it did. The literal meaning of the word was "to change hands."

"Remove the prisoner's shackles," Mux said to the guard, handing him the key. The guard obeyed, returned the key to Mux.

With his hands free but feet still chained, Packer took the ring from the prince's palm, closed his scarred hand around it. He did not know what to say. The wind kicked up again. Then he managed, "Thank you."

"Well, try it on," Mather suggested, a glint in his eye.

Packer slipped the ring onto his right forefinger, a tight fit over the scarred skin there. But instantly the prince, to Packer's amazement, lowered himself to one knee.

"Hagh!" Mux ordered in Drammune, suddenly realizing the absurdity of what he was seeing, and the trouble it would cause him. *Enough!* "Now bind this one," and he pointed at Mather.

The Drammune guard took the shackles to the prince, who was still on one knee, and yanked his arms behind him. "Ixthano," Mux said to Mather with some satisfaction. A ring in exchange for manacles.

"From hand to hand!" the translator informed the crowd.

Then Mux said to the guard, "I want that girl when this is done."

"I want that girl—" the translator boomed, then choked as Mux's fist caught him in the chest. The guard, now quite aware this had been meant as a private command, looked down at Panna as though she had caused his error.

Panna met his eye, and fear stabbed through her. She looked to Packer, who mouthed the single, urgent word, "Go!"

But Panna didn't move.

Mux sniffed. "Valla!" he ordered Mather. *Stand!*

The translator, cowed, said nothing. And the prince did not stand. He did not move at all.

"Valla!" Mux repeated. Now Mather turned his head. His mind had been far away. But still he did not stand.

Instead, in Drammune he replied, "I ask the supreme commander for permission to die on my knees."

Mux rolled his eyes. Was there no bottom to the dishonor these people were willing to bear? "Fine," he announced. "The Transfer is complete. Therefore, Packer Throme shall be your hangman."

The translator, after a nod from Mux, repeated the words. Packer would hang the prince. Now Packer's spirit fell, as though through the trapdoor. "No," he said instinctively.

But Mux had him by the hair with an iron fist, and walked him to the edge of the platform, to his left, stood him beside the wooden lever. He pointed at it.

Packer looked at the machinery of execution. It was a simple length of wood, the kind from which a craftsman might turn a chair leg or a wheel spoke. It was bolted to the edge of the platform, with the bolt serving as a fulcrum. The end that protruded below the platform was positioned against a board that held the trapdoor shut. Pull the lever, release the trapdoor.

The crowd had heard his words, and a fierce whisper rose and fell, as though each needed to confirm for his neighbor the truth of the same dark rumor at the same time. He wants Packer to hang the prince! And then the Vast crowd went silent again as Packer eyed the lever before him. But he knew he couldn't do it. He wouldn't do it. Not for any reason, for any purpose.

"Now!" Mux ordered. He drew his sword. It hissed like a snake.

At that moment Prince Ward walked out onto the Green. He saw the gallows across a sea of the Vast, saw dark clouds building in cumulonimbus piles above it. He was followed closely by Bench Urmand, limping but upright, and then all four of Bench's regulars.

At any other moment the Drammune guards might have stopped them, six men of fighting age wearing jackets in the sweltering heat. But not this moment. There were two reasons for their inattention. First, the Drammune watched the gallows as intently as the Vast did, to see the hero hang the prince. But second, this small party was lost within a steady flow of citizens that had been arriving to join this multitude ever since Packer had entered the Green. Word had spread, somehow, as it always seemed to spread in this city. They came out of respect, they came out of anger, they came out of hiding, they came out of the woodwork. And they came armed. Knives, clubs, blackjacks, pistols, whatever they could hide. They packed the Green until there was barely room to stand, thousands upon thousands of Vast irregulars.

The heart of Prince Ward rose as he squinted at the platform. Packer Throme was alive! And he was not being hanged! He was being forced to execute someone else, but who was it? Some kneeling, dark-haired figure with head bowed. It looked a bit like Mather, but that was not at all a familiar pose for the crown prince. It was impossible to tell.

Ward turned, looked at Bench. The former sheriff's face was now a ghastly white. It looked bloodless, except around his eyes which were dark, almost black. But he seemed alert. Ward said nothing, thinking that Bench looked a whole lot like Ward felt.

Prince Ward had not had his drink. He had gone to the King's Arms for that purpose, looking for the easy way out, trying to find the crevasse that would hide him from the trek up this enormous mountain. But the place had been gutted. The Drammune had found it, finally, had taken all the weapons, then smashed or emptied whatever kegs and bottles they did not want. Ward had cursed them at first, then a moment later he had thanked them, and then a moment later he had thanked God and run to see if he might still find a duty left to perform.

He met Bench and his men in the tunnels, following a lamp taken from the prison wall, hoping to find their way to the Green. They were headed the wrong direction, but Ward turned them right, took them back through the King's Arms and out to the street, where they joined the traffic into the Green, and into the crowd.

But what was to be done now? Bench's look asked the question. Ward shrugged.

Packer looked down again toward Panna. She nodded vehemently, quite certain what his appointed role was in this drama. Everything about her said, "Hang the prince!" This angel was prepared to deliver judgment.

And there was Father Bran Mooring, right beside her! Packer's heart surged within him. He had not even noticed his mentor from his Seminary days. Behind the ever-present smile, the priest's eyes prayed, "Have mercy."

"Now!" Mux ordered again, pressing the point of his sword to Packer's back. But the yellow-hair still did not pull the lever. Mux pressed harder, convincing Packer and all who could see that the Drammune commander would run out of patience quite soon, and run him through.

Packer ignored the pain, looked out over the crowd once more. They were expectant, and he knew what they expected. He was a hero. They wanted heroics. And then an image came to his mind. He didn't invite it, in fact he tried to block it. But it came nonetheless. His training had been too thorough, his habits of mind too rigorously ingrained. It came in a flash, but it was all there.

The translator stood beside Mux, between Mux and Mather, behind Packer and to his right. He had a sword sheathed on his hip. Packer had seen it, and though it hadn't registered before, now it hung before his eyes as though he had contemplated it for an hour. The man was right-handed. The sword was on his left hip, close to Packer. The handle was covered in dark, stained leather. The scabbard was ill-fitting; it was made for a larger sword.

It would come out easily. The translator would die without knowing what had happened.

The three remaining guards were in a rough semicircle behind the prince. The two guards who had walked Packer up the stairs were both huge, strong, with good balance. But they were not quick. They had caught him when he stumbled, twice, and so Packer knew their reaction times. Precisely. His mind worked it all out in a flash, the moves he would need to make, the affect of the chains on his feet, what Mux would do, the order in which all five of the Drammune would die. He couldn't help but see all of it, plan all of it, watch all of it unfold.

He recalled, and felt, the smooth power and unstoppable energy that had taken back the decks of the *Trophy Chase* from the Drammune. He had done that against much greater odds. The warrior within him now rose up, swelling his soul, to set all this right.

But Packer stopped the warrior within him, right there. He remembered the sickness, the vileness that had consumed him the last time. He had prayed the wrong prayer. He had asked to fight, rather than for God to fight, the battle. No, he would not make the same mistake. He could not fight, or pray to fight. God had sent the Firefish. What would God send now? He didn't know, but he knew he had to pray the right prayer this time. His hand burned. "You are not your own, you were bought with a price," he said aloud. And the following words came to his mind. *Therefore glorify God in your body.*

Mather's lips stopped moving, and he looked up at Packer.

Prince Ward and Bench Urmand saw the same thing at the same time. They saw the kneeling figure raise his head, face now visible. "Oh no," was all Ward could say. Bench said nothing, but his pistol was in his hand and he was pushing through the crowd toward the gallows. His men were behind him.

Mux pressed the point of his sword into Packer again.
Packer fell to his knees.
Panna's chin slumped down to her chest as hope ebbed from her. She had no prayers left. Packer had given up again. Now he would die.

Packer did not know how to glorify God, and he confessed that fact now. But here before this Vast throng, he did know one thing: He could not fight. And then the words of another verse came to mind, the words of Christ Himself: "My grace is sufficient for thee: for my strength is made perfect in weakness." Packer would not perform the violent acts the people expected, up here on a stage so they might cheer him as a better pirate, a better mutineer than the Drammune. He had already broken faith with the world. So he asked God to work, to fight, to answer prayer, just as He had done at sea: to make His strength perfect in Packer's weakness.

Mather watched Packer fall on his knees, and he smiled within. He bowed his head again, feeling that God was in that act. He saw an image, then, clear and precise as though it were a waking dream, of a bloodied man carrying a cross up a hill, struggling under its weight. He saw that man spread on a cross beside him, His eyes alight even as His body died, saying, "Today shalt thou be with Me in paradise."

And Mather vowed to stay on his knees, awaiting that moment.

Mux laughed at Packer, mocked him for falling to his knees, joining his prince in humiliation. "A nation of cowards! A great hero to your people! Do you believe because you are on your knees that your God will save you?" he asked to Packer's back. He looked up at the crowd, held his sword high. "Where is your God now? Tell me!" And then to Packer, "Where are your Devilfish now, Packer Throme? Call them!" He turned to the translator and nodded smugly. The translator boomed out the words.

The wind kicked up once again, and this time a gentle rain came with it, pattering across the platform. Mux looked to the sky. He saw no lightning, heard no thunder. He sneered. Then he raised his sword. The Ixthano meant nothing now. By refusing to change places, to become the hangman, Packer had disavowed it. But before he executed this Vast hero, something in the crowd caught Mux's eye. He looked at it. He cocked his head to one side.

The sea was parting. Something was approaching in the falling rain, coming toward the platform as though swimming through this sea of Vast natives. At the leading point of this thing was a pale, pale face with black eyes and a grimace that bared pearl-white teeth. It was a man, or a specter of a man, who held a pistol high in his hand, pointed toward the sky. He limped. He looked like death itself.

Mux frowned. The rain came down, heavier now. Behind the walking dead man were four crimson Drammune helmets, glistening with rainwater. The men who wore them stared back at Mux, and fire was in their eyes. They were not Drammune. Each held two pistols aloft, one in each hand. Without a word, as he watched, all weapons were lowered and aimed at Fen Abbaka Mux. Behind these four, snaking behind in a wake that fanned out in back of them, were many others, many Vast citizens, all rabid enough, and all following in a moving wedge.

Mux shook his head to clear it. The wind gusted. Mux suddenly felt he was on the deck of a ship, looking out over the sea, as a Devilfish swam toward him.

Bench's four warriors wore helmets they had taken from the four guards in the prison. They also wore armor, the vests of the Drammune, under their jackets. They were protected, all but invincible. Only Bench was not; he had refused the armor, insisting his men take it, knowing his own time was short. He would lead this team to claim back both Packer Throme and Prince Mather, and the honor of Nearing Vast.

Mux lowered his sword and pulled out his pistol, intending to shoot the dying man, the living skull who led this otherworldly attack. But Mux was slow—too slow. Three well-aimed musket balls struck him in the chest, and one creased his cheek. He didn't go down, and he didn't return fire. Instead he ducked to a knee behind Packer Throme, who was still praying for the miracle that God had already delivered. The attackers ceased fire, but kept pressing toward the front. The crowd before them cleared, and now the warriors ran toward Mux. No further shots came from the attackers. "Charnak!" Mux shouted to his forces on the perimeter, and on the Rampart.

They all opened fire on the raiding party. Finally, the command had come, the order these guards had hoped to hear. The gunfire echoed through the dark square. The raiders went down.

Mux put a hand to his right ear. Part of it was missing. He looked at his own blood, running down his fingers, vanishing in the rain. "Kill all who resist," he bellowed, motioning generally toward the crowd, meaning to include every Vast native there. Now he had Packer by the hair again, hauling him to his feet. The thought crossed his mind that this yellow-hair would protect him from the Devilfish. Mux held the boy in front of him with one hand, aimed his pistol at the attackers with the other. Then he descended, still using Packer as a shield.

Only two of the raiding party stood again, and when they did they continued toward the platform. All five had been struck several times; only this pair had been fully protected by the Firefish armor. Bench Urmand remained on the ground.

Packer saw the weapon in Mux's hand. It did not occur to him to attempt take it away. This was now God's battle. It was Bench Urmand's battle. It was Mux's battle. But it was not Packer's.

The guards on the platform followed their commander down the stairs. As Mux reached the bottom, a hail of gunfire exploded from Bench's men, lightning from the human Firefish. Several guards were hit, but only the translator tumbled off the stairway, dead.

"Sir! What about the prince?" the last guard shouted down through the growing chaos.

Mux blanched. He had forgotten all about the puny double-crosser. "Hang him," he said simply.

The guard reached back and pulled the lever.

The crowd roared as the trapdoor opened, not as Vast crowds traditionally cheer, but as a wounded, enraged animal. And then as one entity they rushed the platform. It was a storm surge, moving under and into the scaffolding, swallowing up Bench and the five raiders. Hands reached up to the prince, too late to catch him, trying to raise him, while other hands pushed on the wooden beams, the legs of the structure, pulled on them, back and forth until the gallows rocked, cracked, and then came down. The prince went down with it. The hands of his people held him, touched him, offered up prayers and breathed out oaths in sorrow and in anger. The noose had done its job. Mather's neck was broken.

Mux hustled Packer to the prison entrance. Guards on the Rampart shot down anyone who came near, creating space for Mux and his prisoner and the three guards. With one fist the supreme commander still gripped Packer's mop of hair, with the other he held his pistol, still unfired. Inside the iron double doors he forced the boy back down to his knees, closed and bolted one door, then turned to the three guards. "You two, go get that girl." To the third he said, "You go find the prince. If he's not dead, kill him."

They looked at him wide-eyed, then turned grim, nodded, and headed back out to the melee.

The sky was black-dark now, and the rain came in solid sheets. The low rumbling of thunder could be heard, but very little gunfire. The noise of the Vast crowd, however, was everywhere, shouting, rumbling, exulting, echoing.

The three Drammune guards drew their swords as they ran. Two skirted the mob, headed to the right. They didn't need to dive into this mass in order to find Panna; they would stay on the perimeter. But the third had no choice. He had his sword in his hand as he waded back in, toward the fallen platform.

The Vast crowd that was gathered at the wreckage of the gallows turned their faces toward the single warrior. Their prince was dead, and the Drammune had killed him. They moved as one toward this crimson enemy who now dared to confront them. The warrior swung his blade once, but the sheer numbers…there were thousands of these salamanders. These Pawns.

These piranha.

Mux watched the crowd swallow the lone warrior up. The guard went down as fists and knives came up. The pack engulfed him. The knives turned red.

Drammune guns above continued to fire, but the pace had slowed dramatically. Mux looked at the Rampart walls. The men he could see through the downpour were not firing, but fussing with their weapons. The rain had made loading dry powder first difficult, and then impossible. Flints sparked harmlessly. Powder fizzed and popped in a bad imitation of good armament.

Just then the bloody dregs of the Vast rose up from their kill. They turned in unison toward Mux. He slammed the iron door and bolted it. He looked out through the bars. The Vast storm surge now moved away from the broken scaffold. The enormous, unyielding tide receded, then surged again in a mass up toward the lip of the amphitheater, toward the line of guards to Mux's right. Mux heard a voice, Huk Tuth's voice, from upon the Rampart calling for reinforcements, ordering all men down to the Green. Good. Reinforcements would be needed.

Mux had left the main mass of his troops outside the Rampart walls to protect the Old City from the counterattack he still believed was planned by the sly Vast leaders. He had ordered what he believed were more than enough guards to manage these beaten dregs of Vast society. But now he knew he had miscalculated. And only now, finally, did the idea occur to him that if the reinforcements did not arrive quickly, his men might not prevail.

Mux raised Packer to his feet and hurried down the stone stairs, the boy's leg chains clattering, and into the safety of the prison itself.

He tried not to think that somehow, in some way, Packer Throme had once again called forth the Firefish.

CHAPTER 25

The Turning

Ward moved with the crowd in the midst of the melee, helpless to do anything. He had not followed Bench and his men forward as they attacked. He had a pistol in his own belt, but he had little skill with it, and no armor. He would let the raiders raid. But now he was a part of the throng, moving without willing it, soaked in the downpour, pushed along in their frenzy through the growing mud, yet untouched by their emotion. He was thinking only that his luck had not changed one bit.

Packer was alive, maybe, but definitely not rescued. Mather was hung, and most likely dead. Bench and the raiders were almost certainly dead; the Drammune on the perimeter and on the Rampart walls had aimed exclusively at them. And so here was the perfect end to his far-from-perfect mission: the Vast crowd in a total uproar, screaming, mad, their emotions completely overruling their senses. It was as if something had been released into them, and thus into the world, that would not be stopped without great loss of life.

So Ward gave up. He didn't even bother to curse himself. He was beyond that now. They would all die here in the rain, surrounded by the Drammune. This was nothing but mass suicide.

As he surveyed the chaos, his heart fell into his shoes for the stupidity of it all. But at that moment he caught sight of a priest's hood, not ten feet from him, worn by someone who clearly was not a priest. As he watched, the hood fell back and revealed a girl with long, dark hair. It was Panna Throme! He suddenly found himself setting his sullen sights on a new objective. Panna Throme might still be saved.

Packer did not struggle against his captor. He could have taken the man's pistol or his sword, could have killed Mux with either. But Packer would not. He had trusted God, and God had done something, something enormous. He still wasn't sure what, or where it would lead, but he was sure it was God and not Packer doing it, and he was not about to intervene.

Packer's chains signaled far in advance of Mux's entrance that they were coming. When Mux maneuvered Packer into the main hallway of the prison, he stopped short. Two Vast dragoons blocked his way. Each had a sword in his hand.

It was laughable to think he could rescue her, Ward told himself as he began moving toward Panna, attempting just that. He hadn't been able to spring Packer out of prison when he had a secret entrance and five trained raiders. How could he possibly extricate Panna from this horde? But chasing her was better than being moved along, wondering when he would be shot or trampled.

He pushed through the throng after her. But he quickly realized she was doing an expert job of escaping without his or anyone else's help. She pushed her way through the crowd also, but then ducked down, invisible for a time, only to pop up again ten yards away.

The crowd pressed, moved, fists now raised in defiance. They attacked, fell, screamed their rage. Then the cacophony grew into a chant. It was hard for Ward to understand at first, but then he caught the words. "For the King, the Prince, and Packer Throme!" It had a cadence, a rhythm that seemed to energize them even further. He felt it himself. "For the king! The prince! And Pack-er Throme!"

No gunshots could be heard any more. It was all the crowd. It was the storm and the sea in one voice, boiling up from the earth, crashing down from the heavens.

Ward saw Panna near the leading edge of the throng, just as it surged toward a line of Drammune soldiers. The citizens were trying to break through, perhaps to flee, perhaps simply to attack; it was impossible to tell.

The Drammune guards watched the approaching onslaught, quit

reloading, and raised their swords and pikes. But it was the Vast citizenry who prevailed. A dozen men and women fell, but then a dozen Drammune soldiers went down before the combined wrath of hundreds of citizens. The Vast were pressing, screaming, rabid. They had opportunity now, but they did not seek escape. Those closest to their Drammune enemies saw the fear in their eyes, and that fear stoked their own anger. And suddenly they believed they could prevail.

Drammune weapons were snatched up, helmets and armor were yanked away, cheers that broke the chant rose first, then guttural roars, and then spine-chilling shrieks. The crowd was now a full-fledged mob. They could not be stopped. They would do what they would do. A hundred more Drammune warriors poured into the Green, prepared to do what they were trained to do.

Ward stood wide-eyed. He watched as Panna Throme bent down and came up with a Drammune sword. She held it high above her head, and moved with the crowd toward the newly arrived reinforcements.

"No, no, no!" Ward said aloud, and made a mad effort to reach her, throwing people out of his way, pushing, trying to get to her at any cost.

The mob overran the Drammune. Swords flashed, and a few shots rang out from those fresh troops who had not yet fired. But even a hundred reinforcements were quickly lost in this sea.

When the tide moved on, Prince Ward found Panna. She was hunched over a Drammune warrior, her back to Ward. Her sword went up, came down, went up, came down again. Ward grabbed her wrist. She turned on him, snarling. Then distantly, behind her wild eyes, there was recognition.

"Panna," Ward shouted. "Let's get out of here."

She shook her head. "They killed Packer!" Her mouth was turned down, her lower teeth visible, her rage unappeased.

"No, he's alive! Mux took him, but he's alive, Panna."

Her face softened some. Reason began to return to her. "He's alive?" She had been standing near the front of the crowd, had watched Packer go to his knees. She knew then he would die. She couldn't watch. Shots were fired, and the crowd pressed, and Mather was hung. But then her memory was a blur. The chant had started, and she remembered taking it up. Now she looked at the bloody sword in her hand. Ward gently pried it from her grip.

"Let's go," he said urgently.

She nodded.

Fen Abbaka Mux looked around for his troops, his guards, the ones he had left here in this dungeon. Anger rose in him; how could they allow two dragoons to stand here, armed? But he did not speak; he did not have time. At that very second, giving him not a moment to consider, a pike entered the base of his neck from behind. He let go of Packer and fell to his knees. Three swords found their way past his armor.

Stave Deroy's big hands let go of the pike as Mux fell to his knees. Then those same hands picked Packer up by his shirt at the shoulders. "You all right, Mr. Throme?" Chunk asked him, great concern in his voice.

"There she is!" someone shouted in Drammune. Ward turned around to face two Drammune warriors. They were after Panna. Ward now had Panna's sword in his hand. They had swords in their theirs.

He smiled at them. "Parley?" he asked in Drammune.

They charged. He braced for battle, holding his sword up against them as best he could. He didn't think to draw his pistol, and wouldn't have had time even if he had remembered.

But they ran right past him, one on each side, as though he wasn't there. Ward spun around and saw Panna sprinting away. She had seen the weak effort Ward offered in defense, assessed the situation instantly and accurately, and run.

"I'll take that as a 'no,' " Ward muttered, and chased after them.

Bench Urmand sat on the ground, bodies piled up around him. He had gotten two shots off before the Drammune had opened fire from the Rampart. He had been hit in the shoulder and the thigh, and knocked to the ground. He had been unable to stand back up. When the crowd had rushed the gallows, he had been stepped on, trampled, his injured leg kicked and twisted, the wound opened. It smelled of rotten almonds. He breathed hard, and sweat poured from him, mingled with the falling rain. He shivered. When the surge had moved off it had left him in this small redoubt of the dead, with the broken boards of the destroyed platform serving as some further protection.

He used his hands to move himself a few feet toward a four-foot high piece of the gallows, then he propped his back against it. He was almost but not quite in a seated position, his legs straight out in front of him. His tongue stuck to the roof of his mouth, and it took an effort to pull it away. He winced as a pain shot through his leg.

He would die here. He knew that now. He couldn't last another hour. So why had he come, he asked himself? Why had he insisted?

But he knew why. He was no minister of defense. He had skills, but they were not about musters and proclamations and evacuation strategies. Certainly not about crowd control. Only too fitting that he be trampled to death, he thought. No, he had insisted on leading this mission because he did not want to die of the rot, or the fever, talking out of his head, lying on a dirty bedsheet in a farmer's field while his Army cowered, waiting their turn to follow the same path.

He looked at Mather's body where it lay just a few feet from him, the noose still around his neck. The rope had been cut by some citizen trying to save him. But his neck was already broken. He had no doubt died instantly. Why had he stayed on his knees even as gunfire erupted? Why hadn't he tried to stand up, move off that trapdoor?

Bench didn't understand that behavior at all. Both the prince and Packer had put up no fight, none whatsoever. And Packer was supposed to be this legendary warrior who could inspire his people. All talk.

Bench would have fought to the death; that was simple fact. The Drammune commander, he'd have fought to the death, too. Bench loved his country, and served his king and his prince, but he had to respect the Drammune. They knew how to fight.

The sound of a musket shot brought him back to the moment. But it was on the other side of the Green. He took stock. Two of his men were dead for sure. One of them lay on his back not an arm's length away, eyes blank and dull. He was little more than a boy, a dark-haired kid with fire in his belly, name of Camble Canady. He had been with Bench when they'd served papers on Scat Wilkins. He must have been hit with a dozen musket balls, probably more, the way they bounced off that armor. He just kept going. But it only took one to find its target. The other raider he could see was Gildon Trouth, a tough old coot, hard as a leather saddle horn, now on his face fifteen feet away. Like Camble, Gildon still held his pistol in his hand. They were good men. He was proud of them.

Bench's hands felt cold and far away as he reloaded his pistol. When he finished the task, he laid the weapon down on the wet, muddy grass beside him. He hoped he had kept the powder dry while reloading, but he doubted it. Then with a pained effort, he found the pistol tucked into his waistband at his back. And then with an even greater effort, he pulled the two-shot derringer from his boot.

He closed his eyes for a moment, collecting his strength. What else did he have? Nothing of any value now. He looked at his dead comrades, wondered if they still had unfired weapons. Didn't matter. He had at least three shots, maybe five if the powder didn't fail him. That would be enough.

Ward followed the Drammune guards at a dead sprint. He still had his sword in his hand, but now he remembered his pistol; in fact he could think about almost nothing else because he was losing it down his pants as he ran. He fished for it as he turned the corner that opened up onto the greensward near the Seminary, and then he stopped. He pulled the pistol free, finally, and aimed.

Panna was still running at full tilt across the grass, down the hill toward the little cottages, but from this angle, above them, he could see she had actually opened up space. She was faster. But Ward was winded. His lungs heaved; his hand was ridiculously unsteady. He'd just as likely hit Panna as anything else.

This mission was going precisely as well as the last.

He watched Panna cross the street, run through the iron gate and toward a little cottage with broken windows and a door that hung open. She had a good twenty or thirty yards on them now. But why run in there and be cornered, Ward wondered? That cottage…She was last seen at a priest's cottage; isn't that what Mather had said? Yes, and the dragoons had searched it. That's where she had disappeared.

Then it hit him. A chill ran down his spine. There was a hiding place in there.

He threw away his sword, turned and sprinted for the King's Arms. For the first time in a very long time, he prayed. It was a simple prayer, but as earnest as any ever prayed by a Sennett of his generation. *God, save that woman.*

Panna heard the footsteps behind her, kept running in a panic.

Her heart beat so fast she thought it might explode. Her lungs burned. She needed to make it to the cottage, to the kitchen, to the stove, to safety.

She entered the priest's home at a dead run, and as she did it occurred to her she would be found this time. Surely, this time they would not stop searching until they found the secret shaft. But she had no other choice now. She hit the stove at a run, slamming the cold iron aside. She climbed down the ladder, stopping just long enough to pull it over her. It slid easily, as though oiled; she wondered at that, not realizing it was her own strength in the full boil of emotion that made it seem so easy. She climbed down to the bottom, trying to control the sound of her own breathing.

At the top of the shaft, she could hear the footsteps enter the cottage slowly, the voices cautious but gruff and commanding. Calling for her. Then she heard shouting, anger. Then the voices spoke softly among themselves. And then she heard the breaking of windows, of doors. Shattering of wood.

They were taking the little cottage apart, piece by piece.

The Drammune soldiers were baffled, but they were not deterred. They had a mission, orders given directly and personally from their supreme commander, and they would obey or face his wrath. The girl had come into this house. There were no other doors. Windows were broken, and so she might have escaped through one of them, but they were sure they would have seen her. She had gone in; she hadn't left. She was here, somewhere.

One man went outside to walk the perimeter of the house, to look for some means of escape, a cellar, a roof hatch. He checked the toolshed and then brought his comrade a shovel and an axe and a hammer. Both men began in the living room. Every floorboard was tried, pried, overturned. Every wall was attacked and hacked. Then they moved to the bedroom. The bed was overturned, the wardrobe smashed, the floorboards uprooted, the ceiling joists prodded, pried, and broken.

Then they went to the kitchen. The floors and walls and cupboards were treated to the same depredations. And then finally, when all else was a shambles, they turned simultaneously and looked at the stove. The only thing not ransacked. The two men pulled it toward them, muscling it off its track, and stood, sweating, panting, and in no good mood, looking down into a dark well.

"Tai!" one of them called. He pulled a pistol and pointed it down the hole. "Tai ar nocht!" *Come out or die!*

No answer came back.

They held the lamp over the hole; it helped only a little. It was impossible to see the bottom of the pit. The man with the pistol grunted his displeasure, then climbed down.

A moment later he climbed out, and put his pistol back into his belt. He took off his helmet, ran stubby fingers through dark, sweaty hair.

"Zona," he said simply. *Nothing.*

Bench looked around him, trying to find a Drammune soldier to shoot. But he couldn't see one. Where had they gone? He wiped at his eyes, squinted against the rain. He looked up at the Rampart. No one. He couldn't see clearly, apparently. Across the space of the Green the Vast crowd was now milling about, kicking and stabbing at various things they came across lying on the ground. But where were the Drammune? It baffled him.

He closed his eyes. He heard a gurgling sound in his own throat, but it didn't worry him. It was comforting, almost like a snore. He was very tired...very tired.

A moment later, his pistol slipped from his hand onto the wet ground.

Panna followed Prince Ward through the dark passageway. "Glad I remembered this little offshoot," he said breathlessly, putting a hand to his chest. He was still recovering from his sprint back to the King's Arms, and then through the passage that led to the priest's little cottage. "I knew it went to the Seminary somewhere, but I was never tempted to follow it. Mind those cobwebs."

"Father Mooring doesn't think it leads anywhere," Panna told him as she brushed the gray webs aside. "He just keeps potatoes down there."

Ward laughed. *Potatoes.* Why did that strike him as funny? He was giddy with this sudden, unexpected success, he supposed. "Well, that door may not even open from his side. The system was built for escaping the palace."

Ward stopped where two cramped paths intersected, and he studied his choices. "This way." But before he moved, he held up the lamp, looked at Panna. He put one hand on a knee, resting. "Did you see what happened out there?"

The question surprised her. "What happened?"

"They tore down the gallows. Did you see my brother?"

"Yes." She let the memory come back. "I don't think he survived."

Ward nodded. "I'm sorry for what he did to you."

Panna took a deep breath. "He has paid for that."

"I suppose he has. But it doesn't excuse it."

"I suppose not." She was uncomfortable with this conversation.

"Nor does it excuse my not helping you. I am sorry for that as well."

Her dark eyes went darker. He had known all along and yet had done nothing. She didn't know what to say.

"Well, let's see if we can get you to safety," he said, starting up again.

"Safety? Where?"

"To the Army, outside the city."

"Without Packer?"

He shook his head. "He was taken to the prison."

"Can't we find him? Don't these paths lead there?"

He looked at her, amazed. "Well, yes. But I brought Bench Urmand and four raiders here this morning and couldn't rescue him. I don't think the two of us could..." He trailed off as she looked at the pistol he had returned to his belt.

She held her hand out, palm up. "Give me the pistol, then."

He was dumbfounded. "Can you shoot?"

"I can pull a trigger."

"No, I'm sorry. I won't let you get yourself killed doing something rash."

"Something rash? You mean, like trying to rescue someone from danger? Is that rash? So what isn't rash—turning away while someone helpless suffers abuse at the hands of someone more powerful? Oh, by all means, let's not be *rash*."

He closed his eyes.

"Never mind, I'll go myself."

He looked at her and nodded. Of all the idiotic things he'd done in the last few days, what he was about to agree to do, he felt, might just top the list.

Eventually the citizens realized they were winning. They had to accept it, incredible though it seemed, because there were no more Drammune soldiers left to kill. A few people had actually seen Huk Tuth order a retreat, and pull all remaining men out of the palace grounds behind a line of Drammune who died providing cover. Fewer still were thoughtful enough to consider that not far off the Green, outside the Rampart, the Drammune were likely to be regrouping.

Instead they looked around at one another in mute amazement. They were bloodied, bedraggled, utterly spent, and victorious. Women, old men, lunatics, brigands, vagabonds, many of them wounded, many now wearing ill-fitting helmets and vests torn from their vanquished foes, others proudly brandishing enemy pikes and swords and battle-axes. Among the survivors were priests, a few even wearing snatched-up helmets and armor, most of them carrying some sort of weapon, if only a carving knife. And all as bloody as any around them.

Smiles broke out. Congratulations where offered. But the elation of battle was already giving way to the reality of near-total physical and emotional exhaustion.

"What now?" someone asked.

"They'll come back with more—many more," Dirk Menafee answered. The grizzled bounty hunter seemed sure of himself, so everyone nearby looked to him for answers.

"Do we stay? Or do we run?"

A huge man in Drammune armor lay on his back in the main hallway, blood pooled around him. Prisoners lined the cells, watching, but no guards, Drammune or dragoon, were in sight.

Ward tiptoed up to the dead man. "It's Fen Abbaka Mux," he said flatly.

Panna looked around. "What in the world happened?"

"The dragoons got him," one of the prisoners offered.

Panna looked at the prince. Then she looked back at the gaunt face of the prisoner. "What dragoons?"

Prince Mather's skin was gray and lifeless, beaded wet with the rain, which had now dwindled to a fine mist. Packer closed Mather's unseeing eyes. Then gingerly, he loosened the rope from the prince's neck and carefully removed the noose. As he looked at Mather, the evil this prince had committed on earth could not stay in his mind. "He did a noble thing at the end," Packer said.

Chunk hung his head dutifully, shuffled uncomfortably, nodded his agreement. He had no idea what Packer was talking about. "What now, Mr. Throme?"

"We can't leave him here." He looked up, surveyed again the battlefield, the mass of Vast citizens milling about aimlessly. "The Drammune won't stay gone long. Can you carry him back to the prison?"

"Sure I can." And the big dragoon very gently gathered his prince in his arms.

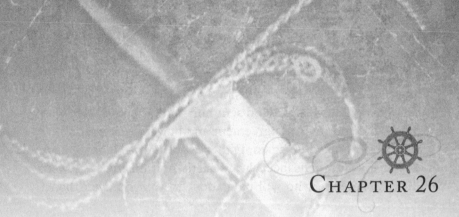

CHAPTER 26

Reunion

"Hey, isn't that Packer Throme?" someone asked. All heads turned. "It is! It's Packer!" The entire crowd moved slowly over the battlefield toward him. Another voice started the chant again, "For the King, the Prince, and Pack-er Throme!" but it died away as they saw the big dragoon with Prince Mather in his arms.

Then Packer saw a little priest at the front of the weary throng, eyes beaming. The pirest ran to Packer and threw his arms around him.

"Father, what are you doing here?" But what Packer meant to ask was why Father Mooring's arms and chest were covered with blood.

"The Lord has been moving in mysterious ways," he said brightly.

"Have you been fighting?"

The priest laughed. "Lord no, that's not my calling. No, no. I've been praying."

Packer was dubious. Finally, Father Mooring looked down at his own deeply stained robes, the blood on his hands and arms. "Oh, and healing," he added. "I've been healing as best I can." Packer glanced around and now saw the makeshift bandages worn by several within sight, an arm in a rough sling fashioned from a bloody shirt, a leg wrapped in a shirtsleeve.

Then on the ground behind the priest, near the shattered gallows, Packer saw Bench Urmand. He was barely recognizable, pale and gaunt, eyes closed within black eye sockets. Two of his men knelt beside him. Packer moved quickly toward them, knelt at Bench's head, and put a hand on his neck.

"Gone," one of the raiders said simply.

Packer lowered his head. "God sent him here," he said. "He won the day." All around nodded agreement and bowed their heads.

When Packer looked up again, Father Mooring was looking back at the prison entrance. His face, always alight, now positively glowed. "Well here's someone who will be gladder to see you even than I was."

Packer stood and saw Prince Ward. And then Ward stepped aside and there was Panna, walking toward him. She moved with a grace that was wholly her own, perfect in Packer's eyes. And she was well and whole, wet hair hanging down across her shoulders, down the front of her robe. She stared only at him. Her eyes were alive and dancing, her expression a blend of gratitude and pure, focused determination. He was undone.

She walked up to him, looked up into his eyes. She put her arms around him, one hand behind each shoulder, and she kissed him. "I love you with all I am," she said. But before he could answer her in kind, she slapped him on the cheek. This was by no means her wicked, dream-inducing straight right jab, but it was a good bit more than a love tap. "And I'm absolutely furious with you!"

His look was all amazement. Oohs and whistles rose from the onlookers.

"*Let me die?*" she demanded. "That's the best you could come up with?"

Packer winced and rubbed his cheek, offering her a shrug and half a smile, searching in vain for any sign of playfulness. "It seemed right when I said it," he managed, rather lamely.

Her look remained grave. "The one honorable thing Mather ever did, and you try to take his moment of glory for your own?"

"I was just..." he started.

But finally she smiled. There was much sadness wound up in it, but it was an invitation he would not pass up. He kissed her gently. The crowd aahed and someone whistled again, this time hitting a few approving notes.

"Doogan Blestoe!" the priest scolded. "What are you doing here?"

Dog just grimaced. He was standing on his own, no crutch or cane or walking stick, but he stood straight as a board and did not move his arms. "Heard there was a fight. Sorry I missed it."

"But Dog—" Father Mooring started.

"I'm fine," he countered, sounding as ill-tempered as ever. He glanced at Packer and Panna, still embracing. "Just so long as nobody tries to hug me," he said, adding just the smallest trace of a wince.

"Look, I hate to interrupt these warm reunions, but we really ought to be leaving," Ward said brightly. "The Drammune shall certainly return." He surveyed the strewn battlefield. "And when they do, I doubt they'll be any too pleased with us."

Packer nodded, then took off the ring Mather had given him and held it out. "I believe this should be yours, by all rights."

Ward glanced at it, then smiled at Packer. "Mather gave that to you."

"Yes. But Your Highness—"

Ward waved him off. "We'll talk about it later. Right now, we've got to get everyone out of here."

Prince Ward led the ragtag mob into the prison, and through the torture chamber, and then into the corridors underground. All of them came. Packer and Panna, at just about everyone's insistence, took the lead position just behind the prince. Dog was close behind, continuing to walk by himself, but he never strayed far from Father Mooring. It was clear Doogan Blestoe drew strength from his new-found friend.

Dirk Menafee agreed to join the rear guard. This meant staying with the dragoons until every last citizen, lame, limping, carried, or carrying was in ahead of him. "Let's go, let's go!" the bounty hunter kept saying irritably, quite sure the Drammune would appear in force before all these charity cases disappeared into the wall of the chamber.

After the citizens came the prisoners, hobbling, leaning on the priests for support or carried by them, but grinning ear to ear almost to a man. "I love this war," one of them said happily as he limped past Dirk.

The Hand That Bears the Sword

The bounty hunter snarled at him.

When Huk Tuth did return to the Green in force, with his soldiers marching six abreast and prepared for mass slaughter, he found it abandoned. The Drammune had blocked the streets. They had posted lookouts. They had trapped the rabble within the palace grounds, up against the Rampart. Where had they gone?

An injured Drammune soldier pointed them toward the prison. "In there," he said in a pained gasp. "They went in there."

Tuth grew alarmed. He knew that Fen Abbaka Mux had last been seen entering the prison with Packer Throme.

The soldiers found the double doors locked and barred, but eventually they gave way to Drammune persistence. Tuth and his men entered the prison ready for anything, but found nothing. Nothing except the body of the Supreme Commander of the Glorious Drammune Military, laid out on his back in the torture chamber, with the bodies of four other warriors, the Drammune guards, laid out beside him.

It had been Dirk's idea to drag them there, the crafty sometime criminal knowing quite well that their commander would be the focus of all their attentions, and the mass of wet Vast footprints might then be ignored until there were so many wet Drammune footprints that the evidence of an exit through a solid stone wall might be obscured.

It worked just that way. As far as Tuth and the Glorious Drammune Military knew, the ragged, rabid Vast irregulars were simply gone, vanished along with the prisoners. And every one of the Drammune knew what this meant. It meant that the second battle for the City of Mann, the Battle of the Green as it would be called, was over. And the Vast had won.

No one in a Drammune uniform now doubted that the rout of the first day had been staged, that it was all a ploy, just as Fen Abbaka Mux had said it was. These were a dangerous people who feigned weakness as they called on their God, whom they credited then for answered prayers. Of course it was all a ploy. Or coincidence. If some Vast truly did believe in this sort of magic, it only gave them strength. The fact was, they knew how to fight, and they fought like dogs foaming at the mouth.

It gave them pause. If the meanest citizenry of Nearing Vast could

The Hand That Bears the Sword

muster such ferocity in the face of overwhelming firepower, if their dregs could defeat Drammune regulars, take down the Drammune supreme commander, and then disappear without a trace, what was possible from their actual military?

And they all knew that the Vast armies must surely be lying in wait somewhere outside the city, plotting their next move.

The bird flapped onto the window ledge of the Hezzan's throne room, lit on the floor, and sat still, legs folded under it. Talon studied the pitiful thing carefully. It was exhausted. She rose and approached it. This one was smaller than the falcon she had seen in Abbaka Mux's cabin, but a Drammune scroll was tied to its leg, and it had clearly traveled a great distance. She knew it came from her Armada.

The bird did not move as she bent over it, nor as she picked it up, nor as she untied the pouch. "Call the falconer," she told her guard, who left dutifully.

Talon sat back down on her throne and read the words of Huk Tuth, her alarm growing with each sentence, then with each word. The *Trophy Chase*, draped with impenetrable armor. Firefish tamed by the Vast, attacking on command. A yellow-haired warrior who stood, unarmed, at the prow of the ship, directing the Firefish. There could be no doubt about his identity.

She put the note into her lap. Tuth was not known to exaggerate. The words were simple, the story lean. It rang of truth. But how could it be true? Somehow Packer Throme, with or without Scat Wilkins or Lund Lander or John Hand, had been aided in battle by a Firefish. He had learned something, the Vast had learned something new about these beasts. They had learned not just to hunt and kill them, but to tame them as well. But how?

Then she wondered. Had they found the feeding waters? Had Packer spoken the truth after all? And as soon as she asked herself the question, she knew the answer. He had told the truth all along. The *Trophy Chase* had ventured into the beasts' very lair, their home, perhaps their spawning grounds, and there had discovered some secret that could turn them, that could tame them. And if they had learned such a thing, if they had taught a Firefish to attack on command, what would that mean to this war?

Her heart pounded. If they could tame one, why not two? Why not a dozen? And even one Firefish could destroy an Armada. This was what came of letting Packer Throme live. And yet, she found that even now she did not want him dead. She did not regret, could not regret that he had bested her with weakness. He had shown her the true nature of power in the universe. What might that boy be capable of accomplishing, humbled as he was before his all-powerful God? Weakness, utter weakness, clothed with perfect, absolute power from above...

Talon looked across the room at the sword that hung on the wall, in a place of honor. It was Packer Throme's sword, the work of Pyre Dunn, left behind when Packer had dropped it on the decks of the *Camadan*. She considered all these things at once: his sword, his Firefish, his God. The beasts had provided defensive armor, and now they were providing an unstoppable offensive threat as well.

Talon called for her scribe, the late Hezzan's scribe. "Write these orders." She began dictating, the scribe working diligently, dunking his quill and gliding lines of ink onto the parchment as Talon spoke.

Satisfied after reading over it, she called for the falconer. "I want that falcon to take this message back to Huk Tuth, just as soon as she has rested enough to make the journey." The falconer put out his hand for the scroll, but Talon shook her head. "When she is recovered, come find me. I will send her across the sea myself."

The empress of the Kingdom of Drammun sat alone on her throne, one thought consuming her. Whoever controlled the Firefish controlled the world.

John Hand found that hunting Firefish was easier than commanding his new Fleet. He had taken the *Trophy Chase* and her crew, hoping to escape the Bay of Mann and skirt the Drammune, avoiding any encounters until he could organize and attack on his own terms. In this he had been successful. He had also hoped to put his fledgling Fleet through a few brief maneuvers, quickly getting the captains of the sixteen other vessels into battle formation, making sure they were comfortable with receiving his orders through signals and flagmen, so that they were ready to pounce on the flanks of the Drammune Armada. In this he was not so successful.

He found that, while these ships were well-maintained and sea-worthy, and their captains were good and seasoned seamen, their lack of experience with the discipline of naval warfare left them far short of a fighting force. There seemed to be as many reasons for this as there were ships. The *Blunderbuss* was the slowest tub John Hand had ever personally seen at sea, so much so that he was sure if he went aboard he would find her crew mired in molasses. The *Wellspring* was captained by a man who apparently felt he could improve on any order given, and prided himself in taking the initiative. The vessel *Danger* was only such to herself. And *Forcible* was anything but. *Candor* was ever needed, rarely found. *Bonny Anne, Gant Marie, Gasparella,* and *Black-eyed Susan* discussed the admiral's orders among themselves before responding, and then politely made suggestions about their preferred approach. *Rake's Parry,* on the other hand, anticipated orders, rushing ahead without them. *Homespun* had a fire break out aboard. *Poy Marroy* struck a reef that damaged her rudder. Only the *Swordfish, Campeche* and, of course, the *Marchessa* responded quickly, with anything like discipline, and with anything close to precision.

Hand scanned the seas with his telescope, shaking his head. Andrew Haas stood beside him, glumly awaiting orders. The men in the rigging, including Smith Delaney, and the men on deck, including Marcus Pile, watched forlornly as the Vast ships wove to and fro, almost colliding, then veering far from their appointed spot in the ranks. Delaney chewed his lip, then spoke to no one in particular. "Just get in a billowin' line. How hard is that?"

Mutter Cabe, the only one who heard him, responded. "Well, we better get to battle soon, that's all I know. Otherwise, that Fish is going to start makin' dinner of one of ours instead one of theirs."

"No great loss, I say." But Delaney scanned the seas. The Firefish was nowhere in sight, and hadn't been for days. Delaney was glad of that. He did not like to think what might happen if that beast rose up at the prow again, and Packer Throme wasn't there to look it in the eye.

The ink on the scroll dried as it sat, waiting for delivery across the sea. The terms were terse, the language tight and simple, but the sign and seal were unmistakably those of the Hezzan of the Drammune. It said simply that the war was over. The Drammune troops would be called off, brought back across the sea. The Hezzan gave three very simple conditions, which she was rightly sure would be impossible to reject.

First, the King of Nearing Vast would immediately dispatch an envoy with plenipotentiary powers to the shores of Drammun to draft and sign a binding treaty of alliance. Second, that same diplomat would arrive in Hezarow Kyne aboard the warship *Trophy Chase*. And third, as sign and symbol of the goodwill of the Vast people toward their new allies, that ship would carry aboard it the leaders of the Firefish trade, who would share all they knew. In exchange, the Drammune would similarly reveal to the Vast all the secrets of their own fishing industry.

A simple request. Transparent, of course, but considering the alternative cost in mutual loss of life, hard to reject. It would bring to Drammun immediately and in peace what otherwise she would need to wait for, fight for, and hope could be salvaged from battle. What would happen, once Talon knew the secrets of the Firefish, would happen.

She was rightly confident that when the falcon reached the shores of Nearing Vast, the war would be over.

The small cottage in the woods was little more than a shack, but it had a door that locked and windows that closed and shutters that shut and a candle that burned. Packer and Panna had been tucked inside for some much-needed rest, and some much-desired privacy. Guards were stationed far enough away to be discreet, close enough to protect the pair from almost anything. Prince Ward had made sure the couple would not be disturbed.

The larger house some twenty-five yards away served as headquarters of the Army of Nearing Vast. Inside it, young General Jameson, the old and recovering general Mack Millian, Prince Ward, and a number of their lieutenants were busy planning. They had taken care of the details of their own Army's defensive positions, and then had turned to plans for the burial of Prince Mather. When that was done, they started their offensive strategy, to take back the City of Mann.

The officers and the prince gathered around a large map laid out on a kitchen table and weighted down with coffee mugs. They drew lines with their fingers and discussed troop strengths, but they had quickly come to an impasse, and opinions differed as to how they might break the logjam.

"We need a king," Ward suggested, rubbing his temples. He felt sick again, dried out and hollow.

"Yes," the elderly General Millian agreed. His head was bandaged, and though he was somewhat pale he appeared quite vigorous for an injured man of eighty-three. "I must tell you in all honesty, I am extremely uncomfortable making such plans with no input from King Reynard."

"My father has gone to the Mountains," Ward reminded them.

"Then we must fetch him," General Millian insisted.

"I'll go," General Jameson offered.

Ward sighed. He knew Reynard Sennett would not come back. And even if he did return, the people would not much like what they saw in him.

Just then a knock on the door introduced Packer Throme. He looked rather tired, but determined.

"Ah, Packer! Excellent timing. I see you haven't gotten much rest yet," Ward said good-naturedly. "Not surprised. I understand this little war interrupted your...what do you call it...honey month? Highly inconsiderate of us all."

Packer turned crimson as the others laughed good-naturedly. But the room went silent as he pulled a ring out of his pocket. "I came to give you this. It is not mine by right."

They had all heard about Mather's last moments. Panna and Packer had both told Prince Ward all they could remember, and Ward had passed much of it on to these men. Now Ward looked at the ring, but did not move to take it from Packer.

"Tell me again what Mather said when he gave that to you." Ward's tone was a shade more ominous than Packer would have preferred. Packer hesitated. "I'd like these gentlemen to hear it from you," the prince said, more gently.

Packer swallowed. "He said he gave it gladly."

"Gladly?"

Packer nodded, then thought a moment. "No, *freely*. He said he gave it freely."

"What did he say about the ring? What did he say it represented?"

Packer nodded. "He said it was the sign and seal of everything he owned. But it should be yours, sir. I'm not a noble. I'm the son of a fisherman."

Now Ward smiled. He spoke softly. "That ring, Packer, is not Prince Mather's."

Packer studied it. Of course it was; it was the same ring.

But before he could protest, Ward said, "That is the king's signet."

"What?" General Jameson feared that Mux and his hordes had somehow reached King Reynard even before the events of the morning. "How could that be?"

Ward picked up a coffee mug, looked into it. Empty. No help there. He cradled it in both hands, then looked mildly at the urgent faces surrounding him. "Two days ago my father wanted to abdicate, and to name Mather king. Mather declined. It's quite apparent the ceremony happened anyway. King Reynard passed that ring, and all it represents, to his firstborn son."

No one spoke. Packer shook his head.

Ward's voice became gentler yet. "The dominion Mather passed to you, Packer, was not that of a prince."

Packer just stared at the ring.

Mack Millian spoke up gruffly. "But you said that the Transfer ritual was Drammune law. We're not obligated by it, surely."

Ward nodded. "But in Nearing Vast the king may pass his title to anyone he chooses. No death required, no ceremony necessary. All he need do is freely give his signet, with all it represents, before two or more witnesses. I believe the small gathering this morning qualifies."

Packer, wide-eyed, was now insistent. "You take it, then. I freely give it to you."

The prince held up a hand. "Ah, but Packer, the recipient must also agree to take it. You have done so. I have not, and will not."

"But why not?" Packer pled, still offering the ring on his scarred palm.

"I have thought about that since you first showed it to me. I recognized whose it was immediately. I've thought about it all day, and I have many reasons for my decision. The most important is, I believe

The Hand That Bears the Sword

Mather wanted you to have it. It was his abdication, every bit as valid as my father's. I have no right to question it. But as you offer it to me, I can tell you that I absolutely do not want it, and will not accept it."

Packer started to protest again, but Ward cut him off. "Why? Because I believe you will not abuse it, and I am quite sure I can't say the same of myself. Even if I did want it, Packer, I would have to tell you I cannot take it now. This nation is at war, and it needs a leader who will inspire the people. That, my friend, is not me. It is you."

The other men in the room now stared at Ward Sennett. What they saw in him amazed them. They saw character.

Now the Prince of Nearing Vast lowered himself to a knee. "Packer Throme of Hangman's Cliffs, you are by all rights the King of Nearing Vast." Then he bowed his head. "And as such, I swear to you my allegiance."

And then all the men in the room did the same.

When Packer reentered the tiny cottage, Panna was waiting for him, eyes questioning.

Packer held up his hand, the ring firmly in place on his right forefinger. Then he walked past her, sat down heavily on the rickety bed, and stared at the signet. A pain shot through his damaged hand.

Panna saw the troubled look and sat down beside him. "Packer, what does that mean? He wants you to be a prince?"

He turned his eyes toward her, but he was far away. "Panna..." He didn't know how to say it.

His look struck something deep into her heart. Fear...wonder... both...she couldn't identify it. Finally she spoke. "What, Packer? What is it?"

"Somehow..." He took a deep breath. He held it a long time. Then he said in a rush of breath, hardly more than a whisper, "Somehow I just became the King of Nearing Vast."

The Hand That Bears the Sword

ABOUT THE AUTHOR

George Bryan Polivka was raised in the Chicago area, attended Bible college in Alabama, and ventured on to Europe, where he studied under Francis Schaeffer at L'Abri Fellowship in Switzerland. He then returned to Alabama, where he enrolled at Birmingham-Southern College as an English major.

While still in school, Bryan married Jeri, his only sweetheart since high school and now his wife of more than 25 years. He also was offered a highly coveted internship at a local television station, which led him to his first career—as an award-winning television producer.

In 1986, Bryan won an Emmy for writing his documentary *A Hard Road to Glory*, which detailed the difficult path African-Americans traveled to achieve recognition through athletic success during times of racial prejudice and oppression.

Bryan and his family lived in Texas for a dozen years, then moved to the Baltimore area, where he worked with Sylvan Learning Systems (now Laureate Education). In 2001 he was honored by the U.S. Distance Learning Association for the most significant achievement by an individual in corporate e-learning. He is currently responsible for developing and delivering new programs for Laureate's online higher education division.

Bryan and Jeri live near Baltimore with their two children, Jake and Aime, where Bryan continues to work and write.

Be sure and watch for the third book
in The Trophy Chase Trilogy,

THE BATTLE FOR VAST DOMINION
coming January 2008.

Harvest House Publishers
Fiction for Every Taste and Interest

Mindy Starns Clark
THE MILLION DOLLAR MYSTERIES
A Penny for Your Thoughts
Don't Take Any Wooden Nickels
A Dime a Dozen
A Quarter for a Kiss
The Buck Stops Here

Brandt Dodson
THE COLTON PARKER MYSTERIES
Original Sin
Seventy Times Seven
The Root of All Evil
The Lost Sheep

Roxanne Henke
COMING HOME TO BREWSTER
After Anne
Finding Ruth
Becoming Olivia
Always Jan
With Love, Libby

B.J. Hoff
THE MOUNTAIN SONG LEGACY SERIES
A Distant Music
The Wind Harp
The Song Weaver

Susan Meissner
A Window to the World
The Remedy for Regret
In All Deep Places
Blue Heart Blessed

HARVEST HOUSE
PUBLISHERS

To learn more about books by Harvest House
or to read sample chapters, log on to our website:

www.harvesthousepublishers.com

HARVEST HOUSE PUBLISHERS

EUGENE, OREGON